SONYA WAS INTERRUPTED BY SOME KIND OF BLASTER FIRE, WHICH STRUCK HAWKINS IN THE LEFT SHOULDER

The security guard cried out in pain and fell to the cavern ground, grabbing his left shoulder with his right hand and dropping his phaser rifle.

As Corsi raised her own rifle to return fire, Ganitriul said, "A security measure has activated. No energy weapons will fire within the confines of the installation."

Corsi pressed the firing button on her rifle anyhow, but nothing happened. "Dammit," she muttered.

It was then that the lights came back up.

Sonya blinked the spots out of her eyes and found herself surrounded by twelve Erlikka. Some of them were also blinking—with upper and lower eyelids—in response to the greater illumination. Some were holstering their blaster   l-stering large curved, bladed weapon:

"Death to the aliens!" one of them cr

Several more repeated, "Death to the

Then they charged.

STAR TREK®
S.C.E.

Book 1

HAVE TECH, WILL TRAVEL

Keith R.A. DeCandido, Kevin Dilmore,
Christie Golden, Dean Wesley Smith,
& Dayton Ward

Based upon STAR TREK® and
STAR TREK: THE NEXT GENERATION®
created by Gene Roddenberry,
and STAR TREK: DEEP SPACE NINE®
created by Rick Berman & Michael Piller

POCKET BOOKS
New York London Toronto Sydney Singapore Eerlik

POCKET BOOKS, a division of Simon & Schuster, Inc.
1230 Avenue of the Americas, New York, NY 10020

Star Trek® S.C.E. #1: The Belly of the Beast copyright © 2000 by Paramount Pictures. All Rights Reserved.
Star Trek® S.C.E. #2: Fatal Error copyright © 2000 by Paramount Pictures. All Rights Reserved.
Star Trek® S.C.E. #3: Hard Crash copyright © 2000 by Paramount Pictures. All Rights Reserved.
Star Trek® S.C.E. #4: Interphase Book 1 copyright © 2001 by Paramount Pictures. All Rights Reserved.

STAR TREK is a Registered Trademark of Paramount Pictures.

This book is published by Pocket Books, a division of Simon & Schuster, Inc., under exclusive license from Paramount Pictures.

ISBN: 978-1-4767-9272-9

First Pocket Books trade paperback printing January 2002

10 9 8 7 6 5 4 3 2 1

POCKET and colophon are registered trademarks of Simon & Schuster, Inc.

For information regarding special discounts for bulk purchases, please contact Simon & Schuster Special Sales at 1-800-456-6798 or business@simonandschuster.com

Printed in the U.S.A.

These titles were previously published individually in eBook format by Pocket Books.

CONTENTS

CONTENTS

THE BELLY OF THE BEAST

Dean Wesley Smith

CHAPTER

1

Space battles never took this long.

Captain Jean-Luc Picard shook his head in amazement as he stared at the main screen of the *Enterprise* bridge. He couldn't remember how many times he had been in engagements with enemy ships, with the fight usually only taking a few minutes. But not this time. The monster ship floating in front of them had kept them busy for almost two hours, its dark shape and strange configuration seemingly able to take all the *Enterprise* could throw at it, and then some.

And, so far, the *Enterprise* had withstood the enemy's weapons as well.

Punch, counterpunch. Each ship had held its ground, wearing the other down one degree at a time. And wearing Picard and his crew down as well. Dr. Crusher had just reported that sickbay was full with the casualties. Luckily, no one had been killed.

Yet.

Without ' standing, he glanced around the bridge. Commander Riker paced in front of his chair, sweat staining his shirt. Lieutenant Christine Vale at security just looked angry, and Troi fidgeted in her chair, the strain of the last few hours showing clearly on her face. Only Data, his emotion chip turned off, seemed as unruffled as ever. Picard envied that android calmness at times.

"They're powering weapons again, Captain," Data said.

"Target those weapons and fire before they do!" Picard ordered.

Picard could feel the *Enterprise* bump slightly as the phasers fired.

A small section of the alien ship's shields flared bright red.

The alien weapons cut through the redness, pounding the *Enterprise* hard. The inertial dampers fought to stop the rocking and shaking the impact had caused. As he had been doing for hours, Picard held onto his chair with both hands, keeping himself seated.

"Forward shields at thirty-two percent," Lieutenant Vale said. "Holding."

"Slight damage on three decks," Deanna said, glancing at the monitor on her chair. "No injuries."

That fire-return-fire scene had repeated itself at least fifty times over the last two hours.

"We have got to find a way to end this," Picard said, standing and taking a step toward the main screen, staring at the black alien ship facing him.

It was a monster, more than fifty times bigger than the *Enterprise*, and at least as deadly. It was round, like a small moon, and its surface was covered with what looked to be some type of control housing. Two smooth rings circled the outer hull of the ship, each attached to the surface at only four places. The rings were as thick as the *Enterprise* saucer section and twice as wide, with one ring circling around the alien ship's equator, while the other ring went around the ship's poles. Picard had no idea what the rings were for.

Or who had built this strange ship.

Or what powered it.

Or even, for that matter, what was the front, back, top, or bottom of it. The sensors could tell when the alien ship was powering weapons, but little else. The alien shields had blocked every attempt they had made to find out more.

He stared at it, studying the black, equipment-covered surface of the alien ball, trying to come up with any way at all to put that ship out of commission. They had been able to punch through its shields in small areas, but the damage they had done to the surface of the ship seemed to make no difference at all.

And the shields reacted like no shields he had seen before. It was almost as if they were alive, healing damaged areas like water flowing back into a depression. Picard would give anything to learn how they worked.

An hour ago, he had even attacked one of the intersections where the two rings met, hoping that would cause the alien ship problems. They had managed to punch through the alien shields twice, hitting the surface of the ship's rings and blowing hunks out of one area of one ring. The alien shields quickly healed. Nothing changed.

The alien ship attacked, they attacked back.

Stalemate.

Over two long hours of the same thing.

However, for the residents of Blossom IV, the fourth planet of this system, the *Enterprise* had to win. The *Enterprise* had been nearby when the distress call had come in from the agricultural colony. The message said they were under attack from a massive black ball, and taking heavy damage. It had only taken the *Enterprise* fifteen minutes to be on the scene, but Picard didn't want to think about the damage the alien ship had caused to those farmers in those minutes.

The *Enterprise* had come in firing, and the alien ship had turned its attention away from the planet. But if the *Enterprise* was forced to retreat, or was defeated, there was no other help for those colonists. No other Federation ship that could stand up to this monster was nearby.

Picard also couldn't figure out why it had attacked this planet. Blossom IV had no resources, nothing worth taking from the two hundred thousand people farming the rich soil. Yet this unknown ship had suddenly appeared and started to fire on the colony. It made no sense at all.

Nothing about any of this made any sense.

Picard glanced at Data, then turned around to look at Number One. "I'm open to suggestions here, people."

No one said a word.

Picard nodded. None of them had any more idea what to do with this ship than he did. They just didn't have enough information about the alien ship to even try to come up with a plan, and the alien ship's shields were blocking all but the most basic surface scans.

"They are powering weapons again, Captain," Data said.

"Return fire!" Riker ordered.

The blast shook the *Enterprise* again, sending Picard staggering to grab the armrest of his chair.

"Shields at twenty-six percent," Data said.

"We punched a hole in their shields again," Lieutenant Vale said. "It has now closed."

Picard nodded, looking back at the lieutenant's fresh, sweating face. Vale had blue eyes, blond hair, and a button nose that made her look much younger than her actual age. But she was a good tactical officer. Smart and very quick. And, from what he understood, deadly in a fight.

Suddenly, Lieutenant Vale's statement sunk in.

"Data," Picard said, "how long did that hole in their shields remain open?"

"One-point-three-three seconds," Data said.

"Is that enough time to get a probe through and the information back?"

Data glanced up at Picard, his yellow eyes showing just a touch of interest. "It could be done, sir," Data said. "But we would have to be closer."

"Let's do it," Picard said, dropping down into his chair. "Data, you take the helm and get us in close."

Data's fingers were flying over the panel as Picard turned to Commander Riker. "Will, ready the probe and fire the instant you have a hole in those shields."

"Understood."

Picard punched the comm link for engineering. "Geordi, I need the front shields reinforced."

"Yes, Captain," La Forge's voice came back.

"Lieutenant Vale," Picard said, glancing back at the young officer. "I want you firing constantly until I give you the word to stop. Punch as big a hole in those shields as you can. Give Commander Riker a large target. He might need it."

Riker frowned. "I could fly a probe down a gopher hole."

"Make it a big hole, Lieutenant," Picard said.

She laughed. "Yes, sir."

Riker only frowned and shook his head.

Picard sat back in his chair, studying the alien ship, letting his people have a few seconds to get ready. A large empty area of the alien ship's surface seemed to suddenly pop out at him. It was above the equator ring, about halfway to one of the poles of the ship, and was just about the only area of the actual surface of the alien ship not covered with equipment. He hadn't noticed it before because it was painted exactly the same color as everything else.

"Data," Picard said, "take us right at that equipment-free area on the alien ship."

Data glanced up at the screen, then nodded. "Ready, sir."

"Make it so," Picard said.

The *Enterprise* surged directly at the alien ship on what seemed like a ramming course, firing phaser after phaser.

The alien ship returned fire, rocking the *Enterprise* like a child smashing a toy into the ground.

Picard hung onto his seat as the lights flickered and the ship shook.

"Shields at sixteen percent," Deanna said, her voice much calmer than Picard knew she was feeling.

Another blast rocked the *Enterprise*.

"Ten percent. Bulkhead failures on three decks."

"Keep pounding those shields, Lieutenant!" Picard ordered.

The alien shields flared bright red from the *Enterprise* phaser fire and then failed, right over the empty spot. The next phaser blast smashed into the alien ship, ripping open the black skin square in the middle of the smooth surface area.

"Probe away!" Riker shouted.

"Stop firing!" Picard ordered.

The probe slid through the opening, heading for the damage in the alien ship's surface.

"Bull's-eye!" Riker said.

"Nice shot," Picard said, nodding at his first officer's beaming face.

"Information coming in," Data said.

Another blast rocked them, but Picard didn't take his gaze from the probe and the area of the ship's surface they had hit.

"Forward shields failing!" Lieutenant Vale shouted.

"Data, put the aft shields between us and that ship!" Picard ordered. "Take us out of firing range."

The *Enterprise* turned and started to move away as one more blast rocked them, sending Riker tumbling from his chair. Picard managed to hold on, but just barely. That was one of the worst hits they had taken so far.

"Damage on all decks," Deanna said as she held on with both hands, her knuckles white.

"Aft shields holding!" Vale shouted, clearly excited.

If this didn't work, Picard had no idea what they would do next. They had been lucky to get away from this attempt. He just hoped the information they were getting was going to be worth it.

He watched the alien ship, expecting the hole in the alien shields to close back up. Instead, for the first time in hours, something on that massive ship changed. The hole in the shields remained.

"Photon torpedoes! Target that opening!"

Suddenly the shields around the rest of the alien sphere flickered, flashed through blue and green colors, and then drained backward into a dozen holes in the ship, like water flowing down a massive drain.

The alien ship was completely exposed.

Picard could see that a series of explosions was occurring just under the surface of the alien ship, where the last phaser blast had gotten through. They had hit something, and for the moment the ship was vulnerable. But the question was, how long?

"Full scan of that ship!" he ordered. "Give me targets. I don't want those shields coming back up."

"They are not going to, Captain," Data said.

Picard pulled his attention away from the area of the alien ship that was exploding and stared at Data. "Explain?"

"We have destroyed the ship's control room," Data said, studying the data coming in. Then he glanced back at Picard, his yellow eyes intense and level. "All twelve of the alien ship's crew are dead."

"Dead?"

"Yes, sir," Data said. "From the readings I am getting, there are no life signs on that ship."

Picard stared at the now-helpless black sphere floating in space. The longest fight he'd ever been in. And now it was over, that quickly.

It almost seemed wrong.

Almost.

CHAPTER
2

Picard sat back in his chair, a cup of Earl Grey tea in his hand, and waited, trying to get himself to relax just a little more. The last ten hours since the fight with the alien ship had ended had been long and very hectic. There had been a thousand things to do, both on the *Enterprise* and in the colony. He could feel the exhaustion crawling over his body, making his arms and legs ache. The tea helped, but not enough. A decent night's rest was exactly what he needed. And he was going to get it very soon. Only a few more things to do first.

He finished keying in the code on his communications screen, then leaned back and closed his eyes, letting the warmth of the tea and the quiet room calm and clear his mind. This fight had been strange from moment one, and the cleanup of both the *Enterprise* and the colony had been hard. And were far from over. It would take another week before everything onboard was back to complete normal. For the colony, it would take years; a rough count put over a thousand colonists dead and thousands more injured.

No one had any idea why the aliens had attacked. Picard had a hunch it was going to be a question that would trouble a lot of people for a long time to come. Maybe the answer would be found on the alien ship, but he doubted that, with the alien crew dead.

The communications screen in front of him beeped softly, and he opened his eyes as the Starfleet insignia was replaced by the broad, smiling face of Captain Montgomery Scott.

"Capt'n," Scott said, his smile getting even broader. "'Tis good ta see ya again."

"Likewise, Captain," Picard said, putting his tea down and leaning forward. "It has been far too long since we've had the pleasure of your company aboard the *Enterprise*."

"An it's gonna be even longer," Scott said, laughing, "as busy as they're keepin' me around here."

Picard had a hunch Scott was enjoying being busy, especially in his job. During the last months of the war, Scott had been appointed the liaison between the Starfleet Corps of Engineers and the Starfleet Admiralty. And he was the perfect man for the job. He was respected by everyone. Period. And he not only knew how to navigate the world of Starfleet politics, but how to deal and work with engineers of every type. Picard's only thought when he had learned of the appointment was, "Of course."

"I'm afraid," Picard said, "that I'm not going to help your schedule much. I have a big job to dump in your lap."

Scott's grin faded some. "I read your preliminary report and scanned the battle information. That's a strange bird all right. And big." Scott chuckled. "The *Enterprise* always was a giant-killer."

Picard laughed. "We were a little too close to being stepped on by that giant for my blood."

Scott shook his head. "Gonna take a lot more than a big, ugly ball to stop the *Enterprise*. So, what more can ya tell me about that alien monster?"

"Not much, I'm sorry to say," Picard said. "We've been so busy dealing with our own repairs and helping the colonists that we haven't had time to even start to explore the thing yet. I can tell you its metal is resistant to any scanning. We have no idea why."

Scott laughed, the sound deep and rich, then waved a hand in dismissal of Picard's apology. "That's our job, Capt'n."

"I was hoping you'd say that," Picard said. "We're due in the Folnar system as soon as we can get there."

"Don't ya worry, Capt'n," Scott said, "I gotta ship in the area. It will be there inside ten hours. We'll take good care of your friend there."

And Picard knew they would. The S.C.E. were the ones charged with the task of boarding unknown ships like the one they had just fought to sift through the rubble and learn what they could from the alien technology and even the remains of the aliens themselves. At times Picard thought that searching through alien ships for new information, new technology, would be exciting. In a way it was a branch of archaeology, his favorite hobby. Of course, when they were digging through the alien ships, most of the time it was in zero gravity, surrounded by intense radiation, and surrounded by far too many dead bodies.

But he knew that wasn't all that the S.C.E. people did by a long ways. If anything in the galaxy needed to be built, rebuilt, programmed, reprogrammed, assembled, reassembled or just understood, the S.C.E. was who you called on.

In many ways, the S.C.E. was the branch of Starfleet with the most varied and interesting job after these recent times of war, and Picard slightly envied them that.

"Would you mind, Captain," Picard asked, "if my Chief Engineer stuck around and worked with your people?"

"That monster's got La Forge's interest bubbling, has she?" Scott asked.

"Salivating, I think would describe it better," Picard said. "He's made sure all the major repairs to the *Enterprise* were done in record time, just for the chance to get over there and look at those strange shields and hull metal. But with us leaving for Folnar system, he's not going to get the chance, unless he stays with your people."

Scotty nodded. "I can remember doin' that a few times myself. I'll tell Captain Gold he's goin' ta have some help. He'll be happy ta hear it."

"Captain David Gold?" Picard asked. "The *da Vinci* is nearby?"

"Sure is," Scott said. "Speedin' your way at warp six."

Picard knew David Gold from all the way back to their Academy days. Gold had been one of the upperclassmen Picard had beat in the Academy marathon; they had become friends and kept in touch as often as their careers had allowed. Gold was what many called "old Starfleet." He ruled with a solid hand, and always kept the mission and his crew at the top of all priorities. But he had a wicked sense of humor that Picard loved. Gold was married to Rabbi Rachel Gilman, who had a thriving congregation in New York. Picard had lost track of all the grandchildren and great-grandchildren they had.

"I wish I could stay and say hello," Picard said. "Shame to be this close and not get the chance, but we'll be leaving within the hour."

Scotty smiled, the twinkle in his eyes clear from the contained laughter. "Well, you gotta pick up your Chief Engineer sometime, don't ya?"

Now it was Picard's turn to laugh. He hadn't thought of that at all. Geordi would have a shuttle-craft, but meeting the *da Vinci* after the next mission would be even better. It would be a great time to have an enjoyable dinner with Gold, find out how his wife and children were doing, and hear about some of the S.C.E. adventures and discoveries.

"Thank you, Captain," Picard said. "I just might do that. Hope your people find something worthwhile here."

"I'm sure we will," Captain Scott said. "I'm sure you'll be hearing all about it from Gold and La Forge."

"More than likely," Picard said, nodding at the smiling face of one of the legends of Starfleet history. "*Enterprise* out."

Picard leaned back and took another sip of his tea, savoring not only the taste, but also the quiet of the room. After a moment, he brought up on his screen the image of the alien ship. The massive black ball with its strange rings seemed to just hang there, taunting him. Every time he looked at the ship, he felt a sense of dread and unease. Even dead and helpless in space as it was, the ship looked and felt dangerous. Picard just couldn't shake the feeling.

Ten hours until the *da Vinci* arrived. Too long for Geordi to be alone with that thing, even with the colony nearby. Picard sipped the tea, and then clicked off the screen. With a tap on his communication link, he said, "Lieutenant Vale, report to me in my ready room."

If the *Enterprise* could make it a few days without its chief engineer, it could also make it without a security chief. And, that way, maybe he could sleep a little better as well.

CHAPTER
3

Lieutenant Vale's light snoring filled the small main cabin of the shuttlecraft *Cook*. Lieutenant Commander Geordi La Forge glanced over at her and smiled. She had a young and innocent look about her, with blond hair cut in a pageboy style, and round, blue eyes. She stood—in boots—no taller than five-three, and looked slight. But Geordi knew someone didn't make chief security officer in Starfleet without knowing every fighting trick there was. So far, she hadn't had to prove any of her skills, and she seemed cool enough under the pressure of battle. He just hoped this side mission would be no exception. It was certainly going to be interesting having her along.

She was slumped in the copilot's chair, her head back, her mouth slightly open. Captain Picard had forbidden him to enter the alien ship until the S.C.E. team arrived, but the captain had said nothing about landing on its surface and taking readings. No doubt doing nothing but gathering data for ten hours was boring to her, but not to him.

Especially not with *this* alien ship. Frustrating him, maybe, but not boring him.

At the moment, he had the *Cook* parked on a junction where the two rings met. They were very flat and smooth on top, and looked like wide highways leading off in four directions. Each ring was over a hundred meters wide and twenty thick. He had taken a dozen readings, using everything he could to penetrate the thick skin of the rings, but had had little success. The alloys that made up that hull were almost as good as shields when it came to blocking scans. He could tell there were no life signs, could get basic shapes and energy signatures from what appeared to be backup systems, and could tell there was a very wide hallway and lots of rooms in the rings below him, but nothing more. This ship's metal hull, whatever its exact makeup, might be a very important find for the Federation and Starfleet.

It was clear that unless he, or someone on the *da Vinci*, came up with a way to penetrate the hull, they were going to have to learn about this ship the old-fashioned way: by exploring it.

And finding out exactly what purpose these rings served was something he *really* wanted to know.

He turned and eased the *Cook* off its position on the ring and moved across the surface of the giant ship like he was skimming over a moon. Unlike the surface of the rings, the surface of the sphere was almost entirely covered with what looked like equipment. Over the last ten hours, he'd managed to identify some of it; he'd found hundreds of redundant environmental systems, and what looked like energy collectors. He had also pinpointed over one hundred airlocks.

But what was under that surface he had no idea, and it was driving him nuts.

He slowly lowered the *Cook* over what had been the only smooth area of the ship's surface before the final *Enterprise* attack. Now it was a large hole, showing layer after layer of open decks below. The top deck appeared to have been the ship's main control room. It was now mostly gone.

The clear surface wasn't made up of the same material as the rest of the hull, but looked as if it might be transparent from the inside, sort of a one-way window. Only it had been the biggest window Geordi had ever seen. The *Enterprise* could have landed on it and not even started to cover it all. On top of that, to be that big, the material had to be fantastically strong. That interested him as well.

The control room had faced the center part of the massive window. It must have had some spectacular view into space. Now it was nothing but a giant hole.

He scanned down through the mess, trying to penetrate into the open decks the explosion had exposed. This ship looked like it was big enough to hold a city's-worth of beings, yet only twelve had been aboard flying it. Why?

He hoped to find the answer to that question before this was over. And a thousand other questions as well.

Lieutenant Vale coughed lightly, gave a small snort, and turned to her right. A moment later her snoring returned, light and consistent.

Geordi smiled and shook his head in amusement. For a young officer on a strange away-mission, she certainly had a sense of comfort and self-assurance. He never would have been able to sleep in her position.

Suddenly the proximity alert beeped, warning them that another ship was approaching.

Vale snapped awake, coming out of her chair with one hand on her phaser. Her blue eyes were very round, and Geordi doubted she had taken a breath.

"Easy, Lieutenant," he said, holding up his hand to her as he glanced at the sensor readings. It was the *da Vinci*, dropping out of warp. "No sense in shooting who we're here to help."

She glared at him, then stood up straight and stretched, as if nothing unusual had happened.

"Have a nice nap?" he asked, smiling.

"Not really," she said, using one hand to massage her neck.

"Seemed like it was pretty good, considering how you were snoring."

Vale looked at him, at first slightly confused. Then she got this defiant look in her eyes. "I don't snore."

Geordi laughed. "Whatever you say. But I had to turn up the warning signal to make sure I heard it."

"Yeah, right," she said, turning away from him and dropping into the copilot's chair.

He could see a little red creeping up her neck, so he just smiled and said nothing. Having her along was going to be fun.

On the main screen, the *da Vinci* swept in, turning and swooping in the same motion. The sleek ship ended up in a position just above the *Cook*. Geordi was impressed. Their pilot must be good, and very confident, to approach like that.

"*Da Vinci* to *Enterprise* shuttlecraft *Cook*."

"Welcome, *da Vinci*," Geordi said as Captain Gold's smiling face filled the screen.

Geordi knew that Gold was only slightly older than Captain Picard, but he looked older. He was a thick man, with white hair and bushy eyebrows. Geordi could tell from his brown eyes that the man didn't miss much.

"Seems like Picard has left us with a doozy this time," Gold said. "Glad you wanted to stick around and give us a hand."

"Thanks to you and the S.C.E. team for having me, Captain," Geordi said. "Just couldn't leave this one without knowing what makes her tick."

Gold laughed. "We know the feeling. I assume you've gotten some readings in the last few hours?"

"What I *could* get," Geordi said. "It's not giving up its secrets easily."

"They seldom do," Gold said. "We're ready for docking when you are."

Ten minutes later, Geordi had slipped the *Cook* in beside the *da Vinci*'s two shuttles, and he and Vale were headed for the bridge.

"Never been onboard a *Saber*-class ship before,"

Vale said, glancing around the hallway and into a medical lab as they passed. "Feels small."

"Compared to the *Enterprise*, it is," Geordi said. "The *Saber*-class holds a crew of forty at most. But these ships can move and fight, trust me."

"Small and mean," she said, nodding. "I like that."

He glanced at her and decided it was just better to say nothing.

Ahead of them a door brushed open, and a woman stepped out, turning in the same direction they were heading. It took Geordi a moment before he recognized her. It was Sonya Gomez, who had been an ensign on the *Enterprise* ten years ago. He hadn't realized she was going to be on this mission. That's what he got for not checking.

He knew she had done well for herself in those ten years. She had ended up, during the war, as the chief engineer on the *U.S.S. Sentinel*. The *Sentinel* had found itself dead behind enemy lines, but Gomez had managed to get the warp core back up and running and adjust the warp field so that Breen sensors had thought the ship was Cardassian. She was decorated for that, and after the war she had been promoted to Commander and joined the S.C.E. as its commanding officer. Ten years ago he had been her superior officer; now, for this mission, she was going to be his.

"Not even going to say hello to an old friend?" Geordi asked, loud enough for Gomez to hear.

She glanced back and then stopped, a smile covering her attractive face. "Geordi."

She waited and gave him a hug. "I was excited when I heard you were coming aboard." Then she glanced at Vale and extended a hand. "Commander Gomez," she said.

"Lieutenant Vale," Vale said, shaking Gomez's hand.

Gomez looked her over for a moment. "So you're the *Enterprise*'s new Security Chief. Corsi's going to love meeting you."

"Oh," Vale said, "Lieutenant Commander Corsi and I go way back."

Gomez looked at Vale for a moment, puzzled, but when the young security chief didn't go on, she shrugged and turned to walk beside Geordi toward the bridge. Geordi was going to have to ask Vale later about her history with Lieutenant Commander Corsi, the security chief for the S.C.E.

"So what's it like working S.C.E.?" Geordi asked. "Actually running it."

"Wonderful, most of the time," she said. "Gold is a great captain, and we are constantly challenged. I must have a backlog of must-figure-out projects that would last an entire year—assuming I don't add on any more."

"Most of the time, huh?" Geordi asked, smiling at her.

"Climbing inside dead alien ships isn't always fun," she said.

Geordi could tell from the flat expression on her face that there were a few bad memories attached to that comment, so he didn't push it.

"We just spent a week on a hot, desert planet

trying to get a water system up and running for a candidate for Federation membership. I don't think I'm ever going to get all the sand out of places I don't want it to be."

Geordi laughed. "I see what you mean. I hope this project turns out better."

"Oh, trust me," she said, "as long as there isn't sand, I won't care. And, from the looks of the preliminary data the *Enterprise* sent us, we've got a real puzzle on our hands. That's always interesting."

"That's why I stayed," Geordi said. "Thanks for having me."

"As far as I'm concerned, you're always welcome," Gomez said. "The rest of the team is looking forward to meeting you. Your reputation precedes you."

"Not sure if that's good or bad," Geordi said, laughing. And he wasn't. But having Gomez make him feel welcome and wanted was a good sign of things to come.

The door to the bridge slipped open and Gomez led the way in, stepping to the right toward the science station. Captain Gold was sitting in the captain's chair, and the large alien ship filled the main screen.

Besides Captain Gold, there were three others on the bridge. A fit-looking man had the conn under the main screen. A blond Bajoran woman was at the operations station, and a well-muscled Atrean male sat at engineering. Geordi didn't recognize any of them.

Captain Gold glanced around, then smiled and

stood, moving to shake Geordi's hand. "Welcome aboard, Lieutenant Commander."

"Thank you, sir," Geordi said, shaking the firm, strong hand of the captain. Gold was instantly likable, and clearly in charge. Very much like Captain Picard.

Geordi turned and indicated Vale. "This is the *Enterprise's* Chief of Security, Lieutenant Christine Vale."

"Welcome, Lieutenant," Gold said, also shaking her hand.

"A pleasure," Vale said. "And a beautiful ship you have here."

Gold laughed and winked at Geordi. "I like an officer who knows how to say the right things to a captain."

"Better warn Captain Picard," Gomez said to Geordi, moving over to join them. "Captain Gold here has a way of getting people he likes to work for him."

Smartly, Vale said nothing. Geordi was starting to understand exactly why Lieutenant Vale had gone so far so quickly. She was smart and knew when to speak and when not to, a valuable skill in Starfleet.

"Let me introduce you to my bridge crew," Gold said, "then Commander Gomez can get you introduced to her S.C.E. team."

The captain did a quick once-around-the-bridge. The young ensign at the conn was a human named Songmin Wong. He seemed very shy, and just nodded when introduced.

The Bajoran at operations was Lieutenant Ina

Mar. She had to be even younger than Wong, but nowhere near as shy. She had bright red hair and the longest, slimmest fingers Geordi had ever seen. When he shook her hand, he didn't want to let go, or look away from her eyes.

The chief engineer was an Atrean male named Lieutenant Jil Barnak. He was middle-aged, heavyset, and very strong.

Geordi had a sense they were all very good at their jobs. And, being under Captain Gold as the bridge crew of the flagship of the S.C.E., they would see their share of action.

As the introductions were finishing, Gomez turned to Captain Gold. "My first insertion team will be ready to go in twenty minutes. You have any sense of where we should start first?"

Geordi was impressed. Gomez was in charge of the S.C.E., but she respected Gold enough to ask his opinion. Clearly, they had worked this way a number of times in the past. It was the way Captain Picard and Commander Riker worked together at times. Picard was in charge, but he valued Riker's opinion. He didn't always take it, but he valued it.

Gold shook his head. "From everything Lieutenant Commander La Forge and the *Enterprise* have given us, plus our initial scans, I'd say slow-but-sure is best."

"My thinking exactly," she said. "We'll focus on building a map of that thing, identifying important areas, seeing if we can tap into its computers, and then decide what we need to take out."

"What are you thinking of doing with it?" Lieutenant Vale asked.

"Way too early to know," Gomez said. "Towing something that big to a starbase would be impossible on our own, and I doubt we're going to get it up and running again, from the looks of that damage. Often, we just take the information and hardware we think is salvageable and useful and drop the ships into the nearest sun. We'll see."

Gold nodded. "Be careful in there. I think Captain Scott's description of this thing as a monster is right on the money."

Gomez laughed. "I've been getting the same feeling."

Geordi didn't laugh. He had had the exact same reaction to the alien ship since the moment he first saw it. It was an unknown beast, and taming it and pulling out its secrets was going to be something the best team of engineers in Starfleet might just have trouble doing.

CHAPTER
4

Gomez felt the transporter beam release them on an open ledge just inside the hole the *Enterprise* had blasted in the skin of the ship. The boots of her environmental suit snapped her onto the deck, holding her in place in what *should* have been zero gravity. Only she could tell it wasn't. The alien ship's artificial gravity system was still working. Amazing.

As per regulations, Gomez had her phaser drawn. But with just a glance around, she put it away. The force of the phaser blasts had pretty much cleared this area of everything.

"Standard check of suits," Corsi said, reminding everyone of that regulation. They were all in full environmental suits, and after any beam-in they were required to run a quick diagnostic of their suits and report any problems.

Lieutenant Commander Corsi was their security chief, and a stickler for following rules. She got on the nerves of the others on the team at times, but Gomez liked what she brought to the table. Corsi made their missions safer. And Gomez agreed with this annoying regulation, mostly because it was better to discover something wrong with a suit right away than when a situation got rough.

Gomez did the quick diagnostic of her suit, getting full green across the small display over her eyebrows. "Clear," she said.

Geordi, who was beside her, said, "Clear."

She had picked only four of her team for this first mapping session, and, one at a time, as per regulations, they reported in to Corsi.

"Clear," Stevens said.

Fabian Stevens had been an engineer with Starfleet for a number of years, including a long stint on the *Defiant*. He was their expert in tactical systems, which was why she had picked him for this first jump into the alien ship.

"Clear," Duffy said.

Lieutenant Commander Kieran Duffy was her second in command, and as good an engineer as there was. He had served as second in command under her predecessor, Salek. This mission on the *da Vinci* was the first time they had served together since their days on the *Enterprise*, and since they had had an on-again, off-again long-distance relationship, they were both still taking it slow so far.

"Clear," Pattie said.

Pattie's real designation was P8 Blue. She was a Nasat—a member of a large, insectoid race that looked something like a terran pill-bug grown to almost human size—and didn't require an environmental suit thanks to her shell and eight arms and legs. Gomez had picked her for this first jump into the big ship because of the chance of running into any unforeseen circumstances. Pattie was the best they had in getting around in low gravity.

The rest of her S.C.E. crew was still onboard, watching and monitoring everything closely. She could see the *da Vinci* holding over the hole, its presence reassuring her.

"Clear," Corsi said, finishing the drill.

Gomez glanced around at her team and Geordi, all of whom were now holding tricorders, scanning the area around them.

"Seems someone left the lights on," Stevens said. "I've got constant point-nine-three gravity."

"Power's still on in what looks like energy conduits."

"Looks like the *Enterprise* didn't hit the power source," Geordi said, "only the control area and crew."

"Copy," Gomez said, glancing down into the massive hole the *Enterprise* had smashed through the decks. That hole had now become a dangerous fall instead of an easy access path.

Around her the walls of the ship were blackened and twisted, but it was clear that they had been light gray, and the hallways that led away from the destruction were wide and still lit. Gravity inside this big ship and power still on would make it easier to explore, by and large. Just more dangerous.

"It also seems," Stevens said, "that airtight

doors sealed in all exposed corridors. We still might have atmosphere in some sections of this baby."

"This changes nothing, people," Gomez said. "We stay with the plan to map this place slow-but-sure. Pattie, you and Stevens go to the right down that passageway; Duffy and Corsi, go left. Geordi and I will go down. No one gets out of contact. Understood?"

She glanced around at everyone nodding.

"Move out."

"Deck at a time?" Geordi asked her after flipping his comm link so that only she could hear him. "Or all the way to the bottom of the blast hole?"

She glanced down. From the readings they had been able to get, the blast had blown a hole through at least seven of the alien ship's decks. The two decks below the control room deck seemed similar to this one. "Down four," she said. "I'll lead."

Geordi nodded.

She engaged the antigrav controls on her suit and stepped out into the air. The suit held her, and she let herself drop slowly, using her tricorder to record what she could see of each deck. Above her, Geordi was doing the same. All the readings from all the tricorders were being fed back to the *da Vinci*, where the computer was working on building a three-dimensional holo-image of this ship, deck by deck, as well as analyzing all the materials and equipment they saw.

The farther down she floated, the smaller the blast hole became, and the shorter distance the damage extended back into the exposed corridors and rooms. She picked a corridor leading off to her right on the fourth deck, eased herself over into position, and landed, stepping away from the edge to give Geordi time to follow her.

The corridor seemed to curve slightly away from her. It was wide and almost warm-feeling, with decorations covering one area just a few steps away. She waited for Geordi to join her, then pointed to one half-closed door nearby. "Want to give it a try?"

"I'm betting on personal quarters," he said.

"No bet." She had been thinking the same thing. This corridor looked like many personal areas of ships she had been on in the past. Only, if they were right, where were all the inhabitants?

It took both of them to budge the door enough to slip inside the room. It was a very large, very colorful room, with a type of bed against one wall, tables and other furniture in the center, and a private bathroom area to one side. There were no pictures of any of the inhabitants, but clearly, from the size and shape of the furniture, they had been humanoid.

"Wow, this is a lot nicer than my room on the *da Vinci.*"

"Same with mine on the *Enterprise*," Geordi said. "But I'll bet, for this ship, this is small."

"Again no bet," she said.

Geordi moved toward a small room off the main one while she headed to where her tricorder showed her a clear space behind a bulkhead. As she approached, a door in the wall slid silently open, revealing odd, metallic cloth in various shapes and sizes hanging there, with other pieces on the floor, as if tossed there just recently. The metallic fibers scanned to be a variation on whatever metal it was that made up the hull of the ship. Alien clothing, Gomez thought, belonging to whoever built this ship.

She glanced back at Geordi as he came out of the bathroom and saw what she had found. "Okay. The *Enterprise* detected twelve life-forms on this whole ship. But there's room for thousands—maybe hundreds of thousands—of passengers, passengers that were using these compartments. What happened to them?"

"I have no idea," Geordi said, "but from the looks of everything, they haven't been gone long. That room was a bathroom, I think, for someone with anatomy I think we'd recognize. It could use a good cleaning, unless that smell is some kind of air freshener. Looks like whoever left here intended to come back soon."

She had to agree. This place looked as if it had been left only this morning. There was something else—there was a sense of alien luxury to the room. Gomez wished she'd brought Carol Abramowitz along—the alien culture expert. She'd be able to tell exactly what the room was used for. "Let's keep moving."

Geordi nodded.

"Commander?" Stevens' voice called to her over the group channel.

"Go ahead," she said as she and Geordi moved back out into the corridor and she pointed to their right to move farther down the wide corridor.

"We've run into three sealed emergency doors," Stevens said. "In three different corridors. Looks like all the corridors were sealed off when the *Enterprise* ruptured the hull."

Ahead of her, Gomez could see that she and Geordi were facing the same thing in this corridor. Chances were the sealed doors meant the rest of this ship was still pressurized and full of atmosphere. They were going to have to set up a way to get through those pressure doors without causing more decompression. Or get the transporter adjusted enough to beam to the other side. That would be the easiest, if they could figure out a way to get through this metal.

"Commander," Corsi said, breaking in, "if we missed both the gravity and the atmosphere in our initial scans through this ship's hull, we might have missed more crew as well."

"I'm starting to realize that," Gomez said. She knew exactly what she had to do. "Everyone move back to the edge of the blast hole. Gomez to *da Vinci*. Bring us home when you have clear signals."

She and Geordi moved back toward the end of the hallway. Ten steps from the ragged edge, the transporter beam took them. In their first short foray into the belly of the beast, they had learned enough to know they needed to be better prepared before they came back.

And as far as she was concerned, that knowledge was very much worth the trip.

CHAPTER
5

Geordi glanced up as Lieutenant Vale poked her head into the panel he was inside; he was lying on his back, working on a sensor relay over his head.

"Don't you ever sleep?" she asked.

He laughed. "Not lately," he said, dropping the calibration tool on his chest and cracking his fingers.

In fact, now that she mentioned it, he couldn't remember exactly how long it *had* been since he'd slept. He'd been on duty since before the distress call and the fight with the alien ship everyone was calling the *Beast*. Then, almost twelve hours of emergency repair work after the fight; then, ten hours of scanning the *Beast* while waiting for the *da Vinci*. Now they had been back onboard the *da Vinci*, after the first short mission, for almost six hours, working on the sensors and transporter, trying to find a way to get them to work through that alien metal. None of the engineers had slept, and it hadn't occurred to him either.

"Well," Vale said, "you are going to need to take a break pretty soon."

"Friendship talking?" Geordi asked, smiling at her. "Or duty?"

"Both," she said, her blue eyes showing him warmth and caring. "Captain Picard sent me along to watch your back and try to keep you out of trouble, and that's exactly what I'm doing."

Geordi laughed. "Noted. But, as you can tell, my back is safe at the moment."

She laughed and scooted back out of the panel entrance as two people came up behind her.

"Thank—"

"—you," the voices said to Vale. "We—"

"—won't be long."

"No problem," Vale said. "I was finished."

The two faces of 110 and 111 appeared in the entrance to the panel where Vale had been a moment before. 110 and 111 were the names of a linked pair of the computer-dependent race called Bynars. Geordi had heard of these two before meeting them. They were supposed to be two of the best computer experts anywhere, and somehow the pair had been assigned to the *da Vinci* as civilian consultants to the S.C.E.

How, Geordi had no idea, but it was very lucky they were here. Corrections and adjustments to the sensors that would have taken Geordi a day to figure out had taken the Bynars, with his and Stevens' help, a little over two hours.

The only thing that annoyed Geordi about them was that they talked together, never completing an entire sentence alone. After the last number of hours working with and around the Bynars, Geordi could understand that maybe there would be a time when he would become accustomed to their manner of speaking. But that was a long way off.

"Are you—"

"—almost finished—"

"—with the—"

"—relay adjustments?"

"One moment," Geordi said. He did two small final adjustments and checked over his work. The alien ship's metal alloys had been blocking the sensors in much the same way as a shield's harmonics did. But, by running computer models, the Bynars had found an exact band that should penetrate the blockage. Geordi figured it was going to work, but the question was how well. With luck, good enough to focus a transporter beam.

"Done. Coming out." He scooted feet-first out of the panel as the two Bynars backed out of his way.

"We are—"

"—ready as well."

Geordi nodded and tapped his combadge. "Commander, give it a try."

"Affirmative," Gomez's voice came back. "Stand by."

Geordi smiled at the two Bynars, who simply stood like robots and waited. Even Data had more personality than these two at times, and Data was an android.

"Bingo," Gomez said. "Good work, you three. Get back up here, and we'll see what we can see."

Both Bynars smiled right along with Geordi, then waited for him to lead the way, even though it was their ship. Thankfully, as far as Geordi was concerned, they didn't try to make small talk as they walked.

The S.C.E. team had a staging room near the *da Vinci*'s bridge. Usually the room had only a large table and eleven chairs for the captain and the ten senior S.C.E. team members. But for this mission, the chairs had been pulled back against the wall and the center of the table had been rigged up to project a hologram of the alien ship. As they gathered details about the *Beast*, the computer would fill in the three-dimensional map floating above the table's surface.

As Geordi and the Bynars entered the staging room, the hologram was slowly filling in. Not with great detail, but at least with deck shapings and sizes, like a thin sketch. Clearly, the sensors could get through the skin better than before. Not anywhere near as well as he would have liked, but enough for the moment.

Gomez and Stevens were watching, along with Carol Abramowitz, a short, black-haired woman who was the team's specialist in intercultural relations, and P8 Blue, who was a structural specialist.

"We're getting clear images of the top deck area," Stevens said. "And the rings. But the deeper we go into the center of the ship, the worse it gets."

"We will—"

"—continue to—"

"—make adjustments."

"Please," Gomez said.

As one, the Bynars nodded, turned, and left.

Carol stared at the image of the alien ship filling in slowly. "We're going to need to find their central computer. Can you have the sensors locate and pinpoint it?"

"Sure," Stevens said, his fingers going to work on the computer controls.

Geordi watched as detail after tiny detail appeared, thick near the surface, very light and sketchy toward the center. Geordi could tell it was one amazing ship. There had to be far over a hundred decks, with large open areas scattered throughout. And the rings looked more like observation decks than anything else. There were a number of very large, multiroom private quarters scattered in the rings, and a lot of large gathering areas. Clearly the ship had been designed by a race as advanced as the Federation, to carry thousands and thousands of beings.

Suddenly Geordi realized that the surface of the rings was smooth. "Check out the material on the outer side of the rings," he said, pointing. "I'm betting you can see through it from the inside."

Stevens did a few quick calculations, then looked up, shocked. "You're right. Every inch of floor inside those rings had an unobstructed view into space."

"What the hell *was* this ship?" Gomez asked.

"I'm putting my money on a cruise ship of some sort," Carol said.

Geordi knew instantly she was right. It would explain the lush cabin they had been in, and the rings.

Gomez was nodding. "You just might be right. We'll have to wait and see."

Geordi watched as the computer scans slowly filled in detail after detail. The answers to the questions *What happened to the people on this ship?* and *Why was the ship built?* and *Why did it attack a colony?* weren't going to be filled in by the computer scanners, that much was for sure.

"Computer," Gomez said, "at this rate of scanning, how long until a complete image of the ship is finished?"

"Six hours, seven minutes, and ten seconds," the ship's computer said. "At this scanning level."

Gomez nodded. She glanced at Geordi, and then at P8 Blue. "Pattie, you want to stay here and monitor this? The rest of us need some sleep."

"Boy, you aren't kidding there," Carol said.

"Agree completely," Stevens said.

Geordi said nothing. He wanted to stay and keep working, but he knew he needed a few hours' rest at least. After Vale had brought up the subject of sleep, he had been wondering how he would find time to catch a nap. Clearly, Gomez was taking care of her team on all counts.

"I would be happy to," Pattie said. "I find the structure of this alien ship completely fascinating, and would enjoy the time to study this as it forms."

"Thanks," Gomez said. "Inform me and the captain at once if the computer picks up any sign of life at all in there."

"Of course," Pattie said.

"Geordi, you all right bunking on your shuttle for the time being?"

"Expected it," he said. He knew the size of the *da Vinci*, and since they had a full complement, many of the crew were sharing rooms. That was standard for a ship this size. There was certainly no luxury of guest quarters, like on the *Enterprise*.

Or on that *Beast* out there.

Gomez nodded. "The entire team will meet back here in six hours."

Ten minutes later, Geordi crawled into the bunk across the shuttle's small sleeping compartment from Lieutenant Vale. She opened her eyes and smiled. "Glad you are following my suggestion."

"Commander's orders," he said. "Now, no snoring."

"I don't snore," she said firmly.

"Right."

He rolled over on his side to face the bulkhead, trying not to laugh.

"I don't snore," Vale said again.

He didn't respond. A few deep breaths and the exhaustion took him before his mind could start to work again on the puzzle that was called the *Beast*.

CHAPTER 6

Gomez looked from the transporter pad at the worried face of Duffy and smiled. Clearly, he cared as much about her welfare as she did about his. If they could just both relax a little, being assigned together might turn out to be a lot of fun.

"Ready when you are, Commander," Stevens said from the transporter controls. "I've got a clear lock just inside the sealed door on the top deck."

Gomez glanced at Corsi to her right and then Geordi to her left. She had decided that the three of them would beam in first, with Stevens keeping a lock on them until they signaled the all clear. The sensors had shown the atmosphere inside the ship to be breathable, and no life-forms to be seen, at least on the decks closest to the surface. They still didn't have a very clear picture of what was near the center of the *Beast*. She had talked with Captain Gold, and both of them had agreed that they shouldn't risk a large part of the team. The three of them would test the waters first.

"Do it," she said, nodding to Stevens. Then, with a smile at Duffy, she felt the transporter take her.

The inside of the hallway smelled of burnt wires and peaches. She hadn't thought of peaches in a long time. It wasn't a strong odor, but noticeable. The walls in this corridor were painted a soft white, the floor was soft under her feet, and what looked like a computer panel filled one wall about a dozen paces ahead. Behind them, the sealed door led out into the cold of space, where this ship's control room had once been.

Geordi was doing a quick scan of the atmosphere while Corsi scanned for any life-form that might be dangerous.

"Preliminary scans from the *da Vinci* were on the money," Geordi said. "A little higher levels of oxygen than we're used to, but it won't hurt us any."

"No sign of any life," Corsi reported, putting her phaser away.

"*Da Vinci*, can you hear me?"

"Clear as a bell," Stevens' voice came back. "And we still have a clean transporter lock on you."

"We're fine here," she said. "Atmosphere is good. Starting our descent. Have the second team insert."

"Affirmative."

The second team was Pattie and the Bynars, led by Duffy. They were going to beam into a point on the other side of the ship and start down toward the center of the ship, exploring and mapping as they went. Stevens was going to stay on the sensors and let her know when either team reached their point-of-no-return level as far as the transporter went. She figured that level was twenty decks down, but the Bynars said it would be twenty-three. She had a hunch they were going to be right. They usually were about anything to do with computers.

But that left over a hundred decks below that point. At some point, she was going to have to figure out what was worth exploring and what wasn't. Otherwise, they'd be roaming around inside this monster for the rest of the year.

Geordi had moved ahead and was using his tricorder to study the computer panel on the wall. She and Corsi moved over to join him.

The panel looked like a schematic, touch-screen type that was on standby status. It had a red line arching over the length of the panel. It took her a moment to realize that, more than likely, she was looking at a schematic of the hallway they were standing in.

"If this thing really was a type of cruise ship," Corsi said, "this panel should be easy to use."

"I think I can activate it," Geordi said, looking up from his tricorder. "You want me to give it a try?"

"Do it," Gomez said.

Corsi looked worried, her ice-blue eyes slitted and focused, but she said nothing.

Geordi reached forward and touched a spot on the computer panel. The entire thing lit up in bright reds and greens. Gomez had been right, it was a map of the area of the ship on this deck—

hallways, rooms, and all. And it even showed where they were standing, and the fact that there were three of them. Clearly, the *Beast*'s sensors, to a limited degree, were still working.

Geordi studied his tricorder for a moment, then reached up and touched another point on the wall.

"You are on deck one, quarter section red, fifth segment," a computer voice said.

"Our translators picked that up quickly," Geordi said. "The basic language of whoever built this ship must be compatible with our basics."

"Agreed," Gomez said. "Carol's going to love this." She stared at the board, trying to study what it could show them. "Corsi, walk ten feet away and then return."

Corsi did, and, as she moved, the red dot on the map indicating her position moved with her.

"Interesting," Geordi said.

"Can it show us the closest access to deck two?" Gomez asked.

A red line appeared on the screen, marking a path to a door on their right.

"It seems the *Beast*'s translators don't have a problem with our speech, either," Geordi said, laughing.

She didn't join in his laugh. Actually, it gave her shivers, for some reason she couldn't figure out.

"If there was a way to download this information to the *da Vinci*," Gomez said, "we wouldn't have to worry about mapping any of this monster."

"Wouldn't that be nice," Corsi said.

"Especially if we could tap into it and track all the team's movements," Geordi said.

Gomez agreed completely. The sooner they could turn their attention fully to finding out more about who built this ship and what had happened to them, the happier she was going to be. And maybe, along the way, find out if there was anything on board that Starfleet and the Federation could use, like this ship's strange shields.

She flipped open her tricorder, and she and Geordi spent the next minute studying the computer panel while Corsi paced. Finally, Geordi scanned down under the panel, then clicked open a small access area and continued scanning.

"Anything?"

"Maybe," he said.

"Stevens to Commander Gomez."

"Go ahead," Gomez said.

"Any problems down there?" Stevens asked. "I'm not showing you three moving much."

She laughed. "We're fine. Just trying to access a working computer panel. Stand by and prepare an isolated computer storage area for a possible download."

"Affirmative," Stevens said.

"Got it," Geordi said. He attached his tricorder to the inside of the panel under the screen and made a few quick adjustments. "Stevens, are you picking up the signal from my tricorder?"

"I am," Stevens' voice came back strong.

"This could be a large amount of data," Gomez said. "So make sure you have enough space to handle it."

"Affirmative," Stevens said. "Stand by."

As she watched, Geordi made a few more slight

adjustments on his tricorder. Then he glanced up at her. "I'm fairly certain this panel only taps into specific data on mapping and layout of the ship, as well as tracking of passengers. I doubt we'll get into the ship's main computer from here."

"Makes sense, security-wise," Corsi said, "if this was a tourist liner."

"Yeah," Gomez said. "It actually does."

"Ready," Stevens' voice came back clear.

"Starting download now," Geordi said.

He tapped his tricorder and then stepped back. Gomez knew that, if nothing else, the speed of his tricorder was going to make the download a slow process, considering the size of this ship.

"Stevens," Gomez said, "beam us another tricorder and we'll continue exploring. How's the other team doing?"

"Down seven decks, without problems," Stevens answered as the tricorder appeared a few steps away and Geordi retrieved it. "They found a massive hydro-garden still alive on deck five."

"Tell them not to worry about the information panels in the hallways," Gomez said, "since we've already dealt with that."

"Ahead of you," Stevens said.

Geordi laughed. "You have a great team here."

Gomez smiled. "Coming from you, La Forge, that means a lot."

He smiled, then said, "How about, instead of going down for the moment, we go up and check out the rings? Give the computer time to get all the information from the panel directional system."

Gomez looked down the wide hallway that

slowly curved away in the distance. If their guess about this being a tourist liner was right, most of what they would find in the decks below were rooms. And the second team was exploring downward at the moment anyway.

"Good idea. Stevens, change of plans for team one. We're going to see if we can find an access to the rings."

"Affirmative," Stevens said.

Geordi turned back to the computer panel, then stopped. "Let's ask the next one down the hall."

She laughed.

"What, afraid you're going to overload it?" Corsi asked.

"Better to not take chances," Geordi said.

"With unknown technology, I agree completely," Gomez said.

A hundred paces down the hallway, past twenty doors, was another computer board. Geordi touched it and brought it to life. Gomez noted that, again, it showed them as three red dots. No doubt the red meant they were unidentified. If they had been passengers on this ship, more than likely they would have been a different color. And, also more than likely, still another color for the crew.

"Where is the closest access to one of the rings?" Geordi asked the computer panel.

The computer image changed scale slightly and a red line appeared, leading them in the direction they were heading. The line ended in a large, open-looking area.

The hike was like walking ten times the length of the *Enterprise*, with smaller side corridors moving off in both directions about every hundred paces. She could see other, even smaller corridors branching off of each of those side corridors. And doors. Seemingly thousands of doors.

Gomez was getting a real sense of the size of this *Beast*. They were just walking a small part of one area of the outer deck. Their preliminary scans showed there were well over a hundred decks below this one.

"Wow!" Corsi said as the corridor finally opened up onto a massive room.

Gomez had to agree. In all her years, she had never seen anything this stunningly spectacular before. The room was more than large enough to land the *da Vinci* in, with massive growing trees and shrubs scattered everywhere. A beautiful waterfall cascaded down the side of a rock face near the center, giving the room a soothing background noise. There were literally hundreds of furniture groupings on different levels around the space, clearly designed like a massive meeting and resting place.

A slight wind blew through the trees, and the peach odor was stronger here.

"Elevators," Geordi said, pointing at some almost invisible clear platforms that floated upward in continuing columns in five places around the room. A few feet from each upward column were platforms moving slowly downward as well.

All in all, this was one of the most spectacular rooms she had ever been in. But it wasn't just the room that was stunning; it was the sky above them.

Or, more accurately, space.

Open, beautiful space, with the *da Vinci* off to one side, was the ceiling to this room. She knew that a hundred meters overhead there had to be the surface of one of the black rings. But from where they stood, she couldn't tell it.

Geordi shook his head and glanced at her. "No matter what we find in this thing, I'm putting in a vote right now that this *Beast* be towed to a nearby starbase and repaired. It would be a shame to toss this into a sun."

"I'll second that," Corsi said.

Gomez glanced at her hard-edged security chief. It wasn't often Corsi was awed by anything, but clearly this was one of those times.

Gomez had to admit, she was just as awed. And now even more determined to discover where the passengers of this ship had gone. And why the twelve remaining crew had attacked a colony.

Once she found out the answers to those questions, she would make the decision as to what would happen to this fantastically beautiful and powerful alien cruise ship.

CHAPTER
7

For some reason, even though he was now one hundred percent convinced that the *Beast* was an alien cruise ship, designed for tourists, that information didn't calm Geordi's uneasy feeling about it.

After exploring the spectacular observation decks on the rings, which was like walking in open space under the incredible windows, Gomez had recalled all the teams to wait for the results of the computer download.

Twenty minutes later, after the download had been completed, Stevens and the Bynars had meshed the information from the *da Vinci* scans with the downloaded information from the *Beast* and fed it all to the holo-image of the ship in the staging room.

They now had a mostly clear deck plan of the *Beast*, one they could focus in on in very decent detail in certain areas. In other areas, it still showed nothing. It was those black spaces Geordi was the most worried about. Still, the detail of the holomap was going to make their job a lot easier, and let them get to working on the real questions much faster. And Geordi had a sneaking hunch a lot of those questions would be answered in the engineering section of the ship, and by accessing the main computer, not in the passenger sections.

But the problem was that the download from the directional computers on the *Beast* only showed public areas, calling the support areas private. Most of the lower decks were labeled support areas. And since the *da Vinci* scans were still having problems getting all the way to the center of the *Beast*, there were still big empty areas in the center of the hologram image.

"Okay, people," Gomez said, getting the attention of the entire S.C.E. team and Captain Gold, who were all standing around the table, talking and discussing the alien ship.

For Geordi, this was the first time he had seen the entire team together. It was an impressive group of talent and skills Gomez had put together. Top-ranked engineers, two of the leading computer experts in the Federation, respected specialists in intercultural relations and languages, a great flagship with an experienced captain, and some top security people. Geordi was glad he had gotten this chance to work with them.

The only member he hadn't met was the stern-faced Dr. Elizabeth Lense, but he knew her by reputation. She had served on the *Lexington* and graduated from her medical class as valedictorian, the same class that had contained Dr. Julian

Bashir. Dr. Crusher had been raving about a couple of Lense's recent medical papers.

Lieutenant Vale moved over and stood silently beside him as Gomez went on.

"Since the *Beast*'s main control room was destroyed, we're going to have to get to the secondary control room, and the engineering section. From what we've learned from our scans, combined with the computer download, the secondary control room *should be* on deck ninety, and the engineering sections might fill the five decks below that."

"Are those decks still outside of transporter range?" Carol asked.

Gomez glanced at the Bynars.

"We have—"

"—made adjustments—"

"—but cannot—"

"—penetrate past—"

"—deck sixty."

"So we go the rest of the way without a safety net," Gomez said, glancing at Geordi.

Geordi nodded to her, agreeing. He didn't much like the idea of not being able to be pulled out in an emergency, but he'd been in lots of situations over the years where there was no quick escape. This would just be another.

"We do it by the book," Corsi said.

"Agreed," Gomez said. "I don't want any stupid heroics in there, people. We go in, we get what we are looking for, and we come out. Once we determine the place is safe, we can explore more. Understood?"

Everyone except Captain Gold nodded. He just watched, his sharp gaze missing nothing as far as Geordi could tell.

"I'll lead insertion team one," Gomez said, "consisting of Commander La Forge, Lieutenant Vale, 110 and 111. We'll go for the engineering section. Duffy, you, Pattie, Stevens, Faulwell, and Corsi are team two. Find that secondary control room. And both teams are looking for the main computer, or any access to the main computer. Understood?"

Again everyone nodded.

"Good," Gomez said. "We jump in on deck fifty-five and go down from there. I want the two teams to remain separated, but staying close enough to help the other if needed. We jump in ten minutes. Get ready."

The room broke back into talking, and Lieutenant Vale turned to Geordi. "Anything special I need for this kind of mission? I'm afraid I'm not up to date on the S.C.E. insertion team regs."

Geordi shrugged. "I've honestly no idea on the security side. Better check with Lieutenant Commander Corsi."

Vale had a pained expression on her face, and Geordi suddenly remembered Vale had said the two went way back.

"Problem, Lieutenant?" Geordi asked, managing to not smile.

Vale took a deep breath and shook her head. "Meet you in the transporter room."

Then, as Geordi watched, the young security chief moved toward the older woman, who frowned when she saw Vale coming. Geordi waited just long enough to make sure the two didn't come to blows, then turned to head for the transporter room.

He didn't need to ask Gomez what he needed to bring along. Give him a tricorder and a phaser and he was as ready as he was ever going to be. Missions like this were the reasons he had joined Starfleet in the first place. He loved going to new places, seeking out new information, new technology, boldly going where no Federation engineer had gone before.

And in a few minutes, he was going to be getting the chance to do just that again. He loved the chance, so why was he so worried about it?

Behind him, floating above the conference table, beside the two security officers, the image of the *Beast* rotated slowly.

CHAPTER
8

Gomez glanced around, her phaser drawn, as the transporter beam released them deep inside the *Beast*. Both Geordi and Lieutenant Vale had their phasers drawn as well. The room they had beamed into was large and well-lit, but not as plushly furnished as the upper decks. It looked to Gomez to be some sort of dining area. There were chairs and long tables, and some paintings attached to the walls.

"Clear," Vale said.

Gomez and Geordi both put their phasers away.

"Looks like this ship had some economy-class passenger fares as well," Geordi said.

"You didn't expect all the rooms to look like those suites up in the rings, did you?" Gomez asked.

"Actually, I was hoping they would," Geordi said.

"Always knew you were an unbridled optimist," Gomez said, smiling at her old friend.

She glanced around and saw the entrance to

what looked to be a sort of passenger lift. She had had some discussion with Corsi and Duffy about using the lifts, then decided to go ahead. She wasn't sure if she liked the idea, but from what they could tell of the ship's layout, the only other way up and down was to crawl through maintenance tubes. And she just didn't want to do that for over forty decks.

"*Da Vinci*, can you hear me?" she asked, tapping her combadge.

"Loud and clear," Captain Gold's voice came back strong. "And we're going to try to hold a computer lock on you for as long as we can."

"Understood," Gomez said. "We'll stop and check in every ten decks."

She turned and headed for the corridor leading to the lift they had planned to use. Geordi dropped in behind her, with the two Bynars following together, and Lieutenant Vale covering their flank.

At the lift, she touched a glowing red panel underneath a glowing green panel. Duffy's team had figured out during the first insertion that on the lifts, the red meant down and the green up.

A moment later, the door slid open.

She didn't want to step into that large, round lift, but she forced herself to.

Geordi followed easily, clearly not bothered, and the Bynars moved in and stood to one side without comment, but Vale looked as nervous about coming onboard as she felt.

"Stand in the opening for a moment," Gomez said to Vale. "I want to make sure we know how to work this thing."

Geordi moved over beside her, his tricorder out. She touched the upper part of the small computer panel on one side of the lift wall.

"Deck?" the computer voice asked.

"Sixty-five," Gomez said.

Geordi nodded that it was working fine.

"Deck sixty-five," the computer repeated. "Please stand clear of the door."

Gomez motioned for Vale to move inside. As Vale did, the door slid closed.

Gomez glanced around. It didn't seem as if the lift was working. Less than five seconds after the door had closed, it slid silently open again.

"Deck sixty-five," the alien computer said.

Vale, looking confused, instantly drew her phaser and stepped back into the open doorway to make sure it stayed open, scanning the hallway in both directions.

"Fastest lifts I've ever seen," Geordi said, scanning his tricorder.

"We actually dropped ten decks?" Vale asked. "The hallway looks the same."

"Yes—"

"—we did," the Bynars said.

"Efficient—"

"—system."

"Very efficient." Gomez tapped her combadge. "Captain, you still with us?"

"That was a quick drop, Commander," Gold's voice came back, strong and clear. "You all right?"

"Smoothest lift ride I've ever taken," she said. "We'll go for another ten decks."

"Affirmative," Gold said.

Gomez motioned for Geordi to tap the panel again, and for Vale to step back inside.

"Deck seventy-five, please," Geordi asked.

The door slid closed, and Gomez tried to get any sense of moving. There just wasn't any. No slightly increased gravity, nothing. Just as fast as the first time, the door slid open.

"Deck seventy-five."

Vale stepped back into the doorway, checking the hall, phaser still drawn. "We are clearly in the economy class now," she said. "The doors are spaced every ten paces, and there are more side corridors."

"Captain?" Gomez said, tapping her combadge.

"We're barely holding on to your signal," Gold said, his voice much more distant. "We could not beam you out at that depth."

"Understood," she said. "We'll just jump on down to deck ninety-one and see what we can find. Track us as best you can."

"Will do," Gold said. "Happy hunting."

"Thanks," she said.

She glanced around. "Okay, people, we're on our own. Let's go see if we can find the engineering room."

"Deck ninety-one," Geordi said as he tapped the panel.

"Access denied below deck eighty-nine," the computer said. The door remained open, even though Vale had stepped back out of the way.

"I was afraid of that," Geordi said. "We're not crew, so we can't take public transportation into the crew areas."

"Can you override that?" she asked, pulling out her tricorder and moving over beside him.

"I don't know," Geordi said as he popped open the access panel over the control area and scanned it. Vale stepped back into the doorway to keep it open and guard them.

"The process—"

"—is simple," the Bynars said.

Gomez tapped Geordi on the shoulder to have him step back and let the Bynars into the panel. Instantly they went into a fast-speaking, clicking exchange with the computer. When they did that, no translator could keep up with them. They were interfacing directly with the lift's computer.

Geordi glanced at her with a puzzled look, and Vale just seemed stunned as the two Bynars worked and talked to the lift's computer system.

After a moment, they stepped back in unison, as they always walked.

"We have—"

"—allowed access—"

"—to all team—"

"—members—"

"—to all crew—"

"—areas."

"Even the second team members?"

"Yes," 110 said.

"All," 111 said.

"Great work," she said. She signaled for Vale to let the door close.

"Deck ninety-one," Gomez said again.

"Deck ninety-one," the computer said.

This time the door took seven seconds to reopen.

Vale poked her head out cautiously, scanning both directions with her tricorder, keeping her phaser out. Finally she said, "Clear."

Gomez followed her out into the hallway. Here there was no soft surface, no art, just door after door on both sides of the hallway, leading off in both directions. At this depth, the hallways curved much quicker. And the gravity felt just a touch lighter than up higher.

"Crew's quarters," Geordi said, studying his tricorder. "But there are energy signatures coming from ten decks down. I think that might be a warp core I'm reading."

She nodded and tapped her combadge. "*Da Vinci*, are you with us?"

Nothing but silence.

"They will—"

"—be able—"

"—to track us," the Bynars said. "But—"

"—they will not—"

"—be able to communicate—"

"—with us."

Gomez nodded and turned back to Geordi. "Any idea what's in the core of this thing?"

"Getting weird readings," Geordi said, frowning. "It seems to be hollow, more than likely a null-gravity core of some sort, starting at deck one hundred and four. And it's packed loosely with some sort of substance I'm not getting a fix on. We need to get closer."

"So we head to the warp core area," Gomez said, motioning for Vale to come back inside the lift.

"Deck one hundred and one," Geordi said.

Five seconds later, the doors reopened.

"Still clear," Vale said as Gomez and Geordi moved out, tricorders in hand, studying the large room in front of them. This one room seemed to extend and curve all the way around the ship, with only massive pillars holding the decks above it.

Gomez glanced at her readings, then at Geordi, wondering if he was as surprised as she was. The question of how this ship moved through space was answered. This entire deck level was one massive array of black-hole propulsion systems, all clearly designed to work in tandem.

She went to her left, glancing from her tricorder to the marvel around her. This ship was pushed through space by a drive that many races had tried and mostly failed with. From what she could tell, dozens of tiny black holes were dropped into subspace and then returned to normal space a slight distance away, shoving the containment, and thus the ship. From the looks of this, she would bet this ship could have reached speeds faster than the *da Vinci* could, and maintain the speed indefinitely.

"This is an engineering gold mine," Geordi said. "We need to find an interface with the computer."

"Agreed," Gomez said. "But where do we—"

"Excuse me, Commander," Vale said.

Gomez glanced over at the lieutenant. Her face was pale as she stared at her tricorder.

"I think you need to take a look at the core of this ship before we do anything else," Vale said.

Gomez quickly set her scanner to check out

what was below them. Beside her, Geordi did the same.

For an instant, she didn't want to think about what she was reading. The core was clearly null gravity, and she guessed it was normally empty. With this kind of structure and drive, an empty core would be the most stable.

But, at the moment, the massive core of this ship was far from empty.

She looked up at Geordi and the shocked expression that covered his face.

"Humanoid bodies?" she asked.

Geordi nodded. Then, weakly, he said, "Hundreds of thousands of them. All dead."

"I was afraid you were going to say that."

"Oh, no," Vale said, her hand over her mouth at the horror of it all.

"It seems—"

"—we now know where—"

"—the passengers went."

Gomez glanced at the Bynars, then back at her tricorder and the impossible readings she was getting. What had happened here? They had seen no signs of a struggle.

Who had killed these people? How?

And why?

The overwhelming dread of what she knew she had to order next filled her. She took a deep breath, then, as calmly and as in control as she could manage, she said, "Let's go take a look."

CHAPTER
9

The absolute last thing Geordi wanted to do was get anywhere near this ship's core. Not with hundreds of thousands of humanoid bodies floating in it. Yet, he was working with the S.C.E. on an insertion team, and doing the hard jobs was what the S.C.E. did. Clearly, investigating this was going to be one of those hard jobs.

Gomez led them into the lift, and Geordi took a deep breath, trying to prepare himself. Clearly, Vale was as shaken as he was with the idea. The two Bynars even seemed agitated, talking in soft computer clicks between themselves.

"Deck fifty-five," Gomez said.

The lift door closed as Geordi glanced at her. "Thought you said we needed to take a look?"

"We do," she said. "But I'm not sure what I'd be looking at, to tell you the truth. I want Dr. Lense with us."

"She's going to thank you later," Vale said.

"If she doesn't kill you first," Geordi said.

Gomez only nodded as the door slid open. She motioned for Vale to hold the door in position and tapped her combadge. *"Da Vinci*, come in."

"Go ahead, Commander," Gold's voice came back.

"Are you still in communications contact with team two?"

"No," Gold said. "They're on deck ninety, as best our scans can tell."

"Understood," Gomez said.

Geordi watched her. Obviously she had wanted a bigger team to tackle what they were heading into, but it seemed that wasn't really possible. At least not with her top people. And Geordi doubted that she wanted to spend the time to stop on deck ninety and find them.

"Have Dr. Lense beam down to join us," she said.

"She is right here on the bridge," Gold said. "She's ready and heading for the transporter room. Give her one minute."

"Understood," Gomez said. "Out."

They all stood there in silence, clearly thinking of what they were about to see. By the time Dr. Lense appeared, ten paces from the lift, Geordi had all kinds of things imagined in that core. His biggest worry was that nothing he imagined would be as bad as it was really going to be.

"Problem?" Lense asked, moving to join them in the lift.

"A big one," Gomez said, motioning for Vale to clear the door and let it close. "Deck one hundred and four."

"Deck one hundred and three is the last deck above the ship's core area," the computer said. "The lift does not extend down into the core."

"Lucky it," Vale said.

Dr. Lense gave her a sharp look, then turned back to Gomez, but the commander said nothing.

"Deck one hundred and three, then," Geordi said.

Twelve of the longest seconds Geordi had ever lived passed as they waited in silence for the lift to take them down into the belly of the *Beast*. Dr. Lense clearly wanted to know why she had been brought along, but Gomez seemed unwilling to tell her at the moment. More than likely Gomez wanted Dr. Lense to get the readings for herself, to double-check what they had discovered.

The doors opened.

Vale, phaser drawn, checked both ways, then said, "Clear."

"Someone want to explain to me what I'm walking into here?" Lense said.

"Bodies," Gomez said. "If we can find a way into the core area of this ship."

"The passengers—"

"—and crew—"

"—are there."

"Dead."

"But this ship could hold thousands, maybe hundreds of thousands of humanoids," Lense said, staring at the Bynars after glancing at Geordi.

"Yes—"

"—we know."

All Geordi could do was nod at Dr. Lense as the reality started to dawn on her. She quickly pulled out her tricorder and scanned around them, something Geordi had been unwilling to do yet.

"Oh, my . . ." she said, her voice breaking as the tricorder gave her the readings.

"There's an observation port ahead," Gomez said, her voice firm. "Everyone, brace yourselves for this."

She moved ahead, getting to the clear viewport a few steps ahead of Geordi. She staggered slightly as she got in front, as if punched in the stomach, then stopped, took a deep breath, and turned and stared.

Geordi knew his fears had been right the instant he was at the viewport. It *was* worse than he had imagined. The race that had inhabited this cruise ship was clearly humanoid in almost every fashion. Most of them wore bright clothing, and the crew wore white outfits. They all had thick, black hair and large, unblinking green eyes. They looked like an attractive people.

They were packed into what had to be a core area big enough to hold the *Enterprise*. They were all floating, limbs tangled up in limbs, faces moving slowly past the viewport.

Faces frozen in terror and pain.

It was like a giant, slowly moving, zero-g dance of bodies.

Lense was studying her tricorder, a bead of sweat dripping off her forehead.

"Can you tell me what killed them?" Gomez asked.

"No," Lense said, "I can't, exactly. There seem to be varied reasons. None of this makes any sense."

"You're telling us?" Vale said.

"What?" Gomez said, flipping her tricorder into action.

Geordi forced himself, after the doctor's strange comments, to study the mass in the vacuum on the other side of that port.

She was right. He couldn't tell right off what had killed the people closest to the port. Some seemed to show signs of the decompression that came with being tossed alive into space.

Other bodies looked like they had been cut apart in some way. Some bodies were missing arms; others, legs; a few, heads.

Still others had puncture wounds of different types. Actually, the more he noticed, the more he saw that they *all* had puncture wounds.

Then something caught his attention to the right of the port, just inside the core. A movement out there that didn't seem to fit in with the slow waltz of the dead. He studied the area, trying to make himself see only the patterns in the dead limbs and faces.

Then he saw it again. A movement along one of the body's arms.

"There's something moving in there!"

He pointed to the right, and both Gomez and Dr. Lense aimed their tricorders in that direction. Something small and dark was chewing on an arm, swallowing hunks of flesh as it burrowed inside.

Geordi felt his stomach twist as the entity disappeared into the body, leaving a pretty good hole in the dead flesh.

The creature looked like a combination between a crab and a wasp, and clearly was able to function in the nonatmosphere environment of space.

He looked at the body closest to him. There were small holes of different sizes all over it as well.

Suddenly Dr. Lense stepped back from the window, as if it had shocked her. "This is a breeding nest," she said.

"The bodies are food?" Geordi asked.

"Exactly," Lense said. "Placed there for the hatchlings."

"And the eggs have hatched, it seems."

"Less than an hour ago," Lense said, "from what I can tell."

"Which is why we scanned no signs of life in this ship," Vale said.

"Well, there's life now," Gomez said.

The bodies were starting to move more and more as the creatures devoured them, drilling in and out, making the cloth ripple on some. Every time Geordi got a glance at one of the creatures, he wanted to smash it, like a spider crawling on the floor.

How did they get in here, if they were space-born creatures?

Geordi scanned past the bodies at the walls of the core. There were large tubes, big enough to easily fly the *da Vinci* through, that seemed to lead up through the ship, more than likely to hatches on the surface. And around the walls there were docking ports. This core had served more than one function. It was the loading and unloading area, more than likely for supplies. Through one of those ports—that must have been how the creatures got in.

The bodies were floating up into those tubes as well as in the core.

"Can you tell where the main nest is?" Gomez asked.

Dr. Lense shook her head. "I think you're looking at it. The eggs were planted in these bodies. Some of these people were still alive when the eggs were planted."

"Now I know I'm going to be sick," Vale said.

"Where are the adults?" Gomez asked.

"Dead," Geordi said. "I'll bet those are the twelve killed in the fight with the *Enterprise*."

"You mean these creatures are intelligent?" Vale asked. "And twelve of them did all this?"

"Oh, they are intelligent, all right," Dr. Lense said, nodding. She pointed to a body floating beyond about twelve humanoids. "A hive-mind sort of intelligence, more than likely passed down from one generation to the other. There's one of the egg-layers."

Geordi followed where she was pointing and finally saw one of the adult creatures, clearly dead.

"More than likely there was an entire swarm of these things that took over this ship, but they must die when they lay their eggs."

"And now we have a new swarm growing right in front of our eyes," Gomez said. "The offspring of a swarm that killed hundreds of thousands of humanoids for food."

"Exactly," Dr. Lense said.

Geordi tried to imagine a man-sized creature that looked like a crab and wasp coming at him. He didn't like the thought at all. But Dr. Lense's theory did answer one question.

"That explains why this ship was attacking the farming colony," Geordi said.

Dr. Lense nodded. "They were looking for more food, so that more of their young could be born."

They all stood there in silence, watching the creatures grow larger and larger by the minute. Finally, Vale asked, "Now what do we do?"

"We get team two," Gomez said, "and return to the *da Vinci*. The last thing the Federation needs is a swarm of humanoid-eating creatures attacking ships. So, we're going to toss this thing into the sun before any of these creatures can escape."

That will not be allowed.

The voice seemed to fill Geordi's head, making him feel dirty.

All of them, including the two Bynars, had their phasers out at the same instant. But the voice hadn't come from one place. It had come from the hive, and Geordi knew it.

Slowly, Geordi made himself look back at the port. At least fifty of the half-eaten humanoid bodies were now lined up facing the viewport, like soldiers on a field. The young creatures were almost four inches long, and getting bigger and bigger as they ate. Bones were starting to show, and creatures crawled in and out of the eyes and mouths.

And as they ate, the dead bodies seemed to jerk and dance, always keeping in a precise line, staring at Geordi and the rest of them.

"We should—"

"—leave."

"Agreed," Gomez said. "Let's move, people."

That will not be allowed.

Again the hive voice filled their heads.

"Geordi," Gomez said, "you've got four minutes to find a way to block that thing. And by that I mean one minute. Got it?"

"Yes, sir," Geordi said. If he cross-routed the tricorder circuits the way Deanna Troi had once shown him, Geordi thought, he could set up a static field to block the creature's telepathic broadcasts—probably throughout the ship.

Then the time for thinking was over. Geordi ran at full speed right behind Gomez and the Bynars and Dr. Lense. Only Vale was behind him.

CHAPTER
10

Captain Gold was stunned as he watched what he had thought was a dead ship come alive right before his eyes. The shields that he had studied on the tapes of the battle between the *Beast* and the *Enterprise* suddenly flowed from the ship like water, pouring out and covering everything.

"*Da Vinci* to insertion teams."

He waited, hoping for an answer, but he knew that the teams were too far inside the ship to be reached, and now, with the shields up, there was even more interference.

"What are they doing down there?"

"Sir," Ensign Wong said, "it might not be them."

"Shields up!" Gold shouted. "Red alert!"

The instant he gave the order, the ship below started to power weapons. A moment later, the blast rocked the *da Vinci* like a powerful earthquake shaking a building. Gold managed to hold on, but just barely.

"Shields at seventy percent," McAllan said from tactical. "Damage on three decks. No one hurt."

"Take us back and hold us just out of weapon's range!" he ordered. "And work on getting a signal through to one of the teams. I want to know what's happening down there."

He turned to Lieutenant Ina. "Put out a call to the *Enterprise*. I have a hunch we're going to need them back here at top speed."

She nodded.

"Out of range, sir," Wong said. "Holding position, but we're also out of transporter range."

"We'll worry about that when the time comes. Good warning on your part, Ensign."

"Thank you, sir," Wong said.

Gold leaned forward in his chair and studied the alien ship on the screen, trying to make sense out of what had just happened. Only there didn't seem to be any sense to be had. Who, or what, had brought that hulk of a ship back to life? Had his people done it accidentally?

Were his people still alive in there?

From out here, there was no way of telling and nothing he could do but wait, and try to contact them.

The problem was, waiting wasn't something he did easily.

"Sir," Lieutenant Ina said, "the *Enterprise* has responded. They will be back in just under three hours."

Gold nodded. Three hours might as well be three days. The *Enterprise* had barely beat this monster once. He just hoped he didn't have to go up against it full-on. But if he had to to save his teams in there, he would.

"Come on, people," he said. "Tell me what's going on in that *Beast*."

None of his crew answered him. He actually hadn't expected them to.

CHAPTER
11

The *Beast* was alive!

Lieutenant Commander Duffy stared around at the rest of his team. All had surprised and shocked looks on their faces.

The *Beast* was alive, and yet it couldn't be.

They had just spent the last half-hour in what appeared to be the *Beast*'s secondary—and only remaining—control room, getting what data they could and trying to figure out how this ship was run. They had been making some pretty decent progress, considering everything they were dealing with.

First off, the secondary control room was something far bigger than most ships' main bridges. It had seats for twenty crew, and stations that would take them months to figure out what they were intended to run.

Everything in the room seemed plush and done to impress visitors, yet it was clearly a functioning control area. And from what they could tell, when the main control room was destroyed, everything was automatically switched to this room.

Stevens had managed to figure out how to turn on the main viewscreen so that they could see the *da Vinci*, but beyond that, not much else had been tested yet.

Now, suddenly, everything was coming alive.

"Who did that?" Duffy shouted, looking around at his team as board after board became active.

"Didn't touch a thing!" Stevens said.

"Nothing here!" Bart Faulwell replied. The linguist had been trying to figure out the communications panel.

Pattie waved her two top legs in a negative gesture. "I did nothing to cause this, sir."

"Well, someone's doing something somewhere!" Duffy shouted. "Where's team one?"

"Near the core, from what I can tell," Stevens said.

Corsi nodded her head in agreement. She had been standing post near the control room door, and was now looking very worried. "I can barely make out their signatures on my scanners," she said.

"Could they be doing this?"

"Your guess is as good as mine," Bart said, "but I would doubt there's another control room down there."

"This ship's shields are going up," Pattie said, four of her eight legs waving in agitation above a control panel. "I am doing nothing, touching nothing."

"Weapons are powering!" Stevens said.

Duffy couldn't believe this nightmare. How was this happening? How was a dead ship suddenly coming back to life? "Stop them!"

"I don't know how to even start them!" Stevens shouted back as he frantically searched what they had pinpointed as one of the weapons boards. He

looked as if he wanted to touch something, anything, even start punching buttons at random, but
Stevens was a good enough engineer to know that
wouldn't help.

"I can tell you it isn't coming from here!" Bart said.
"All these systems are being overridden somehow!"

As they all watched on the main viewer, the
Beast fired on the *da Vinci*. For the second time in
twenty-four hours, an alien cruise ship had attacked a Starfleet ship.

"*Da Vinci* got her shields up in time!" Bart
shouted, and everyone cheered as the shot fired from
the *Beast* was deflected by the *da Vinci*'s defenses.

Duffy didn't know how, but Captain Gold had
managed to out-think what they couldn't figure
out down here. The guy never ceased to amaze.

"*Da Vinci*'s moving off to a safe distance," Bart
said. "No damage, from what I can tell from here."

"Okay," Duffy said, letting out a long breath he
felt like he'd been holding since everything went
crazy. "Now it's up to us. We're inside this *Beast*
and in the driver's seat. I want control back in this
room, or I want this ship dead in space, flat-
useless. We go after both, people. We shut down
those shields and cut the weapons."

"And if that doesn't work?" Bart asked.

"Then, if we have to, we blow up this monster."

He made sure he caught the gaze of everyone,
to see if they understood.

They all did.

"Let's get to work," he said. "All shortcuts are
allowed. I have a sneaking hunch we don't have
much time."

CHAPTER
12

"We're not getting in that lift," Lieutenant Vale said, her voice firm as they ran away from the viewport.

"Agreed," Gomez said. She held up her hand and had them all stop just short of the lift. Then she turned to Dr. Lense. "In your best guess, how long until those things in there are big enough to get out of that core?"

"And come after us physically, instead of through the ship's systems?" Dr. Lense asked.

"Exactly," Gomez said.

"An hour, maybe a little more, but I wouldn't count on it from the rate of their growth and their food supply in there. It might be only thirty minutes."

Gomez nodded. She didn't much like the answer, but at least the answer wasn't now. They had a little time.

"Somehow," Gomez said, "we have to reach the secondary control room."

"I doubt that's going to help," Geordi said.

"I agree with Geordi," Dr. Lense said. "They are controlling the ship from connections in that docking area, using the power of the hive-mind to tap into the ship's computer and override everything."

"How the heck do you know all that?" Geordi asked.

"This isn't the first time I've seen this kind of thing," Dr. Lense answered. "During the war—one of the Dominion's subject races . . . It wasn't these creatures, exactly, but it's close enough for me to make a guess."

"We—"

"—agree with—"

"—the doctor," 110 and 111 said.

"So we need to cut the power to the docking bay," Gomez said.

"Exactly," Geordi said. "Two decks above us in the engine room would be the place to do that."

Both Bynars nodded in unison. "We can—"

"—cut power there—"

"—easily."

"Access to climbing tube?" Gomez demanded, pulling out her tricorder. "Find us one fast."

"Here!" Vale said, moving to a side panel and yanking off the covering. There was a ladder inside.

"Vale, take point," Gomez said, "Doctor, you follow her as close as you can stay."

"You got it," Dr. Lense said as Vale headed into the tube and started climbing.

"I'll guard the flank," Geordi said.

Gomez nodded and indicated the two Bynars should follow Dr. Lense.

She was amazed at how fast they managed to climb that ladder. By the time she ducked out onto the deck of the engineering area, both the Bynars were at a terminal, using their computer-fast speech to form a connection to the computer.

Vale was guarding them and Dr. Lense, who was studying her tricorder and frowning.

Gomez stopped Geordi as he came out behind her. On the way up the ladder, she had realized that maybe the hive-mind wasn't completely telepathic at such a young age. Broadcasting a thought at close range might be easy, but she wagered that listening to some thoughts two decks away might still have to be done through the ship's systems.

So she whispered in his ear. "I want a way to blow this ship out of space."

"We can do it," Geordi whispered back. "I can set these black-hole engines to cascade. But damn it—I can't help feeling that if Captain Picard were here, he'd have found a way to reason with these creatures. Turning an enemy into a friend is better than . . ."

"Geordi, I wish they were giving us that option. If it'll make you feel better, I'll order you to take this ship down."

Geordi stared at her.

"I outrank you now. This is my call to make."

Geordi nodded and headed off at a run toward the nearest black-hole-drive system. She watched him for an instant, realizing that, more than likely, she had just issued their death warrant.

"Commander!" Vale said. "We need to keep each other covered."

"I'll help the Bynars, you stay with Geordi."

Vale looked relieved and headed off at a run, phaser in hand, after her shipmate.

The Bynars turned slightly as she approached.

"They have—"

"—attacked—"

"—the *da Vinci*. It has—"

"—retreated—"

"—safely."

"Shields are up and weapons charged, huh?" Gomez said. "Well, shut them down. I don't care how you do it, but I want that core and all those bugs' access to the ship's systems shut off."

Both nodded and turned back to the computer, their high-speed computer talk almost painful to listen to.

She turned to Dr. Lense. "Anything getting out of the core yet?"

"Not that I can tell," she said. "But they are growing at a fantastic rate. I'd say we have no more than twenty minutes before they can leave those food sources."

"And after that?" Gomez asked.

"We don't want to be inside this ship after that," Dr. Lense said.

Gomez nodded and glanced at her chronometer, so she knew exactly how long was left.

Three minutes of eternity later, Geordi and Lieutenant Vale came running back into view from around one part of a huge engine. As they approached, Geordi said, "Fifteen minutes."

Gomez nodded and again glanced at her chronometer. They were over one hundred decks inside this ship, with fifteen minutes to escape. Their chances were not looking good.

"We have cut—"

"—power to core—"

"—area. But we must—"

"—remain to monitor. You—"

"—go."

Geordi did a quick scan. "The *Beast*'s shields are down, and weapons have shut down as well. Ship is dormant again, for the moment."

"I'm not leaving anyone down here," Gomez said. Losing someone was just not an option as far as she was concerned.

"We have no—"

"—intention of staying."

"Just need—"

"—five minutes."

Gomez nodded as they turned back to the panel and continued to work, talking to the ship's computer at high speed again. "Geordi, you and Vale stay with them and make sure they get out. Dr. Lense and I will get to the second team and get them out."

"The lift is safe for the moment," Geordi said. "Use it."

"Planning to," Gomez said. "Make sure you give yourself enough time to get to a beam-out level."

"We will," Geordi said.

At a run, she and the doctor headed for the lift. She hated splitting the team, but in this situation, with the second team to think about as well, she had no choice.

She just hoped this choice of no choice didn't come back to haunt her.

CHAPTER
13

Duffy glanced around the plush, massive secondary control room at his team as panel after panel went dead in front of them. "All right, people," he shouted. "Now what's happening?"

Stevens glanced up at him. "Whoever was controlling the ship from the core area has been cut off. The *Beast*'s systems are now dormant again."

"But for how long?" Bart asked.

"That is a critical question," Pattie said.

"More than likely," Stevens said, "not long." He studied the information that was coming over his still-active panel for the moment, then smiled. "Someone in engineering is making sure nothing gets out of the core and retakes control."

"The Bynars?" Bart asked.

"From the speed, I would say so," Stevens said.

"So, what the heck is in that core?" Duffy asked.

"Trust me," Gomez said from the door, "it's not something any of us ever want to meet."

Duffy felt his heart soar. He hadn't let himself

think about the chance of Gomez getting stuck down there. Hearing her voice and seeing her was wonderful.

He smiled at her, and she half-smiled back, but her eyes were almost dead with worry. Something was terribly wrong. Even worse than they had thought. Dr. Lense was with her, but Duffy couldn't see any of the rest of Gomez's team. They must be the ones still below, holding whatever was in the core at bay.

"We have just about ten minutes before we need to be off this monster," Gomez said. "Just in case what we have set up below fails, what can you people do from here to make sure this thing never flies again?"

For a moment there was silence, then, finally, an idea came to Duffy. "The ship's systems are mostly dormant now. We could set up a feedback loop that would only kick in if a system like the shields was brought back on-line."

"Perfect," Bart said. "That would—"

Gomez held up her hand for silence. "No more talk about what you are doing until you are back on the *da Vinci*. I'll explain then."

Duffy nodded, and Gomez smiled a faint thanks.

"Duffy, Faulwell, Stevens," Gomez said, "do what you are thinking about in the next three minutes, and then get to a beam-out level and get off this ship. Not one second longer. Understood?"

Duffy nodded at the fierce look in Gomez's eyes, then glanced at his chronometer. In all the years he had known her, he had never seen her look like that before. Something down there in that core had clearly spooked her good.

"Understood," Duffy said.

"Dr. Lense, you stay with them and get off as well. Corsi, you and Pattie come with me. We're going back to help."

"You only have about nine minutes," Dr. Lense said.

Duffy looked at the doctor, then at Gomez. Nine minutes, and Gomez was going back down with a team. What was happening?

"Set it up and make sure it's going to work. Two minutes and thirty seconds, and then out of here." Gomez nodded to him and then headed off at a run.

He didn't have a good feeling about any of this. But with just barely two minutes to figure out a way to sabotage an alien ship, he didn't have time to think about it.

"Fabe, you take shields," Duffy said. "Bart, weapons systems. I'm going to try to make sure nothing gets out of the core area into space."

He went quickly to work, setting up a feedback loop in the commands to open the cargo doors that led down into the core from the surface of the ship. If something, or someone, were to try to open those doors, the computer would shut them and freeze the door permanently shut.

"Done," Stevens said, with eighteen seconds to spare.

Faulwell went right to the last second.

It took Duffy an extra five seconds over what he had promised Gomez, but he took the extra time anyway. Whatever was in that core had spooked the woman he loved. And she didn't spook easy, so he didn't want it coming out any time soon.

Then, at a run, they headed for the lift.

They asked the lift computer for deck fifty-five, but before the lift stopped, the transporter took them to safety.

There was only five minutes and ten seconds left.

CHAPTER
14

Geordi couldn't believe that Gomez and Pattie and Corsi had come back down. He would have done the same thing in Gomez's place, but it was still insanity, plain and simple.

He glanced at his chronometer. There was less than six minutes to go before those black-hole drives started cascading in on themselves. It was going to cause one major explosion. Not big enough to harm the colony, but enough to make sure nothing survived on this ship. And that meant all of them as well, if they were still here.

"We have to get out of here," Gomez said.

"We must build up—"

"—thirty seconds—"

"—of reserve time," the Bynars said.

Geordi knew exactly what they were doing. They were trying to make sure that everyone had thirty seconds to get up that lift and to safety before the hive-mind regained control of the computer.

"Thirty more seconds and they should have it," Geordi said to Gomez. Then, out of the corner of his eye, he caught a movement—fast, like a bug.

"They're out!" he shouted, pulling his phaser and taking cover.

Gomez and Corsi moved to take cover near a computer bank, pulling Pattie with them.

Vale stayed with him, moving to cover his back.

The two Bynars stayed in position at the computer terminal, never hesitating, standing and working as if nothing was happening around them.

"What is that?" Corsi demanded as Gomez fired, spraying the guts of one of the bugs against the wall.

Geordi was stunned at how big it was. Just a short time before, they had all been less than an inch long, crawling in the skin of humanoids in the core. This one now had to be three feet tall, still almost snow-white, but with deadly looking claws and wings tucked against a hard shell.

Clearly, Dr. Lense had been right about the point when they could stop eating.

Another movement caught Geordi's attention, and he fired on instinct, cutting down a bug as it tried to circle behind them.

"We're running out of time here!" Gomez shouted.

Geordi agreed, but if the Bynars didn't buy them the thirty seconds they needed to get to and up that lift, it wouldn't matter how soon they made a run for it.

Corsi fired, then Vale.

Two more bugs exploded on contact with the

phaser beam. The smell of burning chitin filled the area, choking them and making him cough.

Both Bynars turned from the panel at the same instant. They were done.

"Now," Geordi shouted.

"Everyone to the lift!" Gomez ordered.

But getting to the lift wasn't going to be easy.

Around them, hell suddenly crawled out of the shadows.

The smell was awful, a cross between a rotted corpse and a sewage treatment area. Geordi cut four, then five bugs down to the right, while Vale covered the left, firing almost constantly.

The two Bynars were firing together, first right, then left, bringing down two bugs at a time.

Gomez and Corsi and Pattie were trying to keep the path clear to the lift.

As a unit they moved, firing and making their way closer and closer to that lift door.

But to Geordi, each second seemed like an eternity.

The bugs just kept coming and coming. Geordi had never seen anything like it. Every step they got closer to the lift brought more bugs at them.

When Corsi and Pattie were within twenty paces of the lift, at least a dozen bugs bunched up right in front of them, seeming to not care if they were cut down.

At that point, Geordi and Vale and the two Bynars were almost on top of Gomez and Corsi and Pattie, forming a circle of defense and firing in all directions at the sea of wasp-crab insects. But Geordi knew that if they got stopped for even a few seconds in one spot, they'd never make that lift. These bugs would think nothing of simply overwhelming them with numbers.

"We have to get through this last group!" Gomez shouted between shots, clearly thinking along the same lines he was.

But the creatures seemed to be pouring in faster than the team could kill them. And there was a pile of dead insectoids forming in front of them, blocking their way to the lift. Going around or over was going to be hard, if not impossible.

The smell of burning insectoids was choking Geordi. If he lived through this, he would never get the smell out of his mind and off his skin.

"Corsi—maneuver 14!" Pattie shouted to Corsi.

"That's a zero-g move!" Corsi shouted.

"It will work!" Pattie said.

"Cover them!" Gomez shouted.

Pattie flipped into the air, holding two phasers in her top hands, and came down curled into a hard-shelled ball, all six of her legs out of sight.

Almost in the same movement, Corsi had her with both hands and, with a mighty heave, rolled her at the pile of bugs and bug-parts between them and the lift.

Pattie's hard shell smashed through the bugs like they were tissue paper, sending wasp-like crabs flying everywhere and drilling a path straight to the lift.

As Pattie hit the wall, she uncurled and came up firing, clearing away any bug that was near her.

Geordi and Vale and Gomez covered their flank as the two Bynars and Corsi laid down a constant fire, keeping the bugs back in the cross fire between them and Pattie.

The lift door opened and Pattie blocked it that way with her body, staying low and firing constantly with two phasers.

Geordi figured they just might make it when, suddenly, one of the bugs opened white wings that were under its shell, flapped them for an instant, and then flew at them.

Geordi hit it in flight, but one of its crab-like claws cut Vale across the back, smashing her into the ground.

She was up again almost instantly, but clearly hurt. Even though blood was pouring off her back, she kept firing. She was one tough person, that was for sure.

Corsi and Gomez made the lift and took up covering positions across from Pattie.

Then the Bynars reached the lift and moved to the right of the door, both firing constantly.

Now, more and more of the bugs had unfolded wings and were flying at them.

Geordi shoved Vale into the lift and dove after her.

"Come in low!" Geordi shouted as he and Vale fired high, trying to give the rest cover.

Corsi dove through, then Gomez backed in.

Pattie stepped back to let the Bynars in just as five bugs flew at them at once.

Geordi got one of them.

Vale took another.

Pattie blew another out of the air, and Gomez got the fourth.

But they all missed the other one.

As Geordi watched in horror, one of the bug's claws cleanly sliced off 111's head.

110 screamed in terror and moved to help his mate.

Geordi knew instantly there was nothing anyone could do for 111. She was dead.

Corsi grabbed 110, who was immobilized with shock, then tossed him over her shoulder and into the lift.

He scrambled to get up, to get back out to his mate, but Vale smashed him against the wall and held him down.

"Computer, deck fifty!" Gomez yelled.

The doors started to close as even more bugs smashed at them.

The firing was intense until finally the lift doors closed.

It was like slamming the door on hell.

One moment a desperate gun battle, the next silence, utter and complete, broken only by 110's sudden high-pitched keening, a sound like the death throes of a human computer.

Geordi just stared at the closed door, his phaser ready, expecting the doors to open again on his sure death. But for the longest seconds the doors stayed closed, and just as before, there was no sense of movement in the lifts.

Vale was trying to help the sobbing 110 to his feet when the transporter beam took them.

CHAPTER
15

Gomez stumbled off the transporter pad and tapped her combadge. "Captain, jump to warp and get away from here. Fast!"

She reached over the panel and clicked on the screen. The image of the *Beast* still filled the picture, but it was clear that the *da Vinci* was moving away quickly.

Suddenly, it seemed as if the skin of the *Beast* puffed out for a moment.

Then it shrunk back in on itself and imploded in a blinding flash of white light.

A moment later the screen cleared, showing only empty space. Wonderfully empty space.

She let herself lean against the console. Her knees were weak and her eyes felt as if they had had sand thrown in them. She couldn't believe she was out of that nightmare.

She looked around at her team. Duffy was clearly worried about her, but saying nothing. She would talk to him later, but right now wasn't the time.

Stevens and Bart both looked shaken, but fine.

Pattie sat on the edge of the platform, her eight arms and legs drooping.

Geordi leaned against the wall, his hands at his sides.

Corsi stood, looking almost lost and in shock.

Vale sat on the floor, holding the Bynar in her lap.

They were all out of the *Beast*, except one.

She moved over to where Vale was trying to console the sobbing Bynar. Blood was pooled under her and in her lap from her wounds, and her skin looked white. She needed help and she needed it fast, yet she was trying to help another. Captain Picard had a real jewel in her.

Dr. Lense grabbed Vale and shouted to the transporter technician, "Get Lieutenant Vale and me to sickbay stat." A moment later the doctor and the wounded officer dematerialized.

Just then, Captain Gold appeared in the door, looking worried and relieved at the same time. Then he saw the lone Bynar and he stopped cold.

"Don't tell me," he said.

"We lost one, Captain," Gomez said softly.

"Damn," he said, shaking his head, the news clearly hitting him hard.

She didn't want to let the fact that she had lost someone sink in. Not yet. She knew she couldn't deny it, but she didn't want to face it right now.

Geordi put his hand on her shoulder, then said, "Let's get him to sickbay as well."

She nodded and took a deep, shuddering breath, then leaned down, pulling the still-sobbing Bynar to his feet.

He looked at her, his eyes hollow and empty. "You should—have let—me go—back. I belong—back there."

Gomez glanced at the captain, then shook her head. "No, I shouldn't have. But I am sorry for your loss."

Geordi moved around to the other side of the Bynar and they managed to get him to the bed beside Vale in sickbay.

An hour later, after trying to scrub the smell off her skin in the shower, she sat across from Captain Gold, a drink in her hand, and tried to tell him what had happened, from her point of view.

He let her ramble, let her get it all out of her system the way she wanted to. The way she needed to.

He knew how to listen as well as give orders. And right now, he was the only one on the ship who understood what she was going through.

On the way back to her cabin, she stopped in sickbay. Both patients were sedated and sleeping. She had lost one team member. She would learn somehow to accept that, but she had gotten the rest out safely, and had stopped who knew how many more from dying if those bugs would have gotten out of that core.

The mission wasn't a success, but it wasn't a failure either. They had stopped a menace to the Federation cold—although as Geordi had said, turning an enemy into a friend would have been better. A member of her team had died. More than likely she would lose a second as well, because sometimes Bynar bonded pairs did not survive the

death of a mate. Only time would tell, and she was
willing to give him that time. She owed him that
much.

As Captain Gold had said to her, sometimes the
line between success and failure was very narrow.

She had walked that line this time. It didn't feel
good. But it wasn't all bad either.

CHAPTER
16

Geordi stood in the shuttlebay of the *da Vinci* and smiled as Lieutenant Vale got the shuttlecraft *Cook* ready to launch. She was doing everything by the book, right down to the last detail, and it amused him. He hadn't seen anyone go through this sort of preparation to take a shuttle flight since his days in the Academy.

When the *Beast* had blown up, the *Enterprise* had turned around and gone back to its mission. He and Vale had decided yesterday that she would take the *Cook* back to the *Enterprise* and he would stay and help the S.C.E. team a little more. There were things to do yet, files on the *Beast*'s technology to study, and the colonists needed a lot of help getting back on their feet.

Plus they had to finish reports on those insectoids and brief Starfleet as quickly as possible. Who knew how many more hives of them were out there, waiting to take over some unsuspecting craft.

"Well, I think I'm ready," she said, her blue eyes

full of life and the excitement of taking a long shuttlecraft trip alone.

Geordi could remember feeling the same way on his first long trip alone. Now he would just dread it. It was amazing how a person sometimes grew out of certain things. Long, solo shuttlecraft trips were one of those things.

"Lieutenant Vale," he said, stepping forward and shaking her firm hand. "You did great. Thank you."

She smiled. "Thank you for allowing me to come along. I'm not sure if I'll ever have another nightmare-free night's sleep, but I must say, this was exciting."

"The reason you joined Starfleet?" he asked.

She smiled. "No, Corsi was the reason I joined Starfleet. But that's a long story for another time."

"Now, wait," Geordi said, laughing. "You can't leave me hanging like that."

"You're staying here," Vale said, a very sly grin on her face. "Try to get the story out of her. That should be interesting."

Geordi laughed. "I expect a story when I get back to the *Enterprise*."

"Deal," she said.

She stepped back inside and, with a wave, closed the door to the shuttlecraft.

He waited and watched until she jumped to warp, then turned and headed toward the staging room. He was sure Gomez would have a hundred things for him to do. And right now, that was exactly what he needed. It was going to be fun, spending a little more time with the S.C.E.

Fun and work and maybe a little excitement as well.

FATAL ERROR

Keith R.A. DeCandido

CHAPTER
1

The holo in the center of Ansed's living room showed a comedy program that had stopped production a decade earlier, and for which Ansed owned no recordings. A minute ago, it had been showing archival footage of the landing of the Pevvni ship that had colonized the ninth planet fifty years ago. A minute before that, it had been showing a real-time image of the weather on Hendorf Island.

But, for the life of her, Ansed, First Speaker of Eerlik, could not get the holo to open a simple communications channel.

That was only *part* of the problem.

Ansed looked around the living room—currently illuminated by candles, since the lights no longer worked—and out the window at the hailstorm that should've been stopped by the weather control system. She pulled the blanket around her teal shoulders with her short arms—necessary, as the house's heating system was no longer functioning properly.

The unthinkable had happened. The great Ganitriul was breaking down. And if someone didn't stop it from doing so, the entire fabric of Eerlikka society would collapse.

Suddenly, the staccato slamming of hail against the outside of Ansed's house ceased. She looked out the window to see that the storm had *finally* abated.

There was no chance she'd be able to convince the holo to go to communications mode. She'd tried for hours to contact anyone she could, from her fellow speakers and the priests who kept the knowledge of Ganitriul on-planet, to the Pevvni colony, or even the nearest Federation outpost off-planet. Nothing worked. The priority at this point was to consult the clergy. Ansed feared that even they could do nothing—after all, the transporters and spacefaring vessels were also operated via Ganitriul, so they probably weren't functioning any better than the weather control system, the heat, the holo, or the lights. Still, they were the experts . . .

Left with no traditional method of speaking to the priests, Ansed was forced to go outside and *walk* to the temple. Ansed couldn't remember the last time she'd walked outside, nor the last time she'd gone from place to place in that manner. The necessity annoyed her, and the thought that the situation might continue was frightening.

She almost bruised her forehead on the door, which did not open at her approach as it was supposed to. Sighing, Ansed opened a window. She had closed her living room window for the first time in years today; usually, there was a nice breeze coming in. Now, though, she had to use the window as a door.

Clambering out, she was assaulted by the bitter cold. Since the construction of Ganitriul—long before Ansed's great-great-grandparents were born—the capital city had had an even climate. She was forced to continue to huddle inside the blanket in order to stay warm, since she did not have proper clothing for this weather, and the clothes-provider wasn't functioning any better than any other device.

For three millennia, the computer on the moon had provided every creature comfort the Eerlikka could want or need. Since Ganitriul's autorepair components had been installed a century ago, there had never even been a hint of a problem. Though tourists did make regular pilgrimages to the public parts of the caverns that housed Ganitriul's terminals, there had been no need for anyone to travel to the moon to effect repairs in a hundred years.

Until now.

After an exhausting walk of almost fifteen minutes, Ansed arrived at the temple. It was the only structure in the capital city that still retained the hideous Yarnallian architectural style, and Ansed had to admit to finding it painful to look at. But the priests insisted that the temple look as it had when it was first constructed, and Ansed could not blame them for that.

Of course, the temple's greeter wasn't working properly. She wondered how she would be able to gain the attention of those inside.

Then, noticing the ornate handle in the center of the door, she remembered that the temple still had one of those old-fashioned doors that opened manually. She could only hope that it wasn't locked.

First, she tried to slide the door to the side, the way normal doors worked, but it didn't budge. Then she pushed the door at the handle, but still it did not move.

Pulling, however, seemed to work.

Winded after all the walking and the effort of pulling the door open, Ansed took a moment to compose herself before entering the temple.

"Is anyone here?"

Her words echoed throughout the temple, which was almost pitch-dark.

Maybe this wasn't such a good idea, Ansed thought. She considered turning back and going home to try the holo again—but she didn't fancy the idea of walking any more, and dammit, she *needed* to talk to the priests. At least one of them had to be here. . . .

Suddenly, the lights in the temple came on—at about twice their usual intensity. Ansed's wide eyes were momentarily rendered useless by the sudden onslaught, and she blinked both her upper and lower eyelids furiously to clear the spots that now danced in front of her face.

When her vision cleared, she screamed. Ansed was the foremost political personage on all of Eerlik, and she'd been a respected scholar and politician for years prior to that. She hadn't screamed since she was in her crèche.

But she screamed now.

Seventeen priests and twenty acolytes served in the temple. In addition to their other spiritual duties, the priests were tasked with guarding all the knowledge that related to Ganitriul. If anyone would be able to solve the current crisis, it would be them.

Right now, Ansed stared at a pile of corpses that seemed to number approximately thirty-seven, all wearing the robes of either priests or acolytes. They looked like they had been placed there in a semiorderly pile. Blue blood was splattered all over the bodies, and pooled on the floor around them.

A shiver passed through Ansed that had nothing to do with the unnatural chill in the air. The numerous malfunctions were bad; this was worse. Ganitriul could, in theory, be fixed. But to have all the clergy dead . . .

"Help me! Somebody, please, help me!"

The voice seemed to come from amid the corpses. Ansed felt as if her short legs had grown roots. She couldn't move. Someone was obviously still alive in the midst of the carnage, but Ansed couldn't bring herself to investigate further. This was a task for Enforcement, not the First Speaker.

"Help me, please," the voice said, this time much smaller. Ansed saw someone crawling out from *under* the pile of bodies.

Somehow managing to overcome her fear and revulsion, Ansed made her feet move toward the voice and reached out one short arm to him.

With a grateful expression on his face—at least,

Ansed assumed the expression was grateful; it was hard to tell under all the blood—the young man reached out to grab the offered arm. Now that she got a look at him, Ansed recognized the young man as Undlar, who had only just been ordained a month earlier.

And now it seemed he was the only priest left.

The recognition went both ways, as Undlar stumbled to his feet, gazed upon Ansed and said, "F-First Speaker? Is—is that you?" Ansed noticed that the young man had a very large gash all the way down his right arm, and dozens of cuts and abrasions all over his person.

"Yes, Reger Undlar," she said. "I came to speak to the clergy."

With a sardonic tone that impressed Ansed, given Undlar's physical state, he said, "I—I'm afraid that w-won't really be possible, First Speaker."

"What happened?"

Undlar seemed to deflate. "I—I wish I knew. The—the power—it went out—obviously s-something has gone wrong with the Great One—and then—then we were all assaulted—*brutally*. We—we tried to fight back, but our guns wouldn't—wouldn't work. They had some—some kind of edged weapons."

That edged weapons had been used was obvious, given the types of wounds, but Ansed said nothing.

"We need to get you to a hospital." *And hope their equipment is functioning*, she did not say aloud. Undlar did not need to be reminded of that.

"And then we need to call Enforcement. They probably have their hands full, but this is something that will need to be dealt with right away."

"I—I'm sorry, First Speaker. I—I failed."

"You did no such thing, Reger. On the contrary, you showed tremendous courage." *And you may be the only hope we have*, she thought. Saying that aloud was equally inadvisable.

Supporting the young man—who started shaking as they began to walk—Ansed moved back outside into the cold, hoping that the trip to the hospital wouldn't exhaust her.

For thousands of years, Eerlik had prospered. There had been no reason to doubt that the golden age brought on by the construction of Ganitriul would ever end.

Now, the First Speaker of Eerlik had to wonder if that golden age was over—and if it was, whether the Eerlikka could survive its ending.

CHAPTER
2

Captain David Gold was dreaming of his wife's matzoh ball soup when he was awakened by the duty officer on the bridge of the *U.S.S. da Vinci*. There was an urgent message from S.C.E. Command.

Gold blinked the sleep out of his eyes and said, "Screen on." The viewscreen in his quarters flickered to life, first with the Starfleet logo, then with a familiar visage.

"Did I wake you? Sorry about that, lad," said Captain Montgomery Scott. *"Bloody time differences."*

Gold waved a hand dismissively. "Fact of life."

"I can give you a few minutes if y'need it."

Shaking his head, Gold said, "No need. Rachel's the one who needs four cups of tea to get going. When I'm up, I'm up."

"Good. There's a wee bit of a crisis on a planet called Eerlik. You'll need to set a new course there right away."

Without hesitating, Gold contacted the bridge and requested the course change, with speed at warp 9. "How long'll it take to get there?" he asked the duty officer.

"Fourteen-and-a-half hours at this speed, sir."

"Good. Gold out." He turned back to the image of the head of the Starfleet Corps of Engineers. "So, you gonna tell me what this is all about?" he asked with a small smile.

Although Scotty wasn't biologically that much older than Gold himself—about seven years, which at their age wasn't a significant difference—Scotty had, in fact, been born eighty-one years before Gold, which was the only reason Gold let him get away with referring to him as "lad." Scotty had spent some seven-and-a-half decades in a bizarre sort of suspended animation, as a regenerating transporter pattern, until he'd been freed a few years previous. Scotty had done a fine job of whipping the S.C.E. into shape. After all, who better to supervise Starfleet's "fix-it" squadron than the original miracle worker himself?

In answer to Gold's question, Scotty said, *"I'm sendin' you the full mission profile, but the short version is that Eerlik's in a right fix, an' the S.C.E. needs to get 'em out of it."*

"They're not part of the Federation, are they?"

"No, but we do trade with 'em. Turns out their entire bloody planet is run by one big sentient computer on their moon. Problem is, the computer— they call it 'Ganitriul,' whatever that means—is breakin' down. The planet's in a state o' chaos. The problem is, they're completely cut off from the

moon—whatever's bollixed up Ganitriul is keepin' their transporters, comm systems, an' ships from workin' right. In fact, we didn't get the distress call from Eerlik—we got it from Ganitriul itself."

"Really?"

Scotty nodded. *"It knows it's broken, but it can't fix itself."* Shaking his head, the older man said, *"In my day, when we saw a planet that had been taken over by one'a those— Ah, but that's neither here nor there. Your priority is to get the thing up an' runnin', pronto. No time to report to Starbase 505."*

Gold said, "But I've got crew to replace—and one to drop off."

"Aye, I heard about the Bynars. Extend my sympathies to 110, will you?"

"Of course. And we need a new computer specialist." He had been about to finish that sentence with the words, *to replace 110 and 111,* but that wouldn't be possible. They'd find someone to fill the position, but Gold doubted that he'd find anyone who could fill their shoes. *A damn shame, too,* he thought. The Bynar pairing wasn't even Starfleet; they were civilians, part of an exchange program—although they had agreed to abide by all Starfleet rules and regulations.

Not wanting to dwell on the recent unpleasantness, Gold added with a sardonic grin, "Plus, La Forge is itching to get back to the *Enterprise.*"

"Nothin' worse for a chief engineer than to be separated from his ship," Scotty said with a chuckle. *"I understand the difficulties, lad, but Eerlik's whole bloody socioeconomic structure's collapsin'. They canna wait."*

"I know the drill, Scotty. When they put that funny-looking 'A' on your chest, you dance where they tell you."

"Aye, that you do. Oh, by the way, I took your advice. Had dinner with your wife last night. Lovely woman. Makes a fine matzoh ball soup."

Shaking his head, Gold chuckled. *The universe is full of damn strange connections.* For months, Gold's wife—Rabbi Rachel Gilman, the finest cook on the east coast of the Americas—had been bugging her husband to get "the legend" to come over for dinner.

Returning the chuckle, Scotty said, *" 'Twas a lovely evening. I now know everything there is to know about your entire family. Oh, and your granddaughter's pregnant again."*

"You're kidding," Gold said. *I'm a great-grandfather again,* he thought, with a certain pride.

"She only found out yesterday, and Rachel asked me to pass it on. She really is a fine woman, lad. Pity she's all alone. . . ." Scotty had a slight twinkle in his eye, visible even on the viewscreen across the gulf of light-years.

"Don't even think about it," Gold said with an amused glare. "Otherwise, I'll set her mother on you, and *then* you'll be sorry."

Grinning, Scotty said, *"In any event, she really is a fine chef. You should convince her to make haggis."*

"Sorry, but she's a Jewish mother—she's only allowed to make edible food."

Putting his hand over his heart, Scotty said, with mock indignation, *"My dear lad! Haggis is a delicacy!"*

"I refuse to accept culinary judgments from a man whose idea of a good drink is liquid peat bog."

"Lad, people who live in slivovitz houses shouldn't throw stones." Shaking his head, Scotty said, *"In any event, I'll be off. The Sugihara will be in the area if you need any kind of backup."*

"Good."

"Scott out."

The screen went blank again. "Computer," Gold said, "leave messages for all personnel about our course change, and let the S.C.E. crew know that there's a staff meeting at—" he thought a moment, then finished, "—0800." That left him with three more hours to sleep, and would still give everyone over ten hours to prepare for the mission. "Leave copies of the mission profile with Commander Gomez and Lieutenant Commander Duffy. Oh, and instruct Duffy to compile a complete report on Eerlik, based on the profile."

"Acknowledged."

He thought a moment, then added, "Also, let Lieutenant Commander La Forge know that he's welcome to sit in on that meeting."

"Acknowledged," the computer repeated.

Within three seconds, David Gold had set his head on his pillow and was fast asleep again. A few seconds after that, he was dreaming of drinking a nice slivovitz white with his wife's soup.

Or maybe it was Scotch. . . .

110 stared at the ceiling of the quarters that, until recently, he had shared with the love of his life.

For hours, he had been trying to imagine how he could possibly go on without 111. It was proving to be impossible.

So was getting any rest. Bynars only required a couple of hours of downtime per day, but every attempt 110 had made to try to off-line had resulted in nightmares, where he relived those awful moments when 111 had died. Through their link, 110 had felt his bondmate's death.

He was not sure if he would ever be able to rest soundly again.

The *da Vinci* computer then conveyed a message directly to him through his belt unit—110 had never understood how the others could communicate with a computer by so clumsy a method as voice. According to the message, the *da Vinci* had changed course to a planet called Eerlik, delaying their arrival at Starbase 505, and there was a meeting of the S.C.E. staff at 0800.

110 doubted he would be welcome at that meeting.

He could not stand to remain alone in his quarters any longer. For lack of anywhere better to go, he went to the mess hall. The *da Vinci* was a *Saber*-class ship—there were few places to relax outside one's quarters. The mess hall was really 110's only other option.

His steps, as he moved down the corridor, were awkward. After spending all his life walking in tandem with another, walking alone was proving more difficult than he would have thought.

Only one person was present in the mess hall: Bart Faulwell. He was dictating quietly into a padd.

110 had been hoping to have the room to himself, but he found that he was grateful for the presence of the S.C.E.'s linguist and cryptography expert. Bart—the only alien 110 or 111 had ever met who came close to truly understanding the Bynar language—was a good person, and one that both Bynars had always felt comfortable talking to. Perhaps because he had made the study of how people talk to each other his life's work, he had an easier time communicating than others. Most aliens, at best, saw the Bynars as an odd curiosity; at worst, they were completely uncomfortable around them.

As 110 entered, he heard Bart say, "Love you. 'Bye!" Then he looked up and said, "Oh, hi, 110." Setting down the padd on top of a pile of papers, he asked, "Couldn't sleep?"

"I have not been able to off-line—" he hesitated, then finished, "—since 111 died." He had expected 111 to finish the sentence for him. That was perhaps the hardest thing of all to get used to.

"I guess that isn't surprising, all things considered." Bart pointed to the chair opposite him as he himself got up and angled himself toward the replicator. "Have a seat. You want anything? I was gonna get some coffee."

"No, thank you. I have not eaten since 111 died, either."

Bart shook his head. "I'm really sorry, 110. I wish there was something I could say." He turned to the replicator. "Coffee, French roast, half-and-half, no sugar."

After Bart had retrieved his coffee, he sat back down. 110 had taken the seat opposite the linguist's.

"Why are you up—at this hour?" 110 wanted to cry—each time he paused, he expected 111 to continue the sentence.

"I'm usually up this early, actually. I'm a napper—I get snatches of sleep here and there. Starfleet doesn't always allow for that kind of luxury, but that's the nice thing about this ship," he said with a smile. "I'm allowed my eccentricities."

"That must be—beneficial."

"So," Bart asked after a pause, "what're you going to do once we reach Starbase?"

110 hesitated. "Bynar custom is such—that we must immediately rebond with another—if one of us dies and the other does not. We are—designed to function in pairs."

"Designed?"

Frowning, 110 said, "A poor choice of words. We are not genetically engineered." 110 knew that humans had had bad experiences with such things. "Our evolution has taken us to the point where we function better in twos." 110 was proud of himself: he had gotten through that entire sentence—ironic, given the subject matter—without hesitating.

Bart blinked. "'Better'? That's interesting. I always thought it was *necessary* for you to work in pairs. I was actually kind of worried when I heard we were taking this little diversion—can you survive without her?"

"In the literal sense, I can. Our effectiveness and ability to contribute to society is greatly lessened without a bondmate, however," 110 said easily enough. But then, this had been indoctrinated into all Bynars from the moment they emerged from their birthing chambers. "That is why we traditionally rebond."

"But don't you bond from birth? I mean, how can you—" Bart cut himself off. "I'm sorry, I'm being nosy."

"There does not appear to be anything amiss with your nose."

Chuckling, Bart said, "One of these days, they'll design a universal translator that handles idioms. No, I mean I'm asking a lot of probing questions."

"I do not object. In fact, I appreciate having someone to talk to. Perhaps you could advise me."

"About what?"

"You are in a stable, loving relationship, yes?"

Bart smiled a bright smile. "Very much so, yeah."

"What would you do if your bondmate died?"

Recoiling as if he had been slapped, Bart straightened in his chair. 110 realized he had committed a blunder—he tended to forget how little some aliens appreciated straightforward speech.

Reaching a hand forward, 110 said, "I am sorry if I have—given offense. I—"

Bart shook his head. "No, no, it's okay, really. I'm sorry, I just wasn't expecting that question—though I guess I should've." He took a sip of his coffee. "The honest truth is—I haven't the first clue what I'd do. It's funny; if you add it up mathematically, I've spent more of my time without a mate than with one. And we don't even get to spend that much time together, what with Starfleet and all. But I tell you, I can't *imagine* being alone."

110 leaned forward. "Really? So you *do* understand! We—I had assumed that others did not comprehend or share our total devotion to each other."

"Well, I can't speak for other races, but—well, humans may not have bonded pairs on the same level as you guys, but we can get pretty silly about each other," Bart said with a chuckle.

"Our experiences led us to think otherwise. Commander Gomez and Lieutenant Commander Duffy, for example."

Bart rolled his eyes. "Yeah, well, I don't know what the story is with those two."

"But if something *did* happen to your mate, would you rebond? Find another to love?"

Blowing out a breath, Bart said, "I don't know. I wasn't looking for a relationship when we met, it just sort of . . . happened. So, I suppose it could happen again. But I doubt I'd be in any kind of rush to get involved with someone else—and I *seriously* doubt I could find anyone as wonderful."

"The problem is—" 110 hesitated. What he was about to say would shock his fellow Bynars to their very cores. "I am not sure that I *wish* to rebond."

Shrugging as he took another sip of coffee, Bart said, "So, don't."

"You do not understand—we *must* rebond."

"Hold off, you just said it wasn't necessary."

"Biologically, it is not. Culturally is a different matter altogether. If I do not rebond, I will be considered an outcast from Bynar society. I will lose my name and be deleted from the master file. But the alternative is even more difficult for me to contemplate. Like you, I cannot imagine my life without 111. I would rather die than bond with another."

Tensing somewhat, Bart said, "You're not thinking about—"

Remembering that this was another subject about which humans were touchy, 110 quickly said, "No, I am not contemplating suicide." This was not entirely truthful—110 had wanted very much to die with 111 at the end, rather than have to endure without her, but he hadn't been given a choice. And now, truly, the idea of killing himself was not one he was comfortable with. But at the time . . .

He continued. "From the perspective of my people, if I do not rebond, I will be dead. I do not know if I am ready for that—but I also know I cannot bond with another, at least not now. I will not sully 111's memory that way. That is why I wish your advice."

Bart started to take another sip of coffee, then noticed that the mug was empty. "Y'know, there are few sensations more annoying than trying to take a sip of coffee when there's no coffee in the mug." He got up and ordered another from the replicator, then sat back down.

"You are stalling," 110 said impatiently. If there was one aspect of dealing with aliens that always irritated 110, it was their inability to move at anything like a reasonable speed. Bad enough that they naturally moved too slow, but to then compound it with intentional delay . . .

"Sorry, it's just—I don't know *how* to advise you. But if it means anything, 110, no matter what you do, you've got my support."

110 found himself smiling for the first time since 111's death. "Thank you, Bart. That means a great deal to me."

"Well, I'm glad that this new mission isn't going to be a problem. Heck, maybe the extra time'll help you sort things out."

"I hope so. I wonder what the mission is."

Bart shrugged and sipped his coffee. "They'll tell us at the meeting."

"I do not believe I should attend it. I do not believe that Commander Gomez will want me on the team in my diminished state."

"Don't be silly. Of *course* you should be at the meeting. You're still one of us. Let Gomez make the decision about the team—that's her job. Nothing COs hate more than their subordinates anticipating them."

110 had not thought of that. "I will accept your advice. Thank you."

Grinning broadly once again, Bart said, "My pleasure."

Unfortunately, 110 did not feel any more settled with this decision made. He was quite sure that Commander Gomez would not want him. After all, of what possible use was a single Bynar?

CHAPTER
3

Sonya Gomez entered the briefing room at 0750, figuring Kieran Duffy wouldn't have arrived yet. In this, she was correct—in fact, the room was empty when she entered—and so she went to the replicator with a clear conscience. "Computer, hot Earl Grey tea, please."

"That's not a hot chocolate, is it?" came Kieran's voice from behind her.

Sonya tried very hard not to yell. She also resisted the urge to dump the contents of the now-materializing mug all over the second officer.

Kieran had a huge smile on his face as he approached her from the still-open entrance. "'Cause you *know* what happens when you order hot chocolate."

"Ten years, Kieran. It's been ten years since I spilled hot chocolate on Captain Picard."

"And yet the joke remains funny."

"To you, maybe," she said, dolefully sipping her tea.

"All right, I'm sorry," Kieran said, hitting her with those puppy-dog eyes that she'd never been able to resist. "Forgive me?"

Rolling her eyes, Sonya went to sit at the table. "What'm I gonna do with you?"

"Well, I have some creative suggestions. . . ." Kieran said as he sat down next to her. Sonya noticed that he had a padd in his hand.

The doors parted to allow Geordi and P8 Blue in, which came to Sonya as something of a relief. The conversation with Kieran was starting to get a little *too* comfortable for her.

Geordi was in the midst of a laugh, which didn't surprise Sonya. Pattie had a nasty sense of humor, and Geordi was probably the only person on the *da Vinci* who hadn't heard all of her jokes yet.

Sonya had hoped that the S.C.E.'s next task wouldn't come until after they had stopped off at Starbase for a number of reasons, one of which was that Geordi La Forge wouldn't be onboard anymore. She liked and admired Geordi, and he was certainly of great use on their last mission, but she felt so damned awkward around him. After all, he had been her first CO out of the Academy, and now she outranked him. It didn't seem right, somehow. Geordi himself wasn't making a big deal of it, but Sonya always felt like she was walking on eggshells around him.

Pattie had walked in on her hind legs, as Nasats generally did when they walked alongside other humanoids, since even at full height they were shorter than most. However, once she came into the room, she skittered on all six to her specially designed seat at one end of the table.

"Duffy, Gomez," Geordi said as he went to sit down, nodding to each of them. "Hey, that's not hot chocolate, is it?"

Sonya banged her head against the table. Geordi, of course, had been present for the infamous hot chocolate incident. "No," she said through clenched teeth, "it isn't."

"Good. 'Cause you know what happens—"

"—when I order hot chocolate. Yes, I know."

"See?" Kieran said. "I *told* you it was still funny."

Geordi peered at the mug. "That's Earl Grey, isn't it?"

Sonya nodded as she took a sip.

"That was Sonya's way of making penance," Kieran explained, even though Sonya really didn't need him to. "She avoided hot chocolate like the plague, and started drinking the captain's favorite drink."

"Now I'm addicted to it," Sonya said ruefully.

Pattie made the tinkling sound that passed for a chuckle among Nasats. "The price we pay for the follies of our youth."

Glaring at Kieran, Sonya said, "Some of us pay more than others."

Within minutes, the rest of the S.C.E. crew arrived, as did Captain Gold. They all took their seats around the table.

Sonya couldn't help but notice the empty chair next to 110. That was the other reason why she had wanted to stop off at Starbase 505 before they got their next assignment. 110 was supposed to go home to Bynaus and—if Sonya had her Bynar customs right—rebond with another. Indeed, Sonya hadn't been entirely sure that 110 was going to even attend the meeting, though she was glad he did. He was still part of the team, after all.

The captain said, "All right, boys and girls—and Nasat and Bynar—here's the story. We're heading to a planet called Eerlik. The planet is entirely run by a computer called Ganitriul. It's broken, and we get to fix it."

"They named the computer?" said Fabian Stevens, sounding surprised.

"It's got a personality. Might even be sentient."

Carol Abramowitz shook her head. "And they can't fix it . . . why, exactly?"

Turning to Kieran, the captain said, "Duffy?"

Kieran nodded, touched his padd, and an image appeared on the screen. Sonya looked up to see an image she recognized from the mission profile she'd studied before the meeting: an Eerlikka. As a rule, these teal-skinned people were short, hairless, with almost stubby arms and legs, and very wide eyes.

"Eerlik is a thriving, vibrant planet," Kieran said, "that is technologically quite advanced—at least in some ways. They only recently started venturing into space; the Eerlikka's focus has been more in the direction of technology-for-comfort. They've got very little by way of an urge to explore. They developed space travel several thousand years ago, but never bothered with it much beyond going to the moon and back. About fifty years ago, a sect went out and colonized the ninth planet in their system—"

"How come?" Carol asked.

Trust the cultural specialist to zero in on that, Sonya thought with a smile.

Kieran's eyes went wide. "Uh—not sure, I— Hang on . . ."

And trust the engineer not to have a clue, Sonya thought with a wider smile. Luckily, she had read the *entire* thing, unlike her second officer. "A group of Eerlikka that call themselves the Pevvni broke off from the mainstream religion; they wanted to start over in a new place."

Carol nodded.

"Uh, right," Kieran said. Sonya noticed several people trying and failing to hide smiles. "Anyhow, the Federation made contact shortly after the colony was established. They weren't interested in joining, but Eerlik has a rich supply of uridium, so a bunch of trade agreements were made."

Kieran touched his padd again, and an image of Eerlik's moon appeared. "For the last three thousand years or so, Eerlik has been completely run, maintained, and administrated by Ganitriul, which is a giant computer located on its moon." As he spoke, the display slowly changed to a schematic that showed how the moon had been excavated, and Ganitriul installed. "*Everything* on Eerlik is run by Ganitriul, and it hasn't failed them once. It has some of the best diagnostic software and autorepair components that anyone's ever seen." He looked at 110. "Might even put the master computer on Bynaus to shame."

"That is unlikely," 110 said simply.

Kieran grinned for a moment, then got serious again as he went on. "Like I said, Ganitriul hasn't failed them—until now. Nothing is working right on the planet anymore—climate controls, entertainment, communications, food distribution, planetary defense, everything. It's complete and total chaos."

Bart Faulwell shook his head. "That doesn't really answer the question. What do they need us for? Surely, they can fix their own computer."

Fabian smiled. "Not if they can't get to it. Commander, you said that Gani . . . Gani . . ."

"Ganitriul," Kieran completed.

"Right—that it runs everything. That includes transporters and ships, right?"

Nodding, Kieran said, "That's it exactly. And also communications. The only reason we know there's a problem at all is because Ganitriul itself contacted the Federation Council, asking for help. Eerlik is cut off from any useful communications, and from what Ganitriul said in its message, none of their modes of travel are functioning."

"So it's up to us," Pattie said.

"Why should today be different from any other day?" Captain Gold said with a small smile. He looked at Sonya. "Commander?"

"I think we can keep this down to a two-person team, plus"—she added with a look at Domenica Corsi— "a security detail." The security chief nodded her blond head.

Kieran fixed her with a look, but said nothing. Pattie and Carol were less reticent.

"Only two?" the Nasat asked, at the same time that Carol said, "We're talking about the collapse of a culture here."

Patiently, Sonya said, "The results of the problem are large, but the problem itself is pretty straightforward: fix the computer. If we send a big team down there to do, in essence, one thing, we'll be stepping all over each other. Two of us should be able to handle it just fine—if we need more, we'll call."

"Who'll be on the team?" the captain said before anyone else could say anything—and he spoke in a tone that implied that the discussion was at an end.

"I'll lead it, and I'd like to take 110 with me."

110 sat up straighter in his chair. "Me?"

"You're still our computer expert."

"111 and I *were* the S.C.E.'s computer experts. By myself—"

"By yourself," Sonya interrupted, "you've still got a computer efficiency rating of ten. That's *your* rating, not yours and 111's. She also had a ten, but the point is, the best person in Starfleet has an eight."

"I do not believe that—you will be satisfied with my—diminished performance. You should select someone else."

"That won't be necessary," Sonya said. "You're the right person for this job, 110. Unless you're refusing a direct order, you're on the team."

Sonya's strategy was risky. After all, 110 *was* a civilian. But he and 111 had agreed to be under Starfleet orders for the duration of their time on the *da Vinci*, and until they actually reported to Starbase 505, that agreement was still, technically, in place.

The Bynar took a look at Bart for some reason, then seemed to relax. "I would not presume to go against the commander's judgment. I will accompany you on the mission."

"Good," the captain said. "Meantime, I want the rest of you to read up on the Eerlikka. It's possible they'll need more help from us beyond fixing Ganitriul, and I want us to be ready."

Sonya looked at the security chief. "Commander Corsi, I'll leave the size and personnel of the security detail to your discretion."

"Yes, sir," Corsi said.

"Good," the captain said again. "Oh, and I have one other bit of news."

Sonya leaned forward.

"I'm gonna be a great-grandfather again!"

Several congratulatory noises went around the table. Shaking her head, Sonya got up, finished off her tea, and put the mug back in the replicator to be recycled. Some of the crew stuck around to hear the captain tell of his granddaughter's pregnancy, but Sonya wanted to get started on the day's work. She and Geordi walked out together.

"Nice job, " Geordi said.

"I'm sorry that this'll delay you getting back to the *Enterprise*," Gomez said.

Geordi shrugged. "I'll live. Danilova should be able to muddle through without me a little while longer."

"Danilova?" Sonya said, her eyes going wide. "You mean Raisa Danilova? She's your assistant chief now?"

Laughing that staccato laugh of his, Geordi said, "She made lieutenant last year, and I made her assistant chief after the Dominion War ended."

"But she was the slowest person in that whole engine room," Sonya said, returning the laugh. "She'd spend all day on a sensor recalibration."

"She picked up some speed after you left.

Actually, what mostly got her going was the war. I always kept her out of emergency situations 'cause of her lack of speed, but I didn't have that luxury when we were being pounded by the Jem'Hadar—and something about having engineering falling apart around her lit a fire under her or something. She blossomed into one of my best people."

Sonya shook her head. "Pretty amazing."

They arrived at Sonya's quarters, where she was planning to set out a game plan for the mission. "In any case," Geordi said, "I think the *Enterprise* is in safe hands. Besides, this mission sounds like it might be interesting."

Sonya tensed. After relaxing around Geordi for the first time since they had picked him up at Blossom IV last week, Sonya found herself back on eggshells again. Geordi obviously noticed this—if nothing else, his ocular implants allowed him to notice biological shifts that normal vision couldn't detect—and said quickly, "Hey, don't worry, I'm not trying to horn in on you or anything."

"I know, it's just— This is *my* team, not yours."

Nodding, Geordi said, "Don't worry, Sonya, I know this is your show." He added, with a smile, "And, for what it's worth, I think you're doing a great job."

Letting out a breath she hadn't realized she was holding, Sonya said, "Thanks. Coming from you, that means a lot."

"I'll talk to you later, okay?"

Sonya nodded in reply and entered her quarters.

CHAPTER
4

Five of the Speakers had managed to assemble in Valandriw Hall. Ansed was impressed with their fortitude. Three of them, including Ansed herself, lived in the capital city; the other two had happened to be in Valandriw Hall, working. Another Speaker lived in the capital city, but he was not present; he had sent his son with the message that he'd broken his leg tripping over his furniture when the lights went out.

Rather than take their usual seats, which were spread around the large table intended to seat all thirty-one Speakers, the five of them bunched up at one end of the table, around the head, where Ansed traditionally sat.

Also present in the Hall was a heavily bandaged Undlar, who sat to Ansed's right. He was no longer shaking, but Ansed thought the young man still seemed a bit out of it.

The first order of business was to discuss how Enforcement was dealing with the crisis—and, also, the investigation into the murder of the priests. Both were proceeding as well as could be expected. A clever Enforcement officer had found some old radios and they'd been issued, allowing communication; a top investigator had been assigned to the slaughter.

After that, they turned to the issue of Ganitriul.

"I've just come from the transportation center," said Speaker Biral. "They've been doing tests with inanimate objects. Every attempt has failed—and it's a different failure every time, too. Sometimes the object goes to the wrong place, sometimes it's inside out, sometimes it never rematerializes, sometimes the console goes down, someti—"

"The point is," Ansed put in—Biral had a tendency to babble—"that transporting to the moon is not an option."

Speaker Miko said, "We can't risk taking a ship, either. Even if some of them *do* work now, what if they fail en route?"

"And who do we send?" asked Speaker Torin. "Reger Undlar here is in no shape to travel."

"I can make the journey," Undlar said quietly. "And I believe there is also a way to get me there."

Ansed whirled in surprise. "There is?"

"I believe so."

Miko said angrily, "Why didn't you mention this before?"

"I'm sorry," Undlar said, and the sardonic tone Ansed had noticed earlier returned. "But I've been a bit preoccupied with the brutal murder of my brothers."

Softening, Miko said, "Of course, I'm sorry,

Reger. These are troubling times, and I forgot myself."

"That is all right, Speaker," Undlar said, his voice getting more subdued again. "It's just that—there is a Pevvni trading ship in Brioni Port that might be able to make the journey. It is an experimental ship that has circuitry independent of the Great One."

Ansed's already-wide eyes went wider. "What?"

Shock spread around the table as the other four Speakers expressed similar outrage. "Who approved this?" Biral asked.

Undlar straightened. "We did. The Pevvni came to the clergy with a special request to construct this prototype. They built it as an experiment, in case further dealings with the Federation led to more out-of-system travel beyond the Great One's ability to control."

Angry once again, Miko said, "That should *never* have been approved without consulting the Speakers!"

"I don't see how that matters," Undlar said indignantly. "*We* are the Caretakers of the Great One, and so the Pevvni wisely came to us to gain approval for this prototype. We thought it was a worthwhile experiment, for precisely the reasons they gave."

"And you didn't think to consult us?" Biral asked, his face turning indigo with outrage.

"Reger," Ansed said calmly, trying to keep this from turning into a shouting match, "perhaps you didn't realize the political implications of what you were doing."

"What political implications?" Undlar asked, now looking confused.

Ansed sighed. *Priests are wonderful for spiritual matters, but they can be shockingly naïve.* "One of the reasons why we have remained so stable over the millennia is because we are united under Ganitriul. We have had no war, no upheavals, and no strife for three thousand years."

"The Pevvni colonization could safely be called an upheaval."

Save me from youth, Ansed thought, trying not to groan. Undlar hadn't been born when the ninth planet had been colonized by the Pevvni. "Not at all. It was an orderly process that was debated around this very table, and voted on by the people. Eventually, the Pevvni were granted permission, but the process by which they got there was orderly. To secretly grant the Pevvni the right to construct vessels independent of the system is *not* orderly."

"It was never meant to be secret," Undlar said defensively. "We simply did not see it as a concern."

"Well, you should have," Ansed said, trying—and failing—not to sound condescending. "There are those among the Pevvni who have expressed an interest in breaking off from Eerlik—and from Ganitriul. This is exactly the kind of thing they might use as a weapon against us."

Before Undlar could respond to that, Speaker Talu said, "Ah, First Speaker, with all due respect, is this *really* the time to reprimand Reger Undlar for information that may well save us?"

Ansed was brought up short by Talu's statement, which was delivered in the older woman's usual measured tones. *But then*, she thought, *Talu has always been the voice of reason among the Speakers.* "You're right, of course, Talu. If this ship *does* have circuitry that is independent of Ganitriul, then we must see if we can use it to fly to the moon immediately. If no one objects, we should adjourn to Brioni and see if this ship—"

"The *Senbolma*," Undlar said.

Ansed nodded. "If the *Senbolma* is truly spaceworthy."

"I'm not going out there," Biral said. "It's insane. And just walking from my home left me dehydrated. You're not getting me to Brioni—that's at least a couple hours' walk."

Every other Speaker chimed in with similar responses—even Talu, from whom Ansed had expected more (though she *was* quite elderly). Truth be told, Ansed felt the same way in her heart, but she had a duty to perform, and she would *not* shirk it, even if the others would.

"Then I will go myself," she said, getting to her feet.

"As will I," said Undlar, doing the same, albeit somewhat less steadily.

"That is unnecessary," Ansed said, not relishing the idea of supporting the wounded priest throughout the walk. "It would be a waste, Reger, especially if it turns out that the *Senbolma* is not spaceworthy." She put an encouraging hand on his shoulder, hoping he would forgive her earlier, patronizing tone. "I will send for you if and when it proves to be the case. We will, after all, need your guidance to fix Ganitriul."

Undlar looked like he was about to argue, but

then he cut himself off. "Of course, First Speaker. I will await word from you."

"Excellent. You should hear from me soon."

And if—no, when this is all over, Reger Undlar, we will have a long talk on the subject of appropriate behavior for the clergy. Undlar was the last of the priests left, and whatever new ones were ordained after this would look up to him as their leader, for better or for worse. Which meant that his naïveté would have to be dealt with, and quickly.

But first things first, Ansed thought, steeling herself against the ordeal of another endless hike and heading once more into the cold.

Sonya Gomez took one last look over the schematics that presently occupied the display on her tricorder. Thankfully, the Eerlikka had, several years back, allowed a team of Federation computer experts (including a group of eight Bynars) to inspect Ganitriul, so Starfleet had detailed specs on the installation.

Which was, in a word, *huge.* Fully twenty-five percent of Eerlik's moon had been excavated in order to house the computer. In fact, most of that equipment had fallen into disuse as—typically, with advancing technology—the Eerlikka were able to miniaturize over time. Only about ten percent of the original installation was still active, though the autorepair components included small robots that could cannibalize the older equipment as need be.

All in all, a very efficient system.

She looked up to see that 110 still hadn't arrived yet. She stood in the transporter room with Corsi and two other security people, Drew and Hawkins. Sonya had thought that three security people was a bit excessive to guard a two-person team, but she trusted Corsi's judgment.

"Where the hell is he?" Corsi said, after inspecting her phaser rifle for the fortieth time.

"He'll be here. Cut him a little slack, Commander. He's been through a lot."

"With respect, sir, if he's too wrecked to even show up for a mission on time, then I have to question whether or not he can perform the mission."

"And it's a valid question, but I'd like to give him at least a chance to answer it."

Corsi let out a breath. "Yes, sir."

Just then, the doors parted and 110 entered, walking even faster than normal. "My apologies, Commander Gomez. I—I can offer no excuse."

"I don't expect you to," Sonya said gently. "Let's go."

As she moved to step onto the platform, the doors opened again, and Carol Abramowitz entered. "Yes?" Sonya asked.

"Commander, I just wanted to let you know that speed is of the essence here. I've been reading up on the Eerlikka, and they have two major facets as a culture: they are fanatical about maintaining order, and they pride themselves on being well-informed. Both of these stem from Ganitriul. So it's likely that conditions on Eerlik are deteriorating and going to get worse the more time passes. Don't dawdle down there."

Sonya smiled. "Wasn't planning on it anyhow, but I appreciate the report. Thanks, Carol."

"No problem."

The five of them arranged themselves on the transporter pad. To the transporter chief, Sonya said, "Energize."

They materialized into pitch-darkness. *Oh, great*, Sonya thought. She switched on her wristlamp, and the others did the same. Now the space they were in—which felt cold and stuffy—was illuminated by five light sources that cast odd shadows. Unfortunately, this did nothing but make it *bright*, cold, and stuffy. . . .

Drew played his light over one of the walls. "Rocks," he deadpanned.

"*Hello*," said a voice that seemed to come from everywhere. "*Are you from Starfleet?*" The voice was very pleasant—Sonya couldn't place it, gender-wise, but it set her at ease immediately.

"Yes," she said. "I'm Commander Sonya Gomez of the Starfleet Corps of Engineers."

"*Excellent. I am glad you replied to my call. I am Ganitriul. Welcome.*"

"Thank you."

"*And who are the others? I am registering five life-forms.*"

Indicating the Bynar—though having no idea if Ganitriul could see the gesture—Sonya said, "This is 110, who is part of my engineering team. The others are Lieutenant Commander Domenica Corsi and two of her security team, Stephen Drew and Vance Hawkins."

"*I welcome all of you. I apologize for the darkness, but I cannot seem to get the lights working.*"

"That's all right." She consulted her tricorder, which glowed quite brightly in the near-darkness.

It showed that the main terminal was only a few meters away. "If you don't mind, we'll go to your main terminal and try to determine what's wrong." She started walking in the right direction, 110 on her heels, the security detail behind them.

"I hope you can, Commander Gomez. I am afraid that my own attempts to diagnose the problem have failed. I do not understand why I have been unable to function properly. I should also warn you that there are several security devices that are meant to prevent anyone from tampering with the system. My control over them is sporadic. Please be careful."

The voice was almost pleading. Or maybe Sonya was projecting. Either way, she resolved to watch her step, and was suddenly grateful that Corsi had taken a team of three.

Corsi said, "Ganitriul, which security protocols don't you have control over right now?"

"I am afraid it varies. Are you familiar with my security specifications?"

"Yes."

"At the moment, I have complete control over everything in the immediate vicinity. If that changes—or if you move into an area that I do not have control over—I will inform you."

"Thank you."

Within moments, they turned a corner, and the walls were replaced by what appeared to be a giant, smooth slab of black marble. Corsi, Drew, and Hawkins also shone their wristlamps on it, giving Sonya a better view. The slab, she suspected, was a large viewscreen. In front of it, she could see a very comfortable-looking chair, which was also distressingly close to the ground. Various buttons dotted the wide arms of the chair.

"All right, I give up—what is it?" Corsi asked.

"The main terminal," Sonya said. She pointed at the slab. "That's the viewscreen. The operator sits in the chair, and operates it with those buttons."

Hawkins looked dubiously at the chair. "They sit in *that*?"

"The Eerlikka are fairly short," Sonya said, "with small legs for their height, generally, so this is the right size for them. And the viewscreen can afford to be this large—they have wide eyes and a breadth of vision much greater than we do."

As if on cue, the viewscreen lit up with several images. Some were views of parts of a city being subjected to bad weather—Sonya assumed it was a city on Eerlik. Others showed bits of data in a language Sonya recognized as Makaro, the most common language on Eerlik—she couldn't read a word of it, of course, but she had seen similar writing in the mission profile. In addition, a small hole that looked like some kind of dataport opened in the smooth surface. Sonya could detect no seams. It was as if the hole just appeared, though that could have just been a function of the dim light.

"*I must warn you not to sit in the chair,*" said Ganitriul suddenly. "*The chair is designed to allow only those whose DNA patterns match those of the presently ordained clergy to sit in it. I have been unable to disable that function.*"

"That's bad, isn't it?" Drew said.

"*There is an alternative. 110, you are a member of the Bynar race, are you not?*"

"Yes, I am," 110 said.

"In that case, you may interface directly with my dataport."

110 hesitated. "Very well." He moved toward the dataport.

As he did so, Corsi, who had been gazing at her tricorder, cried, "Wait!"

"What is it, Lieutenant Commander?"

"I'm reading a ton of electricity flowing through that port."

"That is normal," Ganitriul said.

"I really don't think that 110 can handle it."

"Bynar epidermis is able to conduct electrical charges, Lieutenant Commander," 110 said.

"Not this much. We're talking eighty thousand kilojoules."

"That is not what my readings indicate. Please wait a moment." A pause, then Ganitriul continued. *"My apologies. It appears my readings were incorrect. Lieutenant Commander Corsi, please tell me what you are reading now."*

Corsi looked at her tricorder. "Two hundred kilojoules. That's within 110's tolerances."

Nodding, 110 said, "Yes, it is."

110 placed a small hand inside the dataport, which altered its size to accommodate the size and shape of the Bynar's hand. A nimbus of electricity started to form around 110, further illuminating the chamber. Then the Bynar let out a rapid-fire burst in the binary language of his people, which the universal translator simply rendered as a high-pitched whine. Bart had said, when Sonya first arrived on the *da Vinci*, that the translators could

be modified to understand the Bynar tongue, but Sonya had never seen the need. Now she was sorry she hadn't taken him up on it.

While this went on, Drew said, "Sir, I've got some weird readings here."

"Define *weird*, Drew," Corsi said.

"I'm getting occasional life-form readings—but then they just disappear. The tricorder thinks they're Eerlikka."

"My apologies," Ganitriul said. *"Those are sensor ghosts. That is a part of the tour that is given to visitors to these caverns. I provide a recreation of the excavation of the moon, and it includes representations of the workers. The simulation includes sensor readings of the workers. I will attempt to prevent that program from running, but I can make no assurances that I will be successful."*

"Do the best you can, Ganitriul," Sonya said, trying to sound understanding.

Corsi walked up to her and said, in a low tone that only Sonya could hear, "It's a computer, Commander, not a kid with a toy."

Matching the security chief's tone, Sonya said, "It's an intelligent computer. I think treating it with respect is perfectly reasonable."

Shrugging, Corsi said, "I guess."

Sonya noticed the light in the cavern growing dimmer. She turned to see that 110 had removed his hand from the dataport. "I have found the problem," he said as the glow faded from around him. "An invasive program has been introduced into Ganitriul's system."

"Sabotage," Corsi said.

"Yes, Lieutenant Commander."

"I do not doubt your diagnosis, 110, but I do not understand how it came to be. I have no record of any invasive programs being inserted into my system."

"Once we have fixed the problem, I can show you how it was done, Ganitriul."

"Can the program be safely removed?" Sonya asked.

"It is possible, yes. We will need—"

Sonya did not learn what 110 would need, as he was interrupted by some kind of blaster fire, which struck Hawkins in the left shoulder.

The security guard cried out in pain and fell to the cavern ground, grabbing his left shoulder with his right hand and dropping his phaser rifle.

As Corsi raised her own rifle to return fire, Ganitriul said, *"A security measure has activated. No energy weapons will fire within the confines of the installation."*

Corsi pressed the firing button on her rifle anyhow, but nothing happened. "Dammit," she muttered.

It was then that the lights came back up.

Sonya blinked the spots out of her eyes and found herself surrounded by twelve Eerlikka. Some of them were also blinking—with upper and lower eyelids—in response to the greater illumination. Some were holstering their blasters and unholstering large curved, bladed weapons.

"Death to the aliens!" one of them cried.

Several more repeated, "Death to the aliens!"

Then they charged.

CHAPTER
5

Ansed held her breath as the *Senbolma* left the atmosphere of Eerlik. *So far*, she thought, *so good*.

The owner of the *Senbolma* was an old man named Emarur, who expressed a certain reluctance to test his ship in quite this manner. He had been hoping to remain in dock until the crisis passed. However, he could not turn down a specific request from the First Speaker and the last remaining priest, especially since they were willing to share the risk with him by taking the flight.

Besides, the *Senbolma* going to the moon was likely the only way the crisis *would* pass.

The ship's pilot said, "We've cleared the stratosphere. Now entering orbit of Eerlik. We'll have our window to the moon in fifteen minutes. All systems reading nominal." He sounded almost surprised.

"Good," Emarur said from his seat to the pilot's right. The flight deck of the *Senbolma* was small, with only two chairs at one large console. Ansed stood behind Emarur, looking at the amazing vista on the viewscreen in front of her. She had seen pictures of what Eerlik looked like from orbit, but nothing could have prepared her for the experience. No picture had adequately conveyed the deep burgundy of the oceans, the swirling, majestic patterns of the clouds, or the deep brown of the land masses. As they orbited, she saw the Lankap mountain range, just outside the capital city. After a minute, they flew over the teardrop-shaped form of Maryllo Island, where she had been born. Then came the ragged, beautiful Kyepas Coast, where she'd spent so many summers as a girl.

It took her breath away. To see the landmarks of her life this way was staggering.

Undlar was in the small cabin he and Ansed were sharing—space was at a premium on the *Senbolma*—meditating. Ansed was half-tempted to run down, grab him, and force him to look at this view. She certainly was determined, now more than ever, to do whatever she could to save her world.

Emarur turned around to look at Ansed. "Nice view, huh?"

"Yes, it is."

"Never been up here before, have you, First Speaker?"

"No, I haven't." She smiled. "It's funny, I always used to dismiss people who took trips to the moon to tour Ganitriul as silly tourists. Now I'm sorry I never did take one of those trips. It would've been worth it just to see this. I had no idea the oceans were *so* burgundy. And the mountains . . ." Her voice trailed off.

"I never get tired of it, either. Although, personally, I think the view is better back home," Emarur said, referring to the Pevvni colony. He turned back to his console and entered some commands into it. "Compensate for that, will you?" he said to the pilot, then turned back to Ansed. "I have to say, it's weird flying without a net like this. Still, it's kind of thrilling, too."

"Thrilling?" Ansed asked, surprised.

"Oh sure. Not knowing every possible variable, being surprised by a random meteor or another ship in the same orbit. That doesn't happen with Ganitriul controlling everything. Never any worries about that. Makes you get lazy."

"What you call 'lazy,' sir, I call safe. I see no benefit in taking unnecessary risks."

With a wide, infectious grin, Emarur said, "Well, First Speaker, I guess that's why I own a spaceship and you're a politician."

Ansed couldn't help but return the grin. Emarur was right, of course. His reaction made perfect sense for one in his position. Ansed herself had never understood the urge that drove the Pevvni to colonize in the first place, but that didn't mean she would demean it. And it was perfectly possible to thrive without Ganitriul—all the major powers of the Alpha Quadrant did just fine without one central computer. Indeed, Ansed wondered if one computer could administer something as large as the Federation.

Enough, she admonished herself. *Let us first see if one computer will ever administer Eerlik again before we wax philosophical.*

"Approaching window now," the pilot said. "This is interesting. I'm reading a ship in orbit around the moon. Too far away for a positive identification."

"Another ship?" Ansed asked. "That could be the answer. Whoever is on that ship could have sabotaged Ganitriul."

"That certainly would explain everything," Emarur said. "Get ready to head for the moon," he said to the pilot.

Emarur initially kept the viewscreen on the view of Eerlik even as they headed toward the moon. The planet receded as they got farther away. Within a few minutes, however, he switched the view to that of the moon—and the ship in orbit around it.

"That's a Starfleet ship," the pilot said. "Registry is NCC-81623, *U.S.S. da Vinci*, *Saber*-class."

"Which one is *Saber*-class?"

The pilot shrugged. "Don't know. We don't have a database, remember? I just got this from the scan."

"It doesn't make sense," Ansed said. "Why would Starfleet sabotage Ganitriul?"

"Well, we could ask them," Emarur said. He touched a few buttons on his console, and a small whistling noise emitted from it. "This is the *Senbolma*, on behalf of the government of Eerlik, contacting the *U.S.S. da Vinci*. Please state your business."

After a moment, the face of an older human male appeared on the screen. Like most of his race, he had tufts of fuzz on top of his head, though this one's was white and wispy.

"This is Captain David Gold of the da Vinci. *We're here in response to a distress call from Ganitriul."*

Ansed blinked. "From Ganitriul?" She cleared her throat. "Captain, I am First Speaker Ansed."

"A pleasure, First Speaker. If you don't mind my asking, how did you get up here? I was led to believe that none of the Eerlikka ships worked."

"With all due respect, Captain, I would ask that you leave orbit. This is an Eerlik matter, not a Starfleet one." Ansed did not want to give Gold any information. If they were responsible for the sabotage, telling them that this was the only working ship, and that they carried the last remaining priest, would be tantamount to suicide. She had no idea what kind of armament this ship carried, but the Federation was less than a year out of a nasty, prolonged war. While Eerlik had managed to avoid becoming embroiled in the Dominion War, they had heard quite a bit about it. Ansed doubted that any Starfleet ship was anything but fully armed.

"I already have a team from the Starfleet Corps of Engineers in the caverns, working on the problem, First Speaker. If you want us to pull out, that's fine, but my people are the best. Let them do their work."

Ansed was torn. Starfleet's reputation was generally good, but with everything else that was happening, she didn't know who to trust.

Another voice sounded on the speakers, and it was one Ansed was grateful to hear. *"First Speaker, this is Ganitriul. The* da Vinci *is here at my request. Their team has just transported down, and they will arrive at one of my primary terminals in two minutes. Please allow—"*

Then the signal cut off.

Emarur made some adjustments to his console. "I can't get the signal back—but it *did* seem to come from the moon."

Ansed let out a long breath. "My apologies, Captain. When we first saw your ship—"

"Say no more, First Speaker," Gold said, holding up a hand. *"Can't say as I blame you, really."*

"I have one of the clergy on board. I believe that his help will be invaluable in aiding your team."

"Couldn't hurt."

Ansed heard the door open behind her. She turned to see Undlar enter. "Here he is now," she said to Gold. "Reger Undlar, this is Captain David Gold from Starfleet. It turns out Ganitriul asked the Federation for help."

"Yes, well, we were afraid of something like this. Now, Emarur," Undlar said as he unsheathed a knife from under his robes and stabbed Ansed in the chest.

As Ansed collapsed to the deck, blue blood spilling from her punctured heart, she cried out an anguished, "Why?"

Undlar smiled a vicious smile. "You'll never know."

Then her vision went black.

CHAPTER
6

Domenica Corsi shot Drew a look. Drew nodded, closed his eyes, and covered Hawkins' eyes as well. Grabbing the grenade from her belt, she thumbed it on, tossed it into the crowd of advancing Eerlikka, and closed her eyes.

She could see the brightness of the photonic grenade even through her eyelids.

As soon as the lights dimmed, she opened her eyes, and saw exactly what she'd hoped: a dozen Eerlikka blinking furiously, temporarily blinded.

Of course, Gomez and 110 were similarly blinded, since Corsi couldn't warn them about the grenade without warning their attackers, but that wasn't an insurmountable problem. "C'mon!" she cried.

Slinging her phaser rifle behind her shoulder, she grabbed Gomez and 110 by the arm and quickly led them out of the area. Drew led the wounded Hawkins—thankfully, Hawkins wasn't hit in the leg.

"I am all right," 110 said as he gently shrugged out of Corsi's grip and dashed ahead. *Guess Bynars aren't sensitive to bright light*, she thought.

"What happ—" Gomez started, but Corsi cut her off as she led the commander around a corner.

"Photonic grenade. Keep moving, Commander."

Gomez nodded, blinking furiously as she picked up the pace, trusting Corsi not to let her walk into a wall.

With the hand that wasn't guiding Gomez, Corsi held her tricorder, currently showing her a map of the caverns. She led the way with Gomez, 110 right behind, and Drew leading Hawkins behind him. Corsi moved as fast as she could without losing the others. The display also showed that the twelve Eerlikka hadn't moved from the terminal chamber.

No, wait, she thought as the display changed, *now they're moving. And spreading out in what looks like a search pattern, which means they have no clue which way we went. Good.*

She led the team around a few more corners, and then finally into a small cul-de-sac. Like the main terminal area, the walls here looked like big slabs of marble, but these were covered in dust. According to the records in the mission profile, there used to be a terminal here, but it had been consolidated into another unit.

Although the lights had remained on in much of the complex, they'd apparently been removed from this area. The only illumination was provided by the wristlamps, and whatever light was coming in from the corridor.

Switching hers off, Corsi said, "Everyone kill the wristlamps. I don't think they have any scanning equipment, so they'll be searching by sight."

110 walked up to Gomez. "Are you all right, Commander?"

"Yeah, I'm okay," Gomez said, blinking furiously. "This dim cavern is actually helping." Letting out a breath, she said, "Let's get the hell out of here." She tapped her combadge. "Gomez to *da Vinci*. Five to beam up."

Silence answered.

Oh, hell, Corsi thought. She tapped her own combadge. "Corsi to *da Vinci*."

Gomez immediately whipped out her tricorder. "The combadges are functioning normally. And there's no security measure of Ganitriul's interfering. Which means the *da Vinci* can't answer."

Shaking her head, Corsi said, "That fits. We were ambushed—they probably were, too. If they're not answering, they—"

"We know what it means, Commander," Gomez said quickly. "Right now, let's focus on what we can do."

Corsi nodded. Gomez was right, actually. "Drew, stand guard."

Drew nodded, gave Hawkins a quick, encouraging look, then headed out to the mouth of the culde-sac.

Corsi knelt down to check on Hawkins. Conveniently, Hawkins himself had been carrying the mini-medikit. She opened it and treated his wound as best she could. It would do until they got back to the *da Vinci*.

If they got back.

"We need to figure out how to proceed with the mission," Gomez said.

Looking up sharply at Gomez—who looked rather sinister with the light from the tricorder shining up on her face, casting odd shadows on her pale complexion—Corsi said, "Commander, I don't think we should be proceeding anywhere. We're actually in a defensible position right now. There's twelve armed Eerlikka out there, and all we've got are phaser rifles that are basically glorified clubs, thanks to our friend the computer—who's already lied to us."

"I have not lied to you intentionally, Lieutenant Commander Corsi." The voice of Ganitriul startled Corsi, and she got to her feet and raised her phaser rifle on instinct.

Gomez, however, didn't look at all surprised, as if disembodied voices spoke without prompting to her all the time. "You told us those were sensor ghosts that Drew picked up, Ganitriul."

"I believed that they were—just as I believed that the current running through my dataport was safe for 110. I was in error in both cases. It is not something I am accustomed to, but it has become a regular occurrence since this invasive program was placed within me. I also know what has happened to your ship."

"Are they okay?" Gomez asked, sounding concerned.

"They were attacked by a Pevvni ship. For some reason, the Pevvni have constructed a vessel that is beyond my control. This is in direct violation of

Eerlikka law. The First Speaker is on the vessel, as is one of the clergy. Unfortunately, I was unable to maintain contact with either ship, so I do not know what precipitated the conflict. Captain Gold and First Speaker Ansed were discussing working together amiably when I lost contact. The Pevvni ship opened fire moments later. I am unable to detect the da Vinci *any longer."*

"What about the Pevvni ship?" Gomez asked.

"It is still in orbit, but damaged."

Corsi gritted her teeth. She didn't like the sound of this at all. Of course, the *da Vinci* just could have been off Ganitriul's sensors—or those same sensors could have misinformed Ganitriul. *Or*, she thought with a sigh, *the damn computer could be lying to us*.

No matter what, though, the away team was on its own.

Gomez turned to the Bynar. "110, you said that there might be a way to remove the invasive program?"

"Yes, there is. It is possible that we can—that *I* can remove it, but I would need access to Ganitriul's central core. Even then, I am not sure that I am capable of performing the programming necessary to fix Ganitriul. If 111 were here . . ." His voice trailed off.

Corsi rolled her eyes. "The core is at least a kilometer's walk from here, and it's sealed in a large bunker with a computer lock. With the security system on the fritz—"

"Actually, Lieutenant Commander Corsi, the systems that lock and seal the computer core are inde-

pendent of my systems. It was a precaution against precisely this kind of malfunction. That lock will open and close as normal with the proper codes, which I will provide."

Gomez smiled. "That's good planning."

Unimpressed, Corsi said, "That still doesn't change the fact that it's a kilometer from here to there. And I'm willing to bet there are all kinds of entertaining little security measures that you don't have control over, right, Ganitriul?"

"That is true. I can do my best to guide you, but my control is limited."

"Commander, there are only five of us, and one of us is injured. We don't have any weapons aside from three more photonic grenades, and those are only good for a fancy light show. We're not likely to get reinforcements any time soon, if ever. There are twelve people out there with big swords who are trying to kill us. We're better off staying here."

"Maybe we are," Gomez said, "but Eerlik isn't. Remember what Carol told us? The longer we take to fix Ganitriul, the worse off Eerlik is."

"The people hunting us are Eerlikka, Commander. Their leader was on the ship that fired on the *da Vinci*. Maybe they don't want our help."

"Maybe not," Gomez said calmly and confidently, "but until I know that for sure, we have a mission to perform, and we can only perform it at the core."

Gomez was half a meter shorter than Corsi, and significantly smaller in build. And yet, anyone walking into the cul-de-sac at that moment would know exactly who was in charge, and it wasn't Domenica Corsi. The security chief had raised her objections, and they had been responded to—not the way she would have liked, but that was the way things worked. "Whatever you say, sir," she said. "But I can guarantee you that things will go wrong."

At that, Gomez actually smiled. "If things didn't go wrong, Commander, the galaxy wouldn't need engineers." She then looked up. "Ganitriul, are you using a scattering field to jam the weapons?"

"Yes. It is an automatic feature whenever unauthorized weapons fire is registered. Normally, it can only be deactivated by one of the clergy or someone else with sufficient clearance. However, I cannot guarantee that it will last."

Gomez consulted her tricorder. "Here it is; Security Measure 7."

"Correct."

She studied the tricorder for a minute. Unable to stand the silence that followed, Corsi finally said, "What are you doing, Commander?"

"Looking over the schematics of the scattering field. If I'm right, I can adjust the phaser rifles so that they can function anyway. When I was on the *Sentinel*, during the war, we pulled this trick on a Breen platoon that tried to jam our hand weapons. Ganitriul's scattering field has a similar design. We'll only be able to get as high as light stun, but we can do it." She closed the tricorder. "Here's the plan. Drew will continue to keep watch. 110, you keep an eye on Hawkins, make sure he doesn't get any worse. Corsi, go over the map, find us the best route from here to the core. Ganitriul, if there's anything you can do to distract our pursuers, it would be greatly appreciated."

"I can make no promises, but I will do my best."

"Thanks. I'm going to modify the phasers. Shouldn't take more than fifteen minutes. You have your orders, people—get to work."

Sighing, Corsi handed Gomez her rifle, then opened her tricorder. She had a bad feeling about this, but she couldn't fault Gomez, either—she was finishing the mission she was given, which was, ultimately, the right thing to do.

I just hope we live to tell Gold's great-grandkids about it.

"Yes, well, we were afraid of something like this. Now, Emarur."

Alarm bells went off in David Gold's head at the priest's words. He turned to Lieutenant McAllan at tactical and started to say, "Shields up," but he couldn't get the words out before some kind of weapons fire struck the *da Vinci*.

"Shields up, red alert!" he was able to say this time, as alarms started ringing out around the bridge. He also saw the priest stab the First Speaker, and watched her crumple to the deck. *There's a helluva lot more going on here than we thought. I should live long enough to find out what, exactly.* "Return fire!"

"Phaser controls aren't responding," McAllan said. "Arming torpedoes." Pounding a fist on his console, he added, "I can't get a lock."

"They're taking evasive action," said Ensign Wong from the conn position.

"Pursue them," Gold said. "McAllan, target manually—use a damn scope sight if you have to, but target that ship!"

"Yes, sir."

"Damage report."

Duffy's voice sounded over the intercom from engineering. *"I don't know what kind of weapon they're using, sir, but it took out half our tactical systems. Shields are fine, but phaser controls are shot to hell and the targeting systems are off-line."*

"That much I knew. Can you fix it?"

"Working on it."

Gold thought a moment. They had someone onboard who probably knew as much about repairing battle damage on the fly as anyone. "Gold to La Forge. Get down to engineering and help Duffy out, Commander."

"Already on my way, Captain."

"Good." Turning to the tactical station behind him, Gold said, "McAllan, any good news?"

"I can't target them unless we get within thirty thousand kilometers."

"Can you close the gap, Wong?"

"Working on it, sir," said the young ensign. "That ship's as fast as we are at impulse."

From ops, Lieutenant Ina said, "They're firing again, sir!"

After the impact, McAllan said, with surprise, "Shields down! Sir, I don't know what they did, but the shields are completely gone."

"Captain, I can get the shields back on-line, but you've got to give me ten minutes." That was La Forge.

"They're firing again!" Ina said.

"Veer off, Wong, give us distance."

Sparks flew as the weapons fire struck the unshielded ship.

"Stevens to bridge. Sir, if you set course for the second planet in the system and maintain a low orbit, we won't be picked up by their sensors."

"You heard the man, Wong. Set course for the second planet, full impulse."

"Yes, sir," Wong said.

"McAllan, full spread of torpedoes—doesn't matter where they're aimed, they're just cover fire."

Nodding, McAllan said, "Torpedoes away."

"Go, Wong."

"Engaging at full impulse."

"They following?" Gold asked.

"No, sir," said Ina. "They did take some heavy damage, though."

McAllan smiled. "Guess my aim was true."

"We should be so lucky," Gold muttered.

The Bajoran ops officer continued, "They're setting course back for the moon."

"All right, give us a low orbit, and keep an eye on them, Wong."

"Yes, sir."

Getting up from his chair, the captain said, "Gold to S.C.E. Briefing room, five minutes. McAllan, you've got the bridge. Contact the *Sugihara* and tell them to get over here, pronto. And the *nanosecond* something happens, let me know, got it?"

"Got it, sir."

"Good."

He headed toward the briefing room, wondering how the hell the mission had managed to go so bad, so fast.

And why, exactly, one of the Eerlikka clergy had killed the First Speaker in cold blood.

CHAPTER 7

"**W**here are they?" Undlar bellowed. He couldn't believe it. They had *had* that Starfleet ship, and now it was gone.

"Scanners aren't picking them up anywhere," the pilot said.

"Maybe they blew up," Undlar said, though it was wishful thinking.

"Then we'd be reading debris. There isn't anything."

Undlar slammed his fist into a bulkhead. *It had been going so well.*

The pilot continued to lean over his readout. Next to him, Emarur turned to look at Undlar. "I can't believe you killed the First Speaker."

"She was in the way."

"You never told me you were going to kill her— especially not on my ship!"

Laughing, Undlar said, "What did you think I was going to do, Emarur? Ask her politely to go along with the destruction of Ganitriul? Don't be

ridiculous. She had to die, the same way my
brother clergy had to die. Revolutions don't succeed if the people you're revolting against remain
breathing." Undlar closed his eyes and once again
relived the death of the other priests in his mind's
eye. He had so enjoyed killing those self-righteous
imbeciles. "Besides," he said, reopening his eyes,
"the role of naïve young priest was getting tiresome."

Emarur blinked several times. "You killed the
priests?"

"Of course. It's no good destroying Ganitriul if
the people who know how to fix it are still up and
about. Besides," he added with a grin, "it was so
much easier to convince the Speakers that this
ship was built with the clergy's authorization
when I was the only clergy left alive to verify it.
Now then, unless you have any other tiresome
questions, I'd like to get on with this before that
Starfleet ship comes back—or worse, brings
friends. Contact the surface. I need to know if
Hagi has neutralized whatever team Starfleet sent
down."

Emarur glared at Undlar. "I'm the owner of this
ship, Undlar, not you. You don't give me orders."

Undlar moved closer to Emarur and
unsheathed his blade, which was still blue with
Ansed's blood. In a low, calm voice, Undlar said, "I
hired you, Emarur, and I'm the one who paid to
have your precious ship equipped with non-
Ganitriul components. Right now, you've got the
only working vessel in the system. I think, therefore, you should modify your tone before you join

the First Speaker. Now, I repeat, contact the surface."

Continuing to glare at Undlar, Emarur reached back and opened a channel. "*Senbolma* to Hagi."

After a moment, a voice replied, "*Hagi.*"

"This is Undlar," the priest said, resheathing his weapon. "We're proceeding *mostly* according to plan. Apparently, Ganitriul called for help from the Federation, and they sent one of their starships to try to fix our 'Great One.' We took care of the ship, but they sent people to the surface."

"*I know,*" Hagi said. "*We found them at the main terminal, but they got away. We wounded one before the security protocol kicked in and neutralized the blasters. Luckily, we've got the blades, and all they've got are useless energy weapons. They're outnumbered by more than two to one, so they should be dead soon.*"

"Excellent. I will join you shortly."

"*I wouldn't recommend that, Undlar. The security systems are going completely haywire.*"

"Of course they are. Ganitriul itself is haywire. That was the point of the exercise," Undlar said slowly, as if talking to a small child.

"*Yes, but if you transport down and a security shield chooses that moment to activate, you could wind up scattered to the solar winds.*"

Undlar sighed. He hadn't thought of that. "We'll have to land, then."

"I'm afraid not," Emarur said. "One of those torpedoes the *da Vinci* hit us with damaged our landing gear. We can only land with a tow—which is impossible, since, as you so kindly pointed out, we're the only working ship in the system. Well, except for the *da Vinci*, but even if they do come back, I doubt they're going to be accommodating enough to help us land."

Growling, Undlar said, "Fine. Hagi, let me know as soon as you've killed the Starfleeters."

"I will. Hagi out."

Emarur turned to Undlar. "If you don't mind, will you please do something with the First Speaker's body?"

Undlar blinked his lower eyelids. "Excuse me?"

"I don't like dead bodies on my flight deck. Remove it."

"What am I supposed to do with it?"

"Dispose of it."

Undlar's face twisted. He took great pleasure in killing, but the idea of *touching* a dead body . . . "I can't do that."

"You're the one who killed her, Undlar. If you're squeamish about touching the body—well, you should have thought of that before you killed her. Now get that body off my flight deck!"

Emarur stared hard, right at Undlar. The priest was sorely tempted to slice open the ship owner's neck. But that would be foolish. The *Senbolma* only had a crew of two, and if he killed Emarur, Undlar would probably have to kill the pilot, too— and Undlar hadn't the first clue how to fly one of these things. His specialty was computers, after all—it was why, among all the Purists, he had been the one chosen to infiltrate the clergy and infect Ganitriul.

"Very well," he finally said. And, fighting down

his revulsion, he dragged Ansed's limp corpse off the flight deck.

Hagi backed up against the wall, counted to six, and then whirled around, swinging his blade upward in order to catch any humans that might be there in the chest.

There was nobody in the cavern.

"Clear," he said to Yanasa.

"This is ridiculous," Yanasa said. "If we had proper scanners—"

"—they wouldn't work anyhow," Hagi said. "They'd be tied into Ganitriul. Besides, the whole point is to get away from all this dependence on technology. This is the way it *should* be—searching on foot, with a blade in your hands, only relying on your own instincts."

Yanasa sighed, scratching the side of her head. "I still wish we had a scanner."

"Don't worry, we'll find them. There's a dozen of us, and we know these caverns better than they do. We'll—"

Hagi was cut off by a sudden jolt and an invisible force impeding his forward progress. "What the—?"

He took a step back, then gingerly reached forward. His finger tingled with the feeling of a forcefield, and he pulled it back. "Dammit. Let's go back," he said, turning around, but Yanasa was shaking her head.

"No luck," she said, performing the same action and also touching a forcefield.

"We're trapped."

"Yes," Yanasa said, sounding annoyed, "we're trapped. So, what do your instincts tell us to do now?"

"I don't appreciate your tone, Yanasa."

"And I don't appreciate being stuck in a cavern on a moon with a malfunctioning computer. I said from the beginning that it was stupid to leave people here for precisely this reason, but I was outvoted."

"First of all, we needed to secure the location in case something like this happened. Unscheduled civilian and alien ships come to the moon all the time, and one might have been on the way here when Ganitriul went down. We had to be here to stop them. Secondly, the security measures are constantly flipping on and off. The forcefield will come down eventually."

Yanasa rolled her eyes. "And then what? The Starfleet people—"

"Are hitting the same problems we are, only they don't know the caverns, and they're unarmed, except with those useless rifles of theirs."

"Did it occur to you, Hagi, that the same security measure that deactivated their weapons may also 'flip off'?"

Hagi found himself fighting the urge to take his blade to Yanasa's throat. Impatiently, he said, "In that case, our blasters will work as well, and we'll still outnumber them."

"Something else you probably didn't think of, Hagi. The Starfleet people have working scanners. And all the people on their team had gold trim on their uniforms."

Now it was Hagi's turn to roll his eyes. "I wasn't

aware you were such an observer of fashion, Yanasa."

"You really *are* an idiot, aren't you?"

Turning angrily on Yanasa, Hagi said, "I warned you to watch your—"

"Gold trim on a Starfleet uniform," Yanasa continued calmly, as if Hagi hadn't spoken, "means either operations or security. Which means the people here are either technicians, or experts in doing things like roaming around unfamiliar caverns. These people are *professionals*."

"Yes, we are," said a voice from behind Hagi. He turned around to see a tall human woman with blond fuzz atop her head. She stood on the other side of the forcefield from Hagi and was aiming her weapon at him.

Hagi laughed. "If that's supposed to scare me, human, it's not working. That thing in your hands is useless." To demonstrate his point, he took out his own blaster and pressed the trigger. Nothing happened. "And even if it did work, it can't fire through this forcefield."

The human just smiled.

"Ganitriul," she said, "lower the forcefield."

With a sharp glow, the forcefield dissipated. Before Hagi could move to charge at the human, an amber beam fired from the weapon and struck Hagi square in the chest.

All at once his nerve endings flared up, as if he'd been jolted with a massive electrical discharge, and then went dead. He fell to the cavern floor, but felt no impact. He saw another beam go over his head, which, he assumed, hit Yanasa.

How did she do that? he wondered, but could not say aloud. His mouth wouldn't work right.

"All clear, Commander," he heard the human's voice say. "Two down, ten to go."

Another voice said, "Good work, Corsi."

Encouraged, Hagi thought, *They've only gotten the two of us. The others will stop them, I'm sure of it.*

The human woman stood over him now. She was still smiling. She aimed her weapon at his chest and fired.

Sonya watched as Corsi checked over the two Eerlikka. "They're both out for the time being," Corsi said, "but I have no idea how long they'll stay that way. Unfortunately, we don't have anything to tie them up with."

Smiling, Sonya said, "We'll have to just hope that we can get to the core before they wake up."

Corsi got up from her kneeling position, and had started to walk toward Sonya when her tricorder beeped.

Sonya's did likewise, and she checked it. "Ganitriul, why did you put the forcefields back up?"

"*I did not.*"

Corsi had stopped walking, and was looking with annoyance at the ceiling. "Well, something did. I'm trapped in here."

"*I am afraid that there is nothing I can do, Lieutenant Commander Corsi. I am sorry.*"

Behind Sonya, Drew said, "We can't just leave her here."

Sonya looked at Corsi, who simply stared back with her steely blue eyes. She knew that look.

"We don't have a choice," Sonya said to Drew. "We can't afford to waste time trying to get the forcefield down. We have a mission to accomplish."

"But—"

"You heard the commander," Corsi said, interrupting Drew before he could argue further. "I'll be fine here. Just get down to the core—that's the main thing."

Drew sighed. "Yes, *sir*."

Giving Corsi a significant glance, Sonya said, "We will be back for you, Domenica."

Smiling a lopsided smile, Corsi said, "I'll hold you to that, Commander."

Amused at Corsi's inability to be casual, even when prompted not to be by a superior officer, Sonya gave the security chief one last encouraging smile, then led Drew back to where they'd left 110 to care for Hawkins.

"Let's get moving," she said.

"Where is Lieutenant Commander Corsi?" 110 asked.

"She got stuck behind a forcefield. We don't have time to get her out, so we're proceeding."

As Drew helped him to his feet, Hawkins said, "We can't just leave her."

"That's what I said, but Core-Breach herself overrode us," Drew said with a smile.

Sonya set her mouth tightly. "Mr. Drew, *I* gave the order to leave Commander Corsi behind. That's because, in case you've lost track of the chain of command, I'm in charge of the mission. Are we clear on this?"

Swallowing, Drew said, "Yes, sir."

"Good. Now let's get moving."

110 was studying his tricorder. "We need to go twenty meters down this corridor and then climb down a service ladder. That will lead to another corridor. None of the Eerlikka patrols are in that area."

Nodding, Sonya said, "Good. It's about time something went smoothly today."

They walked in silence—Sonya leading the way, 110 right behind her, Hawkins moving semi-steadily next to the Bynar, and Drew bringing up the rear. They reached the ladder without incident and started to climb down.

Sonya reached the bottom of the ladder, followed quickly by 110 and Hawkins.

Then a bulkhead closed between Hawkins and Drew, cutting the latter off from the other three. Quickly tapping her combadge, Sonya said, "Gomez to Drew."

"I'm okay, Commander. It kinda caught me by surprise."

"Did another bulkhead open at the top of the ladder?"

"Uh, yeah, one did. I'll try to cut through."

Looking at her tricorder, Sonya said, "That'll never work; you can only get light stun on the rifles. This bulkhead's made of rodinium."

"Damn."

"Ganitriul, is there any air being pumped into there?"

"There are no air vents in the section that Crewperson Drew is presently in. However, there is enough air to last him approximately three hours and seventeen minutes."

"Drew—" Sonya started.

"It's okay, Commander," Drew said. *"I'll be fine. Maybe the bulkheads'll open up again, maybe the scattering field'll go down—or maybe I'll get through some other way. You just get to the core. And, hey, Vance?"*

Hawkins said, "Yeah, Steve?"

"Keep an eye on them, huh?"

Snorting, Hawkins said, "Don't talk, pal, you'll just waste air. I know that's hard for you, but do your best."

"Hardy-har-har."

"Commander," 110 said, "there is an Eerlikka patrol moving in this direction. It behooves us to continue forward."

Nodding, Sonya said, "Stiff upper lip, Drew. We'll be back for you soon."

Ganitriul spoke: *"Commander Gomez, I do apologize for this turn of events."*

"It's not your fault, Ganitriul," Sonya said soothingly. *Listen to me,* she thought, *trying to calm down an inanimate object.*

"However," the computer continued, *"I do have good news. The patrol that is heading your way is presently coming down another ladder. They are now trapped in the same manner as Crewperson Drew. Assuming the bulkheads do not raise without my consent—which is a possibility—they will remain trapped."*

"That just leaves eight of them," Sonya said.

"And three of us," Hawkins muttered.

Hoping her smile was as encouraging as she intended it to be, Sonya said, "It beats twelve against five, Hawkins. C'mon, let's move."

They continued on in silence for several minutes, 110 providing directions toward the core. Many of the walls, like the cul-de-sac where they'd taken refuge earlier, were occupied by dusty, marblelike interfaces. According to the schematics, this section used to house the weather control systems, and was heavily used up until about a century earlier. Then it was consolidated into a smaller system located one level up.

"Commander Gomez," Ganitriul said, *"I have more good news."*

"That's a nice change," Sonya muttered. "What is it, Ganitriul?"

"I have regained control of Security Measure 7. I can deactivate the scattering field now."

Before Sonya could tell Ganitriul to go ahead and do so, Hawkins said, "Commander, I don't think we should do that."

Frowning, Sonya asked, "Why not?"

"Right now, we've got the advantage. Even with light stun, we're better armed than the Eerlikka, even with inferior numbers. If we turn the scattering field off, we lose that, 'cause they'll be just as well-armed."

"Good point," Sonya said with a nod. She thought a moment. "Ganitriul, is there any way to change the frequency of the scattering field so it will only affect the Eerlikka blasters, but not our phasers?"

"*I might be able to. I will attempt to adjust the field.*"

"Okay. In the meantime, leave it on." She turned to Hawkins. "Good work, Hawkins."

"No problem, sir," the security guard said with a tired smile. "Just doing what Core-Breach'd want me to do—keeping us all alive." Hawkins' dark skin had gone almost gray for a while, but he seemed to be getting his energy back up. Whatever was in the medikit seemed to have done the trick. Still, his left arm hung uselessly at his side, while he carried the rifle with his right. Sonya hoped he'd be able to fulfill Corsi's mandate if and when things got down to the nitty-gritty.

110 had never been more miserable in his life, and he cursed Bart Faulwell for talking him into agreeing to sit in on the meeting. He should not have come on the mission. He should have just stayed in his quarters and tried to figure out what to do when he got back to Bynaus.

Instead, he was walking through a strange corridor—stumbling, really, as he kept expecting 111 to be by his side; he wondered if he would ever be able to adjust to walking alone—being pursued by people trying to kill him, in order to reach a destination. At which point, he would be required to, as humans put it, save the day.

And he didn't know if he could.

The feeling did not sit well with him at all. 110's entire life had been defined by computers. He understood them, lived them, breathed them, *knew* them in a way no non-Bynar could truly comprehend.

Or, more to the point, he and 111 did.

Without her, he suddenly doubted his own instincts. Always, in the past, they had checked each other, each constantly confirming the other's work, providing a comforting redundancy that made them so much more efficient. With her, he would have instantly known what was wrong with Ganitriul, and quite possibly have been able to fix it without requiring access to the central core—though that, in all likelihood, would have been safer in any event. Now, though, he could not even be completely sure if his diagnostic was correct.

That had never happened before.

He wondered if this was how the Eerlikka felt when Ganitriul malfunctioned. To suddenly have all the order and sense of your life be taken away from you . . .

His tricorder beeped. Gazing at the readout, he said, "Commander, I am reading a forcefield around this corner."

As they turned the corner, they saw what the tricorder read.

"Great," Gomez said. "Any way around this?"

110 studied the map of the caverns. "There is an alternate route, but it will add an hour to our travel time. In addition, two of the Eerlikka patrols are on that route. This is the most direct way to the core, and is presently free of any of our pursuers."

"Ganitriul, can you release this forcefield?"

"I can, but at the moment the forcefield is holding back a gas that will render all of you unconscious. I have been unable to vent the gas, which is why I put up the forcefields."

"Damn."

110 asked, "Ganitriul, is there a manual override to the ventilation system?"

"Yes, there is. Would you like me to show it to you?"

"Please," 110 said.

110 heard Hawkins mutter, "Why the hell couldn't it mention that sooner?" as a small panel opened up in the floor.

Gomez smiled at the security guard and said, "GIGO."

"Excuse me?" Hawkins asked.

"Garbage in, garbage out. Old saying about computers. They're only as good as what you put into them. Kind of a nice reminder that Ganitriul, for all its sophistication, is still a machine. It didn't volunteer the information about the manual override because we didn't ask."

Meanwhile, 110 got down on his hands and knees and peered into the manual override. Its operation was fairly complex, but his interaction with Ganitriul earlier served him well—he knew his way around the supercomputer's systems now. He started entering the codes that would allow access to the override controls.

As he worked, the forcefields went down. The air quickly turned an odd shade of green as the gas that the forcefields had held in check started to spread throughout the cavern.

His vision swimming, 110 worked frantically at the console, fighting against unconsciousness . . .

CHAPTER
8

"Talk to me, boys and girls."

Unlike the casual atmosphere of the meeting that morning, David Gold thought the tension in the briefing room of the *da Vinci* now was thick enough to cut with one of Rachel's boning knives.

Gold sat once again at the head of the table, with La Forge and Duffy on either side of him, Abramowitz and Faulwell next to Duffy, Lense and Stevens next to La Forge, and Blue in her usual seat at the other end.

"We got the shields back on-line," Duffy said, "but I don't know how long they'll last."

Stevens put in, "I've never seen anything quite like that weapon they used. I've gone over the sensor data three times—so has Commander La Forge," he added, with a nod to the officer, "and we can't figure out why it knocked out our shields."

"I have some guesses as to how to defend against it," La Forge added, "but until we actually get shot at again by them, I don't have any idea if it'll work."

Gold leaned back and sighed. "So, basically, we're defenseless. What about weapons?"

"They're all fine," Duffy said. "We had to reroute half the—"

"Bridge to captain."

Gold looked up. "Go ahead, McAllan."

"Sir, the Sugihara is in the midst of a rescue operation of their own. Apparently, there's a Talarian freighter whose warp core went critical. They're going to try to finish up as fast as possible, but the soonest they can get here is in twelve hours."

"Damn. All right, McAllan, tell them to do the best they can. Gold out." He looked around the table. "All right, people, you're supposed to be the cream of Starfleet's engineering crop. Let's have some ideas."

"Actually, Carol, Fabian, and I have come up with something, sir," Faulwell said.

"Don't keep us in suspense, man, out with it," Gold said when the linguist hesitated.

"Well, sir, the *Senbolma* has a very simple computer system. Since it's not linked to Ganitriul, it was constructed from scratch. And their cryptography is basically nonexistent."

Abramowitz added, "It's a cultural bias, actually. Since every computer system is linked to every other computer system, they never really had to develop any kind of external computer security, since it's all one machine."

"Right," Faulwell said, "so I think I can write up a program that will break into their ship's computer pretty easily. I was able to get some pretty detailed sensor readings when we were talking to them, and—well, not to gloat or anything, sir, but I'd have a harder time hacking into an old twenty-first century mainframe. A lot of their subsystems aren't even encoded."

Stevens said, "The program works pretty fast. We'd need to get within communications range, but with Bart's program, I can probably get access to their control systems in about a minute, and then we can run the ship from here."

"One minute'll be pushing it," La Forge said. "Especially since they'll see us coming as soon as we leave orbit around this planet, and we won't be in comm range for a good thirty seconds."

"Then it's up to you and Duffy to hold us together, Commander," Gold said. He stood up. "Let's do it, people." As everyone filed out of the room, Gold stopped Lense briefly. "With any luck, we won't need your services, Doctor."

Lense waited until the room had cleared of everyone but herself and Gold before saying, in a somewhat bitter tone, "Let's hope for luck, then. I did join this ship to get *away* from combat medicine."

"I know. We'll do our best," he said in as reassuring a voice as possible.

It seemed to work, as Lense nodded and said, "I know you will, sir. I'll go get sickbay ready."

Domenica Corsi watched as the Eerlikka woman started to stir. Aiming her phaser rifle at the woman's head, Corsi said, "I'd suggest not making any sudden movements, or you go back to sleep."

Sitting up slowly, the woman said, "Don't worry. I'm not eager to get shot at again. How'd you do that, anyhow?"

"What?"

"Shoot me. I thought weapons were deactivated."

Smiling, Corsi said, "Oh, they are. Well, yours are. Obviously, our equipment is better than yours."

The woman shook her head and laughed. "You Starfleet types. Everything has to be bigger with you, doesn't it?"

Corsi couldn't help but laugh at that. "Maybe."

"So why are you still here?"

"Wasn't given a choice." She reached behind where she was standing—never taking her eyes off the woman—and tapped the forcefield. "These kicked in after I took you two down. Ganitriul can't lower them."

"So you don't have control of Ganitriul?"

The woman sounded surprised, and Corsi cursed herself for giving that away. Then again, there was no other reason for Corsi to have trapped herself behind two forcefields, so she would have figured it out before long.

Aloud, she said, "Ganitriul doesn't have control of Ganitriul. You folks saw to that."

"Yeah, we did. And it's working. The Eerlikka are finding out what it's like to *live* instead of having everything handed to them."

Corsi rolled her eyes. "If you're gonna start spouting rhetoric, I'll shoot you again."

To Corsi's surprise, the woman actually looked contrite. "Sorry. Occupational hazard when you hang around with fanatics."

"So why hang around with them?"

"I wonder that sometimes, especially when they pull dumb moves like this."

Corsi frowned, but inwardly she smiled. This was the best way to gather intelligence—casual conversation, don't let the subject know she's being interrogated. "Like what?"

"Leaving people here in the middle of a computer complex that's falling apart at the seams on the off chance that someone might come by was not the brightest of moves."

"It wasn't that off chance—after all, *we* came by."

"Yeah, but we're just as trapped in here as you are. Actually, we're more trapped. Your scanners and weapons work."

Corsi nodded. "Bad tactics."

"Yeah, well, us fanatics don't always think things through," the woman said with a bitter chuckle. "I'm Yanasa, by the way."

"I'm the person holding the rifle. Pleased to meet you." Corsi saw no reason to give Yanasa any more information than needed.

"Okay, Rifle Woman, what's the plan?"

"The plan is, you don't move until I tell you to."

"That's it?"

"That's the only part that concerns you."

A beeping noise filled the air, and then a voice said, "Senbolma *to Hagi.*"

Yanasa looked at the still-slumbering form of her comrade, from whose belt the voice was emitting.

"Hagi, this is Undlar, answer me, dammit!" said a different voice.

Corsi mouthed the words, *Don't touch it* to Yanasa, who obligingly didn't move.

"Something must have happened to him," said the first voice.

"Close the channel," said Undlar. *"Hagi's got the only comm unit. We may have to beam dow—"*

Then it cut off. Corsi sighed. She had been hoping they might say something about the *da Vinci* before they cut off communications, but that would've been too convenient.

"Only one comm unit? That wasn't very bright," Corsi said.

"We only had one hand-unit that wasn't tied into Ganitriul," Yanasa said. "I wanted to wait until we had enough units for everyone, but, like every sensible suggestion I made, I was outvoted." She indicated Hagi with her head. "Why's he still out if I'm up?"

Not seeing any harm in answering that question, Corsi said, "Different people react to stun different ways. You've probably got a faster metabolism than him or something."

"Well, you should be grateful, Rifle Woman, 'cause Hagi's the field leader of this merry bunch, and he'd give you more rhetoric than you'd know what to do with."

"Lieutenant Commander Corsi," said Ganitriul, *"I have successfully altered the settings on the scattering field. The Eerlikka weapons still do not function, but your phaser rifles should now function as normal."*

"Thank you, Ganitriul." Corsi turned to Yanasa and smiled. As she did so, she adjusted the rifle to the heavy stun setting.

Yanasa was just shaking her head. "We weren't expecting this. It never occurred to any of us that Ganitriul would actually work against us. I had thought that it wouldn't function at all, but I guess they underestimated that personality. I honestly had thought it was just an interface, not a separate AI personality unto itself."

Oh, God, not another one who runs off about engineering minutiae at the drop of a hat, Corsi thought. She almost would've preferred the rhetoric. She got enough of this on the *da Vinci*.

Just then, the forcefields went down.

Without even hesitating, Corsi fired on Yanasa. She crumpled to the ground.

Hagi started to stir. Corsi fired on him, too, and he was still.

That ought to keep them out for a while, she thought. She tapped her combadge. "Corsi to Gomez."

No one answered.

CHAPTER
9

Fighting through the haze that was starting to cloud his vision, 110 entered the last of the codes needed to activate the manual override on the ventilation system in this cavern. The next step was to actually get the vents going, but he had to fight his fingers to make them work properly.

He wished 111 was there beside him. Together, they would have worked twice as fast, and gotten the vents clear before the forcefields failed.

But she was dead. He had felt her die. He still could feel it, even now, as his consciousness started to fade. . . .

In the background, he heard two filtered voices. One sounded like Ganitriul, and he caught the words *phaser rifles*, but he couldn't make out the rest. The other was Lieutenant Commander Corsi.

The world started to go an odd shade of green. 110 just wanted to lie down and off-line. But, no—then he'd relive 111's death again. Besides, if he did, the three of them would succumb to the gas, and then they'd be left for dead. It was bad enough that 111 had died; 110 would not be responsible for letting Gomez and Hawkins die as well.

He entered the command.

Within seconds, his vision cleared. His thought processes once again settled into the orderly pattern he was accustomed to. And the green haze faded.

Gomez was coughing furiously, but she managed to get out the words "Good work, 110" between coughs.

"I did what any of us would have, Commander," 110 said, not wanting to take undue credit for something so routine.

"Don't sell yourself short." More coughs. "You're the only one who knew your way around Ganitriul's circuits well enough to perform the override." Yet more coughs. "So stop being so modest and take credit for your work."

110 blinked. He supposed that the commander was right.

So why did he feel like he hadn't done anything special?

"Corsi to Gomez, are you there, Commander?"

Tapping her combadge, Gomez managed to say, "I'm here. We had a bit of a scrape with some gas, but we're okay now."

Prompted by those words, 110 went to the mini-medikit that Hawkins—who was coughing even more than Gomez—had on his belt pouch and removed the medical tricorder.

"Well," Corsi was saying, *"I'm out of the force-*

field, and we've got full weapons now. I nailed both prisoners with heavy stun, so they won't be a factor for a while."

"All right, head for Drew's position and see if you can cut him free from the bulkheads—or at least cut a hole for some air for him. Then get to the core. We'll meet you there."

"Yes, sir. Corsi out."

110 said, "According to the readings, both of you suffered minor damage to your esophageal passages from the gas. It can be repaired when we return to the *da Vinci.*"

"How about you?" Gomez asked between two more coughs.

"No deleterious aftereffects," he said calmly.

Smiling, Gomez said, "Lucky you. C'mon, let's get a move on to the core. How much farther?"

"Approximately fifty meters," 110 said, consulting the tricorder, "then down another ladder, and we will be there, Commander."

The two humans' coughs were now coming at longer intervals, which was a good sign. Gomez said, "Let's go."

Undlar had finally disposed of First Speaker Ansed's body. It had been a revolting task, and one he never wanted to be even remotely involved with again as long as he lived. He swore that, one day, he would kill Emarur for forcing him to commit this depraved action.

But, for now, he needed the owner of the *Senbolma,* so he restrained himself.

As he reentered the flight deck, he said,

"Contact the surface. Hagi hasn't checked in, and I want an update."

Emarur asked, "Is the body—"

"*Yes*, the body is disposed of. I hauled the damn thing to the transporter bay and dispersed her atoms into space. Now, contact the surface!"

Turning his back on Undlar, Emarur opened a channel. "*Senbolma* to Hagi."

There was no response. Angrily, Undlar leaned over Emarur's shoulder and said, "Hagi, this is Undlar; answer me, dammit!"

"Something must have happened to him," Emarur said, showing a phenomenal grasp of the blindingly obvious.

"Close the channel," said Undlar. "Hagi's got the only comm unit. We may have to beam down and see for ourselves."

"Hang on a second," Emarur said, turning to the pilot. "What're you picking up down there?"

The pilot shook his head. "I've been reading the same life signs all along. Some of them are faint, though—they're going deeper into the infrastructure of Ganitriul, and it's hard to get a reading that far down. And some people have dropped out as they went into some areas, and—"

Undlar had no patience for this. "Are there still twelve Eerlikka down there?"

"Yes," the pilot said.

"Are there still five aliens?"

"Yes. Four human and one Bynar, in case you're interested."

"I'm not," Undlar said. "We'll have to—"

An alarm went off. The pilot looked at his readout. "It's the *da Vinci*! It's back—it was in orbit around the second planet."

Emarur frowned. "How could they have been in orbit around the second planet?"

"I don't know, but that's where they're coming from."

"It doesn't matter," Undlar said. "This time we'll finish them off. Arm the weapons."

To Undlar's annoyance, the pilot looked at Emarur first. Emarur nodded, and only then did the pilot say, "Arming weapons. Shields up."

"This time, I want them destroyed," Undlar said.

"Then shut up and let me work," Emarur replied. Then he turned to the pilot. "Fire as soon as they're in range."

"Firing," the pilot said a moment later. Then he grinned. "Their shields are down."

Undlar smiled. He had no idea why their ship blasters were so effective against Starfleet shields, but he was willing to accept that they were.

The pilot said, "Firing again." A pause. "A direct hit, but no hull damage. Interesting—they've managed to partly reconstruct the shields. They're down again, though. They took damage to their weapons, propulsion, and secondary systems." Smiling a bit, the pilot said, "They've got a good engineer or two over there."

Maybe, Undlar thought, *we should consider selling the weapon to the Federation after we take over Eerlik.*

Of course, the Federation might not want to deal with a government that had destroyed one of their ships, even if one could consider it a field test. *So maybe we can sell it to someone else. The Ferengi or the Breen. The Breen would probably love a chance to even the score after the Dominion War. . . .*

Undlar shook his head, bringing himself back to reality. *Time enough for that after we've triumphed*, he thought. "What are you waiting for?" Undlar said impatiently to Emarur and the pilot. "Destroy them."

"Targeting them n—" The pilot cut himself off. "I've lost the lock." He stabbed at his console, but nothing happened. "I can't reestablish."

Emarur cried, "The shields have gone down!"

"What?"

"I've lost helm control," the pilot said, continuing to stab pointlessly at his console.

"Dammit, Emarur, what happened?"

Emarur was also stabbing at his console. "I can't access any ship's system. We've been completely locked out."

"That's impossible!" Undlar cried.

The face of the human captain of the *da Vinci* appeared suddenly on the viewscreen. *"We're the S.C.E., Undlar. Impossible things are our business. Now then, are you folks going to surrender?"*

"Don't be ridiculous," Undlar said. "Fine, you've taken over our ship. Now what? You don't have enough power to do anything to us. Your transporters and weapons and shields are down, so you can't fire on us and you can't board us. It's a stalemate, Captain. And I have righteousness on my side."

"Righteousness? You call cold-blooded murder righteous?"

The human sounded indignant. *Well, let him*, Undlar thought. "Every revolution has its executions, Captain. And this *is* a revolution. We will bring Eerlik out of its decadence and into a new era of greatness. And I can assure you that I will never give up. I will *never* surrender to you!"

"Screen off," Gold said, not wanting to look at Undlar's smug, teal-colored face. "Bridge to engineering. Duffy, La Forge, give me good news."

"Wish I could, Captain," La Forge said. *"I might be able to get the shields reconstituted again, but I doubt it. And the weapons systems were jury-rigged as it is—it'll take at least four hours to fix them now."*

"Get on it," Gold said with a sigh. At least La Forge had been able to reconstitute the shields after the first shot. That was all that had saved them—if he hadn't, that second shot would've done major structural damage instead of "merely" taking out half their systems. *In fact*, he thought, *that second shot would've more than likely destroyed the ship.*

He turned back to McAllan. "Contact the surface."

"Yes, sir." A pause. "Sir, I'm only reading two combadges—Corsi and Drew."

"Gold to Corsi," the captain said.

"Corsi here."

"Situation report, Commander."

"Commander Gomez, 110, and Hawkins are currently approaching the computer core, so they can do whatever they need to do to fix the thing. I'm on

my way there now. Drew is trapped between two bulkheads that fell down. The security systems have been switching on and off—that's how I got separated from the others—but Ganitriul's doing its best to help us out."

"We're not reading Gomez, Hawkins, or 110 up here."

"I'm reading all three of them on my tricorder."

"Good. We're in a stalemate up here with the Eerlikka ship. The sooner you people get Ganitriul up and running again, the better."

"Understood, Captain. Can we get reinforcements?"

"Negative," Gold said, hating the fact that he had to say it. "Transporter's down. I'm afraid you're on your own, Corsi."

"That's fine, sir. We'll get it done."

"Keep me posted for as long as you can. *Da Vinci* out." He looked around the bridge, then hit his combadge. "Duffy, La Forge, how soon until the transporters are up?"

"Maybe six hours," Duffy said.

"Make that the priority. We can end this if we can board them."

From the conn position, Wong said, "Why don't we board them with a shuttle?" The *da Vinci* had two shuttlecraft, the *Archimedes* and the *Franklin*.

McAllan was shaking his head. "Too risky. They'll know we're coming when we approach the shuttlebay and open up the bay doors—and they've got hand weapons. I can't tell what kind they are, but if they're anything like the shipboard weapons, the shuttle will be a sitting duck."

Gold sighed, then looked at Stevens, seated with Abramowitz and Faulwell at one of the rear science stations. "Can you maintain the hold on their computer system?"

Stevens nodded. "No problem, sir. I installed a dozen passwords on all the systems, and they're all in-jokes that only about three people in my family would even guess."

"I doubt they even know what a password *is* in this context," Abramowitz said. "We should be fine."

"Is there any kind of security device we can use against them?"

Stevens shook his head. "They don't have anything like that. Best I can do is either cut off their air supply or their gravity."

"Killing them's only a last-ditch option," Gold said, "and knocking out the gravity'll hardly matter." He sighed again. "All right then, we'll wait." He hated waiting. Rachel always said his impatience would be the death of him. *Hope she's wrong this time*, he thought.

Sonya Gomez felt like someone had scraped her throat with a rusty knife. She didn't particularly want to cough, as it hurt like hell every time she did, but it got to the point where not coughing was worse. So she coughed. And was sorry she had.

This went on for the entire time she, 110, and Hawkins walked the rest of the way to the core.

"Corsi to Gomez."

"Go ahead."

"Good news, Commander—the da Vinci *is okay."*

Sonya had been trying very hard not to think about the fact that they hadn't been in touch with the ship. The idea that she'd never see Kieran again . . .

Aloud, she simply said, "That's good to hear."

"You're too far deep for them to pick you up—and I will be soon. I tried to get Drew out, but one rifle can't cut it without exhausting the power pack. I was able to make a small breathing hole for him, so he should be able to survive until we can get everything under control."

"All right," Sonya said. "We're almost at the core. We'll meet you here. Be careful."

"Always, Commander. Corsi out."

About ten minutes passed in silence, and then Ganitriul's ever-pleasant voice sounded once again. *"Commander Gomez, I am afraid that the scattering field has gone down. Any weapon will work within the caverns now, not just yours."*

"Okay," she said with a sigh. That had been a handy tactical advantage, but they'd have to live without it.

After another five minutes, Sonya figured they had arrived at their destination when they were confronted with a massive bulkhead. "I'm assuming this is the entrance to the core and not another security protocol we have to work around?"

Ganitriul's voice said, *"Yes, Commander Gomez, this is the entrance to the core."*

"I've got the code to open the door," 110 said.

The Bynar walked up to a keypad, which was right at arm level for him. Sonya smiled. *Good thing that the Eerlikka and the Bynars are roughly the same average height*, she thought.

"Commander, a patrol's coming toward us," Hawkins said, looking at his tricorder. Then he dropped the tricorder and picked up his rifle, bracing it against his shoulder, since he only had the one good arm.

"How many?" Sonya asked.

"Only two."

The bulkhead started to slowly slide open.

Blaster fire whizzed by Sonya, only missing her by a few centimeters.

She turned and ran for the opening bulkhead. Behind her, Hawkins lay down covering fire.

A sharp pain seared into her left leg, and she went sprawling to the ground, her jaw colliding with the cavern floor.

Her leg felt like it was on fire, but she managed to clamber the rest of the way into the core with her right leg and arms.

She looked back and saw that 110 had made it in, but Hawkins was still on the ground outside the core, firing at their assailants.

Then the door started to slide shut.

"110, keep the door open!"

"I can't," he said. "Not until it closes again—it's on a strict cycle."

The door slammed shut.

CHAPTER
10

Vance Hawkins did not like the position he was in.

Getting shot at by two people while lying on a cold, stone cave floor with a useless left arm, wielding a phaser rifle designed as a two-handed weapon, and separated from the rest of his team was not his conception of the ideal tactical situation.

So far, his two assailants hadn't struck. Part of that was because he was flat on the floor, which made it harder to hit him than if he were standing up—but not as difficult as if he were behind a wall.

By an annoying coincidence, behind a wall was precisely where his assailants were. There was one on either side of the corridor, hiding mostly around a corner. Thus far, Hawkins had been able to lay down more or less continuous cover fire that kept them around their respective corners, except when they poked their heads out long enough to shoot—another reason why they hadn't hit, as they hadn't been able to aim properly. But sooner or later, they were going to get lucky.

A shot came frighteningly close to his left arm. The magic of modern medicine meant that he could no longer feel the pain, but the limb was also useless until he got back to Dr. Lense's care on the *da Vinci*. Hawkins didn't really like the idea of it being injured further.

The door had slammed shut and showed no signs of reopening. Since Commander Gomez and 110 weren't armed, Hawkins couldn't afford to move from his position, even if it had been open, unfortunately.

No, he thought, *I definitely don't like this position.*

Then he heard something that sounded like "*Urk!*" and a shot went flying a meter over his head. Neither of the Eerlikka had missed by that much before. . . .

The reason became apparent soon enough, when he saw the assailant on the right fall to the ground. Hawkins then saw the most beautiful sight he'd ever seen in his life: Lieutenant Commander Corsi, pointing her rifle at the head of the other Eerlikka.

And she was smiling. The smile that meant whoever she was pointing her rifle at was not going to go home a happy person.

Good ol' Core-Breach, Hawkins thought. *Can always count on her to save our asses.* He started to clamber upright with his good hand.

"Drop it," she said.

The Eerlikka dropped his weapon.

"And the blade."

Reaching into his tunic, the Eerlikka pulled out his sword and dropped it, too.

"Now put your hands out where I can see them and walk very, very slowly forward. Don't stop until I tell you."

As the Eerlikka walked forward, Corsi asked, "What's your name?"

"I—I'm Utaka."

"Well, congratulations, Utaka, you're now a prisoner of Starfleet. Stop walking," she added when they arrived in front of the bulkhead—

—which started to slide open.

The door opened to 110 and Gomez, the latter sitting on the floor, clutching her left leg. She was also bleeding from a gash in her jaw.

"Glad you could make it, Commander Corsi," Gomez said with a small smile. "And I see you brought a present."

"This is Utaka," Corsi said. "Walk inside the core, Utaka."

Corsi led the prisoner into the core. Hawkins followed behind, first shouldering the rifle, then taking out the medikit. He knelt down to check on Gomez.

As Hawkins one-handedly checked over Gomez's leg wound and gingerly applied the appropriate hypospray, the prisoner said, "It's no use, you know. We still outnumber you. We've alerted the others—they'll all be here soon. And that door won't protect you."

Gomez nodded. "I guess they know the code for the door, then. 110, can you change it?"

"Yes," the Bynar said.

"Do it, then shut it. We may as well have some privacy."

Corsi was staring at her tricorder. "Utaka's right. I've got eight Eerlikka moving toward this position."

The door started to slide shut. "I have changed the code," 110 said, "and it's unlikely that they'll determine what it is."

Hawkins finished awkwardly applying a salve to Gomez's jaw. "You should be able to at least limp on that leg now, Commander." He stood, put away the medikit as best he could, then offered his good hand to help her up.

"Thanks, Hawkins," she said, getting to her feet.

"Commander Gomez, all security protocols have gone off-line. I cannot access any of them."

"Does that mean Drew is freed?" Hawkins asked.

"Yes, but it also means that the other two who were similarly trapped are freed—and I will be unable to use any security devices against those who are heading this way."

Hawkins breathed a sigh of relief. He'd been worried about his friend.

"Okay," Gomez said, "we'll have to hope that the door will keep them out."

Corsi tapped her combadge. "Corsi to Drew."

"Drew here. The bulkheads just raised."

"We heard," Corsi said. "Proceed to the core, but with caution. There's a band of eight hostiles coming here, and two more wandering around as well, and I don't want you to get taken down by them."

"Understood, Commander."

Sonya turned to the Bynar. "All right, 110, get to work on the core. We need to end this."

Sonya Gomez looked at the Bynar—and her heart fell. She'd never seen 110 like this: his eyes were dilating, he was fidgety, and he spoke with a motormouth that reminded Sonya uncomfortably of herself as an ensign.

"I—I don't know if I can perform this task, Commander. I'm—diminished without 111, and—"

Sonya put her hands on 110's shoulders. "I understand, but you have to try."

"But it might go wrong. I've been fearing this moment since you first put me on the away team. In fact, to be honest, I've been fearing it since 111 died. Up until now, everything's been simple. The interface with Ganitriul, activating the manual override, changing the code—those were basic tasks that even the most inept Bynar pair can do without thinking, much less one as mature as I, even *without* a mate. I know that I'm supposed to be able to fix any computer problem, but this may be beyond my capabilities."

Great, Sonya thought. *My throat feels like raw uridium, I've got a bum leg and a sore jaw, and now I have to hand-hold a Bynar.*

"Listen to me. It's true that you're not as efficient without 111 as you were with her. But you were never infallible. It may have seemed that way, but you're not. There's *always* a chance of failure. That doesn't mean you don't try. You still know your way around computers better than anyone I've ever met. And, even if it doesn't work, at least you'll have made the effort. If you don't even do that, you'll *never* succeed."

That has to be the hoariest load of clichéd crap I've ever uttered in my entire life, she thought. *Hope it worked.*

110 gazed up at Sonya, who saw only fear in his eyes. The question was, could he get past that fear?

Finally, the Bynar nodded and said, "Very well, Commander. I will try."

Slowly, 110 walked toward one wall. Like all the other interfaces, it looked like a giant marble slab, but this one was lit with a variety of symbols in the Makaro language. 110 activated his belt unit and started letting loose with a rapid-fire stream of binary code.

The symbols started to flash by more quickly. 110 only occasionally actually touched the interface—mostly, Ganitriul was responding directly to the binary code.

Every time Sonya saw the Bynars in action, it amazed her that people could be so in tune with a computer that they could communicate directly with it.

However, having seen 110 and 111 working in tandem, she could tell that 110 was working at about a quarter of the speed. She also noticed that he was getting frustrated with certain elements, and going back and trying something again.

"What's he doing?" Utaka asked.

"Undoing your sabotage," Sonya said.

"How?"

Sonya just smiled. "It's what he does."

Minutes passed, and still the rapid-fire stream of binary code came from 110's mouth. The rhythm of the code started to fall into something like a pattern that Sonya could detect. 110 didn't seemed as frustrated, and did less backpedaling and hesitating.

"What's taking him so long?" Hawkins asked. "I thought these guys could walk through computers like nothing."

"Two of them can," Sonya said angrily. "One of them takes a little longer. Anytime you want to step in and help out . . ."

Holding up his good hand and backing off, Hawkins said, "No, Commander, 'course not. It's just—"

He was interrupted by a loud *thud* against the door.

"My guess?" Corsi said, looking at the door. "The remaining Eerlikka just realized that the code doesn't work, and they're trying to break the door down."

"That's a pretty reasonable guess," Sonya said sardonically. "If they get through, protect 110 at all costs, understood?"

"Yes, sir," Corsi said, taking up position at a forty-five degree angle to the door on one knee. Hawkins did likewise at an equivalent point on the other side of the door.

Smoke started to show through the door. Sonya could now hear the whine of the Eerlikka blasters through the weakening rodinium door.

The pure simplicity of the binary code washed over 110. At first, it was like coming home again.

He was comfortable for the first time since 111 died.

At least, until the first glitch.

It was a simple mistake. He went down the wrong subroutine. A simple error—a misreading of a command.

If he'd been working with 111, it would never have happened.

He continued to navigate his way through Ganitriul. It was a complex system, and one that had many different facets. The Eerlikka had spent the millennia improving Ganitriul, building new processes over the old ones. But some of the older ones were still in place, never having needed to be improved. The newer routines were almost completely compatible with the older ones, adjusted for maximum efficiency.

Although Lieutenant Commander Duffy's statement that Ganitriul might put the master computer on Bynaus to shame had struck 110 as unlikely at the time, he now had to admit that Ganitriul was, in its own way, almost as impressive. For that alone, the Eerlikka deserved commendation.

Once again, he lost his way, this time exploring some of the older programs that regulated the economy, and which hadn't needed any alteration for almost a thousand years. He let his curiosity get the better of him—something 111 would not have tolerated.

Eventually, he found the source code for the invasive program. It had taken far longer than he'd expected, especially since the fruits of the program were all over every system he'd visited, going back to when he had interfaced with Ganitriul at the other terminal.

110 had to admire the simplicity of it: the invasive program simply changed the numeric values, or the operators of random mathematical equations. Addition would become subtraction, values were doubled or halved, a use of two variables would instead be a use of seventeen. The changes were random, and were restored just as randomly. This served to explain why the specific problems were a loss of control and a rearrangement of functions.

Most impressive of all, none of the errors the program introduced would actually cause the system to shut down. After all, if the system shut down, it was easy enough to diagnose the problem at the spot where the system crashed. But as long as the system was still operating—if not functioning properly—it made it that much harder to seek out the problem.

But 110 had found it.

Now he had to get rid of it.

The problem was, he could not simply eliminate the program. That is to say, he could, but that would not solve Ganitriul's problem. Whatever changes the program had initiated would remain once the program was wiped, and it would still not be able to function properly. What 110 had to do was backtrack: find all the changes the program had made, fix them, keep it from making any further changes, and *then*, finally, wipe the program.

With 111, it could have been done easily.

By himself, it would be extremely difficult.

But, as Commander Gomez said, he had to try.

So he did.

The process was slow. He almost missed a few of the equations that had been altered.

In the end, however, he found all the changes that had been made.

Then he eliminated the program.

I did it! he thought, triumphantly.

He turned around to tell Commander Gomez that he had succeeded, only to find himself knocked to the ground by Hawkins. Some kind of blaster fire went over his head.

110 looked up to see a large hole in the door, and an Eerlikka standing on the other side, firing a blaster.

Then a forcefield came up in front of the door. The Eerlikka still fired into it, but the forcefield simply absorbed the impact.

The Eerlikka tried to fire again, but her weapon no longer worked.

"Security protocols activated. Hostile forces have been neutralized," Ganitriul said. *"I once again have full control of all my operations. The hostiles outside the door are now trapped behind forcefields, their weapons deactivated."*

The three humans all broke into grins. "Good work, 110," Gomez said.

110 returned the smile. "Thank you, Commander."

Gomez asked, "Ganitriul, can you show us what's happening with the *da Vinci*?"

"Of course. The da Vinci *is presently in standard*

orbit around the moon," Ganitriul said, as an image of the *da Vinci* and another ship flickered to life on the interface. *"The Pevvni ship is the same one that engaged the* da Vinci *earlier."*

"Can you put us in touch with the *da Vinci?"*

"Yes. I have boosted the signal in your combadge so that it can penetrate the crust of the moon."

Tapping her combadge, Gomez said, "Gomez to *da Vinci."*

"Gold here. Good to hear your voice, Commander."

"Likewise, Captain."

"Assuming that is your voice. You sound like a Horta."

Gomez laughed, then coughed once. "I got on the bad side of some gas. It's nothing that can't be dealt with, sir. In any case, mission accomplished: 110 *has* fixed Ganitriul. All its operations are back to normal."

"Good. We've got a bit of a standoff here—we have control of the Senbolma, *but our transporters and weapons are out. We'd like to send a boarding party over there."*

Corsi said, "Ganitriul, can you send Hawkins, Drew, and me to the *Senbolma?"*

"Yes."

Turning to Gomez, Corsi said, "With your permission, we can be that boarding party."

Gomez nodded. "Permission granted."

CHAPTER

11

It would have been inaccurate to say that it was *all* over, but still, Sonya Gomez was impressed with how quickly things had calmed down. Corsi, Hawkins, and Drew took control of the *Senbolma*, subduing Undlar and his two accomplices in fairly short order. The three Eerlikka were taken into custody by the first Enforcement ship that had been able to get itself into Eerlik orbit. The weather on the planet had stabilized, as had transportation methods and food distribution.

Closer to home, Dr. Lense had treated Sonya and Hawkins—removing the lingering effects of the gas from their throats and patching up their wounds.

There were still plenty of relief efforts that needed to be coordinated, and the *Sugihara* had at last arrived in order to aid in those matters, freeing the *da Vinci* up to resume its course for Starbase 505.

Sonya sat in the mess hall with Carol Abramowitz and Bart Faulwell, who were filling her in on what happened on the *da Vinci* while she was dealing with Ganitriul.

"I'm just glad things will get back to normal," Sonya said.

Carol snorted. "Not much chance of that. The First Speaker's dead, the only surviving member of the clergy is a mass murderer, and now everyone's questioning the efficacy of having one big, vulnerable computer. Even if they do keep things as they are, their entire spiritual base *and* the people who are capable of fixing Ganitriul are all dead. You don't just recover from that by taking out an invasive program."

Bart shrugged. "Maybe they'll decide to join the Federation. Or at least work something out so that some computer experts can be nearby until they can train people. Or something."

"Maybe 110 and his new mate could do that after he rebonds," Carol said.

"Maybe," Bart said, looking down, and suddenly very interested in his root beer.

Sonya frowned, and wondered what that look was about—especially after that odd look 110 had given Bart before accepting the assignment.

Oh well, she thought. *It's not my business.* She polished off her mug of Earl Grey and said, "Still, that's not our lookout. We're the fix-it squad, not the diplomats. We've done what we're supposed to do—now we go on to the next assignment. Or, in this case, to Starbase 505. I'm sure both 110 and Geordi will be happy to finally be heading home."

"Oh, I don't know," Carol said with a smile,

"they were both pretty handy. Maybe they'll stick around."

Returning the smile, Sonya said, "Trust me, nothing will keep Geordi off the *Enterprise* for any length of time. And 110 does have obligations."

"True," Carol said.

Bart continued to stare at his root beer.

110 stared at the ceiling of the quarters that, until recently, he had shared with the love of his life.

He had received accolades, not just from Captain Gold and Commander Gomez, but also from the new First Speaker of Eerlik, a man named Biral, who had gone on for quite some time about how grateful the Eerlikka were, to the S.C.E. in general and to 110 in particular.

And now, finally, the *da Vinci* was headed back to Starbase 505, from which 110 was supposed to take a transport to Bynaus.

110 got up off the bed and stared at the viewscreen, which presently was programmed to show the stars as they appeared when at warp. Humans always liked to gaze at the stars whenever they sought out answers, but 110 and 111 had always found the practice to be pointless.

Now that he was alone—it was just as pointless. The stars had no answers.

If he did not return to Bynaus, he would be an outcast.

If he did return to Bynaus, he would have to rebond.

He found each choice to be repugnant in some

form or other. While he could not imagine *not* being a true part of Bynar society, neither could he imagine living without 111.

At least he knew that he could function without 111. He had fixed Ganitriul. He had saved Eerlik. That, at least, counted for something.

110 lay back down on the bunk and stared at the ceiling.

HARD CRASH

Christie Golden

CHAPTER
1

Our communications system appears to be damaged. I am receiving no response from you. Jaldark, please come in. You need to effect repairs so that we can communicate.

Jaldark, please come in.

Jaldark, respond.

Please.

Tlaimon Kassant sipped a cup of hot *jiksn*. He had the late shift, the solitary shift, and he liked it that way. His people were known for their close-knit bonds and love of socialization, but Tlaimon was considered unusual in that he preferred his own company for a few hours every day. He considered his "oddity" a boon, as he was paid twice as much for being willing to go the entire night by himself. Most Intarians liked to work in huddled groups.

All alone for the night. What a pleasant thing. Easy job, too; watching the monitor for things that seldom happened. Most ships communicated their arrival long before they showed up on the monitor. They were always eager to get to Intar. It wasn't as well known in the quadrant as Risa, admittedly, but then, what planet was?

Tlaimon stretched the retractable tentacles that served as arms for the Intarians and lazily brought the gaze of his multifaceted eyes toward the screen.

The cup of *jiksn* fell to the padded floor unheeded and bounced twice. Its contents formed a pool of sticky lavender fluid. Tlaimon swore a deep oath under his breath, while his two hearts raced with fear at what the screen revealed.

Something large was approaching the city from space. It was several million kilometers away, but it was closing fast. Too fast for comfort. He adjusted the controls swiftly, his tentacles more deft than any humanoid's clumsy digits.

Tlaimon could see the outline now. A ship of some kind, though the computer kept flashing that most frustrating of words, "Unknown," on the screen. It was long and spiky and promised destruction if it continued on its trajectory.

Tlaimon quickly hit the button that would translate his message in every language known to the Federation.

"Attention, alien vessel," he said in a voice that trembled. "You are on a collision course with a major population center of our planet. Adjust your course to bearing one-four-seven mark eight, and you will avoid impact."

The ship didn't change its position one millimeter. Either it was unaware of the impending disaster—for surely it would be destroyed upon striking the planet if it continued at its present speed—or else its crew didn't care.

Unpleasant scenarios crowded Tlaimon's mind. Was this a suicide run? A dreadful first strike that would mean war?

Who would possibly want to make war on us? Tlaimon thought wildly.

There was nothing else for it. Trembling, Tlaimon extended a tentacle and tapped the white button that would alert the government that a disaster was descending upon the capital city of Verutak, with all the inevitability of dusk at the end of the day.

Jaldark, what is going on? I have heard nothing from you. Everything appears to be intact, and yet we remain unable to communicate. Please respond. Please attend to the communication damage.

Are you still receiving this? Jaldark?

Bartholomew Faulwell smiled to himself as he took the items from the replicator. What he was doing had become, over time, a ritual of sorts. He took the crisp, off-white paper, enjoying the feel of it in his hand; picked up the smooth pen filled with just the right shade of black-blue ink. Sometimes, if he wasn't careful, the ink would stain the tip of the third finger on his right hand. It brought him an uncommon rush of pleasure whenever he chanced to look upon that smudge before it wore off, because it reminded him of the ritual, and the ritual brought him closer to Anthony Mark.

Of course, there was no convenient way of getting the actual letters to Anthony. Once Faulwell had composed them, had gotten the words exactly right, he'd read them aloud into a subspace message and, *poof*, off it would go. It was impersonal, but it was the only way. On the rare opportunities they had to meet, Faulwell would give Anthony the letters in a box, as a special gift. But the simple, physical act of writing the letters—all of which he opened with the words "Just a brief note," regardless of how many pages the letter would then go on to become—made Bart feel akin to the myriads of wanderers who had gone before: the sailors of ancient Earth, the early spacefarers, all those who knew distance from those they loved and tried to bridge that distance with the written word.

Words, written or spoken, were almost as dear to Faulwell as Anthony.

He took a breath and settled down in a chair in the quarters he shared with Stevens. He instructed the computer to provide soft, instrumental music as a pleasant background, and began to write.

Just a brief note to let you know that our last assignment was completed successfully. It was not without its tense moments, however! Some days, this mission becomes just a trifle too exciting for a boring old linguist like me to handle. It is always such a pleasure to have a calm moment now and then to write down my thoughts and feelings to you, my dear, and know that, as you read these words, you will, in some small way, share in my adven-

tures. How are you getting along with your new colleague, the one you called in your last letter the "Pompous Windbag?" Has PW come around to your way of thinking yet? I cannot imagine you would be unable to win him over once—

A klaxon sounded. Yellow alert. The slight linguist sagged in his chair and groaned. Time for another adventure.

"Will the following crewmembers please report to the briefing room." Bart listened, but his hopes of peacefully continuing with his correspondence were dashed when he heard his name among those listed. Carefully, he capped the pen and left the letter on the table.

He wasn't usually summoned to briefings unless he was an actual participant in whatever mission they were about to embark upon. Still, he remained optimistic. With any luck he'd return to his letter in a few moments. After all, not every "adventure" on which the *da Vinci* embarked required a linguist.

"And we'll need a linguist," Captain David Gold was saying to Geordi La Forge as Faulwell entered the room. "And there's one now," Gold added, with a lift of his bushy eyebrows as he caught sight of Faulwell. The rest of the crew who had been asked to report were filling the small briefing room, gently pushing past Faulwell to take their seats.

Faulwell smiled weakly. His brief note would have to wait.

Something brushed past his leg; P8 Blue, scurrying toward her specially designed seat. She was

muttering under her breath. Bart wondered what
this mission was about, that it got the normally
calm Pattie so agitated.

He sat between Commander Sonya Gomez and
Carol Abramowitz. Carol leaned over and whis-
pered, "Culture specialist *and* linguist, huh?
Wonder if it's a first-contact situation."

Her dark eyes glowed with excitement. Abramowitz loved first-contact situations, but they
always made the academic Faulwell nervous as
hell. He, more than anyone, knew just how important choosing the right word in delicate negotia-
tions could be. Sometimes, it was literally a matter
of life or death. He figured each of the first-
contact situations in which he'd participated had
aged him at least a year. No wonder his hair was
thinning and turning gray.

110, as always, was the last one to enter.
Sometimes he was quite late in reporting to the
briefings, but Gold had not reprimanded him.
Everyone was sympathetic to 110's situation. Bart
had begun to worry about him, after their recent
conversation. The little Bynar edged into the room
as if fearing an attack, his eyes—so small in his
round, pale face—darting about. Bart remembered how the unified pair used to move—each
step in sync, quickly, but with grace. Now 110
moved jerkily, awkwardly, as if he were uncertain
where to put hand or foot. There was no rhythm in
his movements anymore. In many ways, he
reminded Bart of nothing so much as a broken
toy. He did not take a seat, but chose to stand next
to the door.

Gold's sharp eyes scanned his crew. He nodded, as if satisfied.

"We got the notification from Scotty about fifteen minutes ago. We're going to have to move quickly, boys, girls, and others. We've got a delicate situation on our hands. Commander, if you will?"

La Forge touched a button. Bart felt a sinking in the pit of his stomach as he stared at the image that appeared. A large ship lay like a beached whale in the center of tons of debris. The pile of rubble had once been, if the graceful curves and arcs of the surviving buildings were any indication, a highly civilized city. The vessel was oval in shape, with four peculiar extensions jutting out of its fore and aft sections that looked like spikes. It seemed as if the impact had severely damaged the vessel, but the unfortunate city had gotten the worst of the deal.

Faulwell's mind raced. High population area, doubtless.

"Casualties?" asked Gomez, alert and focused.

"None that we know of, fortunately," said Gold. "It's the capital city of Intar."

"Not Intar!" gasped Abramowitz, her eyes wide with shock. "The Intarians are famous for their friendliness. I can't imagine anyone attacking them."

"They also have an extremely advanced warning system," said Gold. "It was designed so that they could address approaching ships and send them a nice hello. The other, secondary, purpose was to identify drifting space debris that might do some damage. They were able to evacuate the entire city before impact."

Bart felt the tension in his chest ease a little.

"However," Geordi continued, "according to reports on the approach of the ship, everything points to the vessel deliberately crashing into the planet. The Intarians tried to contact it, and when contact failed, they opened fire. Intar doesn't have much of a defense system, and what little they did have seemed to have absolutely no impact on this thing. And while it's temporarily dormant, it's still emitting signals." He tapped the screen with his knuckle. "It's wounded, all right, but it's still alive."

"Any vessel we're familiar with would have been broken to pieces on impact," said Pattie, blinking her multifaceted eyes solemnly. "This is damaged, all right, but preliminary reports indicate it's made out of something we've never seen before. It's got a structure as impervious to damage as—"

"Yours," joked Lieutenant Commander Kieran Duffy.

Pattie looked pleased. "That's not a bad comparison, actually. The difference between that ship's structure and a normal vessel's is, indeed, roughly comparable to the difference between my chitin and your thin human skin." She extended a limb and delicately patted Duffy's hand.

"The first volley in a war?" theorized Lieutenant Commander Domenica Corsi. The chief of security was always looking for the martial explanation, and, sadly, she was often right.

"As I said, I can't imagine a more unlikely target for such an attack than the Intarians," said Abramowitz, frowning a little. "They don't have a lot of resources, other than a pleasant climate and a pleasant people. Nor do they have an extensive weapons array. On Intar, it's pretty much come when you like, stay as long as you like, and don't forget to write."

"Nonetheless, we ought to be prepared." Corsi stuck out her chin a little. "I recommend we proceed with Tactical Code Level—"

Gold held up a hand. "No life signs, Corsi. No one to fight. No one on the long-range sensors hovering about, watching like vultures, either."

"Captain, there's always the chance the ship was crewed by a kind of life-form we haven't yet encountered. Our scans wouldn't necessarily detect them," Corsi pointed out. "Or, it could be a trap." She sat up a little straighter in her chair, utilizing her always-intimidating height to its best advantage, even when seated. "The entire ship could be a threat. A bomb of some kind. It could explode at any moment. I repeat, I recommend—"

"Duly noted, Commander," said Gold, his voice slightly harder than before. "But let's do a little investigating before we declare this planet a war zone, okay?"

Her eyes flashed, but Corsi settled back in her chair. She pressed her lips together tightly. Gomez gave the security chief a reassuring smile, but Corsi would not relax.

"Lieutenant Commander Corsi does have a point." It was Dr. Elizabeth Lense speaking. "The vessel could be automated. It could have been programmed to crash, especially if it's as tough as

Pattie's theorizing. Is there any indication that there was a crew onboard?"

"No way to tell without investigating it with our own eyes," said Geordi. "But that impact was pretty rough. Despite its thick hide, that ship's banged up quite a bit. Unless they were secured and protected somehow, humanoid bodies probably couldn't have survived that kind of crash even if the vessel itself did."

"Nonhumanoid bodies could," said Faulwell, speaking up. His mind was already racing with the possibilities. He needed to narrow it down as much as he could, in order to determine which branch of linguistics would be most effective to research. Armed with at least a rough idea of what to look for, he'd have a better chance translating the data they would retrieve from the ship's computer banks. As far as he was concerned, other than the concern a caring person must always feel at loss of life, he was relieved that there were no living beings aboard that ship to try to talk to.

He noticed that Carol, however, looked keenly disappointed. They'd called her in for her knowledge about the Intarians, not to speculate about the crew of the ship. There would be no first contact this time.

"Early indications are that the environment inside the ship is a nitrogen-oxygen mix, similar to Earth's. But that's no guarantee that the crew was humanoid," said Geordi. He smiled a little. "We'll find out soon enough."

"So, here's the situation." Gold leaned forward and laced his fingers together on the table. "The ship has deliberately plowed into the heart of downtown. It's far less damaged than it ought to be for the impact it took. It is inactive at the moment, but we're still getting signals. No signs of life, but as Corsi astutely pointed out, that doesn't mean that something's not still alive in there. Now, sensors indicate there's only one central command area in the thing. Pattie, you get to examine the outside."

"Certainly, Captain." She wriggled several of her legs. "I could use a little exercise."

Gold continued. "If we can get a transporter lock inside, you five—Commander La Forge, Gomez, Duffy, Faulwell, and 110—will be transporting into a ship about which we know absolutely nothing. Anything can happen, or nothing."

"In short," said Duffy, grinning, "an assignment much like any other."

But Faulwell wasn't laughing. Out of the corner of his eye, Bart had noticed that the Bynar had physically shuddered at the news that he was being assigned to the team. It was, as a Vulcan would say, the only logical choice. 110 was their computer specialist, until Starfleet sent them another one. 110 had been very brave up until now, expressing a willingness to continue with his work despite what had to be—*had* to be—extreme personal grief. But it was clearly taking a toll on the little fellow. He'd already delayed going home once. Now this had come up.

Even as Bart regarded the Bynar with sympathy, 110 straightened, pulled his tiny shoulders back, and resolutely lifted his large, hairless head. Faulwell was filled with admiration.

CHAPTER 2

Jaldark? If you are conducting a test of some sort, you may cease. I am starting to worry. Please, please come in.

The worried face of the Intari Makestru, the leader of his people, appeared on the viewscreen. "Captain Gold," he said anxiously. "You are a welcome sight. We have done nothing, as per orders from Starfleet, but I must say, it's been alarming having this ship just sitting there in our capital city."

"I'm certain it has," soothed Gold. "We're preparing to transport our people over to the ship. We'll contact you once we have the situation well in hand."

"We are grateful." The image blinked out. On the screen now was the strange, seemingly dead ship. Gold took a breath, said a quick prayer, and instructed the away team to report to the transporter room.

* * *

As they gathered in the transporter room, Sonya Gomez was still a bit on edge from the confrontation she'd had with Domenica Corsi. Normally, she got along with "Core-Breach" Corsi better than anyone else aboard the *da Vinci*. But Corsi was still stinging from the rebuff she'd gotten from Gold during the briefing. While Gomez was heading for the transporter room, Corsi had fallen in step beside her and insisted that she be allowed to accompany the away team.

"There's no indication that that will be necessary, Dom," Gomez had said, as sympathetically as she could.

"There's no indication that it won't," Corsi had retorted.

"Look," Gomez had finally said, exasperated, "the captain wants you on the bridge. And I think he's right. Suppose something does go wrong? We'll need you up here, in case that ship proves to be a danger to the Intarians."

When even that logic failed to placate the chief security officer, Gomez had added, "That's an order, Lieutenant Commander."

She disliked pulling rank, especially here, with this crew, where at times it seemed so unnecessary. They had worked together long enough that everyone knew what to do and usually didn't need to be told. She especially disliked having to do it with Corsi, who was generally the one keeping all the rest of them on their toes with regards to regulations, protocol, and proper rank deportment. Corsi had stiffened, drawn herself up to her full and imposing height, fixed Gomez with an icy stare, replied, "Yes, Commander," in a cold voice, and stalked off.

Gomez wasn't superstitious, but this was a bad way to start a mission. Her boots rang loudly as she stepped onto the transporter pad.

"Core-Breach got you?" asked Duffy.

"Kaboom," she replied softly. He grinned a little, then looked away quickly. Too quickly. It would take more time than this to get used to each other again.

Geordi, too, was smiling. She felt a trace of annoyance. She didn't want La Forge to see any division in the ranks, any hint that she couldn't take care of subordinates. She wished Gold hadn't ordered him to accompany the away team. This ought to have been her mission.

It was only now that she realized that 110 was missing. Her dark brows drew together in a frown. "Where is—"

The door hissed open. 110 stood there for a moment, looking around as if lost. Gomez's vexation with Geordi evaporated. Dammit, 110 seemed so very tiny, so very fragile in his envirosuit. So . . . alone. There was something very strange to her about seeing a single Bynar, something *wrong* about it. Like watching a Vulcan laugh at a joke. That wasn't the way this culture was meant to be.

Were they pushing him too hard? Was 110 really ready for another assignment, without a chance to properly mourn and reconnect with his people?

Hesitantly at first, then with more determination, 110 moved into the room. He clambered onto the transporter pad and craned his neck to look up, first at La Forge and then Gomez, with unreadable dark eyes.

"We—I—apologize for being late, Commander."

"Don't worry about it, 110," said Gomez, with more warmth than she had intended to show.

She looked up at Wong, who was awaiting their order to transport.

"Energize," said Gomez.

... Jaldark ... ?

They materialized in hell.

The command center looked like a torture chamber to a horrified Duffy. It was a huge, domed area, but there was no skylight letting in the softening light of the stars. The area was completely enclosed. There appeared to be no exits. All was metal, heavy and cumbersome-looking. Everything seemed the same—the arching ceiling, the consoles, the walls. What little light there was was red and eerie, casting a pulsing, bloody hue over the alien equipment and the macabre centerpiece of the disturbing scene.

For, in the center of the room, its decaying limbs splayed at an odd angle, a corpse was strapped into a chair.

"So it *did* have a crew," said La Forge softly, sadly.

"Or at least a pilot," said Gomez.

Duffy admired the calmness of her voice. Sometimes it was hard to believe this was the same big-eyed girl who'd spilled hot chocolate all over Captain Picard just a few short years ago.

But, of course, she wasn't really the same. She had changed, just as he had, in the intervening decade or so.

Gomez stepped forward and shone her wrist-lamp over the humanoid body.

La Forge and Duffy stepped beside her. Duffy began to take tricorder readings.

"As Commander La Forge reported earlier, the atmosphere in here is perfectly breathable," he said to whoever was listening. "It never shut down after the pilot's death. That's why the body's rotting."

"Let's not take our suits off just yet, shall we?" said La Forge. Faulwell and 110, less interested in the dead body than in the computer that might be coaxed to yield information, stepped over to the consoles and began to analyze them. They spoke together in low voices, Faulwell occasionally bending over to hear 110 better. They seemed to be having a hard time figuring out where to begin. For the first time in a while, Duffy heard the oddly musical sound of the Bynar language, as 110 adjusted the blinking buffer he always kept at his side. Duffy wondered why 110 was talking in his native tongue. Could he simply have forgotten there was no one here who could understand him?

La Forge tapped his combadge. "La Forge to *da Vinci*."

"Go ahead, La Forge," came Gold's voice.

"It appears there *was* a crew on this vessel, Captain," La Forge continued. Duffy examined his tricorder as he spoke. Out of the corner of his eye, Duffy saw something on the floor, and directed his tricorder at it.

"A single pilot," said La Forge. "Humanoid. It appears to be female."

"Injured in the crash?"

"Negative. It looks as though she was strapped into the seat. Hard to say how long she's been dead. Long enough for decay to set in." La Forge stepped closer to the corpse, his face almost touching that of the dead pilot. "No obvious trauma."

Duffy knelt and regarded the piece of equipment on the floor. According to his readings, it was the alien equivalent of a tricorder. Gingerly, he reached to pick it up. It was about the size of an old-style tricorder, and weighed about as much. They could take this back to the ship and analyze it while Faulwell and 110 continued to work on the computer here.

He glanced over at the linguist and the Bynar, and frowned to himself. 110 seemed to be having a hard time cracking the ship's computer, and Faulwell was looking a tad impatient. *I'm sure it would be much faster if 111 was still with us*, Duffy thought. *Although even a single Bynar is usually several times faster than any human in accessing a computer.*

"No, wait," said Gomez. She was squatting on the other side of the humanoid in the chair, examining the fastenings. "Look at this, Commander."

Both Duffy and La Forge moved to shine their wristlamps where Gomez had indicated. La Forge inhaled swiftly, but otherwise gave no indication of how startled he must be. Duffy gaped, seasoned Starfleet officer though he was.

"Correction, Captain Gold," Geordi said. "The pilot appears to be *impaled* upon the chair."

That got Bart's attention. His head whipped around, and he gazed, frowning, at the corpse in the chair. Leaving the Bynar alone for the moment with the conundrum of the computer that would not yield its information, he strode quickly over to the rest of the team.

"Geez, will you look at that? You're right," he said, distaste in his voice. As rigor mortis had set in, the arms had pulled back from the metal of the chair. Three spikes extended from the chair deep into the pilot's arms. "Do you think this was some kind of torture device?"

Gomez shook her dark head, recovering her composure quickly. "I don't know. And we shouldn't make assumptions without all the data," she said. "Captain, I think we should transport this pilot to sickbay and have Dr. Lense perform a complete autopsy." Her eyes flickered to 110. "And 110 seems to be having a tough time figuring out this computer."

"*What?*" Gold's voice was incredulous. "And Earth is having a tough time spinning."

"He's doing the best he can," said Bart, almost as if in defense. "It's still hard for him, by himself."

"I'll send over Pattie and Ina to lend him a hand. Or leg, as the case may be. The rest of you, keep examining that ship. I'll have the pilot beamed over and I'll let you know when Lense learns anything."

"Aye, sir." La Forge, Gomez, Duffy, and Bart stepped back from the chair. The figure shimmered, then dematerialized.

A terrible sound rent the air, a high-pitched scream of agony mixed with an ear-splitting mechanical hum. As one, they whirled to behold 110, his tiny body arched in agony, screaming as his body shuddered and writhed. Blue light crackled around his small frame, enveloping the Bynar and the console on which his delicate fingers were placed. He was caught, writhing, unable to break free. Unable to do anything but cry out.

His crewmembers rushed forward. Before they could get to him, a final burst of energy lifted 110 up into the air and hurled him across the room. He slammed into a bulkhead, and Duffy heard an audible crack as the Bynar tumbled, limp, to the deck. The buffer lay beside him, blinking wildly.

Faulwell was the first to reach him, but by then Gomez was already saying, "Medical emergency! Lock onto 110 and get him to sickbay *now!*"

Even as 110 shimmered and vanished, Duffy felt the ship shudder. The light changed from murky red to bright yellow.

"It's powering up!" Duffy cried, yelling to be heard above the sudden rumbling that filled the control room.

Gomez raced back to the chair and began searching for a control panel. "There's nothing here!" she yelled.

The ship lurched violently. All of them lost their balance and fell heavily to the metal deck. The vessel heaved and bucked, then appeared to move forward.

There was no screen, no way to see what was happening outside this womblike single room. How had the pilot been able to navigate?

"Gold to away team. I'm getting everyone the hell out of there."

"What's happening?" demanded La Forge.

"That ship just woke up, and it's trampling all over downtown. Prepare to beam aboard."

They all appeared on the bridge. Duffy materialized directly in front of a furious Corsi. She towered over him, her face red with anger, and hissed, "Look!"

She pointed angrily at the screen. Duffy stared. His captain hadn't exaggerated. The ship filled the screen. Earlier, they had wondered what function the four protrusions on the otherwise sleek ship might have performed. Now, they saw those strange spikes, seemingly so awkward, in action. They served the vessel as legs, moving clumsily but effectively across the wreckage that had once been a thriving, peaceful city. Thank God there had been time for an evacuation, or by now thousands would probably be dead.

"It looks like it's . . . *walking*," said Bart with faint disgust.

"It is," said Gold grimly. "And I think there's an Intarian ordinance against unleashed ships walking around downtown. Try to make contact one more time, Ina, then, McAllan, it's your turn."

Ina Mar shook her head. "No response, sir. I don't think it even heard us."

Gold sighed. "I hate having to do this. God knows what we'll lose. McAllan, target weapons systems and fire at will."

"Sir, I'm unable to detect any weapons systems at all," replied McAllan in his deep, rich voice, taut now with tension.

"Let me see that," snapped Corsi, shoving McAllan out of the way. Her fingers flew over the console, her body tense and focused on the task at hand. Nobody could concentrate like "Core-Breach." Finally, she looked up, confusion and irritation on her face.

"McAllan's right. It's impossible to distinguish weapons from propulsion or from anything else."

"Maybe it's unarmed," suggested Abramowitz. "Maybe the people who built it are nonviolent. It could have crashed accidentally."

"You saw what they did to that pilot," said Faulwell with unusual vehemence. "That sure wasn't nonviolent."

Duffy quickly took his seat again. Gold leaned forward, resting his head on one hand. He rubbed a finger along his chin as he considered the options. "Let's find out. Corsi, fire a warning shot."

On the screen, their phaser blast appeared angry and red. The ship stopped dead in its tracks. Looking unsettlingly like a dog sitting and begging, its stern section dropped suddenly and it lifted its upper two "arms." Blue-black balls of energy exploded forth and screamed out of the atmosphere, striking the *da Vinci*. The ship shuddered with the impact.

"Shields down thirty-three percent," said Ina.

"It's got weapons," La Forge commented.

"And it's not very nonviolent," said Gold. "We've got to disable it. Corsi, it's all yours."

Corsi's lips thinned. Inwardly, Duffy cringed. He liked to avoid Corsi whenever possible, because it seemed to him that whatever he said or did was exactly the wrong thing. She was utterly intent upon the task at hand, and her blue eyes were like ice now. He was very glad he was not the object of such intense concentration.

Corsi fired. And fired again. And again. Red phaser energy shot through space. Despite her fear for those she was charged to protect and her natural passion, she knew what her captain wanted. For some reason, they had been unable to locate the weapons systems—indeed, any specific system—on the vessel. Now that it had fired on them, however, their targets were clear: the two major appendages. Corsi concentrated her fire on those.

To everyone's astonishment, the heavy attack seemed to have little to no effect. The ship merely resumed its bizarre squatting position, targeted the *da Vinci* with deadly accuracy, and returned fire. The Federation vessel rocked violently. The impact knocked Duffy out of his chair, and he fell heavily for the second time that day. He was bruised and bloody, and something felt wrong in his hand. Once this was over, he'd have to go see Lense.

"Ineffective, sir," said Corsi in a low, angry voice, stating the obvious. She continued to fire on the ship's appendages.

"Evasive maneuvers. Transfer all power to the forward shields. Let's take its hits here. Try different parts of the hull before we back off," said Gold. "Nothing's completely invulnerable." But he didn't sound too certain.

Now Corsi directed the *da Vinci*'s phasers randomly. She attacked the rear appendages, the bow, the stern. At one point, when the ship raised itself again to fire, she got a clear volley in at its underside.

It stumbled. One spiky leg waved frantically.

"That's the spot, Corsi!" cried Gold.

Heartened, Duffy leaned forward as Corsi fired again. The ship collapsed. It clambered to its "feet," but Corsi knew where to aim now and was merciless. After five more rounds, the ship teetered for a moment, fell heavily, and lay still.

Silence on the bridge. The ship was motionless; they had disabled it. Duffy let out his breath. He hadn't been aware he'd been holding it. All at once, he became conscious again of the alien piece of equipment he'd been clutching in a death grip.

"Captain," he said, "I recovered this from the vessel. I think it's a tricorder of some kind. We may not have been able to access the main computer, but this might have something on it worth knowing."

Gold's eyes lit up. He and Geordi exchanged looks, and La Forge grinned.

"Duff-Man found a key," said La Forge with a trace of pride. After all, Duffy had been under his command at one time. Duffy grinned back.

"La Forge, you and Faulwell start trying to figure out how to use this key. Nice work, Duffy."

"Thank you, Captain." It made the terrible pain in his hand worth it.

"Permission to go to sickbay to check on 110," said Gomez.

"Granted," said Gold. "You two," he said to

Faulwell and La Forge, "get on this tricorder immediately. Now," he continued, rising and walking down to the screen, "little ship, are you really disabled, or do you still have a trick or two up your sleeve?"

Duffy held his injured hand and watched Gomez leave. He knew why she was going, and he understood. It wouldn't kill him to wait until she'd finished with 110 to get his injury treated.

CHAPTER
3

Dr. Elizabeth Lense hated this part of the mission. She'd much rather be attending her other "patient." The dead one, lying on a biobed, awaiting examination with the patience of, well, the dead. But 110 needed her attention now.

The Bynar was spasming on the bed, his eyes rolling back and forth underneath tightly shut lids. He wasn't breathing. Lense went into automatic pilot, making the right judgment calls and movements without even thinking about them. *Get him breathing. Stabilize the erratic heartbeat. Monitor brain-wave activity.* Her hands flew over the small, prostrate figure, attaching monitors, sensors, hypospraying concentrates of this and that.

At that moment, the ship rocked violently. It would appear as if the hitherto dormant ship had been awakened. Lense swore softly under her breath. Sickbay lost power momentarily, and the emergency backup mechanisms kicked in.

She had a brief flashback to a similar scene aboard the *Lexington* in the middle of a battle. Voices were crying out her name, shrieking in agony, begging for help. There had literally been blood almost everywhere in sickbay. Patients with injuries from fractured skulls to severed limbs to sucking chest wounds filled sickbay and overflowed into the corridor. There hadn't even been the chance to set up the shuttlebays to handle the sheer volume of wounded. The stench of so much blood had been almost unbearable.

Eighteen of the dead and injured had been her own staff. She and the EMH, an efficient but cold and sarcastic image, had been the only ones able to treat the wounded.

She remembered Jenson, dying in her arms even as she buried her hands almost to the wrist in his wound, trying to hold closed a slippery, severed artery with her fingers because she couldn't reach her tools. And Galloway, who kept refusing treatment in order to bring in others more gravely injured than she, breathing her last quietly in a corner, when she couldn't bring in any more.

Lense had been able to save about a quarter of them. One lousy quarter of the screaming, bloody people who had begged her for help, pleaded with her to ease their torment.

Damn it. Damn it all to hell.

"Stay with me, 110," she whispered, although she knew the Bynar could not hear her. She couldn't treat him when the ship was this chaotic. The best she could do was make sure he didn't fall off the bed, and that the pieces of medical equipment strapped to his little body stayed put.

For what seemed like an eternity, the ship shuddered under attack. Finally, it appeared that the worst was over. The power surged back on.

Lense turned her full attention to 110. The cortical stimulator was doing its job, and the spasming slowed, then stopped. A quick glance at her tricorder told her that the immediate danger had passed, though only a complete examination would reveal what, if any, permanent damage the Bynar had incurred.

She took a breath. She could use an extra pair of hands. "Computer, activate the EMH," she ordered. At once, the slim, somewhat elegant figure of Emmett appeared.

"Good morning, Doctor—oh, dear," said Emmett. "What happened?"

Lense noticed that his dark eyes had quickly taken in everything she had done before he asked his question. Good. She had never had so apt a pupil.

As he spoke, the door to sickbay hissed open. Lense turned her head quickly and saw that it was Sonya Gomez.

"Can you fill us in, Sonya?" she asked.

Gomez stepped closer, looking down at the Bynar with her arms folded tightly across her chest. "No one's really sure," she said. "He was attempting to interface with the computer aboard the alien ship when it appeared to send a massive shock throughout his system. He was caught in it for a few seconds, and then it shot him across the room. We had him beamed up the instant he was released."

Lense extended a hand for Gomez's tricorder, which had captured the whole event. She reviewed it in silence, Em peering over her shoulder.

"Who was working with him, or was he by himself?" asked Lense, handing the tricorder back to Gomez.

"Bart was with him at first, but he came over to look at the pilot's remains after we noticed the—the holes."

Lense glanced up sharply at the hesitation in the other woman's voice. As a previous victim of burnout herself, she was always keenly alert to the manifestation of the symptoms in others. But Gomez appeared to be all right.

"Holes?" Lense demanded.

"Of course. You've been so busy keeping 110 stable, you haven't had a chance to look at the body," said Gomez. "There were holes in each of the arms. It was impaled on the chair."

Lense glanced quickly over at the pilot's body. Sure enough, there were three holes in the lower arms. Gomez was clearly a little rattled, and who wouldn't be, upon discovering a body that had seemingly been impaled on sharp spikes in the command center of an alien vessel that had just gone on a city-wide rampage? Gomez wouldn't be human if *that* hadn't unnerved her at least a little.

"The pilot's not going anywhere," she said with a touch of black humor. "Right now, I'm more interested in 110. Did he do anything, touch any specific button? He had to have triggered something, or else the computer would have exploded the minute he tried to interface with it."

"You'd think so," said Gomez, moving hesitantly to stand beside the Bynar. "And he probably did, but no one was watching."

"What about his own tricorder?"

"He hadn't activated it. He never does." She looked miserable. "Captain Gold's reprimanded him about it before. It's just not in the Bynar nature. Between their evolved brains and the buffer they carry with them at all times, they seem to have everything they need."

"Perhaps when they're on Bynar, but not when they're all the way out here," snapped Elizabeth. It could take days to translate the information stored on 110's omnipresent buffer. But only the Bynars could figure out that gibberish. "If he'd recorded what happened in a way we could understand, we'd be a lot closer to knowing how to help him."

"The pilot," said Em slowly.

Lense and Gomez turned as one to look at him. "What about the pilot?" demanded Gomez.

Em seemed a little uncomfortable at suddenly being the center of attention. "Well," he began, "according to your tricorder, Commander, the incident occurred as the pilot's body was being transported out. We've seen that it was attached in some fashion—you used the word 'impaled'—directly to the ship. Perhaps there were sensors that were triggered when the body was removed from the chair. The ship has to be operating on automatic commands. Maybe the removal of the pilot activated it."

"Very good, Emmett!" said Elizabeth. She was proud of the EMH's deductive reasoning, but a little embarrassed that she hadn't figured it out herself. A quick glance at Gomez confirmed that the other woman shared her discomfiture.

Lense turned back to the supine figure of the Bynar. "There are first-degree burns on his hands and face," she said. Whatever had happened to him had been bad enough to burn right through his protective gear. "Em, can you take care of those for me, please?"

"Certainly, Doctor," Em replied, and began to run the dermal regenerator over the injured flesh while Lense continued.

"There appears to be no permanent damage to the brain. If he'd been human, there might have been, but Bynar brains are set up to be able to handle bursts of computer-generated information. Their limbic system can take an awful lot, more than almost any other humanoid species could. Whatever the ship's computer did to him seems to have caused no lasting damage. You may tell Captain Gold I expect a full recovery. One more piece of the puzzle."

"Can you awaken him? The captain will have a lot of questions."

Lense hesitated. "Let's give him some time. I want him more stable before I force him into consciousness. While we're waiting, I can begin the examination of the pilot." She nodded her curly, dark head in the pilot's direction. "She should have a great deal to tell me about her race, if not necessarily her ship."

Gomez lingered, looking anxiously at the still Bynar. "Sonya," said Lense gently, "I'll let you know the minute we learn anything."

Gomez nodded her head, knowing a cue when she heard one. "Thanks, Doctor." She turned and exited, running smack into Duffy.

"Sorry!" Gomez said.

"No, it's my fault. Wasn't watching where I was going."

Lense looked at the two of them. It wasn't a secret they had once been involved. And, judging by their awkwardness around each other when they weren't in the midst of a mission, they hadn't figured out what to do about that past involvement.

Duffy was wincing and clutching his hand. "Oh, no, did I hurt you?" said Gomez.

"No, no," Duffy protested through clenched teeth. "I was heading down here to get this fixed."

"I'm sure I didn't help it any," said Gomez. "Sorry, Kieran." She hastened out.

Lense smiled. "Let me take care of that for you." The injury wasn't serious, just a bad sprain. When she was done, Duffy flexed his hand and gave her a grateful look.

"Thanks, Doctor. See you, Emmett."

"See you, Lieutenant Commander Duffy," said Emmett with perfect correctness, if too much formality. Lense would have to work on that with him.

Lense turned back to the task at hand. Her gaze traveled up and down the small, slight frame on the bed. Space had not done its usual fine job of preserving the body in this case. According to what the away team had reported, the ship had continued to maintain atmosphere, and the body had decayed normally. At the moment, it was safely encased by a forcefield; Starfleet SOP for the *da Vinci* in bringing any nonliving organic matter aboard.

Lense glanced at the readings. Nothing dangerous detected. She could safely eliminate the forcefield, but she would keep the body in stasis. Otherwise, the smell would be unbearable, and she wanted to prevent the body from decaying any further. She touched a button, then stepped beside the body.

A thought occurred to her. "Emmett," she said, "have you ever performed an autopsy?"

"I am perfectly capable of performing an autopsy." He looked offended. "It's a standard part of my programming."

She held up a placating hand. "Of course, you *know* how to do one, but have you ever actually done so? On an alien, about whom we know nothing?"

He looked a little excited. "No, I haven't."

"You'll find this fascinating," she assured him. "I've been doing some comparative research on how this used to be performed in the old days, and how it's done in other cultures. A few hundred years ago, they had no holographic technology. If you wanted to find out how someone had died, you had to literally cut them open."

The sensitive hologram stared, mouth slightly open. "That's . . . barbaric," he stammered.

"Well, naturally, we think so, but that's only because we have other methods to gain information," she replied. "And there's something about actually seeing inside a body, touching it, weighing the organs. It makes you respect death a little more, I think."

"I prefer to respect life," Em replied primly.

"Of course you respect life. Every doctor does. But on this mission, you and I are dealing mainly with the dead. You'll need to cultivate respect for them, too."

Em's face furrowed. "But, Doctor, surely dealing with a holographic representation shows more respect to the body than cutting it open."

"Yes—after a fashion. But let's begin. You'll see what I mean eventually."

Despite everything that had happened, Lense couldn't help laughing at the expression on Emmett's dark face. "Don't worry. We won't be dissecting the body, I promise!"

Em looked very relieved. Still chuckling, Lense gave instructions to the computer. "Computer, prepare to construct an accurate holographic replication of the body on the biobed. All weights and textures must be exact."

The biobed closed over the body and a lavender beam washed through the form.

"Prepared and awaiting data," replied the computer in its cool female voice.

"Project the alien's skeletal structure," Lense ordered. "Keep it in the same position as it would normally be if held in place by tissue."

Immediately, the skeleton appeared on the

empty bed. It could easily have been mistaken for that of a human, save for the narrower jaw, extreme indentations of the skull at the temple point, longer finger bones, and a rib cage that extended almost to the hip.

"What conclusions do you draw from this?" she asked Em. He carefully examined the skeleton, leaning in to peer at it, his hands clasped behind his back.

"No, no," said Lense. "A good doctor uses more than just his eyes. Touch it."

Em was hesitant. "We are not programmed—"

"You'll need to learn to exceed your programming here, Emmett. Go ahead. Touch it. Like this. Computer, adjust image to permit removal of individual bones without disturbing the construction." Lense stepped forward and picked up the skull. She ran her fingers over it, feeling the smooth, slightly oily texture.

"This is unusual," she said, caressing the indentations in the skull. She handed it to Emmett. "What do you make of it?"

"Perfectly circular," he said, emulating her and running his fingers around the holographic skull. "It's unlikely that this is a natural development."

"Part of the torture that we think may have been performed?" It was a leading question, but she wanted to push him.

"No," he replied with certainty. "The indentations are too old, too well-integrated into the skull structure to have been inflicted upon an adult. These modifications were begun when the patient—" His face fell a little, realizing that there was no "patient" to treat, only a body to examine. "When the, ah, subject was in infancy and the skull was more malleable."

"Good," approved Lense. "What else?"

Em was starting to get as excited as she was about this old-fashioned method of examination. "There are similar stresses in the radius and ulna. They've been manipulated over a long time to draw away from one another. Again, I would say this was begun in infancy. Perhaps for decorative or ritualistic purposes."

"Good. And the rib cage? What does that indicate?"

"The extended rib cage indicates the strong likelihood of a multiorgan cardiovascular system, and perhaps other extra organs humans do not possess. And the lengthy fingers indicate that this race is probably quite dexterous."

"You catch on quickly," said Lense. "Computer, add internal organs, except for the brain."

Blue light traveled down the skeleton, leaving in its wake an intriguing jumble of soft tissue. Lense nodded to herself. Emmett's theory of two hearts had been dead-on. There were a few extra organs that they did not recognize. She went through them one by one, removing them and handing them to Em for his comments. The functions of most of them were immediately recognizable, despite the unusual shapes, textures, and colors. All humanoids had hearts, lungs, and organs that performed the functions of kidneys and livers. They might have different shapes and colors, and be located in different parts of the body, but they were always there. She frowned when they examined the digestive system.

"It's unusually atrophied for a humanoid of this size," she said. "What could be the reason for that?"

Em frowned. "Perhaps this alien has evolved to the point where it does not require fibrous foodstuffs in order to obtain its nutrients."

It was a fascinating development, and one Lense had never before encountered, but it had no direct bearing on their real purpose. They could save that for later. Time to look at the brain.

"Computer," she instructed, "replicate the alien's brain."

It appeared on the table, beside the skull. Lense was shocked. It looked, on first examination, no more complex than that of an average human. She had begun to wonder if this species was more highly developed, but apparently not.

Em, too, seemed a little disappointed. "It looks a great deal like a simple human brain," he said.

"Let's look a little closer. Computer, separate the brain along the two hemispheres." The computer complied, and Lense picked up one in each hand, scrutinizing them carefully. "The corpus callosum is severely degraded," she said, confused. That slab of white nerve fibers was what transferred important information from one hemisphere to another. Thus degraded, it made it highly unlikely that the pilot could function.

"It doesn't look damaged," said Em. "Perhaps the brain transferred information by some other method."

Lense nodded, though she had her doubts. There were a few things common to all humanoids, and the corpus callosum was one of them. This body was becoming more intriguing to her by the minute.

Further examination of the brain only whetted her appetite. Other parts of the brain were degraded. Some seemed to be completely missing. Other areas were so developed as to be completely unrecognizable.

"This is absolutely fascinating. We'll have to come back to this later, but I want to complete the procedure so that you're familiar with it. Computer, add musculature."

Again, the pilot's muscles were not as well-developed as she would have expected. She glanced over at the actual body. It seemed fit and strong. Why, then, were the muscles so atrophied? This was not a result of decay, for the computer was programmed to extrapolate on how the musculature had been in life. She thought about the brain with its missing corpus callosum. Something strange was going on here. She asked Emmett what he thought.

"The muscles could be artificially stimulated," he suggested.

She smiled a little. She'd caught him in an error. "But then the muscles themselves would show us that stimulation, wouldn't they?"

He nodded, confused. "Then I have no theory," he said, apologetically.

"Neither do I, not yet. Let's see if the skin tells us anything. Computer, apply the epidermal layers."

And this was when it always started to get to

her. Once you had skin, you had a face, and once you had a face, you suddenly had a person. This face was a sweet one.

"It is a shame she died so young," said Emmett softly. Lense shared his regret. The girl on the table, eyes closed softly as if in sleep, was only an adolescent. In human years, Lense put her age at about fifteen. Just a girl, a child. She must have been attractive in life. Large eyes, with greenish freckles on skin that was almost human-colored, but a bit chalkier. Long brown hair with green highlights pooled around her head.

But there was something not right. Something was missing.

"Wait just a minute," said Lense. She glanced back from the actual body to the holographic replication. "Look at the temples."

Emmett followed her gaze. "They're not sunken on the actual body," he said.

"Exactly. Why do you suppose that is?" Without waiting for an answer, she went to the body and gently touched the temples. Her questing fingers found something hard and spherical.

Lense's heart began to race. Firmly, she told herself not to jump to conclusions. "Something has been embedded here," she said. "The computer didn't replicate it because we didn't ask it to. The good old sense of touch comes through again. Computer, scan the body. What is the source of the spherical nodes on the cranium?"

"Cybernetic implants," replied the computer, utterly unperturbed by the direness of the words.

Lense swallowed. "Purpose?"

"Unknown."

"Display on holographic replica. Remove skin layer."

She caught her breath as the computer complied. The pilot lay before them, devoid of the skin that softened the emotional impact. Two silver spheres were nestled in the carefully cultivated nodules in its skull. The eyes, while organic, had also been augmented with implants. A thin silver wire ran like a shiny nerve along the pilot's body. This, then, was the reason the muscles had atrophied. Artificial constructs had assisted them in doing their job. The missing corpus callosum was present and accounted for. It—and other parts of the brain—was utterly artificial.

She could see now the three cones that had been inserted between the bones of the lower arms. That was why the radius and ulna had separated so much; these metal cones had been implanted, and had forced them to grow apart.

Lense recalled the chair upon which the away team had found the pilot sitting. When the pilot sat in an erect position with her hands on the arms, these holes lined up perfectly. It was almost as if she were plugged directly into the ship. . . .

Sweat broke out beneath her arms, and she started to tremble as the realization struck her. It all fell into place now, and made terrible sense. Even the atrophied digestive system now seemed logical.

"Oh, my God, Emmett," Lense said softly, lifting her blue eyes to meet Em's puzzled gaze. "I think we've found a Borg."

CHAPTER
4

Beneath closed lids, 110 saw. Dreamed. Downloaded information.

1110100001001001001000001111101101110 . . .

"Coffee?" asked La Forge, standing next to the replicator in engineering.

"Thanks. Half-and-half and sugar," replied Faulwell. La Forge returned, carrying two mugs. Bart reached up to accept the one Geordi extended to him. "We're not supposed to have these here, you know."

Geordi smiled. "Last person I let have a beverage in engineering was Sonya. Picard, as you may have heard—"

"—ended up wearing it," Bart finished, sipping the hot beverage. "Wish I could have been a fly on the wall that day."

Geordi winced. "No, you don't. I'd rather have faced a phaser blast than Captain Picard's glare. Poor Sonya just about died."

"But look how far she's come. She's soared through the ranks."

"Hmm," said Geordi with mock seriousness. "Perhaps the secret to advancing in rank is to spill hot chocolate on one's commanding officer."

"If that's the case, I'll stay where I am," said Bart, trying to envision Captain Gold's reaction to such an incident.

"You know," said Geordi, "you are starting to have quite the reputation yourself."

Bart was startled. "Me? Oh, no."

"Yes, you. I've an ear for languages myself, so I pay attention to developments in the field. And I've heard your name come up more than a few times. There's nothing that says you can't go through the Academy."

"Oh, no. That's not for me." Bart concentrated on his drink. "I'm quite happy as a noncom."

Geordi regarded him for a long moment with those odd, artificial eyes. "If you ever change your mind, let me know."

"Yes, sir."

"Download complete," came the computer's voice.

"Damn. And just when my coffee was exactly the right temperature," said Geordi in a mock-mournful tone. "Come on, Bart. Time to see what's on this thing."

At that moment, Geordi's combadge chirped. "Commander La Forge, Faulwell, get to the briefing room at once."

They exchanged glances. "Captain Gold," said La Forge, "we've just finished downloading the information from the tricorder. We're about to try to decipher it."

"And I want you to, but not right now. It'll have to wait. On the double, gentlemen."

Faulwell had always thought that the expression of one's heart leaping into one's mouth was a bit over the top. But when he looked at what a tight-lipped, pale Dr. Lense had to show them, he realized that the old cliché was actually quite true.

Borg.

Hard to believe that one word, comprised of four letters, could produce such violent emotions. But then, Bart had always respected the power of words. Now, as he gazed at the replicated body on the viewscreen, with its lengths of cables and artificial implants, all he could think of was a giant cube sweeping down to assimilate them all.

"What do you think, Geordi?" Gold asked, his calm voice breaking the horrified silence that filled the briefing room. "You've had some experience with Borg technology."

Geordi licked his lips. "I don't know, Captain. This technology is different from any Borg technology I've encountered before. Take a look at the delicacy of that cable, the seamless way the artificial has been integrated with the organic in the brain. Borg technology was . . ." He searched for the right word. "Crude, but efficient. It got the job done, but not much more. This is almost elegant. Then again, if there's one thing you can count on with the Borg, it's that they're always improving. Upgrading."

"Assimilating," said Duffy, managing the complicated trick of putting a sneer of disgust and respect into the single word.

"Exactly," said La Forge.

"But it was my understanding that the Borg travel in groups—in a collective, or subdivisions, in a unimatrix. Never just alone like this," put in Gomez.

"Again," said Abramowitz, "that's always been true . . . so far. But don't forget the Borg queen. She is quite definitely an individual."

La Forge nodded agreement. "And there was an adolescent male Borg who came aboard the *Enterprise* several years ago, who was able to understand the concept of the individual. We even named him. Called him Hugh. Got kinda fond of the guy, actually."

"I remember reading about that," said Abramowitz. "Because of his interaction with the *Enterprise* crew, he was unable to fully reintegrate into Borg society. He joined with others who split off from the collective, right? What became of him?"

"We don't know," said Geordi. "I like to think that he and his group are all right, but who knows with the Borg? They could have reassimilated him and studied this thing called individuality. They could have found the group and reassimilated them. When you think about it, the Borg are already a blending of organic being and machine. It's not that big a step to link an individual with a vessel to form a new collective of one unified mind—instead of a humanoid simply being implanted with cybernetics and linked together, link that mind directly with a personal, mobile machine. With a ship."

Carol sank back in her chair. "It does sound exactly like something the Borg would do."

"The ship's ability to withstand the crash also points to Borg technology," said P8 Blue. "It powered up well enough when it wanted to. Self-repair, just like a Borg cube."

"Let's think like the Borg for a moment," said Gold. "Not that it's a pleasant task. What would be the advantage to the Borg of forming such a collective? Tying only one mind to one machine? What's the point in that?"

"Easier maintenance," said Gomez at once. "One person, one ship. Elizabeth, it looked as though that pilot was able to disengage from the ship. Is that right?"

Lense nodded. "They could join, and I'd imagine they could separate. There was no indication that the pilot required any sustenance while joined. The entire digestive system had shrunk. I suspect the pilot didn't even eat as we understand the term, but got her nourishment somehow through her connection to the ship."

"Again, exactly like the Borg," said Gold, frowning. His bushy black eyebrows stuck out over his eyes like alarmed caterpillars. "She would regenerate. As long as the ship had power, she could live."

Lense nodded confirmation. "And yet, she died and the ship continued on. There was no trace of injury or illness, so there must have been some kind of malfunction that was localized and didn't spread to the ship."

"So," continued Gold. "Easier maintenance might be a reason. What else?"

"A single-person vessel could travel places that a more standard Borg ship couldn't," said Abramowitz, clearly warming to the subject. "It could scout out races for assimilation, then alert the more aggressive cube."

Bart felt cold. All this made terrible sense.

"There's your explanation as to why someone would attack Intar," said Corsi. "The Borg are hardly tourists. You know their mantra. 'We are the Borg. Resistance is futile. Prepare to be—'"

"Stop it," said Bart. He hadn't intended to speak, but the words came out of his mouth. Everyone turned to stare at him. He felt his face grow hot.

"Faulwell is right, Corsi," said Gold gently to his chief of security. "This isn't a laughing matter. Very well. I'd say that, while we can't be absolutely certain that this is the latest version of the new, improved Borg, it's a possibility. I'll alert Starfleet Command, see what they want us to do about it. Gomez, I remember right before we beamed you out, you said something like, 'There's nothing there.' What did you mean by that?"

"There were no control panels," said Gomez.

"That's right," said Bart. "No buttons, no lights, nothing to indicate how the pilot controlled the ship. I guess we know now. There's no need for control panels when you can maneuver a vessel with your thoughts."

Gomez frowned and her brow furrowed as she tried to recall exactly what there *had* been. "At least," she amended, "no control panels as we understand them. Now that I think of it, there might have been some other ports where the pilot could have linked, other than the chair." She looked a little embarrassed. "We were so distracted by the pilot, and then we were transported out. We didn't have time to conduct a more thorough investigation. I'm sorry, sir."

Gold waved off her apology.

"That's why I couldn't locate where the tactical and propulsion systems were," said Corsi. "With most ships, there are separate sections where the various pieces of equipment are installed. Here, it's all spread throughout the ship, controlled by the pilot's mind."

"Heavens above," said Gold, with feeling. He rubbed at his eyes with his hand. "No chance of learning anything without a whole Starfleet team of Borg experts swarming over that ship, then. La Forge and Faulwell, you two are now the indispensable crewmen. So far the information on that tricorder is the only information we've got. Translate whatever is on there. I want concrete data, not theories, when some admiral starts trying to pull rank and questions our actions and conclusions. Understand?"

"Yes, sir," said both Bart and Geordi at once.

"You're pretty quiet," La Forge observed as he and Bart stood in the turbolift.

Bart shrugged. For some strange reason, all he

could think about was the unfinished letter to Anthony Mark sitting in his quarters. If this thing was indeed a Borg ship, as was looking more and more likely, who knew what would happen? He wondered if he'd even have a chance to finish the note, let alone see Anthony Mark again.

"Finding a completely new type of Borg threat isn't something that happens every day. Not even in this job," Bart added, in a weak stab at humor.

"Listen, I've survived a lot of up-close-and-personal encounters with the Borg," La Forge said, "and while they're definitely to be taken seriously, they're not totally indestructible. Besides, the captain must think there's at least a chance that it's not a Borg ship, or else he wouldn't assign you to this."

Bart brightened at that. "True," he said. If Gold had expected the tricorder information to be recorded in standard Borg, the computer would already know how to translate it. The particular skills of a linguist wouldn't be required.

When they began their work in earnest, Bart was heartened by the fact that the language recorded was not Borg. After working with the computer, he narrowed it down to a branch of the Taklathi language, with some of the grammatical structure of the Nemar and Olisu thrown into the mix. By cross-referencing with languages as varied as Xlatitigu and Pe, he was able to establish a root structure from which the universal translator could extrapolate. He loved these moments. They were positively exhilarating, and it was a refreshing change to work with someone who, like him, respected and enjoyed language.

Finally, the tricorder was adjusted and linked with their system. After a burst of static and snow—which gave Bart a bad moment, thinking they'd shorted the whole thing out—it began to transmit information onto the screen. Their eyes widened in shock at the first image, and the shock did not diminish as they watched. Engrossed, they listened to the entire recording with a growing sense of horror.

At last, it was done. Geordi turned to regard Bart, who felt exhausted and emotionally drained after viewing the information.

"The captain needs to see this. Heck, I think *everyone* needs to see this." Geordi's voice was heavy and somber.

Bart blinked rapidly and swallowed hard. "It's pretty awful. How much of it do you want to show them?"

"All of it."

CHAPTER
5

Lense regarded the still form of the solitary Bynar. She didn't want to do this, but Gold had insisted. 110 had had the most direct contact with the computer system of that ship. He had information that had been downloaded into that buffer of his. He knew things the rest of them didn't, things that Gold needed to know.

She sighed. "Em, bring him around."

Emmett pressed a hypospray to the Bynar's neck. It hissed gently, and 110 opened his eyes. Lense squeezed his newly healed hand gently and smiled down at him.

"Welcome back, 110," she said softly. "How do you feel?"

He blinked slowly. "As well as can be expected."

With the tenderness Lense had come to expect from the surprisingly sensitive hologram, Em leaned forward and eased the Bynar up into a sitting position. 110 blinked, seeming a little dizzy, but, otherwise, he appeared to be fully recovered.

"We—I must speak to Captain Gold," he told Gomez.

"And he wants to speak to you. Let me run a few tests first, to make sure that—"

"You do not understand," insisted 110. He turned his dark eyes to her. "The vessel is *alive*. It is in pain. And it is very, very angry."

110's shocking announcement stunned everyone except Bart and Geordi, who exchanged glances.

"Before we act on the information 110 has given us," said La Forge, "I highly recommend we watch this."

"Time is speeding by, Commander," said Gold. "I've got the *Enterprise* and the *Lexington* on their way here even as I'm having this pleasant conversation with you."

"I understand the situation, sir," Geordi continued, speaking urgently, "but trust me, you all need to see this first. And I mean *see* it, not just have me brief you on it."

Gold's brown eyes narrowed, and he regarded La Forge intently. Geordi didn't flinch from that scrutiny. Duffy wondered what the hell was on that recording that would make La Forge buck Gold so openly.

Finally Gold nodded, cursorily. "You waste my time, La Forge, and I'll let Picard know about it."

"Understood, sir, but I'm certain you won't consider your time wasted."

"Well, then, start the thing going. I feel my hair falling out."

Geordi pressed the control button and took a seat.

With such a dramatic lead-in, everyone assembled leaned forward, expecting to see something staggering. The static and snow stabilized, formed itself into the face of a young woman. While Duffy knew intellectually that it was the face of the greatly decayed corpse now being held in stasis in sickbay—their possible Borg—this lively, animated visage bore little resemblance to the still death mask of the decaying body they had found in the chair.

By human standards, he guessed her to be between sixteen and nineteen, if she was even that old. She was grinning. The recording device, which she held in her hands, was not steady, and she occasionally moved out of the center, but this inefficiency, which Duffy would have thought intolerable to a Borg, seemed not to trouble her one bit.

"I'm recording these on a portable device because I don't want Friend to know about them," she said. Her eyes were a beautiful shade of leafy green, her teeth white and straight. But what broke Duffy's heart more than anything was the smattering of greenish freckles on her small nose. Judging by Abramowitz's expression, Carol, too, was mourning the loss of such a vibrant young woman.

"Don't get me wrong—I love sharing things with Friend," the girl hastened to add. "I love it when we link up, and I've got the whole ship's sensors at my hands."

She looked a little smug. "I don't need a primitive viewing screen to see, or a console to program, not when I'm joined with the computer. To be able to experience so many things that, as an organic being, I'd never otherwise know is indescribable. And he—yeah, I know it's not alive and it's got no gender, but I think of the ship as a he—is so *close* to me when we're joined. I've never known anything like it, not even in a relationship with another Omearan. But there are things I want to say, so I can look back at them later, and I can't be entirely honest when Friend is so completely joined with me. So, I guess these are secret journals."

She giggled. To his surprise, Duffy felt tears sting his eyes. He had thought they'd be looking at boring but informative impersonal logs, stuff that would reveal the horrors and atrocities committed by this ship and this pilot, not the most intimate confessions of a young girl's private thoughts. He felt like a peeping Tom. But there was nothing for it. This was, so far, the only information they had on the ship and its pilot, and they needed to keep watching, hard as it was.

One thing was becoming rapidly apparent. Their assumption about the pilot had been all wrong. Whatever she was, this giggling, endearing child on the viewscreen was no Borg.

The girl rambled on about how hard it had been for her to say good-bye to her family. "I didn't want to tell Friend about it, because it'd upset him. He's really sensitive to my happiness. It's nice to have things like that matter to someone else so much." She smiled, her green eyes soft with affection, and continued.

"We wouldn't normally get tapped for so deep a mission, but after the war, we're really short of pilots," she explained. "So here Friend and I are, alone together in space, searching for an uninhabited but fertile planet so we can get off that toxic rock. Start new lives. I tried to explain to Friend about how great it feels to walk on soft grass in your bare feet, but he didn't quite get it, I think."

Another journal entry described a severe bout of homesickness. A third had the girl, who finally identified herself as Jaldark, describing how she and Friend had navigated a treacherous asteroid belt unscathed.

"It was the most amazing sensation, to be linked with him while we did that!" Jaldark enthused, practically bouncing up and down in her chair. "I just love Friend *so much*. He's the most wonderful ship. I'm so glad I'm bonded with him for the rest of my life. He seems to be so much easier to get along with, temperamentally, than the trainer ships, but maybe that's because they are constantly bonding and breaking bond with new pilots. Maybe they never get to settle into being themselves. Poor things."

The grin—the wonderful, wide, endearing grin—crossed her face again. "I guess I'm just the luckiest girl in the universe."

But you weren't, Jaldark, Duffy thought, feeling slightly sick. And sure enough, on the next tape, the trouble had already begun. Jaldark looked thinner and paler. There were deep circles under the green eyes, and she wasn't smiling.

"Something's wrong," she told her recorded journal without preamble. "Friend can sense it, but I'm not telling him any more than I have to in order to maintain function. He knows we're turning around and heading back toward Omearan space at our top speed, but I don't know that we'll make it in time. I hate lying to him like this."

She swallowed hard, licked dry lips, and continued. "I think it's the implants. I've passed the rejection window, so it can't be that. They'd never have let me go on a deep-space recon mission if there was a possibility that they'd be rejected. But they're failing somehow. I can't get sustenance from Friend anymore."

Jaldark pressed long, thin fingers to her unusually deep temples. Twin implants pulsed beneath the skin at her touch.

"I have these terrible headaches. And the arm sheaths—they ache whenever we join." She looked dreadfully unhappy. "That means that, whenever we join, I'm in a lot of pain. So, of course, I come up with excuses not to join as often. Friend hasn't said anything much, but I know his feelings are hurt. He's the last person— well, thing—I'd ever want to hurt, and I just hate it that this is happening!"

Tears welled in her eyes, trickled down her freckled cheeks. She wiped at them angrily. The gesture afforded Duffy a good look at what Jaldark called the "arm sheaths." They were three conical tubes that had been implanted on both lower arms.

The spikes on the chair that Duffy and the others had first assumed were torture devices, and later thought were evidence of Borg technology, were links with the ship's computer. They created a way for a lively young woman to be close to a machine that had transcended its hardware and become a friend; a way to attain the sustenance that would keep Jaldark alive.

There was nothing sinister about the spikes anymore. There was nothing sinister about anything now—only sorrow.

Still crying, Jaldark reached and turned off the recording device. But there was one more entry. Kieran didn't want to see it, but, along with the others, he couldn't look away.

Jaldark looked awful. She had lost a lot of weight and was obviously very ill. She was silent at first, but in the background they could all clearly hear "Friend's" voice: slightly metallic, but filled with concern.

"Jaldark?" Friend called. "Please respond. Are you angry with me? Is there something wrong? I am an Omearan Starsearcher, a top-of-the-line vessel with extensive and flexible programming. I am certain there is something I can do to help you. Please respond, Jaldark. Please respond."

"Do we have to watch the rest of this, Captain?" Surprised, Duffy tore his gaze from the haggard girl on the screen to look at the speaker. It was Corsi, the last person aboard the *da Vinci* he would have expected to have a problem watching this recording. She seemed to have a skin thicker than Pattie's shell. And she was doing her best to look annoyed, not pained; irritated at time wasted, not about to cry. She hid it well, but he could see it, and he suspected everyone else could.

It seemed like Core-Breach Corsi had a heart after all.

"I think we owe it to Jaldark and Friend, yes," said Gold. "It's a little bit like sitting *shiva.*" He stabbed a forefinger at the screen, where Jaldark was burying her face in her hands and sobbing openly as Friend's queries became more plaintive and frantic.

"This is a brave little girl here, who never had the chance to grow up into the brave woman she ought to have been. We may be the only ones who see what she went through, how courageously she handled it. We have to bear witness." Gold's brown eyes were serious. "We crawl over corpses in alien vessels all the time, take their dead ships, examine their bodies. I hope we never forget that they were once people. She's reminding us. Friend is reminding us."

Corsi said nothing, only leaned back in her seat and fixed her gaze on the table.

Jaldark lifted her head and stared into the viewscreen. She was shaking. Her hair, once long and lustrous, was dull and stringy. The implants in her temple, which had once pulsed to a steady, slow rhythm beneath the skin, were flashing erratically.

"I don't think I have much longer," she said in a voice thick with tears. In the background, Friend continued to call for her. "The pain is so bad I can hardly stand it." She bit her lip and closed her eyes as, Duffy guessed, another wave of pain racked her skeletal frame. "I think I'm going to die. But I can handle that. It's Friend I'm worried about. He's supposed to autodestruct if anything happens to me. They said Starsearchers aren't designed to function on their own. They told us the ships need an Omearan mind to link with in order to make ethical decisions. They warned us that they could be dangerous without a pilot. But I don't believe that. I don't think Friend would hurt anybody, unless they hurt him first."

She took a long, shuddering breath and leaned into the recorder. "I can't kill Friend, I just can't. That would be the most selfish act I think I could possibly perform. I know I'm supposed to, but I won't do it. I won't. I've deactivated the autodestruct mechanism. Friend won't be able to reengage it on his own. He's going to live, even if . . . even if I don't."

She smiled a little, a taut, pained smile. "That's what friends do, isn't it? They help each other. If anybody finds this, please take care of Friend. Send him home. The coordinates are in the computer. Help him find a new pilot. He's going to be so lost without . . . me to take care . . ."

Jaldark whimpered. More than a scream, that tiny sound rent Duffy's heart. Watching this was torture. Jaldark's chest hitched. Her free hand went up to press tightly at a flashing implant. When she was able to speak again, it was through tightly gritted teeth.

"Tell him I'm sorry. Tell him I love him. Tell him it will be all right. He's just got to be brave."

She began to gasp, as if her body could no longer absorb oxygen. Her brilliant eyes rolled back in her head, and the recording device slipped from a suddenly limp hand to bounce on the floor. There it lay, recording only the base of the chair until it ran out of bytes, while, out of sight, Jaldark quietly gasped until she made no more sounds, and the plaintive voice of Friend kept demanding, "Jaldark, please respond!"

La Forge reached over and wordlessly turned off the screen. For a long moment, despite the urgency of the situation, no one spoke.

"Rest in peace," said Gold solemnly.

"Do you see?" said 110 softly. "The ship—Friend—has lost its only companion. Jaldark told us that the ships are supposed to autodestruct if anything happens to the pilot, but Friend does not have that option. It was not designed to be alone. It does not know what to do. Like its pilot, it is a young vessel, with little experience, and it is terrified. We must not destroy it. We must help it. And I volunteer to be linked with it as Jaldark was."

Gold looked at him sharply. "110, forgive me if I step on your toes here, but—you've been deliberately avoiding such an intimate link with anyone. That's why you're putting off going back to Bynaus. Assuming I will even let you, which is not an assumption you ought to be making, why do you want to do this? You barely survived your last encounter with that ship's computer. We've got trained specialists on the way right now. They'll figure something out."

110 looked solemn. "Because, Captain Gold, I

am already partially linked to Friend. When I attempted to access the computer when we first boarded, I engaged some sort of circuit with it. It has downloaded a link to my brain, but a very inefficient one. Bynar brains are already constructed to link smoothly with computers, and contain a great deal of information. I am the only one capable of establishing communication that could convince it that we are no threat. It is up to me to stop the ship."

"We've already stopped the ship."

Slowly, 110 shook his large head. "No, sir, we have not."

At that moment, Gold's combadge chirped. "McAllan to Captain Gold. The alien ship is powering up. It's left the planet surface and is heading right for us."

CHAPTER
6

Repairs are complete. All systems fully operational. Jaldark is not on board. Accessing search parameters. Searching planet surface . . . Jaldark is not present on the planet surface. Alien vessel in orbit about planet. Unable to penetrate shields for search.

Conclusion: Jaldark has been taken by the alien vessel.

Action required: Jaldark must be recovered immediately.

Jaldark, I am coming. I am coming, my Friend. I will not let them harm you.

Gold was still in a solemn mood from the tragic recording he had just seen as the turbolift doors hissed open. But once he stepped on the bridge, and saw the expressions on the bridge crew, he put his pity aside.

It was tragic that Jaldark had died alone, in pain. And he sympathized with the ship's loss, if it was, as 110 kept insisting, sentient and capable of emotion. But that didn't mean he was willing to make the ship feel better by letting it blast the *da Vinci* to bits.

"Shields up. Red alert," he snapped. He took his seat and gazed at the image on the viewscreen.

It seemed impossible, but there it was. That ship had been badly damaged when it crashed into the planet, and they'd believed that they had completely knocked out its weapons systems. And yet it looked like they hadn't even scratched the thing. It was, as McAllan had said, heading straight for them, and if Gold imagined that the ship was seething with deadly intent and aching for revenge, he knew he wasn't guilty of anthropomorphizing.

"Status report," he demanded.

"One minute, the vessel was dead; the next, it's completely repaired and heading right for us," said Wong. "We can't tell for certain, of course, but I would guess its weapons systems are intact."

At that moment, a green bolt of energy narrowly missed them.

"I'd say you're right," said Gold. "But that was obviously a warning shot. If that ship wanted to hit us, it would hit us. Open a hailing frequency. Attention, alien vessel. This is Captain David Gold of the *U.S.S. da Vinci*. We mean you no harm. Let's open a dialogue."

At once, a metallic voice echoed throughout the bridge. "Omearan Starsearcher 7445 to the *da Vinci*. You have my pilot. Return her at once, unharmed. Then we will open a dialogue."

Dear God, thought Gold, *he doesn't know she's dead*.

"Captain," said Gomez softly, "I don't think Friend will respond too happily if we beam that body over."

"Agreed," said Gold. "Suggestions?"

"Let me attempt to link with it," said 110 at once.

"110," said Gold wearily, "that ship might just as soon crisp you as talk to you."

110 lifted his head and regarded Gold evenly. "As we—as I have told you, Captain Gold, I am already linked with it, though it is not a two-way communication. Its pain is my pain. The only way I will lose that pain is if I can speak with it. And that is the only way Friend will ever accept what has happened to Jaldark. The news must be given to him gently, in a way he can understand. Otherwise, he will attack in anger. When he crashed into the planet—it was not an accident, Captain. He was in despair, and could not engage his self-destruct mechanism." He winced a little. "Please. This is the only way."

"110," Geordi said gently, "there's no guarantee that you will be able to form a proper link with the computer."

The little Bynar smiled at that. "There is, as you humans like to say, only one way to find out."

Geordi and Gold exchanged glances. Gold reached a decision. "Gold to Dr. Lense. Would it be possible to adjust 110's brain and body in order to render him able to link with the ship?"

"I think so. If you'd wanted to do this with a human, the answer would be no, but the Bynar brains are much better candidates for such a link.

And, judging by his brain-wave patterns, I'd say that there seems to be some kind of connection established between them already. It would take some surgery, but I—"

"110, get to sickbay right now," ordered Gold. At once, 110 scampered to obey. "Wong, reestablish link. Attention, Omearan Starsearcher 7445. We would like to send an ambassador to your command center to speak with you."

"Return my pilot. Then she and I will speak with your ambassador."

Gold took a deep breath. Time for a little white lie. "Your pilot is unwell." It was true. Dead was about as unwell as one could get. "She is currently in our sickbay." Also true. "We have boarded you previously."

"I remember." The metallic voice was angry now. "When you kidnapped Jaldark."

"We brought her to our ship, yes. But while we were aboard you, while you were inactive, you established a link with one of my crew."

Silence. "Yes," said the ship, haltingly. "I remember."

"We think we can further adjust him so that he may link with you. We can explain everything to you most efficiently in that fashion."

A long silence. Gold felt sweat gather on his brow. He let this ship take its time.

"I will permit such a contact," said the ship after what felt like an eternity. Gold briefly closed his eyes in relief. "You should be aware that your crewmember will be vulnerable. If I do not like what I hear, I will not hesitate to kill him."

Was it a bluff, or the truth? Either way, it seemed as though this was something 110 was intent on doing. And, much as Gold hated to admit it, it seemed as if it was their only hope. The *Enterprise* herself would have a hard time fighting an opponent that was virtually indestructible. And the little *da Vinci* was certainly not equipped to handle it.

"We are explorers, not warriors," said Gold. "We have no intention of harming you. You will realize that once you link with my crewmember."

"There is no deception possible in the link," agreed the ship. "All your plans will be revealed."

"We have nothing to hide," Gold declared.

"Then you have nothing to fear." Abruptly, the ship terminated the transmission.

Gold sank back in his chair, debating. He thought about contacting Starfleet and telling them to cancel the arrival of the *Enterprise* and the *Lexington*. Gold now knew the vessel wasn't a Borg ship, and there was a chance that it wouldn't even prove hostile. What was it Jaldark had said? That she was certain Friend wouldn't hurt anyone unless someone hurt him first.

But if 110 couldn't convince the ship—Friend—that Jaldark had already been dead for weeks before the *da Vinci* found her, then Gold imagined the vessel would consider itself grievously hurt. They'd need the *Enterprise* and the *Lexington* then. Hell, they might need every vessel in the fleet if the repaired ship went on a rampage again. It had done enough damage while still repairing itself. At full strength . . .

Gold chuckled a little. His father had had a wise saying that he would always trot out when David would start fretting about things that might happen. "Don't go borrowing trouble," he would say. And Gold realized that's exactly what he was doing.

They had the tricorder recordings Jaldark herself had made. They had the body, which was in an advanced stage of decay. And they had 110. If these weren't enough to convince the ship, then they'd just have to deal with the consequences.

"Lense to Gold."

"Go ahead."

"110 is tolerating the implants for the moment, but I don't know how effective they'll be. I also don't know how long it will be before his body starts rejecting them. I'm sorry, sir, but it's the best I can do."

"Then, as always, Elizabeth, your best is good enough for me. 110, how do you feel?"

"The implants are . . . uncomfortable, Captain. But it is a necessary pain. Faulwell has given me Jaldark's tricorder. I hope to be able to interface with both it and Friend's central computer system."

"Good luck, 110."

"Thank you, Captain Gold. It has been an honor to serve you."

Gold didn't like the way that sounded. He didn't like it at all. But there was not a single thing he could do. It was all up to the Bynar now.

He only hoped the little guy was not planning to go out in a blaze of glory.

* * *

When 110 materialized in the command center of Friend, part of him felt like he was coming home. Odd, since the last time he had been aboard the vessel it had attacked and nearly killed him. He stood for a moment in the command center of the sentient ship, looking around. There was no dull, blood-colored hue. Instead, Friend had given him lighting that was quite comfortable to his eyes and enabled him to see perfectly. The entire scene was much less sinister than it had been when the away team had beamed over earlier.

Various panels here and there had indentations or spikes. He knew that these were ways to join with the ship if he needed to fire the weapons, or enhance propulsion, or effect repairs. Over there, where he had foolishly begun trying to tap into the ship's computers, he had triggered Friend's angry arousal.

But for everyday operations, for companionship, for nourishment, the chair was the central joining point.

Jaldark had died in that chair—and lived in it. 110 wondered if the fluttering in his insides was nervousness or anticipation. Probably a little of both. He had never joined with a computer the way he was about to join with Friend, and he was uncertain as to what to expect.

"Please sit in the command chair," came Friend's metallic voice. "It is the most efficient way for us to link."

Slowly, one hand reaching to touch the buffer at his side for reassurance, 110 climbed into the chair. Even though Jaldark was an adolescent of her species, she had been much bigger than the little Bynar. He had to hold his body in an awkward position for the holes Lense had made in his arms to line up with the spikes on the arms of the chair.

For an instant, 110 knew terrible fear. Then, resolutely, he maneuvered so that the spikes inserted into the arm sheaths.

Information flooded his brain at a speed that even 110 found difficult to process. Frantically, he thought, *Slow down, slow down!* To his surprise, the ship obliged. It wanted to tell him everything at once, but it tried to curb its urgency. The information came at a rate that would have killed a human, but, with effort, 110 was able to comprehend it.

The ship's designation was Starsearcher 7445, but Jaldark Keniria had taken to calling it Friend. Their people, the Omearans, had just emerged from a bitter and devastating war that had nearly destroyed their planet. Their foe, the Sarimun, were advanced technologically, but lacked the advanced traits of mercy and a desire for peace. The attack had been rebuffed, but the Omearan world had paid a dreadful price.

The strongest advantage the Omearans had had was the Conjoined, the term used to refer to the linking of Omearans with the Starsearcher vessels. It was a position of tremendous honor among their people. Only one in ten thousand was born who was able to withstand the pairing. Rejections of the cybernetic grafts were the norm. Once a child had been identified as a good candidate, the process began, in infancy. The still-forming skulls were carefully manipulated to eventually house the spherical implants. One by one, strands of cables replaced nerves and muscles. The child was weaned to eat food only occasionally, and to take most of its sustenance from the same fuel that propelled the Starsearchers. It was a union of the most intimate sort.

Once a child pilot entered adolescence, it was bonded with the ship that it would have for the rest of its life. Such pilots considered themselves blessed, and the ships, which had also been carefully programmed with emotions and their own intelligence, adored their pilots.

Originally designed for peaceful purposes, the Starsearchers and their pilots had been altered for war. Thousands were lost in the war, and the pilots grew younger and younger, less and less experienced. By the end of the war, only a few pilots were left. They were sent off to various parts of the quadrant, to search for a planet the Omearans could safely colonize.

Thus it was that Jaldark, all of fifteen in human years, had found herself alone with her malfunctioning implants in the darkness of space. All alone, except for Friend.

Humans could not possibly understand this, thought 110 in wonder. They were so very separate. Even in their marriages, which he understood brought physical union, they remained two separate entities, with their own personalities and uniqueness. The humanoid races that had developed telepathy might have moved closer to comprehension, but even they could not share information so profoundly. Bynars could; clearly, the union of ship and pilot was closer to that union experienced by the Bynars than anything the crew of the *da Vinci* could conceive.

But . . . you do? Friend's "voice," in his mind, quivered along the implants that served for nerves, tingling where 110 was physically impaled upon the ship's spikes.

110 let his memories be the answer. It was his turn to flood Friend's chips with images. Friend was silent as it absorbed the information. 110 thought of Bynaus, of his joining with 111, of the grace and speed and efficiency with which they worked together. He let Friend in on the intimacy of computer linkage with another living being, something he knew Friend understood only too well. Organic being, computer bytes, joined in two beings who were not really two, but one.

I understand, came the response, but not even in words, not anymore. The Bynar and the sentient ship had surpassed such clumsy methods of communication now that they trusted one another. Steeling himself for the fresh wave of pain, 110 relived 111's death. The emptiness, the aching, the repeated, increasingly frantic queries to a mind that was already gone. Oh, yes, he knew loss such as Friend had experienced.

Friend's agony washed through 110, and the Bynar experienced it as if it were his own. He swam upward, drowning in the linkage, long enough to press the button on the tricorder. He forced his eyes open. He would have to watch Jaldark's logs for the second time. Through the link they had established, Friend would then also see them. He would see, and believe.

So much information coursing through his brain, along his artificial nerves! Jaldark's childish face appeared on the screen, saying words that pierced both vessel and Bynar.

I love sharing things with Friend . . . I love it when we link up and I've got the whole ship's sensors at my hands. . . . To be able to experience so many things that, as an organic being, I'd never otherwise know is indescribable. And he is so close to me when we're joined. I've never known anything like it . . . He's really sensitive to my happiness. It's nice to have things like that matter to someone else so much. . . . I tried to explain to Friend about how great it feels to walk on soft grass in your bare feet, but he didn't quite get it, I think. . . .

She was wrong, came Friend's thoughts. *Through her, I knew. I knew everything. . . .*

It was the most amazing sensation, to be linked with him . . . I just love Friend so much. He's the most wonderful ship. I'm so glad I'm bonded with him for the rest of my life. . . . I guess I'm just the luckiest girl in the universe. . . . Something's wrong . . . Friend can sense it, but I'm not telling him any more than I have to in order to maintain function. I don't know that we'll make it in time. I hate lying to him like this.

110 had thought the ship's pain difficult to deal with, but the raw rage almost stopped his heart.

Why did she not tell me? There were things I could have done, systems I could have shut down, that would have made us much more efficient!

She did not wish to burden you with her fears and pain, 110 replied.

We were joined! *I was supposed to share her fears and pain!*

But Jaldark had been a humanoid, and augmented and technologically enhanced as she was, she remained a humanoid. She didn't understand that Friend would have been more comforted had she confided in him. Perhaps she would have learned this, as she grew older. But perhaps that wisdom might also have made her less compassionate, and she would not have disabled the ship so that it could not self-destruct.

I think it's the implants . . . they're failing somehow. I can't get sustenance from Friend anymore. . . . I have these terrible headaches. And the arm sheaths . . . whenever we join, I'm in a lot of pain. So, of course, I come up with excuses not to join as often. Friend hasn't said anything much, but I know his feelings are hurt. He's the last person—well, thing—I'd ever want to hurt, and I just hate it that this is happening!

The ship could not form coherent thoughts anymore, but 110 did not need it to. For the first time since 111's death, he let his own grief surface. In the bonding, they were more than two. Now that she was dead, 110 felt as though he was less than one. She had taken so much of him with her when she died.

I don't think I have much longer. The pain is so bad I can hardly stand it. I think I'm going to die. But I can handle that. It's Friend I'm worried about. He's supposed to autodestruct if anything happens to me. They said Starsearchers aren't designed to function on their own. They told us that the ships need an Omearan mind to link with to make ethical decisions. They . . . could be dangerous without a pilot. But I don't believe that. I don't think Friend would hurt anybody, unless they hurt him first.

Friend had been lost in his own pain, but now 110 felt the Starsearcher's attention focus fully on the dying Jaldark's words. 110 wanted to linger in his own bittersweet misery, but was pulled along with Friend. He, too, really began to listen.

I can't kill Friend, I just can't. That would be the most selfish act I think I could possibly perform. I know I'm supposed to, but I won't do it. I won't. I've deactivated the autodestruct mechanism. Friend won't be able to reengage it on his own. He's going to live, even if . . . even if I don't. That's what friends do, isn't it? They help each other. If anybody finds this, please take care of Friend. Send him home. The coordinates are in the computer. Help him find a new pilot. He's going to be so lost without . . . me to take care . . . Tell him I'm sorry. Tell him I love him. Tell him it will be all right. He's just got to be brave.

Friend's shock now felt as strong as his suffering. *That is against all the rules. Jaldark was the reason I was unable to self-destruct? She did it deliberately? Why, why? We were supposed to die together!*

110's narrow chest hitched. So were Bynars. Linked unto death, it was not at all uncommon, nor frowned upon, for a remaining Bynar to die upon losing a partner. Sometimes, more often than not, such a death was chosen, self-inflicted. It was the only way in 110's culture to avoid being forced to take another mate. It was the only way to remain Bynar.

But 110 did not want to take another mate. For a while, he thought, as Friend had, that he wanted to die. For what was life without 111, without his friend and mate and ultimate companion, who lived in his affections and mind and soul? But there had been no chance for suicide, and, to 110's own astonishment, his body refused to simply quit on its own. There had been the computer to help, and the Pevvni to fight, and then Friend's plight to attend to.

While 110 was sorting through this, Jaldark quietly died on the screen. He expected the ship to lose control utterly, and braced himself for the throes that would surely come.

Instead, Friend remained strangely still. 110 realized that the ship was focusing on him and his thoughts.

You did not die.

No, 110 replied. *I kept living. I kept working.*

For what reason? Your loss was as great as mine. Why did you live?

For a long moment, 110 could not form an answer to that, because he truly did not know. Finally, the answer came, and with it, a sudden easing of the pain that had been his constant companion since that terrible moment.

Because 111 wished me to continue.

As Jaldark wished me to continue, thought Friend. 110 felt the ship's own pain subsiding ever so slightly. *But why? Starsearchers cannot function*

on their own. We need a pilot. We could be danger-
ous. I was *dangerous. I destroyed buildings and*
fired upon your ship. I could have killed you. I was
not constructed to attack, only to defend.

Physical pain began to penetrate 110's consciousness, distracting him from the thoughts he
was only now beginning to process. The implants.
Dr. Lense had warned him about this. Because he
was a Bynar, a member of a race that already had a
great deal of integration with computers, he could
tolerate the implants to a certain degree. A normal
human could not. But he was not Omearan, and
the implants had not been part of his body since
infancy; it was starting to reject them. Once the
pain began to increase, Lense had said, he only had
a matter of moments before he would go into
shock.

Faced with dying like the unfortunate Jaldark,
in the same position, 110 realized that he very
much wanted to live.

I can help you, sent Friend, with a sudden sense
of urgency. *I can enable you to make the transition.*
You could help me by becoming my new pilot. You
understand. And . . . I could help you, too, because I
understand.

The pain in his head increased. 110 wondered if
all Starsearchers were this compassionate. He
understood now why destroying Friend had been
anathema to Jaldark. And, oh, it was appealing,
wasn't it? It was the perfect solution. He would not
be alone, and yet he would not dishonor the memory of all he had shared with 111 by so quickly
selecting another mate. And poor Friend desper-

ately needed him. He was right. They could help one another. Heal one another.

It was ideal. And it was too easy.

Friend sensed his rejection before 110 even had a chance to phrase it. He hurried to explain his reasoning.

Jaldark said you had to be brave. She said everyone thought that the Starsearchers couldn't function without a pilot. But you proved them wrong. Look at you right now, interfacing with a completely alien species. You're making ethical judgments. You can be an individual. As . . . as I can be. If we are both brave enough.

But what is a ship without a pilot? I serve no useful purpose.

The pain was increasing. Morbidly, he wondered if the same white-hot agony that was racking his body was what Jaldark had undergone. He had to transport out and have the implants removed before they caused permanent damage. But he didn't want to leave, not yet. 110 willed himself to hang on for just a little while longer.

That is a false conclusion, arrived at by incorrectly analyzing the data. You could help to complete the mission upon which you and Jaldark had embarked. If you will let the Federation help you, they can assist your people in searching for an undeveloped world to colonize.

In reply, 110 received such a violent jolt of fear and loathing that he almost passed out from the force of it. *Other races hate us! They tried to kill us!*

But I don't hate you, 110 thought. *The Omearans have encountered only a few other alien races. There* are thousands in this quadrant alone, and every race is different. Many of them have joined the United Federation of Planets, for their mutual benefit. I know my captain wants to assist you, and—once he knows what it is you are seeking—help the Omearans as well. You must be able to sense my sincerity.

Yes. The ship's reply was slow, halting. 110 supposed he couldn't blame Friend for his suspicions. But the pain was worsening. He needed a decision now.

Friend, the implants are hurting me. I must leave you.

No, please, please stay, just a while longer. . . .

I cannot. While it is right and appropriate for us to mourn our lost bondmates, we must continue. Alone. We have tasks to perform, things that only we can do. Things that our bondmates would want us to do.

I . . . I understand. I will do what Jaldark wanted me to. I will be brave.

Right before the darkness claimed him, 110 knew in his heart that both 111 and Jaldark would be proud of their decisions.

CHAPTER
7

"Welcome back," came the kind voice of Emmett.

110 blinked. "You beamed me out in time," he said. It was a statement, not a question.

"And only just," came Captain Gold's booming voice. His face moved into 110's line of vision. "What were you thinking? You were supposed to come back the minute the implants started to hurt. You could have died down there!"

110 smiled softly. No. Friend would not have let him. None of his friends would have let him die. Another time, another place, yes—one day, he would die.

But it would not be today.

"So," said Gold, his anger diminishing, "what happened with the little Bynar and the great big ship?"

"What is Friend doing now?" countered 110.

"Sitting quietly in space. It wants to make sure you're all right."

"He will be," said Lense. "I would recommend

you take it easy for a while, though, 110. No more joining with strange ships. In fact, you should leave the computers alone for at least a day."

"The *Enterprise* has arrived," Gold said. "They came, even though I called off the alert. They figured, they were this close, they might as well pick up Geordi and you, and take you back to Starbase 505."

"No." The firmness of 110's reply surprised everyone. "I will not go to Starbase 505. I will not rejoin."

"What?" Gold appeared stunned. "But—you *have* to. You're a Bynar."

"I am," agreed 110, "but I am also myself. An individual. Captain, my bond with 111 was profoundly deep. The severance of that bond was dreadful. I know what my customs demand, but I do not wish to obey them. I do not want to bond with anyone, at least, not yet. That is why I did not bond with the ship."

"What?" Gold said again. 110 felt a faint flush of humor. He was certainly startling his captain with these revelations. "The ship tried to force you to bond with it? Be its new pilot?"

"Force? No. Friend would not force anything on anyone. He and the people who built him are very peaceful people, Captain. But the offer was made, and I almost accepted." He felt a sudden pang of wistfulness. It would have been sweet, to have bonded again, to feel the comforting presence of that Other who was yet one's self. But this solitary state had lessons to teach, lessons 110 knew he was ready to embrace, hard though they might be. "I will remain here on the *da Vinci*, if you will have me. If not, I am certain that Bynaus would be happy to provide you with another joined pair. They would certainly be more efficient than a solitary Bynar."

"Your contribution is unique, solo man," said Gold warmly. "As are you."

110 cocked his huge, round head. "Soloman? Is that an Earth term for one who is unmated?"

Gold chuckled. "Not an official term, no."

110 considered for a moment. If he refused to rebond, he would not be permitted to use his designation of 110 anymore. He needed a new designation—a name, as the humans called it.

"Soloman," 110 said softly, liking how the awkward words sounded on his tongue. "May I then take the name Soloman? I will need one, now that I am unbonded."

"Soloman it is," said Gold. "Now, what's up with Friend?"

As best he could, utilizing the clumsy and inefficient method of the spoken word, the newly dubbed Soloman tried to convey what had transpired. He was frustrated at his lack of ability to convey the nuances, the intimacy of the joining with the ship, but Gold was a wise human. He seemed to understand what could not be spoken, only sensed. He listened intently, his dark eyes intense under his bushy brows.

"Do you think Friend trusts us?" he asked.

"He has bonded with me, and I trust you. Therefore, he must trust you also."

Gold nodded. He rose, and patted Soloman's leg. "Let me see what I can do."

* * *

"Hello, Jean-Luc, you old son of a gun. Late as usual. You missed all the excitement."

The normally formal visage of Captain Jean-Luc Picard broke into a smile. Gomez didn't think she'd ever seen that before, and, for a moment, was mildly startled to hear Gold speaking to Picard in such a fashion. But Picard seemed unoffended; in fact, he appeared pleased.

"Seems like, the last time, *you* were called late on the scene, David," he replied.

Gold laughed, a short, quick bark. "Starfleet called us in to clean up after the *Enterprise*. Run any marathons recently, Jean-Luc? You're looking a little soft around the middle."

"Not for some time," Picard answered, "but I could still beat you, old man." His dark gaze flickered to Gomez. "Commander Gomez, Lieutenant Commander Duffy. A pleasure to see you both again. So, David, I understand you called the *Enterprise* and the *Lexington* all the way out here on a wild-goose chase."

"And we caught the goose," Gold said. "Wong, please transmit the information we learned about Friend to the *Enterprise*."

"'Friend'?" echoed Picard. "An odd name for a ship, especially one that did so much damage to an innocent planet."

"It's a long story, Captain," said La Forge, "but one with a happy ending, I hope. This isn't a Borg vessel, but the ship was designed to uniquely bond with its pilot. It's sentient. It—sort of panicked when its pilot died. Went a little crazy. They were searching for a new homeland for her people. They seem like a benevolent, peaceful race, and I'm hopeful that the Federation might be able to lend them a hand in that quest."

Picard had been listening intently, and now he nodded. "We'll do what we can. If this species is, indeed, as peaceful as you say they are, then I'm certain we'll be able to assist them. I understand that your last few missions have not been without cost, David. I'm sorry for the loss of 111."

"Thank you, Jean-Luc. I'll pass that on to Soloman."

Gomez almost giggled at the expression on Picard's patrician mien. "I beg your pardon?" asked the captain of the *Enterprise*.

"110 won't be coming back with me, Captain," explained Geordi, stifling a smile of his own. "He's decided to stay on with the *da Vinci*—unpaired. Captain Gold has nicknamed him Soloman."

Picard frowned. "You run a bit of a lax ship, Gold."

Gold appeared unruffled. "You know what we do, Jean-Luc, what we deal with every day. My team's sharp enough when it counts, and that's what matters to me."

Picard relaxed. "As it should. I've worked with some of your crew, and you know I think they're among the finest in Starfleet."

Gomez felt a blush suffuse her cheeks.

"Mr. La Forge, I'm certain you'll be reluctant to rejoin our boring old vessel after serving with this crew. But we need you back here."

"Aye, sir. I'll be there right away."

"Picard out." The screen was filled with the image of the *Enterprise*, awaiting Geordi's transport.

"Geordi La Forge," said Gold expansively, "the door is always open. We could use someone like you more than occasionally, you know."

La Forge smiled. "Thank you, sir. It's been quite the experience." He looked over at Gomez. "Commander Gomez, it was good to see you again."

Sonya smiled, a warm, genuine smile. She'd worried about clashing with La Forge, about him stepping on her territory. But he was a good man, and had been a good friend. She was glad she had been granted the opportunity to work things out with him, and found herself realizing she was going to miss him.

"It was wonderful to see you, Lieutenant," she said, and the words could not have been more sincere. "Give my best to everyone over in engineering, will you?"

"You got it. Picard looks like he's itching for me to get back, so do me a favor. Say good-bye to Bart and Soloman for me, will you?"

She nodded and followed him with her eyes as he stepped into the turbolift. He almost bumped into Soloman.

"Whoa!" exclaimed Geordi. "Shouldn't you still be in sickbay?"

"I must say good-bye to Friend. And I am glad to have the chance to say good-bye to you, Geordi."

"Take care of yourself, Soloman," said Geordi as the turbolift doors closed.

"Captain . . . may I?" asked Soloman.

Gold nodded. "Wong, contact the ship. Go ahead, Soloman."

Gomez watched intently, her gaze flickering between the screen, on which Friend appeared, and Soloman. "How are you feeling, Friend?" the Bynar asked.

"I am a little afraid," the ship admitted in a halting voice. *And we thought that thing was a killer on a rampage. Thought it was Borg. How wrong can you be?* Gomez thought to herself.

"So am I," said Soloman. "But I think we have chosen the right path, you and I." He hesitated. "If you would like, we could transport Jaldark back to you, so that you may deliver her body to her people. Or else we can send her to the stars, as is the custom with Federation ships."

Gomez couldn't believe it, but her eyes prickled with tears again. It had been a long, long time since any mission had moved her this deeply. Perhaps it was because one of their own had been so profoundly affected. Or maybe it was because they had seen the young, lively Jaldark before her death. Regardless, the whole thing was stirring up deep emotions inside her.

"I . . . I think I would like to have her with me. I would like to take her home, one final time."

Soloman turned to Gold, who nodded. "We will transport the body in a sealed coffin, Friend. We will handle her with all respect and honor," said the captain.

"I am sorry for my attack on your ship, Captain Gold," apologized Friend. "You are kind to forgive me."

Gold cleared his throat. Gomez shot him a quick glance. His face revealed nothing, but that one sound told her that even her grizzled captain was moved.

"It wasn't the ideal first-contact situation. But the second contact worked out pretty well," Gold replied.

"I am being hailed by the *Enterprise*. They are ready to depart."

"Soloman," said Gold, very softly. "If you want to change your mind, either about Friend or about returning to your homeworld, now's the time."

"No," said Soloman firmly. "I know what I want, what I need. I can do this, and so can you, Friend," insisted Soloman. "Farewell."

"Farewell," echoed the ship. The *Enterprise* powered up, and Friend obediently moved into position alongside it. Both ships jumped into warp, and were gone.

CHAPTER
8

Captain's personal log, supplemental: We started with a dead ship, then a live ship, then a dead pilot, then a Borg. We ended up with a formal first contact that could save an entire species, if it's handled right, and saw two individuals display strength and courage as they chose to stand alone. You know, Picard and the others can have their Galaxy-class behemoths. I'll stick with this little vessel and its crew any day. Look what we get to do.

Gomez was surprised to see someone else awake at this hour when she entered the mess. The lighting was dim; after all, it was well past midnight. But even in this faint light, she could tell it was Duffy. He seemed as surprised, and as uncomfortable, as she. They exchanged awkward smiles.

She stood in front of the replicator for a long moment. Gomez almost didn't make the order she'd intended to make. She'd rarely requested this over the last ten years as it was. But she wanted it badly tonight.

"Cocoa, hot," she finally instructed the replicator. "With whipped cream," she added quickly, and took the steaming mug the replicator offered.

"Whipped cream, huh?" commented Duffy. "You must be having a rough night."

Gomez smiled, feeling suddenly, absurdly shy. She had wanted to be alone, to think about things, but now she was glad Duffy was here. She had always been able to talk to him before. She wondered if that, too, had changed.

"May I join you?" she asked.

"Certainly," he replied. She took the seat opposite him, and then suddenly laughed as she saw what he had ordered.

"Macaroni and cheese?"

"The ultimate comfort food. Like hot chocolate," he said, forking up another mouthful. "Just like my mother used to make, if Mother had been a replicator. Good for what ails you."

Sonya took a sip, enjoying the chocolaty, sugary hit of the smooth beverage on her tongue. It had been too long. Ever since "the incident," as her spilling encounter with Picard had been dubbed by some wag, she had refrained from ordering the infamous beverage in front of others.

But Duffy was more than just someone she supervised. He'd been her friend, just like Geordi had, and then, he had become something more. He was someone she could trust, someone she could drink cocoa in front of when she really needed it, without fear of being teased.

What he had just said suddenly registered. "Comfort food? Why do you need comfort food?"

Now it was his turn to look away shyly. "You know."

Sonya supposed she did. It was time they talked about it, at least a little. She was tired of this unresolved business getting in the way.

"What happened with 110—I mean, Soloman—and Friend," she said softly. "Watching poor, young Jaldark dying alone, in pain, while her ship kept crying for her. And Soloman teaching it how to be by itself."

He nodded, still not meeting her eyes. "It kind of brought home . . ."

"That we're here, but we're not together anymore," Sonya finished. "I know." She gestured toward her mug. "Why do you think I'm drinking this?"

"It was one thing when you got promoted and left," said Duffy, leaning forward and talking quickly. "I mean, we said our good-byes, and we moved on."

"Yes," Sonya said. It had been hard—harder, she supposed, on Duffy than on her. She had a promotion to look forward to and to provide distraction—a new ship, a new mission. He had remained on the *Enterprise*. Until they had both ended up here, on a ship far too small for them to avoid each other. "And then, here we are again."

He nodded. "And this time, you're my boss."

"Another wrinkle in an already very wrinkled relationship."

"Very wrinkled."

"I've missed you."

He looked up at her quickly. She held his gaze. Her heart began to beat faster. "I never got involved with anyone else," Sonya continued.

"You were probably just too busy," said Duffy, but his voice shook, just a little.

"I'd have made time for you," Sonya replied.

"You could now."

"Can I? Can I, really? Oh, Kieran," she sighed, and she reached across the table to grasp his hand. "I'm tired. I don't want to think about this right now. I just want to be with you, eat our comfort foods, and enjoy each other's company."

He smiled, and, as she remembered, he looked just like a little boy when he grinned that grin. "Sounds good to me," he said.

Gomez felt warm inside. They'd broken the ice, and she had learned something that was very important to her. Kieran Duffy was still her friend, despite the time and distance that had developed between them. There would be an opportunity to explore this further, if it was what they both wanted. For now, she laughed, and clinked her cup of cocoa against his bowl of macaroni and cheese.

Alone in his quarters, Bart reread the letter he'd just finished writing to Anthony Mark. It was long, eight pages' worth of small, neat script. He had told his partner everything. About their fear of the Borg, about finding Jaldark's log, about Soloman and his new name, about the sorrow and joy both sentient ship and unpaired Bynar were discovering in their newfound solitary lives. He frowned, crumpled up the heavy cream-colored paper, and tossed it over his shoulder. It was all wrong. It was full of details, of description. Those were the things he'd tell Anthony Mark later, over a delicious candlelit dinner in his quarters on Starbase 92.

Right now, he needed to say the important things. 111's untimely death and Jaldark's heartbreaking story had taught him that. There was no need for a long letter.

He selected another sheet of stationery, and began again.

My dearest Anthony, just a brief note to tell you how much I love you. Good night.

CHAPTER
1

Nostrene could sense the tension permeating the room, though he himself refused to display any outward indications except that of perfect calm. His posture contrasted with that of his crew and the scientific advisors bustling about the command deck as they made last-minute adjustments or ran final tests. Consoles and viewscreens displayed a vast array of data, each one dedicated to some facet of the monumental experiment currently under way.

"Holding at light speed minus three," reported the subordinate manning the helm with no attempt to hide the excitement in his voice. Nostrene could not blame the younger officer, who was serving aboard ship on his first assignment and was displaying much of the same excitability and enthusiasm he himself had at that age.

"Report current status, Dlyax." In response, one of the scientists stationed near the front of the command deck turned to face Nostrene, the deep red hue of his crystalline body reflecting the harsh illumination emitted from the deck plating.

"Commander, the drive system appears to be functioning normally. Our diagnostic scans show no anomalies or irregularities. It is our consensus that the test can proceed without further delay."

Of course they would think that, Nostrene mused. *Their reputations are being tested here today as much as any new propulsion system.*

Tholian ships had enjoyed success with their ability to attack from positions of stealth and to utilize their much feared energy web generators, draining the power and crushing the hull of even the sturdiest enemy vessel. But it had been Nostrene's experience that ships controlled by enemies he'd faced in past battles had possessed definite advantages in speed. While Tholian vessels had been able to travel faster than light for generations, they never had been able to achieve speeds comparable to those recorded by ships of other races. The vessels most frequently underscoring this shortcoming, to Nostrene's chagrin, belonged to the United Federation of Planets.

This concern had been brought to the forefront during the recent war between the Federation and the Dominion. Alpha Quadrant forces had nearly succumbed to the might of the so-called "Founders" and their legions of genetically engineered soldiers, the Jem'Hadar. The Assembly's tenuous state of peace with the Federation had strengthened during the conflict, allowing the Tholian people to largely observe the war. That position fit securely with the nonaggression pact they had established with the Dominion. Though it had not been popular opinion to state publicly at the time, Nostrene was certain that Tholian forces would have fallen quickly to the vastly superior strength exhibited by the Dominion. Fortunately the war had ended, with the Founders and the Jem'Hadar being forced back into Gamma Quadrant space before his suspicions could be tested.

Such concerns could soon be put to rest, however, should the experiment they were conducting here today prove successful. Tholian vessels would be regarded as among the fastest in the Quadrant. Additionally, the ability to channel newly harnessed stores of power would lend additional strength to the defenses and armament of their ships.

Satisfied with Dlyax's report, Nostrene said, "Very well, resume acceleration."

As he gave the order, his eyes shifted from screens displaying information transmitted by the ship's network of sensors to the command deck's main viewscreen. The stars as rendered by the computer remained still, but he knew that in a few moments they would twist and distort as their ship crossed the threshold into subspace.

"Light speed minus one," his helmsman called out, and Nostrene braced himself for the impending quantum shift. He knew it was an absurd notion, as the ship's inertial dampening systems prevented him or anyone else on the ship from feeling the effects of acceleration. But it was something he had always done, almost instinctively, since childhood. It added to the thrill, he thought. In his mind's eye, he saw the subspace field erupting into reality as the ship stretched, extended and distended into infinity.

"Plus one," the helmsman said. "Continuing to accelerate." Except for the subordinate's reports of the ship's progress, all else was silent on the command deck as engineers and scientists continued checking the telemetry fed to them by the ship's sensors. This was the easy part, in actuality, with the difficult tasks yet to come. First the ship had to accelerate successfully to its uppermost obtainable velocity. Then endurance tests would begin as the crew determined how long the ship could sustain that measure of speed. If those experiments were successful, then the celebrations would begin in earnest, and merely wary adversaries would now have reason to fear the Tholian Assembly.

Nostrene's reverie was broken by the first in what quickly became a series of alarms coming from the observation stations at the front of the command deck.

"Commander," Dlyax said, "we are experiencing a power fall-off."

Moving toward the forward stations, Nostrene replied, "What is causing it?"

The scientist was keying commands into his console and studying the rapidly shifting patterns of light on his suite of monitors. "I cannot ascertain the cause. All systems are functioning normally, but there is an unexplained power drain in the drive system."

For a moment, Nostrene was worried that the ship might be rendered inert in space. "How serious is this drain?"

"It is not severe, Commander, but it is enough to disrupt our subspace field."

Given the choice between slowing to sublight speeds on his own or being ripped from subspace by a malfunctioning propulsion system, Nostrene preferred the first option. "Decelerate to light minus eight." Turning back to Dlyax, he said, "Initiate a diagnostic check of the drive systems."

Another voice called out from behind him, "Commander, our sensors are registering some unusual readings."

Now what? Was the entire ship falling apart?

"What is it?" he asked as he made his way to the sensor officer's station.

The subordinate manning the station did not look up at his commander's approach. "I have detected a disruption in space at bearing four point nine relative to our current position. It wasn't there during my initial scans a few moments ago, Commander."

The report was far too vague for Nostrene's tastes. "Be more specific."

"I cannot, Commander. The sensors are behaving quite erratically. They report it as an object, yet I cannot verify the readings."

If an object had been detected so close to the ship, Nostrene knew that automated defensive systems would have alerted the crew to possible danger. That none of that had happened deepened his concern. Was an enemy who could render themselves invisible to sensors attacking them? Was a Romulan ship out there, attempting a covert strike?

"Is there a flaw in the sensor equipment?" Nostrene asked.

"Not that I have been able to find, Commander," the sensor officer replied. "It is as if this region of space is physically deteriorating."

"A localized phenomenon?" There were no intelligence reports of anything unusual encountered in this area. It was a lightly traveled region, one of the reasons it was selected as the site of the experiment in the first place.

"Put that area on the main screen," he ordered.

All eyes turned as the image on the forward screen changed. At first Nostrene saw no discernible difference from the field of stars that had been there previously. It appeared tranquil, almost the very image he carried in his mind even when he was planetbound to tide him over until he could return to space once again.

"There," the helmsman said, pointing at the screen. "Upper left quadrant."

Nostrene saw it too. Amid the blanket of stars beckoning to them, a dark area had appeared. It was small but opaque, and therefore contrasting sharply against the starfield.

"Magnify that area," Nostrene said, stepping closer to the screen. The image shifted again and now the dark area dominated the center of the screen. It was irregular in shape, its edges fluctuating with no noticeable pattern. Everyone on the command deck watched as the patch of darkness expanded, then contracted to almost disappear entirely before repeating the process all over again.

"It looks like a hole in space," the helmsman said.

Nostrene agreed. In all the years he had traveled space he had never seen anything like what was displayed on the screen.

"I am detecting spiking radiation levels coming from that area, Commander," the sensor officer reported. "They are slight, but there nonetheless."

"Is there a danger to the ship?" Nostrene asked.

The subordinate took an extra moment to confirm his readings before replying. "Negative, Commander, at least so long as we maintain this distance."

"Commander!"

Nostrene's attention snapped back to the screen at the call in time to see the interior of the "hole," as he had come to think of it, shift as a blue-green field of energy appeared.

"Enlarge that," Nostrene ordered, and the image appeared to jump forward. The energy distortion became more detailed and he could see static discharges and rippling effects as the field undulated within the confines of the dark area.

"Are you saying the sensors register none of that?" he asked.

"That is correct, Commander. We see it, but our sensors give no indication that it exists at all."

In front of him, the helmsman nearly came out of his chair as he pointed to the screen. "Commander, look!"

On the viewer, the energy field wavered and expanded violently as, out of the nothingness that was the dark hole amid the stars, an object began to materialize, quickly taking on form and substance. With the image magnified as it was, Nostrene easily made out seams between scarred hull plates and areas where bare metal now shone through what had once been a brightly painted finish.

A ship.

"Sensor readings?"

Behind him, the sensor officer studied his console and shook his head. "I have managed to tune the sensors to at least detect the vessel, but readings are inconclusive at best. There are no signs of life or power sources. I believe the ship to be a derelict, Commander."

Nostrene suspected as much, having already recognized the design of the ship as soon as it had become visible. He hadn't seen such a vessel except in historical documents, but there was no mistaking the large, saucer-shaped hull supported by a pylon above a smaller cylindrical secondary section and the pair of long nacelles resting on their own support pylons. Though the design had been refined and improved over the many years the Tholians had been aware of it, the basic tenets had remained the same.

Behind him, his weapons officer confirmed his suspicion. "Commander, our tactical database identifies it as a Federation *Constitution*-class starship. According to our information, that model of vessel was retired from active service long ago."

"Are there any indications of other ships in this area?" Both the weapons and sensor officers replied with negative reports.

"So what is it doing in our space?" Dlyax asked, staring at the ghostly image of the ship.

Nostrene had no answer. Learning of the ship's presence in Tholian space would certainly put some government officials on edge. Despite the warming of relations with the Federation, distrust and even contempt for its principles continued to simmer within the ranks of the Assembly's elder statesmen.

Seeing the ship on the screen, however, his instincts told him such worries were unfounded. If the ship was indeed a derelict, then it was likely that neither the Federation nor the Assembly had any knowledge of its whereabouts, let alone the circumstances surrounding its appearance here and now, long after such a vessel would have been retired from normal service.

Such judgments, though, were not his to make.

"We must report this discovery," he said finally. "They will know best how to proceed."

CHAPTER
2

As he traversed one of the numerous corridors of Starfleet Headquarters, Captain Montgomery Scott felt as though red-alert klaxons were sounding but only he could hear them. His eyes couldn't help but be drawn to officers mingling or casually going about their business. He returned a few polite nods but didn't stop to talk or even smile back when their glances met his. There was no time for niceties.

It was a key difference between Headquarters and serving on a starship, he had learned. People here could be on full alert, but hardly ever at the same time.

His combadge chirped for his attention, followed by a female voice. "Captain Scott, please report to Briefing Room 23 immediately."

"Aye, lassie," he said as he tapped the badge, "and since we last spoke, where did ya think I might be goin'?"

The question went unanswered. "I'll tell them you're still on your way, sir."

"Scott out." He sighed as he severed the connection. Whatever it was that awaited him in Briefing Room 23 must be important indeed to have his assistant page him twice in as many minutes.

Probably some politician with his nose all out of joint.

Scotty didn't break stride as he turned toward a pair of doors that parted at his approach. As he entered the briefing room, the first person he saw was a man wearing civilian clothes and the puckered expression he normally associated with a typical Federation diplomat.

Ach. Some days it just doesn't pay to get out of bed, he thought as he braced himself for what was sure to be a long day. As he made his way to one of the empty chairs surrounding the conference table, Scotty put on his "admiral's smile." It was the one that allowed him to bite the inside of his cheek when a politician inevitably said something to irritate him.

In addition to the civilian eyeing him impatiently, Scotty noted the unfamiliar Starfleet commander also seated at the table. An Andorian, the commander's rich blue skin contrasted sharply with the dark colors of his uniform. Scotty decided that the commander, like a growing number of officers he ran into these days, looked like he'd just graduated from the Academy.

Does his mother know he's playin' Starfleet?

As quickly as the thought surfaced, Scotty admonished himself. Not everyone could be an eighty-year old captain with fifty or more years in Starfleet, after all.

"Good morning, Captain. Thanks for joining us on such short notice," said the third person in the briefing room and the only one Scotty recognized, Admiral William Ross.

The admiral presented an imposing figure dressed in his dark Starfleet uniform. Jet black hair, cut short and liberally speckled with gray, added to a severe expression dominated by piercing blue eyes. Ross was one of the few flag officers Scotty respected implicitly, due primarily to the fact that the admiral had risen through the ranks while serving in the fleet instead of occupying staff positions. He had commanded vessels and people in peace and in war, and he had earned the trust of those he led.

Ross also knew that most issues faced by commanders in the field rarely if ever resembled the tidy tactical problems presented to cadets at the Academy. It gave him a wisdom shaped by experience that Scotty usually found lacking in other officers in similar positions. It also made Ross in high demand at Starfleet Headquarters, especially during critical situations. If the admiral was here now, then something big had to be brewing.

"Aye, Admiral," Scotty said as he settled into one of the conference chairs. "What have ye got?"

"We have a developing situation that requires not only your department's expertise, but your own as well."

Ross indicated the Andorian and the civilian. "This is Commander Grelin, our liaison with Starfleet Intelligence, and this is Mr. Marshall of the Diplomatic Corps."

Considering the presence of Grelin and Marshall, Scotty hardly believed whatever was happening was going to be a routine matter for the Starfleet Corps of Engineers, the department he had been appointed to oversee by Ross himself.

The assignment had come as part thoughtful gesture and part impassioned plea, with the admiral seeing a singular opportunity to take advantage of Scotty's vast experience and unique perspective. After all, how many other officers could lay claim to having served aboard Starfleet vessels more than a century ago?

After his rescue almost eight years before from the wreck of the *U.S.S. Jenolen*, where he had been suspended in a transporter beam for seventy-five years, Scotty had flirted with self-pity at being removed from his friends and loved ones by nearly a century. It hadn't taken him long, however, to embrace this new era and all the challenges it presented. The offer from Ross had come soon afterward, but Scotty really hadn't needed an invitation to return to Starfleet. In his heart, he had never truly left.

Ross said, "Captain, Starfleet was contacted earlier this morning by representatives of the Tholian Assembly. They reported the presence of what appears to be a derelict Federation starship within their territorial borders. I don't think I need to tell you how upset the Tholians are."

It was an understatement, Scotty knew. The Tholians had always been protective of their region of space, only rarely allowing foreign vessels to cross their boundaries. Relations between the Assembly and the Federation had improved in recent years, but they were still nowhere near what Scotty would call "stable."

"This is of great concern to us," Marshall said, insinuating himself into the conversation in that manner all diplomats seemed to employ and which almost always annoyed Scotty to no end. "Just seeing one of our ships in their space is enough for the Tholians to declare all-out war."

"I don't think the situation is that extreme, Mr. Marshall," Ross countered. "One of the few good things that came out of the Dominion War was better diplomatic relations with the Tholians." He didn't bother to shield the skeptical look on his face as he added, "At least, that's what we keep hearing from the Diplomatic Corps."

"Those relations came at a very high price, Admiral," Marshall said, bristling at Ross's jab. "We intend to cultivate them, not jeopardize the peace every time one of your captains steers a ship where it's not supposed to go."

Ross didn't rise to the baiting. "Sir, Starfleet has not authorized any vessel to enter Tholian space. This incident was a complete surprise to us, just as it should have been. The ship in question hasn't seen active duty since stardate 5685.5."

The date struck Scotty with the intensity of a physical blow. All of the puzzle pieces fell into place as the completed picture became clear to the seasoned engineer.

"The *Defiant*," he said, his voice almost a whisper.

"That's impossible," Grelin blurted, his antennae twitching noticeably in alarm. "The *Defiant* is currently docked at Deep Space 9. They couldn't possibly have traveled to Tholian space in such a—"

"Laddie," Scotty said, cutting the Andorian off, "did they stop teaching history at the Academy altogether, or are ye just too accustomed to hearin' five-digit stardates?" He turned to Ross. "Now I know why I'm here, sir."

Ross couldn't suppress a smile. "Gentlemen, in 2268 the *Constitution*-class *U.S.S. Defiant* was lost with all hands when it traveled into an interspatial rift in an area of space subsequently claimed as a territorial annex of the Tholian Assembly. According to the Tholians, the rift reopened two weeks ago, and the *Defiant* has been scanned drifting in and out of it nine times since its initial reappearance. The average duration of its visibility is three hours and twelve minutes, though the intervals are by no means consistent.

"In more than a century, just one Federation starship has encountered the *Defiant* since her disappearance. That ship had the only opportunity to learn what happened to the ship and her crew." Ross indicated Scotty with a gesture. "We're just lucky enough to have a member of that ship's crew with us today." Steely blue eyes fixed on the engineer.

"Scotty, do you want another crack at her?"

The *Defiant*. It was one of many memorable missions Scotty had been a part of as a crewmember of the original *Enterprise*. It also was one of a handful of mysteries they'd encountered that remained unsolved. Leaving the *Defiant* locked in the spatial rift had never set well with him. The vessel numbered among the original *Constitution*-

class starships, and it was one of two such vessels that Scotty had seen lost or destroyed during his tenure aboard the *Enterprise*.

Three, counting the ol' girl herself, Scotty reminded himself.

Constitution-class ships held a special place in his heart, as such a vessel was where Scotty had served his first tour as chief engineer. The fleet museum contained a *Constitution*, and he'd traveled there many times in recent years. He enjoyed walking the decks or inspecting the bridge and, on rare occasions, treating himself to the warm familiarity of her engine room. Her powerful warp engines may have been silenced long ago, but Scotty could close his eyes and almost hear their comforting throb of power.

Hoping his voice wouldn't break, he said. "Aye, that I do, sir."

"Admiral," Commander Grelin said as he leaned forward in his chair, "what's to say this isn't some kind of ploy to lure us into a trap?"

By way of reply, Ross thumbed a keypad on the tabletop that activated the briefing room's main viewscreen. It promptly displayed an image of the century-old starship, glowing a fluorescent blue seemingly from within and winking in and out of sync with the universe.

"This was relayed to us from one of our Epsilon deep space reconnaissance stations that was re-tasked to monitor the region," Ross said. "We've no reason to believe what we're seeing isn't authentic."

Scotty remembered that day, ages ago, when he had first laid eyes on the missing ship. "Admiral, that's just what she looked like from the bridge of the *Enterprise*."

"This invitation to reclaim the *Defiant* doesn't come lightly," Ross said. "The Tholians aren't excited about a Federation ship working in their space, but they want this situation resolved before word of the rift and the ship spreads to every sight-seer and salvager in the quadrant. They're grateful enough for our assistance during the Dominion War that they're allowing us an escorted attempt to get the *Defiant* back. We're going to take it."

Marshall nodded. "We're looking forward to working with the Tholians in such an atmosphere of cooperation. It is an unprecedented endeavor and could do much to improve our relations with the Assembly. But know this, gentlemen: I believe the progress we've made with the Tholians is far more important than the recovery of some relic that's remembered only by history buffs."

Diplomats, Scotty huffed to himself. "Mr. Marshall, I dinna know about all the political ram-ifications, but surely ye'd agree that it's important to bring the ship's crew home for the final respects they deserve."

Marshall was unmoved. "I don't think it's important enough to risk war."

Scotty could sense himself falling victim to what he dubbed the "Robert Fox Syndrome." It was a term coined by his longtime friend Leonard McCoy and used to describe a longing desire to launch an insufferable politician from a photon torpedo tube. Whereas Scotty might have been tempted to indulge that inclination in his younger days, age and wisdom instead told him he would be better off if he simply returned his attention to Ross.

"Admiral, I'd like to head out there and help with recovery. No one alive knows the ins and outs of a *Constitution*-class ship better than I do."

"If time wasn't an issue, I'd agree," Ross replied. "But the Tholians aren't a patient people, and they're already complaining that we're taking too long. Given the difficulties we're likely to encounter during the mission, both technical and political, it's vital that whomever we send to lead this mission be an innovative thinker as well as a level-headed diplomat. There are two ships with S.C.E. detachments in range of the *Defiant*: the *Musgrave* and the *da Vinci*. Your opinion?"

"I'd send the *da Vinci*, sir," Scotty said. "Captain Gold has the temperament to handle the Tholians, and if anybody can get the *Defiant* out of that mess, it's Commander Gomez and her team."

Ross stood, signaling an end to the meeting. "Very well. Proceed as you think best, Captain, and keep us informed."

Walking toward the door, Marshall halted abruptly and turned on his heel to face Scotty. "Remember, Captain, that preserving the peace between the Federation and the Tholians is more important than a single starship, whether it's the *Defiant* or the *da Vinci*."

Not replying to the diplomat, Scotty instead looked to Ross. The expression on the admiral's face confirmed to the engineer that he, reluctantly, agreed.

CHAPTER
3

As he absently swirled his drink, watching a wedge of lime chase stray ice cubes, Kieran Duffy's mind drifted for what he believed would be the last few minutes he might grab for himself until their return to Federation space.

Not that the mess hall of the *U.S.S. da Vinci* was the most intimate of hideaways. Crewmembers popped in and out for a cup of coffee or a bite to eat as if the place were each person's home kitchen. Everyone stopping in took a second to be friendly or at least acknowledge his presence, Duffy noticed. The *da Vinci* carried a lot of camaraderie even for a Starfleet vessel, but Duffy didn't find that surprising. After all, there were only forty-two people onboard, and most of them numbered among Starfleet's top engineers.

And there goes one of them now, Duffy thought as he caught sight of the one person for whom he wouldn't mind breaking from his reverie. Sonya Gomez's form flashed past the mess hall door, then reappeared as she back-stepped into the doorway. Her eyes narrowed, then her smile widened a bit.

"I thought that was you," she said as she walked toward his table. "I wondered why I hadn't seen you around."

Duffy shrugged. "Not much for me to do yet, really. Got a minute to sit?"

"I'll take a minute," Gomez replied. "I'm getting a drink. Need a refill?"

"Thanks," he answered. "It's quinine water, not so—"

"Not soda water," she finished for him. "Over ice and with a lime twist. Same vile stuff you have every time you sneak away to think."

Gomez returned from the replicator moments later with a clinking glass in one hand and a steaming mug in the other. She set Duffy's fresh drink before him as she took the seat across the table, raising her mug in a quick cheer before sipping from it.

"We all have our vices," Duffy said, smiling at the smell of Earl Grey tea coming from the mug. "So, are you ready to, what were the captain's words again? 'Step aboard history'?"

Gomez snickered, but only good-naturedly. Captain David Gold was an even-tempered man who rarely allowed his emotions free rein. But the news that the *da Vinci* crew had been assigned to recover the *Defiant* had sent the captain into a near fit of excitement. History, mystery, and legend all converged on the area of space the *da Vinci* was rapidly approaching, and Gold had made no apologies for wanting to be the first one there.

"He hasn't been this keyed up for a mission in a long time, has he?" Gomez asked. "He's acting like an ensign on his first assignment. But to answer your question, we're ready. The captain's been at my side almost every minute since the initial briefing." She grinned mischievously. "I did manage to shake him, though."

"And your lucky successor was?"

"Why, Carol, of course. She's got her hands full dealing with our Tholian escorts, but I don't think it's helping with the captain talking into one ear while she listens to the Tholians with the other."

As the team's intercultural relations specialist, it fell to Carol Abramowitz to guide them through the delicate dealings with the Tholian vessel that had greeted them at the Federation border to escort them through Tholian space. Things had been touchy at first, with Captain Gold exercising more care and diplomacy than was normal even for him. Given the Tholians' penchant for requiring utmost precision and adherence to protocol, however, it made sense to enlist Abramowitz's expertise and greater grasp of Tholian idiosyncrasies.

"Oh, and I imagine they're a chatty bunch, those guys," Duffy said. "Maybe I could tell them the one about the Tholian, the Leyron dabo girl, and the tuning fork?" Noting the lack of amusement in Gomez's expression, Duffy grinned and took a sip of his drink. "Uh, maybe not."

"Not retreating into humor now, are we?" she asked.

"Meaning?"

Gomez stared at him until he met her gaze.

"Meaning are you avoiding thoughts of what we're supposed to do here?"

"Sonnie, I'm begging you," Duffy deadpanned as he grasped her free hand, "don't take the mission. How will I ever explain to the kids why Mommy never comes home for dinner anymore? You and your daredevil plans. You don't see the looks I get from the other guys at the tongo club every week." He gave her a grin.

"Ha ha," Gomez said as she took back her hand. "Pardon me for trying to connect with you."

"Okay, no more wise guy," Duffy said. "What would you have me say? Of course I've run through all the scenarios in my head and yes, I'm nervous for you . . . for every one of you who are beaming over to the *Defiant* during interphase. But whatever works out . . . here, well, I think we've both been around long enough to know the risks and costs to our personal lives."

The admission, uncertain yet heartfelt as it was, caught Gomez completely off guard. How long had it been since she and Duffy had talked, really talked, like this?

Her giggle came from nowhere, and Gomez found herself abruptly covering her mouth, struggling to keep her composure from dissolving completely. It was too late, though, as she saw Duffy's expression fall.

"Kieran, you're sweet," she said, choosing her words carefully. "But that wasn't what I meant at all."

Duffy straightened in his chair, the brush-off stinging him almost as much as it used to back on the *Enterprise*. Determined to save the moment, he quickly fumbled for a witty retort.

"Oh, well, this has got to be the first time in my life I've misunderstood a woman's intentions." Was it enough of a cover?

He should have known better.

"It seems we have a new issue on the table." Gomez drew a breath only to giggle again, but quickly rallied to maintain her bearing. "I can't say I haven't missed this kind of talk with you, but we really don't have time to get into this right now. Can we put it in stasis for the time being?"

"Consider it frozen," he said, almost too quickly.

For now, he added to himself.

The pause in their conversation threatened to become too long, but then Gomez pressed forward.

"What I wanted to know was how you're planning for your end of the mission."

Duffy shrugged again and sipped from his glass, hoping to avoid looking Gomez directly in the eye. He felt certain that, had she looked hard enough, she would see through to the doubt he hid within him.

He hoped to sound nonchalant. "Seems pretty cut and—"

A tone from the *da Vinci*'s communications system interrupted him, followed by Captain Gold's voice.

"All senior officers and mission specialists to the briefing room. We're approaching the rendezvous point."

"You were saying?" Gomez asked as they both rose from the table and headed out of the mess hall.

"Oh. It seems pretty cut and dried," he finished as they proceeded down the corridor. "You guys have the hard part in prepping the *Defiant*. I'm just minding the store."

"But that's just it, Kieran." Gomez dropped her voice, a tone Duffy knew she used when she wanted his full attention. He obliged, pausing in his step.

"It's not standard procedure for the captain and me to be off the ship at the same time. We both know that the *da Vinci's* center seat is not where you want to be."

For the second time in their conversation, Duffy hoped that his wince was more internal than external. During his time on the *da Vinci*, Duffy had worked his way up the chain of command, earning the confidence of Captain Gold to the point of his being recognized as third in line to the big chair. But that line had never stretched so far as to put him in command during an actual S.C.E. mission. Duffy had taken the conn on a few occasions, his previous one lasting less than an hour as Captain Gold accompanied Sonya to a debriefing on Starbase 42. When he was in charge, Duffy himself had joked, the *da Vinci* might as well be on autopilot.

I've never even recorded a captain's log entry.

Duffy shifted on his feet as Gomez's words hung in the air. Everyone on the *da Vinci* saw Duffy as a lighthearted but skilled officer, one who led more by example than authority. It was an image he had worked hard to project. He never wanted to be one of those engineers who thought he knew a ship better than its captain did. He didn't sit at his station on the bridge, secretly hoping for a catastrophe or crisis that might place him in the center seat.

Was his attitude merely avoidance? Or was it fear?

Even he didn't want to plumb for the answers to those questions, at least not now, lest he wonder whether Captain Gold's confidence in his abilities was warranted.

"You know that I'm in this whole thing for the puzzle, Sonnie. I like cracking the nut, coming up with answers in the nick of time, and doing what I'm told." He paused to swallow, maybe a bit too hard. "Captain Gold told me that I'm sitting in command on this end, so that's what I'm going to do. I'll be fine."

"You don't have to say that for my benefit, Kieran. I know you will." Gomez reached out to give his hand a squeeze. "I just want to be sure *you* know you will."

"The big red button on the chair fires the phasers, right?" He smiled at her generous laugh, which put him more at ease. "Thanks, boss."

Gomez dropped his hand and walked toward the briefing room's door, turning her head just enough so Duffy could hear her whisper.

"You know, I'm liking the sound of that 'boss' stuff more and more."

He followed her into the room and saw that,

save one other, the meeting was waiting on them. Then he felt a small shove against his calf.

"Excuse please, many pardons," P8 Blue said as she pushed her hard-skinned form almost between his legs. Skittering in on all eight limbs as she was wont to do when hurried, the Nasat then shot up to her hind legs and walked to her specially designed seat at the table's end opposite Captain Gold.

"You may begin now," she said to Gold, who smirked at Duffy and gestured him to the remaining seat with a nod of his head.

Once everyone was settled, the captain said, "Thank you all for your efforts these past hours, and for indulging my hands-on curiosity. I'm sure it's obvious to you that I've more than a passing interest in our rescue of the *Defiant*. Commander Gomez, let me reiterate that this is your mission. You have the final say as to whether I beam over with you or stay here and direct things on this end."

Duffy almost laughed aloud at the thought of Sonya actually telling the captain he should sit this one out.

"Sir," Gomez began, "I'm counting on your knowledge of that class of starship to help once we get there. You're hardly just a sightseer, and I'm going to put you to work."

"In other words, no putzing around," Gold said, laughing.

With a final gesture to Gomez, Gold said, "Lead us through the final check, if you would, Commander."

Gomez turned to glance up and down the table as she spoke. "Well, we've already covered the historical and political aspects of this mission with Captain Scott. Now it's time to get down to the nitty-gritty." She looked over at P8 Blue. "Pattie, why don't you bring us up to speed on what we're facing."

Consulting her padd, the Nasat said, "Everything we have gathered through long-range scans corroborates the data provided by the Tholians. The *Defiant*, for all intents and purposes, exists simultaneously within our universe and another. The ship is drifting in a rift between the two. As it moves in and out of this rift, it appears to lose molecular cohesion. Consoles, deck plates, everything on the ship gives up its physical qualities in one universe to regain them in the other. We will have to exercise extreme caution while moving around over there. I cannot be more precise, as this is as much as I have been able to determine from the data available to us. Many pardons."

"That's fine for now, Pattie." Gomez turned her gaze to the ship's chief medical officer. "Dr. Lense, just what is this going to do to us physically?"

Elizabeth Lense leaned forward in her chair. "I've reviewed the medical logs from the *Enterprise* and determined that we have two issues to deal with. First, those of us on the *Defiant* will get the full experience of interphase, which is sure to bring on nausea and dizziness, muscle weakness and slowed response times to all outside stimuli."

Duffy couldn't help himself. "Sounds like what happened to me after breakfast."

Ignoring Duffy, Lense did not even give him the satisfaction of an irritated look. "Based on what I learned from the *Enterprise* logs, the humanoids among us on both ships have an added concern. Our proximity to the area of interphase puts us at risk for irregular, paranoid and ultimately psychotic behavior, something we might as well call space madness." Lense glanced at Duffy, as if she expected him to chime in again. He held his tongue as she rose from the table.

"Dr. McCoy believed it was this condition that killed the *Defiant's* crew, but he was able to develop a counteragent to the interphase's effects on his ship, one that my team has already begun to administer to our crew." She held up a hypospray. "I can give all of you your first inoculations now, if that's not an interruption, Commander."

With Gomez nodding assent, Lense rose from her chair and walked first to Duffy and placed the hypospray to his neck.

He leaned to one side and asked, "So what's in this stuff, Doc?"

Lense grinned slightly, thumbing the hypo before answering Duffy's hanging question. Through the hiss of the spray, she said simply, "Theragen."

Duffy's eyes widened in shock and he slapped his hand to his neck, nearly toppling his chair over in his haste to scramble to his feet.

"What? That stuff's pure poison!" Basic Starfleet combat history was rife with accounts of 23rd Century Klingon biochemical warfare and their use of theragen as a nerve gas, one quickly and painfully deadly to humans. Not an honorable way to fight a foe, Duffy believed, but times were different then.

Gold laughed aloud, as did Gomez and the others in the room. "Mr. Duffy, Dr. Lense has assured me that it's merely a derivative. It's perfectly safe and may even carry a slight intoxicating effect."

"That's correct," Lense added. Her right eyebrow rose in an almost Vulcan fashion as she added, "Dr. McCoy also saw fit to include a recipe for mixing the counteragent with Scotch, based apparently on field testing by the ship's engineer, whom we all know, of course." The doctor's deadpan delivery evoked another chorus of laughs from the group.

"Well, if it's good enough for Captain Scott," Duffy said, "far be it from me to say no to a nip of the hard stuff, Doc." He tried to laugh it off but his adrenaline needed another moment to simmer.

As Lense made her way around the others, she paused at P8 Blue's seat. "Pattie, I want to monitor the interphase's effects on you before your inoculation. I don't think the theragen is necessary."

"I will report any irregularities at once, Doctor."

Satisfied with Lense's report, Gomez turned her attention back to the group. "So those of us headed to the *Defiant* are ready. The plan is for Soloman and me to install a series of portable generators to the *Defiant*'s systems, as she's sure to be completely drained of power. It won't restore full functionality, but we should be able to activate the maneuvering thrusters and gain limited control of some shipboard systems. Pattie will verify the ship's systems to make sure they can handle the power and prepare ship's thrusters to help coax us out of the rift, assuming they will still work.

"Dr. Lense, your job is to keep an eye on us and gather what data you can on the physiological effects of the interphase phenomenon." The physician confirmed the instructions with a single nod.

"Captain, I need you to get whatever information you can from the *Defiant*'s logs and pass anything to me that might help us."

"That's hardly an order, Commander," said Gold and smiled. "You have no idea how much I want to hear the answers to our questions about the *Defiant* in the words of Captain Blair himself."

She then turned to Duffy. "Commander, what have you got for me?"

He almost stammered, knowing she playfully chose those words to catch him off guard before the whole team. It went a long way toward calming the fresh wave of butterflies that had formed in his gut.

"I wish I could say we're going to be as busy as your team. We've modified the *da Vinci*'s tractor beam to work in conjunction with a molecular stabilizing beam emitted from our navigational deflector. The specs come from Starfleet, and all of our computer models match what we were told to expect from them. Captain Scott worked on the calculations himself, and he hasn't let us down before. We're good to go, Commander."

Gomez smiled just enough for him to take it personally, then turned to the ship's cultural liaison. "Carol, what's your take on the Tholians at this point?"

Carol Abramowitz shrugged her shoulders just a bit as she drew in a breath. "This is my first time dealing with a Tholian who wasn't a training hologram. My contact on the Tholian ship is curt bordering on rude, guarded with information beyond any specific requests, and quite snippy when I don't report regularly and precisely according to his timetable." She shrugged. "In other words, business as usual."

Gomez stifled a snicker. "We all appreciate your extreme patience here, Carol. Your role in keeping the Tholians calm and informed on our actions is as important as anything any of us will be doing. I might sug—"

A tone from the comm system silenced Gomez and Lieutenant Commander Domenica Corsi's voice followed it from the speakers.

"Captain Gold? This is ahead of schedule, but we're in visual range of the rendezvous point."

Gold answered, "We're on our way." Duffy turned to catch the captain's eyes widening and a hint of a grin creeping across his mouth.

Duffy was one of the first to step onto the bridge, only to stop in his tracks and fixate on the *da Vinci*'s main viewer. A pair of hands on his shoulders guided him to one side and without looking he could tell the touch was Sonya's. At any other time he might have reacted or commented on her touch, but his attention was riveted to the viewscreen and the captivating image cast upon it.

The area of torn space itself was unremarkable,

unless one stopped to notice that no stars shone there. What seized Duffy was the shimmering lines and apparition-like form of the starship drifting within the rift, hanging askew in relation to the *da Vinci*, with the top of its primary hull flat enough to clearly read the dead ship's name and registry number: *U.S.S. Defiant*, NCC-1764.

The low number bespoke the antiquated status the vessel held, Duffy knew. Here was a vision straight out of history, a physical manifestation of the challenges and adventures that had more than likely inspired every member of the *da Vinci*'s crew to enter Starfleet and see what mysteries the universe held for themselves.

The electric-blue glow infusing the century-old starship bathed the *da Vinci*'s bridge and the dozen or so people gathered there. As they watched, the *Defiant* continued to fade and solidify, winking in and out of existence.

As far as this universe is concerned, thought Duffy, *the* Defiant *is both real and unreal.*

"Sensor scans are inconclusive," Corsi said as she vacated the command chair, "but readings indicate she hasn't been there too long. We can't confirm any power sources or atmosphere." She directed a wry smile toward Gomez. "I'd watch my step if I were you, Commander."

"Away team, to the transporter room," Gold said. "It's time to go to work. Mr. Duffy, you have the conn. Take care of my ship."

The order from Captain Gold raised a chill on Duffy's skin, but one fueled by responsibility, not alarm. His attention turned to Gomez as she and the others moved toward the turbolift. His eyes found hers as she smiled just a bit and held his gaze.

Just for her, Duffy puffed out his chest and winked.

As the doors closed, Duffy blew out a long breath. For better or worse, the bridge was his.

CHAPTER
4

As the transporter beam released her, Sonya Gomez experienced a momentary feeling of weightlessness before the magnetic locks of her boots pulled her back to the deck.

"No gravity," she said, confirming her suspicions that many of the *Defiant*'s systems would be off-line or without power. That was to be expected, of course. Not even considering that the ship had been out here for over a century, log reports from the *Enterprise* had described the draining effects of the rift on their own power systems. It made sense that after so many years, the unprotected *Defiant* would have ultimately succumbed to the influence of spatial interphase.

The only illumination in the engineering section was that provided by the helmets of the five away-team members' environment suits. As powerful as they were, the lamps didn't do enough to drive away the enveloping darkness of the large chamber for Gomez's taste. Dust and dirt floated all around them, free from the restraint of gravity. It gave the room a murky feel that Gomez likened to disturbed silt on an ocean floor.

"What was that?" Gold called out, detecting movement from the corner of his eye and jerking around in response. As his helmet lamp shone on the source of the movement, he felt bile rise in his throat.

Drifting unencumbered in the open space of the cavernous chamber was a skeleton, what Gold presumed to be the remains of a *Defiant* engineer. It still wore the black pants and red shirt common to engineering and security personnel on Federation starships in the 2260's, though the boots that completed the uniform had fallen away from the skeleton's feet. No doubt they were still floating elsewhere about the room.

"Oh my God," the captain whispered.

"Captain, there's something else," Lense added, her tricorder beeping in her hand. "The majority of what we see floating around us isn't dirt or dust. It's what's left of the decomposed bodies of the people who died in this compartment. I'm picking up similar readings throughout the ship."

Gomez shuddered at the thought of maneuvering through the interior of this dead ship, the remains of its crew floating all about her, stepping through it and having it settle on her suit as she walked. She had prepared herself to deal with looking at the bodies of dead crewmen during the mission, even decomposed ones. This unanticipated twist, however, made an already tense and depressing situation even more morose.

Perhaps sensing the pall that had been cast over

the room by their discovery, Gold said, "If we weren't sure why we came here, then we should be now." He indicated the drifting skeleton. "If nothing else, our job is to make sure that these men and women finally get to go home."

"Only trace amounts of oxygen in the atmosphere," Gomez said as she consulted her tricorder. "We won't be able to work without our suits if we can't restore life support."

Gold nodded. "The ship's been out here a long time, so there's no telling what long-term effects the rift had on her. Plus, we don't know what she's been exposed to on the other side of the rift."

"Perhaps the ship's computer . . . recorded data received by automatic sensors before power . . . was lost," Soloman said. Formerly known as 110, the Bynar had changed his name after finally coming to terms with the tragic loss of his mate, 111, during an earlier mission.

110 had wrestled with the question of whether or not to return to his home planet and seek out another mate, but had finally decided against it. No other would ever be able to replace the one with whom he had shared so much. So rather than do something that would, in his eyes at least, diminish the memory of his life's love, 110 elected to remain with the *da Vinci*. But a Bynar without a mate was not a normal occurrence and by remaining unbonded, the use of his designation would not have been proper. 110 therefore decided that a new mode of address was needed. Captain Gold had inadvertently provided that by referring to the Bynar's unique status as a "solo man."

"We'll have time to examine the computer records later," Gomez said. "But first we have to get some power back into this old girl." She activated her suit's communicator. "Gomez to *da Vinci*."

"*Da Vinci*. Duffy here."

"Kieran, everything's clear here. Send over our equipment."

"Aye, aye, Commander. Stand by."

A few seconds passed before transporter energy flared into existence and a group of cargo containers materialized. Equipped with magnetic locks, each crate remained on the deck instead of floating freely. In addition to the collection of tools and instruments she had insisted on for the mission, Gomez's expression brightened at the sight of the five portable generators.

"How did you manage the fifth one?" she asked Duffy. She could almost hear the smile coming over the comm circuit as he replied.

"Hey, an engineer isn't supposed to reveal all of his secrets. At least, that's what Captain Scott always says."

When Duffy had asked about her equipment needs for the away team, Gomez had decided that four of the generators would probably be sufficient for their plans, but five would be better. It had been necessary to outfit each of the devices with special shielding to protect them from the detrimental effects of the rift, a time-consuming procedure. That Duffy had expended the extra effort to prepare a fifth generator, especially with the limited amount of time he'd had to complete his original tasks, pleased Gomez to no end. She was thankful to have the added cushion, just in case.

"Well, thanks just the same. Dinner's on me when we get back. Gomez out."

As she severed the connection, Gomez noticed P8 Blue studying her tricorder, a frown creasing her face.

"Pattie, is something wrong?"

Looking up, the Nasat replied, "I have detected an anomalous reading. It appears to be a shielded power source. The indication is very faint, but it is there."

"Where is it?" Gomez asked.

"Deck 20, portside cargo hold."

Frowning, Gold said, "Odd place for a power reading on an otherwise dead ship. Why didn't we detect it from the *da Vinci*?"

Gomez turned so that her helmet lamps cast illumination past the heavy mesh grating separating the main engineering deck from the ship's massive impulse engines. She found it an odd sensation to stand in the heart of a starship and not hear the comforting hum and feel the pulse of the vessel's engines. The silence only seemed to strengthen the aura of death surrounding her.

"The rift might be acting as a kind of dampening field," she said. "The *Enterprise* logs detail how they were unable to get worthwhile sensor readings, also." She turned to Pattie. "You didn't find other power sources anywhere on the ship?"

The Nasat shook her head. "I am sorry, no. The warp core is completely inert and will require a cold restart to bring it back on line."

"No, thank you," Gomez countered. "After a hundred years, I'm not doing anything with those engines until they've been thoroughly checked out, preferably by a starbase dry-dock crew. Our first order of business is restoring partial power, enough to maneuver us out of the rift. We'll also try to get enough power to the main computer and access the databanks containing log entries."

"The best place to accomplish that is the science officer's library computer station on the main bridge," Gold said. "I can have Mr. Duffy transmit the *Defiant*'s prefix code from the Starfleet tactical database and give me direct access to the whole shmeer."

Gomez wasn't sure who had come up with the idea behind the prefix code, which allowed a ship commander to assume remote control of another starship by establishing a link between the vessels' computers. It had proven to be a tactical advantage on certain isolated occasions, she knew, but she was convinced it provided a much greater use for engineers, especially those sent into an abandoned or derelict ship such as the *Defiant* had unfortunately become. Once the code gave Captain Gold access to the ship's main computer, he would be able to retrieve anything contained within its vast memory banks, including secured sections containing Captain Blair's personal log.

"But you'll have to get there the hard way, sir," Gomez told Gold. "I won't be able to spare enough power to access the turbolift control network." She looked around the immense engineering chamber. "They built these old *Constitutions* tough enough, but their original duotronic systems were never intended for exclusive automation."

"Dr. Richard Daystrom did attempt to . . . rectify that shortcoming," Soloman said, "but his multitronic computer project was . . . a failure."

"That's certainly an understatement," Gold replied. He remembered reading how Daystrom's lauded attempt to follow up his revolutionary duotronic computer systems had ended in fiery tragedy. During an experiment in which the original *Enterprise* had been outfitted with Daystrom's prototype multitronic system, the M-5, the new computer had experienced massive malfunction. After locking the *Enterprise* crew out of the ship's critical systems, M-5 took the vessel on a murderous rampage. It had ended with the near destruction of four other *Constitution*-class starships and the deaths of nearly a thousand Starfleet personnel.

"Well, we're not out to automate the *Defiant*," Gomez said. "We just want to be able to generate enough thrust to help the *da Vinci* pull us out of the rift, if necessary. Besides, I don't like the idea of not being able to move under our own power if the need arises."

She turned back to P8 Blue. "Pattie, I want you to check out that power reading on Deck 20. Take Dr. Lense with you."

Lense looked up at that. "Commander, I was hoping to investigate sickbay and see if the ship's doctor recorded any useful information about the physiological effects of interphase on the crew."

Shaking her head, Gomez replied, "I haven't forgotten about you, Doctor, but I'd rather not have Pattie roaming the ship alone until you're certain the rift won't have any adverse effects on her. Besides, anything the *Defiant*'s doctor recorded will be accessible from the bridge."

Having stepped away from the team to consult his tricorder, which Duffy had prepared by downloading the technical schematics of the *Defiant* into it, Gold looked up and asked, "All the way from engineering to the bridge by way of the Jefferies tubes?" The smile he directed to Lense was good-natured enough, though. "Oy, I guess I should have seen that one coming. Well, at any rate, the good doctor here will be thrilled to see me get my week's exercise quotient during this mission."

The access panel opened with minimal effort on his part, swinging away to be swallowed by the darkness beyond the hole it revealed. David Gold directed the illumination from his helmet lamps through the opening, becoming the first person in over a century to gaze on the abandoned bridge of the *U.S.S. Defiant*.

He'd toured the *Constitution*-class starship that was interred at the Fleet Museum several times, of course. With its display placards and directional signs to guide visitors, however, the vessel on exhibit had seemed to be exactly that; an elegant mock-up rather than a functional ship of the line. This was different, much different.

The consoles, the turbolift doors, the railing

surrounding the command well, everything was infused with bright colors that were only slightly diminished by the layer of dust covering everything. It was a striking contrast to the bridge of the *da Vinci* and other ships on which he had served. By current Federation standards, the *Defiant*'s systems were hopelessly outdated, but Gold could see in the archaic equipment how the various systems had evolved over the century separating this ship from her modern-day descendants. He could almost feel the history of the era from which this vessel hailed wash over him.

"Gold to Gomez," he said as he activated his communicator. "I've made it to the bridge. What's the status on power?"

"Almost there, Captain," Gomez said over the connection. "Soloman should have the main computer on line a few minutes after that."

"Excellent," the captain said as he stepped from the access crawlway onto the starboard side of the upper deck next to the main viewscreen. His boots made a satisfying clank as their magnetic seals attached him to the deck.

As with engineering, thick dust hung in the air. At least, that's how Gold preferred to think of it. The bridge appeared deserted, but he knew better. He'd read the reports filed by Captain Kirk on their investigation of the *Defiant* and so was prepared when his light fell on the two skeletal bodies floating near the bridge's far bulkhead.

Gold figured the skeleton swathed in the gold shirt was the decomposed body of the ship's commander, Captain Blair, the golden braids on the sleeves of the dust-coated, century-old uniform shirt providing the only hint. The other skeleton wore a red shirt, with no other clues to its wearer's identity.

Gold idly wondered where the rest of the bridge crew might have gone. Did they abandon their posts while in the grips of the madness brought on by the interphase phenomenon? Were they lying somewhere, their fallen bodies bearing silent witness to the carnage that had eventually overtaken the rest of the crew? Gold was surprised to feel himself shiver at the thought.

And then he nearly had a heart attack when the lights came on.

"Gottenyu!" The exclamation burst from his lips as the overhead lighting snapped on and consoles all across the room began their various start-up sequences. True to her word, Gomez had restored power to the bridge. Life flowed through the *Defiant's* nerve center once more.

"Gomez to Captain Gold," the engineer's voice sounded in his helmet. "You should have power restored up there."

Gold sighed as he chuckled to himself. "Thank you, Commander. Now I just need a moment to get my own power source restarted."

"In a few more minutes I'll have life support restored to that deck, Captain," Gomez said. "It'll make working up there easier and allow us to conserve the oxygen supplies in our suits."

Taking another look at the bodies of Captain Blair and the unknown crewman hovering in the absence of gravity, Gold's expression sobered, though there was no one around to see it. The restoration of the *Defiant*'s normal atmosphere was sure to have a debilitating effect on any decomposed remains exposed to it.

"Stand fast on that for the moment, Commander, and send Soloman up to the bridge at his earliest opportunity. We have one task to complete before we get started."

The mission, Gold decided, could wait. Captain Blair and his crew deserved at least that much.

CHAPTER
5

Deep in the bowels of the *Defiant*, Dr. Lense and P8 Blue succeeded in forcing open the reinforced double hatch. Unlike most of the other doors they had encountered on their journey from the ship's engineering section, this one had proven more difficult to get past. That wasn't surprising, considering its double thickness and magnetic seal designed to hold even in the event of a ship-wide power loss.

It was also heavy.

"That's some door," Lense said, accentuating the fact.

"It has to be," Pattie replied as she retrieved the manual opener from the surface of the door. "In the event of an explosive decompression in the cargo bay, this door is the only thing separating the rest of the ship from vacuum. This class of ship was in service long before automatic safety forcefields became common. They are strong, but not too strong for us." She hefted the door opener one last time before returning it to its carrying pouch on her belt. Normally used in emergency situations, the device was also one of the many helpful implements employed by engineers on starships to carry out their normal range of duties. It was a standard component of every S.C.E. team member's tool kit.

"Lense to away team," the doctor said into her communicator. "We have arrived at the cargo bay."

"Understood," Gomez replied. "Be careful in there. There's nothing that says a hatch or two can't fail unexpectedly if the ship is tossed around by the rift."

Lense directed a questioning look at Pattie, who shrugged in reply. "It has been known to occur on derelict vessels."

"Wonderful," the doctor sighed. "Let's just get this over with."

As with the rest of the ship that they had traversed so far, this area of the *Defiant* was devoid of any appreciable atmosphere and was wrapped in darkness. Getting here from engineering hadn't been the most pleasant of journeys, either, as they had been forced to walk past more skeletal remains of crewmembers drifting in the zero gravity as well as the particles and residue saturating the air. Though Lense was a physician and used to seeing bodies in all manner of decomposition, she would be more than happy to return to the *da Vinci* and its quite living crew.

The pair swept the immense chamber with their helmet lamps, chasing the black away as the illumination shone across the bizarre sight of cargo containers drifting freely about the chamber. Dust littered the air as well, further hampering their vision, and in some instances the grime covered shipping labels and other markings on various containers.

Pattie's eyes widened as one reading on her tricorder changed. "I have located the anomalous power source." She pointed off into the depths of the cargo bay. "That way."

With Lense following, Pattie stepped cautiously into the hold, her attention riveted on the information being relayed by her tricorder as the pair continued past containers and other equipment. While some of it was still strapped to the deck or fastened to storage shelves, the majority of the room's contents floated about the room free of any restraint.

Inspecting the label on one container, Lense shook her head. "This one is full of replacement components for computer workstations." She pointed to another. "That one has parts for engineering control systems. This stuff could fill a museum exhibit."

"Perhaps it will, one day," Pattie said as she continued to consult her tricorder. "Starfleet may see fit to honor the *Defiant*'s crew by interring the ship in the Fleet Museum as part of a memorial. Such an action would seem appropriate." She turned a corner and headed toward the bay's far bulkhead. Moving in and around more drifting containers and components, the insect-like engineering specialist abruptly stopped.

"This is it," she said simply. It was an understatement.

Unlike the drab gray square and rectangular containers dominating the rest of the cargo hold, the object Pattie and Lense now beheld was octagonal in shape and painted in a dark black that shone through the thick dust covering it. Pattie guessed that the object was half again as long as a Starfleet standard quantum torpedo tube while being nearly twice as wide. Secured to the deck with restraining bands, the item sat atop a suite of six stocky legs. Bending down near one end of the squat device, Pattie waved her tricorder over one of the legs.

"Soil residue," she said as she examined the unit's readings. "Whatever it is, it was intended for use on the surface of a planet or moon."

Lense wiped dust from the surface of the object, looking for some clue to its origin or purpose. "There doesn't seem to be any external markings. Do you have any idea what it might be?"

"Components of this device look similar to technology possessed by the Tholians," Pattie said. "Or at least the configurations carry basic Tholian tenets of design." She pointed to one of the object's eight side panels. "These appear to be energy emitters of some kind." She shook her head. "It is remarkable that its power cell is still functioning after all this time, and despite the debilitating effects of the rift. We may be able to learn something useful about the protective aspects of its internal shielding."

Lense frowned as she studied the squat device. "No means of propulsion, nothing that appears to be a weapon. What could it be?"

For that, Pattie had no answer. Lense mentally

filed their exchange among her reminders as to why she preferred medical science to engineering: At least her patients could assist in their own diagnoses.

Sitting at the engineering station on the bridge of the *Defiant*, Sonya Gomez couldn't deny the feeling that she'd stepped backward into history.

As she ran her hands along the glossy black console and let her fingers trace over the rows of multicolored buttons, she realized how Captain Gold had been enamored with the idea of boarding this vessel. The sensation had begun to assert itself earlier, down in the engineering section, but it was nothing compared to what she had felt when she set foot on the bridge.

Her trained eyes had inspected every station, every control, and come away impressed. The design of the *Defiant*'s nerve center, like many of the systems she'd seen so far on the ship, were ones that held up surprisingly well despite the gap in technology they represented. She had been very satisfied with what she had found in engineering.

"So you're saying she'll hold together?" Gold asked, a childlike grin dominating his features.

Gomez nodded. "Most definitely, sir. The maneuvering thrusters are operating well within acceptable parameters, even though they've been out of commission for a century. It'll be more than enough to help the *da Vinci* pull us out if necessary. They certainly knew how to build these old ships."

In addition to restoring power to the thrusters, Gomez had also returned power and life support to the bridge, allowing the away team to remove their environment-suit helmets. Of course, Gold had let her activate the automatic air scrubbers first, while he and Soloman had taken the time to remove the remains of Captain Blair and the unknown crewman he had found on the bridge. Gomez for one had been thankful for that. During the time it had taken her and Soloman to install the generators, they had encountered more skeletons of the engineering crew. The ghastly sight had begun to unnerve her more than she wanted to admit.

"Captain," Soloman said from where he sat at the science station, "I have obtained access . . . to the ship's main computer. We now have access to the entire data storage network, including the . . . captain's logs."

"Excellent," Gold replied. "Maybe now we can finally find out what happened to this ship. See if you can find anything in the logs about the rift." He paused for a moment before adding, "Or Tholians, while you're at it." Noticing Gomez's questioning look, the captain shrugged. "A hunch."

She turned to watch Soloman set to his task. Bynars as a race interacted with computers as easily as humans conversed with one another. On their home planet, the central computer system was highly regarded throughout the Federation as one of the pinnacles of information processing capability. Like others of his species, Soloman was used to computers possessing far greater power and speed than those of a century-old starship.

Despite his best efforts, however, Soloman was still adjusting to working as a lone entity, rather than being able to divide responsibilities with his bondmate. In the weeks following 111's tragic death, Soloman had at times found himself confused, hesitant, even resistant to the idea of working alone. Tasks once regarded as routine while working in tandem with 111 suddenly seemed insurmountable. Gomez knew that it had taken no small amount of courage to rise to the challenge of continuing on without 111's support. That was one of the things she admired about the Bynar.

She also wondered idly if Soloman would experience any additional frustration at being forced to deal with the *Defiant*'s antiquated equipment. The commander couldn't suppress a smile at the image of the Bynar throwing up his hands in exasperation and loudly announcing his refusal to work under such intolerable conditions.

Soloman did no such thing, of course. Instead, he turned back to Gold after only a few moments of scanning the *Defiant*'s computer records.

"Captain, I believe I have found . . . what we are looking for." He keyed a series of controls and was rewarded with the main viewer's activation. The image on the screen coalesced into the figure of a human male who Gold recognized as Captain Thomas Blair.

"*Captain's log: stardate 5684.7. Sensors have detected a trio of Tholian vessels on an intercept course. We can outrun them, but long-range scans indicate other ships in the region. We are plotting an evasive course to get us back to Federation space. The area we're traveling through is uncharted, but sensors have detected nothing that might present a threat to the ship.*"

"Little did he know what he would find," Gold said as the image froze.

Gomez nodded knowingly. "Our sensors have trouble detecting the rift, and we have better equipment and know what to look for. The *Defiant* never had a chance." She could almost feel her blood chill as she regarded the image of Captain Blair. After studying the man's service record during the journey here, Gold had mentioned that Blair had been about fifty standard Earth years old at the time of his command. But the log entry made the *Defiant* captain look older still.

From the science station, Soloman said, "Captain, there is more."

"Let's have the whole megillah, then," Gold replied. After a brief pause, the image of Captain Blair reappeared.

"Captain's log: supplemental. The ship has come into contact with an unidentified phenomenon unlike anything on record. Science Officer Nyn believes it to be some kind of interdimensional corridor that may actually connect our universe with a completely different one. In addition to affecting our onboard power systems, Dr. Hamilton reports that members of the crew are being struck with what she describes as a frantic paranoia. Her medical scans show that in all of the victims, an area of the brain has been affected in a similar fashion. She hasn't isolated the cause yet, but the attacks didn't start until we entered this rift. We need to leave this place, but our sensors can't seem to detect an exit from this hole in space we've fallen into."

In the next entry, Gold and the others could

now clearly see the exhaustion and near panic on Blair's face.

"The incidents of unrest are escalating, both in number and violence. Four crewmen have been killed and Dr. Hamilton was severely injured when she was attacked by one of her own nurses. Without her help, I don't think we'll be able to find a cure for whatever is affecting the crew. Science Officer Nyn is unable to find a way out of this rift. We have been pulled into and out of our universe on three separate occasions, but in each instance we were unable to break free from whatever is holding us here. Nyn has a plan to—"

On the screen, a crewman wearing a red shirt suddenly lurched into the picture, his hands lunging for Blair's throat. The captain bolted from his chair to parry the attack, but the crewman had the advantage in both speed and strength.

"Oh my God," Gomez breathed. Like Gold and Soloman, she too was transfixed by what quickly became mortal combat on the viewscreen, with Captain Blair fighting futilely against the onslaught of the obviously crazed crewman. None of the away team could bring themselves to speak another word as the struggle continued onscreen.

Finally, Captain Thomas Blair succumbed to the greater strength of his opponent, his body sagging in defeat before he and the crewman fell out of view. The log entry continued to play, the only thing discernible being the unpleasant sounds of struggle continuing out of range of the log recorder's visual pickup. That only lasted for a few moments, though, before it mercifully ended.

Soloman was the first to speak, his voice quiet and tentative. "They never had a chance . . . trapped in the rift as they were. What a tragedy."

"That explains why Starfleet never learned what happened to the *Defiant*," Gomez said. "First they were hiding from the Tholians, probably maintaining communications silence. Then they fell into the rift with no hope of getting a signal out. And the *Enterprise* never had the chance to review the captain's logs." She paused momentarily, gathering her composure when she realized how profoundly the images on the viewer had affected her.

"What a terrible way to die."

Gold nodded. "Well, we mustn't let our emotions get the better of us. There will be plenty of time later to answer all the questions the *Defiant* and her crew have left us. For now the best thing to do is to concentrate on getting the old girl out of this mess and heading home."

Gomez agreed, upset with herself at allowing what they had encountered to bother her. It wasn't normal for her to react in such a manner to the unexpected or the unpleasant. Why should now be any different?

Her attention was drawn to the chirping sound of their suit communicators and the voice of P8 Blue.

"Captain Gold, we have found the source of the power readings," the Nasat said. "I think you will find this to be most interesting."

Gold couldn't help a small smile as he replied. "What on this ship isn't?"

CHAPTER
6

Despite the reports from the *Enterprise* and from his own colleagues—reports of lunacy and bloodshed that he supplemented with horrific images in his own mind—Duffy could not look upon the *Defiant* as a dead ship anymore.

His eyes surveyed the century-old starship's glowing image on the *da Vinci's* main viewer. Hanging silently in space, the all but powerless craft shimmered in its eerie blue shroud, more of a specter than a starship. Duffy propped himself against the bridge railing, vaguely recalling stories of ancient sailors on Earth's seas and their reports of phantom schooners sailing not on the waves but in the skies. Had more people the same opportunity to view this hapless ship as did he and the *da Vinci's* crew, he thought, the *Defiant* surely would become the stuff of legend.

But the surreal ship now housed very real members of his own crew, whose mission was to restore life to the *Defiant*. At least, they were to restore enough of it to allow his team to pluck the ship from more than a century of interspatial limbo.

If nothing else, we'll bring home some answers to questions that have baffled Starfleet officers for decades, including Captain Gold.

As he thought of his captain, Duffy swung his glance to the empty command chair in the center of the *da Vinci's* bridge. Technically in command of the vessel for almost three hours, Duffy still had not brought himself to sit in that chair. When he wasn't working, he lingered around it, appraising it as he used to size up the antique sofa in his grandmother's home as a child. Every holiday, his family would take the shuttle to Denver for a big meal and overnight stay. During each visit Duffy would find a way to sneak into the sitting room and plop down on that rickety sofa when no one was looking, just to know that he did it. Duffy smiled to himself as he eyed the seat cushion of the captain's chair. His little game dulled some of the tension in his mind.

Hey, Grandma, take a look at little Kieran now, he thought as he sauntered over to the chair, turned around, bent his knees and—

"Mr. Duffy," called Fabian Stevens from one of the science stations at the rear of the bridge. "I've got the latest structural integrity readings from Commander Gomez if you want to see how they fit the models."

Duffy's rear hung over the seat for a moment before he straightened and wondered if Grandma had been watching after all.

Fabian Stevens was the one crewman on the *da Vinci* who Duffy had the most fun with, whether it was knocking back a synthebeer in the mess hall or puzzling out the answer to a technical problem. Stevens struck Duffy as, for lack of a better term, the most regular guy on board. He had also confided to Duffy his own personal interest in this mission as the *da Vinci* sped through Tholian space.

The tactical expert's assignment previous to S.C.E. had been to Deep Space Nine and its attending starship, which bore the same class designation and name of the very ship they intended to salvage. Upon receiving that posting, Stevens had studied with keen interest the logs and history of the original *Defiant* and had been caught up in the mystery and tragedy surrounding the vessel's loss. As an engineer, he relished the idea of applying his technical prowess and that of his fellow teammates to retrieve the fabled ship and finally bring her home.

Stevens likened their mission to the ongoing effort by Lieutenant Reginald Barclay and the Pathfinder project to contact the *U.S.S. Voyager*, stranded in the Delta Quadrant with her crew valiantly trying to get home. While the stakes for this mission certainly weren't on the same level, Fabian Stevens felt as strongly about this mission as Barclay had about bringing the *Voyager*'s crew home safely.

As he made his way toward the science station, Duffy decided to put Stevens' question back on him. "Well, how do things look to you?"

"How technical do you want to get, Duff?" Stevens grinned. He tapped several commands into his console to bring up a graph with a series of fluctuating bars. "We've finished our modifications to the deflector dish, and with even a low-strength infusion from the beam, we should have a nice stable area of the *Defiant's* hull to latch onto with the tractor beam." Stevens tapped once more and the bar graph dissolved. "Curse me for being overconfident, Duff, but this ought to go pretty smoothly."

Duffy nodded to Stevens and smiled, shrouding his sincere hope for a trouble-free mission in a quip. "Smoothly? That would be a refreshing change." As he turned away from the science station, he became aware that he was the object of someone's attention, and that someone wasn't happy.

Of course, I'd have to consult a calendar to figure out the last time ol' Core Breach was happy, Duffy joked to himself as he turned his attention to the *da Vinci's* security chief, Domenica Corsi.

"Concerns, Commander?"

Corsi maintained her stiff stance near the security console, moving no muscle except those needed to deepen her frown. Duffy decided to meet her there rather than forcing her to call across the bridge; that would be the more "captainly" way to handle it. As he took one step toward her, however, Corsi made it clear she wasn't above raising her voice.

"You seem pretty relaxed, Commander Duffy."

He hustled his step to meet Corsi, hoping his

proximity might prompt her to tone down. "I want everyone to relax, Corsi, including you. Okay, mostly just you." He decided to add a smile in order to ease the remark's effect.

Unfazed, she replied, "Never mind that we're in hostile space with a Tholian ship off our bow. You don't even have our shields up or our weapons charged."

"That's at Carol's and Captain Gold's recommendations," he countered. "We do that, and the Tholians will be sure to get curious. And just what would we say in response? That we're nervous?"

"You know it's against regulations." As if sensing her own breach of protocol, Corsi lowered her voice. "I want people to be prepared on the bridge, not calm and folksy as you would have them."

Bristling at the implied criticism, Duffy snapped back, "Tell you what, Commander—next time, you can sit in the big boy's chair."

He caught himself, his ears ringing with reminders of Sonya's advice against getting baited by Corsi. On the surface, the crew almost universally saw the security chief as a hard-nosed stickler for protocol and procedure. But, as Sonya said, a person such as Corsi was never bad for a captain to have at his or her disposal. Duffy knew that in a pinch, he could turn to Corsi for advice and that he could count on her to act quickly and correctly.

And one thing he did not want now was her noticing his unease with command.

"Wait a minute," Duffy said and stalled. "That was uncalled for." He tried another smile, holding his hands out in supplication. "Listen, I'll toe the command line if you remind me of regulation breaches later, okay?" Corsi nodded, seemingly placated for the moment, and Duffy again noted one of the reasons that he would never pine away for the center seat.

It's not a starship that a captain has to manage so much, he reminded himself. *It's her crew*.

A hail from the *Defiant* pricked up Duffy's ears. The voice was Sonya's and she was just whom he wanted to hear, if only as a mental pick-me-up.

"*Defiant* to *da Vinci*. Commander Duffy? We're ready on this end."

Duffy smiled. "And ahead of the Tholians schedule by, oh, twelve minutes and change. They ought to appreciate your efforts, Commander."

He looked in the direction of Carol Abramowitz, who was seated at the communications console. As a cultural specialist, she was pretty used to the post although it wasn't her usual one. Duffy had seen her talk the crew's way through plenty of encounters before; Carol's background made her the perfect blending of a diplomat and a crewperson with Starfleet training at heart.

"Carol, alert the Tholian commander that we'll be starting our operation momentarily," Duffy said, stifling a more natural urge to phrase things as requests rather than orders.

She nodded and tapped the console before her. "Commander Nostrene, this is the *da Vinci*. I know this is—"

"You are twelve minutes and eleven seconds premature for your next scheduled communication," came a reply in a synthesized voice that Duffy recognized as the echoing timbre assigned by the computer to all Tholian communications. He'd had plenty of opportunities to hear the native tongues of races across the Alpha Quadrant: the guttural barking of Klingon, the almost lyrical qualities of Vulcan and Romulan, and the clicks and grunts peppering High Tellarite that almost always made him chuckle. But he had never heard the actual sounds of the Tholian language. Sonya once likened it to the screech of a tritanium blade on glass.

"Yes, Commander, but forgive our haste as we need to inform you that we are ready to begin the salvage operation," Abramowitz said in an even, almost apologetic tone. "Our away team is prepared, and we know that time is of the essence for you and the Assembly."

"Understood," replied the computer voice that Duffy assumed was Nostrene. He figured the Tholian commander must have drawn this plum assignment from his higher-ups through to the bitter end, as Nostrene's name was attached to the Tholian reports passed through Starfleet Intelligence to the *da Vinci*. Nostrene's ship had been the first Tholian vessel on the scene of the rift's reopening and the *Defiant*'s reappearance.

"Just to remind you, Commander," Abramowitz said, "we expect this to be a routine maneuver. We will project a pair of beams from the *da Vinci*. A narrow, bluish one will be our tractor beam and will come from the front of our ship. The wider, yellowish beam that will stabilize the molecular integrity of the trapped ship will come from our deflector dish. Neither beam will affect your ship.

With any luck, we'll need just a few minutes to pull the *Defiant* free. Then we'll be on our way."

"Proceed," was all Nostrene said before cutting the channel.

Duffy exchanged an amused look with the cultural liaison. "I'm really going to miss these stimulating conversations when this is all over." He was about to order Stevens to begin when his combadge chirped, startling him from speaking.

"Gold to Duffy. I need to interrupt your operations a moment."

Duffy felt his pulse quicken at the captain's words. Had something gone wrong? Not according to readings on their end. He tipped his head toward the bridge's ceiling, as if that might make him more audible to the crew on the old starship. "What is it, Captain?"

"Have Carol patch me through to the Tholian commander," said Gold. "And feel free to listen in. You all may find this interesting."

Duffy and Abramowitz met each other's gaze as if on cue. He nodded once to her as she tapped commands on the console before her. "Commander Nostrene, please prepare for communications from Captain Gold on board the *Defiant*." She paused for a moment until the Tholian commander signaled his readiness to proceed, then said, "Captain Gold, go ahead."

"Commander Nostrene," Gold said, "we've discovered something onboard the *Defiant* that I believe will make this operation one of historical significance for both our peoples. We are transmitting for your interpretation our tricorder readings of a device we found stowed here. We'll be pleased to turn it over to you for return to the Assembly as a token of our appreciation for your help in retrieving this starship."

Duffy noted Abramowitz's quick tapping as she not only forwarded the tricorder data to the Tholians but recorded it in the *da Vinci's* memory banks as well.

The speakers rang with the computerized timbre of Tholian voice. "Received and acknowledged."

Abramowitz, focused on readings from her console, said, "Captain, the transmission's been cut from their end."

Duffy smirked and spoke up himself. "I'm sure there's a Tholian word for 'thank you' somewhere in our linguistics records. In any event, Captain, we're definitely interested in seeing everything you've found over there."

"Maybe not everything, Mr. Duffy." The sober tone of his captain's voice gave the engineer pause before the full realization of Gold's remark hit home. The *Defiant* was, after all, more than simply an unsolved mystery or engineering challenge. The ship was also a tomb, the final resting place of more than four hundred men and women who had given their lives in service to Starfleet. Above all else, Duffy reminded himself, that one fact could not be forgotten in their haste to accomplish the recovery mission.

Gold's voice interrupted his thoughts. "Commander, if you're ready on your end, let's get this show on the road."

Duffy tried to exude some confidence, for

Gold's benefit as well as his own. "Once more unto the breach and all that, Captain. We'll have you out in no time."

"Mazel tov, Mr. Duffy."

As the connection was severed, Duffy started toward Stevens' station, then paused. A quick check of the bridge showed that everyone was at their stations, ready to go. They all knew their jobs and had everything under control. With that taken care of, he realized it was time for him to step up and do the job Captain Gold had given him, and there was only one place where that could be accomplished.

Tightening his lips, he turned instead to the steps leading to the captain's chair. Without a hesitation or flourish, he settled into the center seat. He imagined the chair embracing him, the authority and responsibility it represented reaching out to envelop him and fuel him with the confidence he needed to see this mission through.

Hey, this doesn't feel so bad.

"Mr. Stevens," he said, not looking away from the viewscreen, "ready the navigational deflector."

As Stevens tapped at his console, Duffy spoke again. "*Da Vinci* to *Defiant*. Commander Gomez, alert the away team that we're bringing you out. Prepare your thrusters, please."

Gomez was quick to reply. "Ready on your mark, Commander."

Stevens signaled his readiness as well. Duffy paused a beat to center himself, then, "Go with the deflector, Mr. Stevens."

Duffy watched the main viewer as a wide, sparkling beam burst from the bottom of the screen and shot arrow-straight to the *Defiant*. The gold hue of the beam mingled and swirled with the neon-blue glow of the trapped ship's saucer section, stirring colors and flashing energy in ways that Duffy had never seen. In the center of the maelstrom grew a patch of dirty white. As he stared, the white took on definition as precisely spaced crosshatches of black appeared within. He watched the very hull of the *Defiant* integrate at the deflector beam's touch.

"Commander," Stevens' voice broke across the nearly soundless bridge, "she's emerging from the rift and the hull is phasing as projected. We have enough room now to grab her."

Duffy spoke more loudly than even he expected. "Tractor beam at maximum, Fabian. Now!"

He watched a thin blue beam etch a path across the gold of the existing one. While they appeared intertwined from the bridge, the tractor beam actually skated meters above the dish emission, narrowing its proximity to the integrity field as it approached the *Defiant* and struck the ship exactly where the white hull plates coalesced within the colorful swirl. The patterns worked to soothe Duffy a bit as he turned his attention to the pair of consoles before him.

"Pull us back, Mr. Wong. One-quarter impulse."

Ensign Songmin Wong tapped Duffy's orders into his helm console and Duffy felt the *da Vinci* lurch, rocking him forward in his seat. As he leaned back in the chair, Duffy saw the integrated area of the *Defiant's* saucer growing at a much faster rate than before. The ship waxed into whiteness as if emerging from an eclipse.

Could it be this simple, even after all these years?

Duffy called out to the viewscreen, "Sonya, how are you doing?"

The speaker came to life with a laugh. "We're fine, Kieran. Even with the heads-up, you guys still managed to knock Pattie off of her feet. You need thrusters?"

"Seems to be good on our end without them," Duffy said, nearly able to read the markings on the underside of the *Defiant's* saucer section, faded but still stark against the white of the hull. "We've almost got the pri—"

Wong interrupted. "Commander, I'm getting some resistance now. It's growing, almost as if something's pulling harder the farther we get the *Defiant* out."

Here's where the fun begins, Duffy cracked to himself. "Is this new?"

Stevens answered first. "Not new. The pull from inside the rift was slight from the very beginning and was almost undetectable." He checked more readings. "Yeah, it's growing exponentially, Duff. We'll have to fight to get her free."

"Kick it up to half-impulse, Mr. Wong," Duffy said, "and intensify that deflector beam, Fabian. I don't want to rip a chunk out of the saucer just to win a tug-of-war."

Duffy didn't want to contemplate a stalemate just yet as he hoped the away team could help. "Stand by on thrusters, Sonya. Seems as if we'll need all of the kick we can get."

CHAPTER
7

Tholians were not known as a race that wasted a lot of movement. Their unusual physiology, evolved over millennia spent on their home planet, did not lend itself to ease of mobility beyond the confines of that world. Conditions aboard ship favored their life support needs, of course, but generations spent exploring and colonizing other planets had long since conditioned Tholians to conserve their energy for only the most appropriate of occasions.

Nostrene, however, cared for none of that as he paced the length of his private quarters. He had decisions to make, and precious little time to make them.

His analysis of the data supplied by the Starfleet engineers regarding the device they had found in the abandoned ship's cargo hold had led him to believe that the mechanism was of Tholian origin. However, he had not recognized it, and his surprise was compounded when a search of his ship's computer yielded no useful information.

That revelation had prompted him to transmit the data and his report to the High Magistrates personally.

Their response had been alarming.

"We are to destroy the derelict?" asked Taghrex, Nostrene's second in command. From where he stood near the computer station terminal set into one wall of the room, he studied the message Nostrene had just received from the High Magistrates on the home world. He made no effort to hide the astonishment in his voice.

"That is the command of the Magistrates," Nostrene replied. "As soon as we are able to achieve a weapons lock, we are to either capture or destroy it as circumstances permit. Either of these options will obviously require us to destroy the recovery vessel as well."

"We risk retaliatory action from the Federation," Taghrex said. "Is that truly a wise course?"

Nostrene did not reply immediately, instead taking an additional moment to study his subordinate. Like Nostrene, his body was of a similar reddish hue as befitting someone of noble upbringing. Taghrex had served with distinction under him for many cycles, more than the Tholian commander could easily remember. He would make a fine leader one day, of that Nostrene was sure, once he learned to curb his rash impulses to openly question the wisdom or dictates of those superior to him.

Taghrex was correct about one thing, Nostrene decided. Their next action could well anger the

Federation, perhaps endangering the fragile peace that had been established between the two governments.

As if sensing that he may have overstepped his bounds, Taghrex said, "If the Magistrates are willing to risk such a response, then the situation we face now must be dire indeed."

Much better, Nostrene mused. There was potential in the young officer yet. "You are correct," he said. "It seems that the Starfleet engineers have stumbled across something that should not exist, at least not any longer."

Part of a prototype defensive system, the land-based web generator had been designed to capture the inhabitants of a planetary installation without harm to them or the structures they occupied. At least, that was what the Assembly's official position had been. Once seized, prisoners from captured areas could then be easily transported to facilities properly designed to detain them while Tholian forces moved in to occupy the newly acquired territory. However, the system had only been employed once outside of strictly controlled testing environments, and the results had been catastrophic.

The official conclusion from the investigation following the incident was that the system's designers had not adequately foreseen the radical physiological differences encountered in the wide variety of life forms in this region of the galaxy. Having read the report that the Magistrates had sent along with their message, Nostrene considered the findings to be ludicrous.

How could scientists of such caliber create a revolutionary nonlethal weapon, designed for use against all manner of species, and not take into account the biological varieties inherent in such an attempt? It was incomprehensible to him, though it was an opinion he doubted he would ever share with anyone else.

In this particular case, the "radical physiological differences" encountered had been Klingon, and not even a military target, but instead a civilian agricultural colony. The Empire had been furious to learn of the settlement's destruction, swearing vengeance on those who had been slaughtered. The true nature of what had happened had never been discovered by anyone, and the Magistrates had kept it that way all this time.

"Only now, the secret is threatening to be revealed because of the Starfleet engineers," Taghrex concluded, absorbing what his commander had told him with degrees of awe and uncertainty.

Nostrene nodded. "During their investigation, the surveyors of the colony discovered that one of the generation system's emitter arrays was missing. We now know that the Federation ship currently trapped in the rift took it. Reports did place the vessel in that part of space. They must have come across the colony, investigated it, and found the destruction wrought by the web generator."

"And since Federation scientists like to study everything in painstaking detail," Taghrex said, "they took the emitter array with them, having no real idea as to what it was they carried."

"And they remain ignorant, it seems," Nostrene

replied, knowing that it had fallen to him to take maximum advantage of that ignorance in order to protect the Assembly's interests.

He knew that the political ramifications of the next few moments went far beyond the simple angering of the Klingons. While the Empire might very well respond with hostility to the news, the Assembly could ill afford to alienate the Federation at this time. Diplomatic relations had reached a critical juncture, and the Magistrates feared that negative repercussions from any revelations made here today could put the Federation into a difficult position. They could well be forced to choose between their alliance with the Klingons and the progress they had made with the Tholians. It was not difficult to believe that any decision would not be in the Assembly's favor.

Avoiding such a predicament seemed the only logical choice to make, the Magistrates believed. They considered the destruction of one or even two Starfleet vessels a small price to pay, and had issued the order to Nostrene.

But being a seasoned commander, Nostrene would not act rashly. In order to succeed, his plan of attack would have to be bold and focused, with the first priority being the destruction of the derelict ship and the emitter array. That way, even if he failed to defeat the recovery vessel, the damning evidence harbored by the trapped ship would no longer be an issue.

His thoughts were interrupted by the sound of the intraship communications system.

"Commander," the sensor officer called out

from the command deck. "The Federation ship has increased power to their tractor beam. They seem to be experiencing difficulty pulling the other vessel free."

So the operation is turning out to be more difficult than anticipated, Nostrene thought. Perhaps the Starfleet engineers would fail in their attempt to retrieve their trophy. If that were to be the case, he would not be surprised. Nostrene had always considered it the height of arrogant presumption for anyone to think that mechanical devices created by fallible beings could have any real influence on natural phenomena such as the interdimensional anomaly holding the forsaken starship.

Of course, he fully expected arrogant presumption to win out today, and for that he knew he must be prepared.

Moments later, he and Taghrex walked onto the command deck. His eyes scanned the main display screen and saw that the Starfleet recovery vessel's tractor and deflector beams were still active and concentrated on the center of the rift.

"What is the status of the trapped ship?" he asked the sensor officer.

"It is difficult to be certain," the subordinate replied. "The rift is still blocking our scans. But the ship is approaching the threshold of the opening, and the Starfleet engineers tell us that there will be a moment of molecular disruption as it moves through that barrier. Once that process has begun, our sensor readings should improve."

How much time would he have before he was forced to act? He could not risk attempting to arm weapons until he was certain a lock could be obtained on the trapped ship, otherwise he risked alerting the recovery vessel's crew. Likewise, he could not even order the ship's defensive screens activated, as that would also make their Starfleet counterparts suspicious.

"Commander," the sensor officer called out again, "scans of the *Defiant* are improving. She has engaged low power thrusters. They have managed to restore limited power to the vessel and it appears they are trying to assist the rescue operation." The subordinate spent several moments studying the sensor information before issuing his next report. "The forward edge of the vessel's primary hull has begun to emerge from the rift, Commander."

Nostrene did not have to look to know that Taghrex was staring at him, waiting for his instructions. Though he may have voiced concerns over the Magistrates' directives earlier, the Tholian commander knew that his second in command would carry out his orders without question when the time came to act.

That time, Nostrene admitted, had come.

Gomez took one final look at the status readings displayed on the bridge's engineering console monitors before nodding in satisfaction. The power generators they had brought with them were working perfectly, and thruster power was available. It wasn't much, but with the *da Vinci* already applying the full force of its workhorse engines and tractor beam, it should be enough.

"I'd find a seat, everyone," she said as she stepped

down into the command well and made her way to the helm console. "This could get bumpy."

Gold heeded her advice and lowered himself into the captain's chair. It wasn't as comfortable as his chair on the *da Vinci*, a fact compounded by the bulky environmental suit he still wore. Looking to his right, he saw that Soloman remained seated at the science officer's console, his wide eyes watching the main viewer.

And for good reason, too. The sight on the screen was a kaleidoscopic furor of energy as the *Defiant* struggled against the interdimensional forces holding it inside the rift. Gold thought he could faintly see stars beyond the multihued chaos dominating the screen, though. He told himself that it wasn't his eyes playing tricks on him. They were making progress.

He continued to tell himself that even as the deck beneath his feet, already vibrating noticeably since the *da Vinci* had locked on with her tractor beam, began to tremble with increasing fervor.

"You weren't kidding," Gold said to Gomez as his hands instinctively grabbed onto the arms of the captain's chair.

Gomez replied without turning her attention from her console. "It will probably get worse as we start to cross the threshold. That's when the molecular shift will occur as we move out of the rift and back into normal space. Besides, I couldn't spare the power to the inertial dampening field. We'll feel pretty much every bump in the road from here on out."

"We are approaching the barrier, Commander,"

Soloman reported, his face bathed in blue as he peered into the science station's viewfinder, which filtered and displayed all relevant sensor data at the command of the person operating it. "Transition should occur in five seconds."

Gold found himself counting to himself as the interval passed, the bucking of the ship continuing to increase with each passing second. On the screen, the stars he thought he had seen earlier were now quite distinct. Another few moments and they would be free of the rift.

It's going to work.

The thought came, of course, just before everything went to hell.

Gold felt his stomach lurch and his teeth rattle as something seemed to reach out and smack the entire ship, hull plates and bulkheads rattling and shaking as the *Defiant* twisted first one way and then another. The sounds of protesting metal were nearly deafening in the small confines of the bridge.

"What the hell was that?" Gold yelled above the din.

Knuckles white as she held onto the helm, Gomez shook her head. "I don't know. It felt like—"

"We are under attack," Soloman interrupted, fighting to read the sensor telemetry even as he too gripped onto his console for support. "The Tholians are firing on us!"

"What?" Gold replied, scarcely believing his ears even as his mouth formed around the words to order evasive action, experience and instinct beginning to take over. His brain took an additional instant to catch up and remind him that the *Defiant*, even if not in the grip of the *da Vinci*'s tractor beam, currently had all the maneuverability of an elephant in a closet.

"Gold to *da Vinci*," he called into his communicator, his thoughts quickly turning to his ship and the vulnerable position they were in so long as they maintained their hold on the *Defiant*. Duffy would have to disengage if he were to have any chance of protecting the *da Vinci* should the Tholians attack her.

There was no response to his call.

Repeating the attempt achieved the same results, and Gold turned to Gomez. "I can't raise the ship."

It was Soloman who replied, still continuing to study the sensor displays. "The Tholians' weapons fire has caused a . . . disruption in the rift, Captain. Communications have been . . . disabled."

Damn. Gold wondered about Duffy and the pressure he must be feeling right now. It was one thing to learn the rigors of command from classroom study and even from time spent aboard ships in space. It was quite another thing to be tried by fire under combat conditions. Many hopeful commanders had failed this particular type of test. How would Duffy respond to the challenge dropped so unceremoniously into his lap?

Before he could consider that answer, the ship shuddered again as the *Defiant*'s unshielded hull absorbed the brunt of another attack. The shock tore Gold from the chair and tossed him forward without warning. He threw his arms out in a desperate effort to protect himself from the impact of being thrown into the unmanned navigation console.

It never came.

Air was forced from Gold's lungs as he crashed into the deck, coming to rest at the foot of the stairs leading to the bridge's upper deck.

"Captain!" Gomez cried as she bolted from her seat, moving around the helm console to kneel next to Gold.

Rolling onto his side, the captain realized with astonishment that he was lying *in front of* the navigator's station. He looked at the console that he was sure he should have fallen into and was stunned at the sight before him.

"Sonya," he said, his voice a horrified whisper, "look."

Before them, the captain's chair was clearly visible *through* the surface of the helm console, itself looking like a hazy, semitransparent film draped across the command well.

"Molecular shift," Soloman called out from the science station. "They're occurring . . . all across the ship. I suspect it is a reaction to . . . the weapons fire inside the rift."

The ship rocked again under yet another assault and Gomez was knocked from her kneeling position to the deck. Everyone reached for handholds as the *Defiant* endured the latest round of punishment, shaking violently once again.

"We can't take much more of this," Gomez said. "Without shields, they'll cut us to pieces."

Gold pulled himself to a sitting position. "Any chance you can divert power?"

"The shield generators are completely inert and I'd have to go to engineering to get them back online. We don't have that kind of time."

"Captain," Soloman said. "The *da Vinci* has severed her tractor beam." The Bynar turned from the console, his expression one of deep concern. "We are being pulled back into the rift."

CHAPTER 8

"They're firing! The Tholians are firing on the *Defiant!*"

A backhand from an enraged Brikar could not have spun Duffy around in the *da Vinci*'s captain's chair with more force than did the voice of Ensign Wong. He had turned away from the viewscreen for only a moment to better focus on data coming from Fabian Stevens at the science station. But in that moment, his worst-case scenario, the one he had tucked even deeper in his mind than thoughts of phaser-cutting the *Defiant*'s primary hull free from the ship should the rift pull too tightly on its warp nacelles, leapt fully formed from his imagination to the main viewer.

Duffy felt time slow as he stared at the screen, watching the inevitable. A reddish blob of energy, writhing and expanding, closed on the *Defiant*'s saucer section and spread across it. The crippled starship rocked a bit in response, jostling hardly at all in the perspective provided by the viewer.

But with no shields? That had to hurt.

"They've gone space crazy!" Wong shouted. Duffy wasn't so sure about that, but he was willing to let the whole bridge crew assume that the Tholians had fallen prey to the effects of the interspatial rift. He saw no immediate need to speculate on the true motivations of the inscrutable race of crystalline beings.

What the hell is going on? What did we do wrong? As the *Defiant* reeled from her blow, the Tholians struck again, this time with a disruptor burst that appeared even more intensely red than the first. Words stuck in his throat as Duffy saw the old ship rock even more violently than it had from the first attack.

"Duff, I'm having trouble holding the tractor beam on her," called Stevens from the science station.

"Then don't hold it."

The words were Corsi's, startling Duffy nearly as much as had the Tholians' attack. His head snapped around and he stared at the security chief, his mouth already open to ask her if she was out of her mind.

But he reined in his words before they could be uttered. He just as quickly dismissed his first instinct that Corsi was challenging his authority and instead remembered Sonya's advice to hear Corsi out, especially in a fight. Duffy had always thought she meant the next time they laid over at a club on Argelius II.

He scolded himself. *Don't joke; listen to her. She doesn't think you're weak, she's just trying to help.*

"What do you mean?" he asked Corsi.

"The *Defiant* has no shields. They'll be ripped apart out here, but maybe they'll be safer in the rift." She kept her tone civil, Duffy hoped out of respect for his command. "And besides, we won't be able to maneuver as long as we're locked on with our tractor beam."

Duffy knew where she was going, and cursed himself for not reacting sooner. The rescue operation was transforming rapidly into a tactical situation. The fate of the *Defiant* as well as the *da Vinci* could well rest on the decisions he made in the next moments.

"Shields up!" he yelled before attempting to temper his voice with the same confidence he heard in Captain Gold's orders under fire. "Fabian, disengage the beams. Mr. McAllan, lock weapons on the Tholian ship, but hold your fire."

Without missing a beat, the *da Vinci*'s tactical officer tapped the commands into his console. "Aye, sir."

As he directed a final glance at Corsi, Duffy hoped his next words were tinged with enough appreciation for her to pick up.

"Recommendation noted, Commander."

Corsi did not give him the smug look he half expected from her, but instead offered a nod and a grim, tight-lipped smile. "Let's just hope it works."

In the cargo hold on deck 20, the attack on the *Defiant* was felt with an even greater intensity than on the bridge.

P8 Blue and Lense found themselves in a hell-storm as cargo containers and equipment across the bay began to shift and tumble in response to the second assault on the ship. The lack of gravity, protective forcefields, and inertial dampening systems only exacerbated the situation as boxes sailed around the room, bouncing off the deck, bulkheads, the ceiling, and each other.

"Look out!" Lense cried, pulling the Nasat out of the path of a cargo crate as it rushed past where she had been standing the instant before.

"What is going on?" Pattie asked as the pair rested against the bulkhead, catching their breath while trying to keep an eye on the legion of errant debris pervading the chamber.

"Somebody's shooting at us," Lense said. "Probably the Tholians."

Pattie looked at the doctor askance. "Why? How can you be sure?"

Cursing for what seemed like the hundredth time at her helmet interfering with her ability to wipe the perspiration from her face, Lense replied, "I don't know why they'd want to attack us, but I've been on ships that were shot at enough to know what it feels like."

And she'd certainly had her fill of that during the Dominion War, a course of events she had not counted on after graduating first in her Starfleet medical class. Such an accomplishment normally allowed the honored individual to choose their first duty assignment, and Lense had opted for Starfleet Medical Headquarters on Earth. She'd enjoyed that posting for a few years as she concentrated on research before deciding on a change of pace and requesting assignment to the *U.S.S. Lexington*. But then valedictorian status and personal preference gave way to the needs of the service as war erupted between the Federation and the Dominion. She'd always felt more than capable of handling any situation that life might confront her with, but that resolve had been sorely tested as she faced enough death and desecration against living tissue to last her several lifetimes.

You signed on with the da Vinci *to get away from war and the horrors it inflicts on the body,* Lense reminded herself. *So how did you end up here?*

"Unless Gomez can figure out a way to get enough power for the shields," Lense said, "we're a sitting duck out here."

Any reply Pattie might have had was stifled as the *Defiant* shuddered against a third vicious impact to its hull. The shock from the attack sent the pair stumbling again for something to hold on to.

"Pattie!" Lense yelled out. The Nasat turned in her direction too late to avoid the cargo container careening off the deck and heading directly for her. She was directly in its path, trapped between it and the bulkhead. The tumbling box was moving fast enough and was of sufficient size that Lense feared Pattie would be severely injured if not crushed by its impact.

The Nasat's eight limbs went out in a futile attempt to stop the wayward container, but could offer no resistance as it struck her full on. Lense saw Pattie's head snap back, the box having struck her in the helmet and upper body and driving her toward the bulkhead behind her with the container in fervent pursuit.

Lense lunged forward to help, reacting instinctively rather than with any real course of action in mind. As she moved, she looked to the bulkhead that Pattie was about to smash into.

She saw *stars*.

"No!" was all Lense could shout before Pattie and the cargo container made contact with the bulkhead.

And passed through it *as if it wasn't even there*.

For a split second, Lense's mind refused to accept what she had just seen. The *Defiant*'s hull had begun to destabilize around them, and Pattie had fallen outside of the ship itself!

"Pattie? Do you read me?" she called into her communicator, but received no response. Was the Nasat injured, or worse? Had her suit sustained damage in the collision with the cargo container? Was she losing oxygen?

Don't just stand there, her mind screamed at her. *Move!*

And before she realized what she was doing, Elizabeth Lense leapt straight from the figurative frying pan into the proverbial fire.

Though the bulkhead's surface had turned transparent with the consistency of a membrane or thin gauze, she noted no strange sensation of passing through any such barrier as she leapt through the destabilized hull section and into open space. The first thing she saw as she emerged from the ship was Pattie, her body limp as she drifted slowly away from the *Defiant*.

"Pattie, can you hear me?" she called out even as she activated her suit's maneuvering thrusters, pulsing the small jets of compressed gas. It took a moment to orient her body so that she was moving in the correct direction as she called on skills that she hadn't given a second thought to since her days at the Academy.

The Nasat did not respond to her latest call, and Lense concluded that she must have been knocked unconscious. How serious was the injury? Did she have a concussion? Could she be treated here, or would she require transport back to the *da Vinci*?

All of these questions and many others flooded Lense's mind as she closed the gap. After another moment, she was able to reach out and grab an errant leg, her gloved hand closing around the fabric of Pattie's environment suit.

"Gotcha," she whispered, sure that Pattie was unconscious when the Nasat did not react to having her leg grabbed. "Don't worry, we'll get back to the ship and . . ." The sentence faded away incomplete as she reoriented her body to face the *Defiant*.

Elizabeth Lense had never been outside a starship before. The closest she had come was an observation port at SpaceDock orbiting Earth, looking through plexisteel windows at vessels berthed in various parking slips. While those ships looked big from that perspective, the derelict before her now was positively *huge*.

"What the hell am I doing out here?" she asked aloud as she pulsed her thrusters again, pushing her and Pattie closer to the ship. Lense stretched a hand out as several more seconds of maneuvering brought the vessel's hull within reach.

Then it and the rest of her body made contact with the tritanium surface, discovering that the hull was as solid as a starship's skin was supposed to be.

Of course, her mind taunted, reminding her that even in the 24th Century, Murphy's Law still applied: Whatever can go wrong, will go wrong.

They should make that *the S.C.E. motto*, Lense decided as she set her feet and activated the magnetic seals on her boots. Once secured to the hull, she surveyed the area of the ship in her range of vision. She had returned to the *Defiant* near the midpoint of the secondary hull, yet there were no signs of airlocks or other entries into the ship that she could see. Where were they located? Other than the shuttlebay doors at the rear of the ship, she had no idea. She hadn't consulted the *Defiant's* technical schematics prior to beaming over.

Adjusting her hold on Pattie, she turned the Nasat in order to look into her helmet and saw that she was still unconscious. An area the size of a fist appeared to be swelling over her left eye, and Lense saw that the bruise was already beginning to turn a dark blue.

"Pattie, can you hear me? I need you to wake up." A moment's scan with her tricorder confirmed her suspicion: Pattie did indeed have a concussion. She would need medical treatment, and soon, something Lense would not be able to provide so long as they were stuck outside the ship.

"Damn it," she whispered, turning her head to face the front of the ship when her attention was caught by something else. It was the rift, the barrier marking the entrance to interspace. Unlike the black void surrounding the *Defiant*, the rift itself was a spectacular clashing of colors, colliding and mixing to form a frenzied chaos.

And it was shrinking. The rift was closing back up! While Lense stood by, a powerless spectator, the tear that had brought together two spatial planes was slowly healing itself. They and the *Defiant* would be cut off from their companions and in fact from their entire universe.

"Well, this was certainly a bright idea."

"The rift is sucking them back inside?" Duffy spoke to no one in particular. The question was unnecessary, though, as everyone on the *da Vinci*'s bridge could easily see the *Defiant*'s regression into interphase.

The numbing sight almost made Duffy not notice that there was still a Tholian ship nearby, and that it was at this very moment turning itself toward the *da Vinci*. As Corsi had predicted, things were about to go completely to hell.

"We're not shooting first," he said, willing to telegraph his strategies to the bridge crew in the hope that they might better understand his command decisions. Turning his attention to Abramowitz at the communications station, he said, "Carol, open a channel and find—"

"Incoming fire!"

Wong's warning drowned out the rest of Duffy's

order as the ensign frantically punched commands into his console in an attempt to move the ship out of the line of fire. On the screen, the hellish red burst of energy grew until it washed over the entire image.

The next instant the *da Vinci* pitched upward, throwing Duffy nearly out of his command chair and catching Wong completely off his guard. The ensign's head slammed into his console with a sickening sound that Duffy heard even over the klaxons and warning signals erupting across the bridge. He rushed forward, catching Wong's slumping body before it dropped to the deck.

Even as he eased the ensign to the floor, though, it struck Duffy that no orders were being given to respond to the attack.

That's because you're not giving them. The realization jerked him back to his first priority.

"Corsi, take the helm. McAllan, fire phasers. And a torpedo." He paused. "Hell, two torpedoes." Frustration and confusion enveloped every word that left Duffy's mouth. "And turn off those damned alarms!"

As McAllan tapped out the necessary commands, Duffy continued tending to Wong. He tapped his combadge. "Bridge to sickbay. Copper? Wetzel? One of you, up here now!"

From the tactical station, McAllan called out, "Looks like we got them, Commander."

Duffy turned to the viewer in time to see the Tholian ship listing to its portside, shunted from the offensive position it had held only seconds before. He could see an ugly black puncture wound on the side of the vessel's hull, evidence of the damage the *da Vinci*'s barrage had caused.

"Nice shooting, Mr. McAllan," he said. "Carol, open a channel. I want to know what . . ."

The words died in his throat as, on the viewscreen, energy glowed from the stern of the Tholian ship. Reorienting itself in a sluggish maneuver, the vessel pivoted on its axis and pulled away from the *da Vinci*, moving quickly out of the viewscreen's coverage.

"They're moving off," Corsi said from the helm. She turned to look at Duffy, her eyes asking the obvious.

"We're not chasing them," he said simply.

Though he noticed the mild slump in her shoulders, Corsi's tone was all business. "They'll be back, you know, and they'll bring reinforcements. Tholians don't like getting their butts kicked."

"It's worse than that," Abramowitz added as she stepped down to assist Duffy with Wong. "They'll view the attack on them as an act of aggression. We may have just caused an interstellar incident."

"Well, that'll certainly make Captain Gold's day," Duffy said as he rose to his feet. The attempt at humor fell flat, he knew, almost flinching at how weak the words sounded even as they left his mouth. Getting into a political hotbed with the Tholians was no laughing matter, and he imagined how the Federation Diplomatic Corps would blow its collective stack once word of the altercation got back to them.

No time for that now. Get it together, Duff.

"Our first priority is to get the *Defiant* out," he said. "Fabian, reestablish the tractor be—"

His voice fell off as he focused on the main viewer.

The *Defiant*, and the rift, were gone.

To be continued in

Star Trek®: S.C.E.

Book Two

Miracle Workers

ABOUT THE AUTHORS

Born, raised, educated, and still residing in the Bronx, **Keith R.A. DeCandido** is the co-developer of *Star Trek: S.C.E.* with John J. Ordover, and he has written or co-written several eBooks in the series. Besides *Fatal Error*, *Cold Fusion*, and *Invincible*, he has also written *Here There Be Monsters*, and more of his *S.C.E.* scribblings will be available in electronic form in 2002 and 2003 (some in collaboration with David Mack). Keith's other *Star Trek* work includes the novels *Star Trek: The Next Generation: Diplomatic Implausibility*, *Star Trek: Deep Space Nine: Demons of Air and Darkness*, and the two-book cross-series tale *Star Trek: The Brave & the Bold* (coming in 2002); and the comic book *Star Trek: The Next Generation: Perchance to Dream* (reprinted in the trade paperback *Enemy Unseen*). He has also written best-selling novels, short stories, and nonfiction books in the worlds of *Buffy the Vampire Slayer*, *Doctor Who*, *Farscape*, Marvel Comics, and *Xena*, and is the editor of the forthcoming anthology of original science fiction *Imaginings*. Learn more than you ever really needed to know about Keith on his web site at the easy-to-remember URL of DeCandido.net.

Kevin Dilmore counts himself as very thankful for the person who, at age nine, tipped him off to the fact that *Star Trek* was a live-action television show before it was a Saturday morning cartoon. A graduate of the University of Kansas, he works as news editor and "cops and courts" reporter for a twice-weekly newspaper in Paola, Kansas, where he lives with his wife, Linda, and daughter. Kevin also covers "nonfiction" aspects of the *Star Trek* universe as a contributing writer for *Star Trek Communicator* magazine as well as the Internet site StarTrek.com. He is looking forward to his next writing project with Dayton Ward, the *S.C.E.* trilogy *Foundations*, to be published in 2002. Kevin always will be proud that the formula for transparent aluminum was devised by the user of a Macintosh computer.

Award-winning author **Christie Golden** has written eighteen novels and sixteen short stories in the fields of science fiction, fantasy and horror. Besides her *Star Trek: S.C.E.* work in this volume, she has written eight *Star Trek: Voyager* novels (*The Murdered Sun*, *Marooned*, *Seven of Nine*, the *Dark Matters* trilogy, and the *Gateways* novel *No Man's Land*) and one *Star Trek: The Next Generation* novel (*Double Helix: The First Virtue*, in collaboration with Michael Jan Friedman). She is also the author of three original fantasy novels, *King's Man and Thief*, *Instrument of Fate* (which made the 1996 Nebula Preliminary Ballot), and *A.D. 999* (under the pen name of Jadrien Bell, winner of the Colorado Author's League Top Hand Award for Best Genre Novel of 1999); the TSR novels *Vampire of the Mists* (which launched the Ravenloft novels and introduced the popular Jander Sunstar character), *Dance of the Dead*, and *The Enemy Within*; the *Warcraft* novel *Lord of the Clans*; and the short stories "The White Doe" in *Buffy the Vampire Slayer: Tales of the Slayer* and "In the Queue" in *Star Trek: Gateways: What Lay Beyond*. In 2001, she wrote a special addendum to the *Star Trek: Voyager* finale novelization, in which she takes the characters in new directions. Golden will continue writing *Voyager* novels even though the show is off the air, and is eager to explore the creative freedom that gives her. Golden lives in Denver, Colorado, with her artist husband, two cats, and a white German Shepherd. Her web site is www.christiegolden.com.

Dean Wesley Smith is the bestselling author of over 60 novels and hundreds of short stories. He has been nominated for every award in the science fiction, fantasy, and horror fields, and has won the World Fantasy Award and a Locus Award. His most recent novels are the movie novelization for *Final Fantasy* and (with his wife Kristine Kathryn Rusch) *Star Trek: Voyager: Section 31: Shadow* and the first original *Enterprise* novel. He works and plays poker on the Oregon coast.

Dayton Ward has been a fan of *Star Trek* since conception (his, not the show's). After serving for eleven years in the U.S. Marine Corps, he discovered the private sector and the piles of cash to be made there as a software engineer. His start in professional writing came as a result of placing stories in each of the first three *Star Trek: Strange New Worlds* anthologies. In addition to co-writing *Interphase*, Dayton is also the author of the *Star Trek* Original Series novel, *In the Name of Honor*. He and Kevin Dilmore are also writing the forthcoming *S.C.E.* trilogy *Foundations*, to be published in eBook form in the summer of 2002. Though he currently lives in Kansas City with his wife, Michi, he is a Florida native and still maintains a torrid long-distance romance with his beloved Tampa Bay Buccaneers. Feel free to contact Dayton anytime via e-mail at DWardKC@aol.com.

Look for STAR TREK fiction from Pocket Books

Star Trek®: The Original Series

Star Trek: The Next Generation®

Star Trek: Deep Space Nine®

Section 31: *Abyss* • David Weddle & Jeffrey Lang
Gateways #4: Demons of Air and Darkness • Keith R.A. DeCandido
Gateways #7: What Lay Beyond: "Horn and Ivory" • Keith R.A.
   DeCandido

Star Trek: Voyager®

Mosaic • Jeri Taylor
Pathways • Jeri Taylor
Captain Proton: Defender of the Earth • D.W. "Prof" Smith
Novelizations
Caretaker • L.A. Graf
Flashback • Diane Carey
Day of Honor • Michael Jan Friedman
Equinox • Diane Carey
Endgame • Diane Carey & Christie Golden

#1 • *Caretaker* • L.A. Graf
#2 • *The Escape* • Dean Wesley Smith & Kristine Kathryn Rusch
#3 • *Ragnarok* • Nathan Archer
#4 • *Violations* • Susan Wright
#5 • *Incident at Arbuk* • John Gregory Betancourt
#6 • *The Murdered Sun* • Christie Golden
#7 • *Ghost of a Chance* • Mark A. Garland & Charles G. McGraw
#8 • *Cybersong* • S.N. Lewitt
#9 • *Invasion! #4: The Final Fury* • Dafydd ab Hugh
#10 • *Bless the Beasts* • Karen Haber
#11 • *The Garden* • Melissa Scott
#12 • *Chrysalis* • David Niall Wilson
#13 • *The Black Shore* • Greg Cox
#14 • *Marooned* • Christie Golden
#15 • *Echoes* • Dean Wesley Smith, Kristine Kathryn Rusch &
   Nina Kiriki Hoffman
#16 • *Seven of Nine* • Christie Golden
#17 • *Death of a Neutron Star* • Eric Kotani
#18 • *Battle Lines* • Dave Galanter & Greg Brodeur
#19-21 • *Dark Matters* • Christie Golden
   #19 • *Cloak and Dagger*
   #20 • *Ghost Dance*
   #21 • *Shadow of Heaven*

Enterprise™

Star Trek®: New Frontier

Star Trek®: Starfleet Corps of Engineers (eBooks)

Star Trek®: Invasion!

Star Trek®: Day of Honor

Star Trek®: The Captain's Table

Star Trek®: The Dominion War

Star Trek®: Section 31™

Star Trek®: Gateways

#1 • *One Small Step* • Susan Wright
#2 • *Chainmail* • Diane Carey
#3 • *Doors into Chaos* • Robert Greenberger
#4 • *Demons of Air and Darkness* • Keith R.A. DeCandido
#5 • *No Man's Land* • Christie Golden
#6 • *Cold Wars* • Peter David
#7 • *What Lay Beyond* • various
Epilogue: *Here There Be Monsters* • Keith R.A. DeCandido

Star Trek®: The Badlands

#1 • Susan Wright
#2 • Susan Wright

Star Trek®: Dark Passions

#1 • Susan Wright
#2 • Susan Wright

Star Trek® Omnibus Editions

Invasion! Omnibus • various
Day of Honor Omnibus • various
The Captain's Table Omnibus • various
Star Trek: Odyssey • William Shatner with Judith and Garfield
    Reeves-Stevens
Millenium Omnibus • Judith and Garfield Reeves-Stevens

Other Star Trek® Fiction

Legends of the Ferengi • Ira Steven Behr & Robert Hewitt Wolfe
Strange New Worlds, vol. I, II, III, and IV • Dean Wesley Smith, ed
Adventures in Time and Space • Mary P. Taylor, ed.
Captain Proton: Defender of the Earth • D.W. "Prof" Smith
New Worlds, New Civilizations • Michael Jan Friedman
The Lives of Dax • Marco Palmieri, ed.
The Klingon Hamlet • Wil'yam Shex'pir
Enterprise Logs • Carol Greenburg, ed.